BODY LINE

The new Bill Slider Mystery

David Rogers was a doctor, handsome, charming and rich. He lived the lifestyle of a consultant, expensive clothes, top restaurants, exclusive clubs, until someone killed him in the hallway of his lovely million-plus-pound house. But when Bill Slider and his firm are thrown into the mystery, they soon discover that nothing is as it seems, for though David's girlfriends are plenty, none of them can tell Slider anything about where he worked or what exactly he did...

*Cynthia Harrod-Eagles titles available from
Severn House Large Print*

THE COLONEL'S DAUGHTER
HARTE'S DESIRE
THE HORSEMASTERS

The Bill Slider Mysteries

GAME OVER
FELL PURPOSE

BODY LINE

A Bill Slider Mystery

Cynthia Harrod-Eagles

Severn House Large Print
London & New York

This first large print edition published 2011
in Great Britain and the USA by
SEVERN HOUSE PUBLISHERS LTD of
9-15 High Street, Sutton, Surrey, SM1 1DF.
First world regular print edition published 2010 by
Severn House Publishers Ltd., London and New York.

British Library Cataloguing in Publication Data

Harrod-Eagles, Cynthia.
  Body line. -- (A Bill Slider mystery)
  1. Slider, Bill (Fictitious character)--Fiction.
  2. Murder--Investigation--Fiction. 3. Police--England--
  London--Fiction. 4. Detective and mystery stories.
  5. Large type books.
  I. Title II. Series
  823.9'2-dc22

  ISBN-13: 978-0-7278-7967-7

Severn House Publishers support The Forest Stewardship Council
[FSC], the leading international forest certification organisation. All
our titles that are printed on Greenpeace-approved FSC-certified paper
carry the FSC logo.

MIX
Paper from
responsible sources
FSC
www.fsc.org
FSC® C018575

FALKIRK COUNCIL LIBRARIES

Printed and bound in Great Britain by the
MPG Books Group, Bodmin, Cornwall.

For Ali and Giles, with love.

ONE

The Wrath of Grapes

'You look terrible,' Slider said as Atherton slid into the car.

'I feel terrible. I'd have to be dead three weeks to feel better than this,' Atherton said. His voice gave him away – he sounded as if he'd been smoking forty a day for a week. 'You, on the other hand...' he added resentfully.

'You shouldn't mix your drinks,' Slider said mildly.

'I'm sorry, but I can't sit in a jazz club and sip wine. It isn't hip.'

'If you were any more hip you wouldn't be able to see over your pelvis.'

With Emily away in Ireland covering the elections, and Joanna doing a concert in Harrogate, Slider and Atherton had had an all-too-rare-lately boys' night out. They had gone to Ronnie Scott's for a Charlie Parker evening: Gilad Atzmon on sax, with a septet backing. Later on some of the Central boys coming off duty had arrived and the session had turned into a long one, moving from Ronnie's to the flat of one of them nearby.

'It was a good evening, though,' Slider said.

Atherton agreed. 'I can't remember when I last heard live jazz.'

'When I worked Central, I often used to slip into Ronnie's at the end of a shift. Heard all the greats back then – met quite a few of them, too. The atmosphere's not the same, though, now they've banned smoking.'

'True. Without the fog you can actually see the performers across the room.'

'Yes, but...' Slider let it hang.

'I know,' said Atherton. 'It's weird. I hated smoky pubs and bars, but without smoke ... It's like waking up with someone you picked up when you were really, really drunk.'

'It's a long time since I did that,' said Slider.

'At least you went home to a bed and a missus. The kits had been shut in on their own all day, so when I got home they wanted a vigorous work-out. They were wall-of-deathing round the house until dawn. Once every circuit they'd land heavily on my stomach and bawl, "Get up and play!"'

Atherton had inherited two Siamese, Shredni Vashtar and Tiglath Pileser, from his previous relationship. They had originally been intended to cement it – ha ha. Fortunately, Emily loved cats; and even more fortunately she was a free-lance journalist and worked from home a lot. The kits liked company.

'Well, you smell nice, anyway,' Slider said, catching a breath of Atherton's expensively subtle aftershave. 'Maybe too nice for police work. A blast of Old Corpsebuster can make a big difference to that all-important first impression.'

'Oh, blimey, it's not a stinker is it?' Atherton said. They were on their way to a murder shout. 'I don't know anything about it, only the address. Three Hofland Crescent.'

'Where's that? It doesn't ring a bell.'

'Back of Sinclair Road. I know *where* it is, but I don't think I've ever been there.'

'So it could be anything. Could be something that's been down a cellar for a week,' Atherton said. 'And I haven't had any breakfast yet.'

'Maybe just as well.'

Shepherd's Bush was not beautiful, but it had something to be said for it on a bright, breezy March morning. Clouds were running like tumbleweed across a sky of intense, saturated, heraldic azure. The tall, bare planes on the Green swayed solemnly like folkies singing Kumbayah. All around, the residents – young, old and middling – were sleeping, getting up, planning their day, thinking about work, school, sex, shopping, footie. Some were perhaps dying. One was dead in what the police called suspicious circumstances, and that, fortunately, was unusual. Homicide, even in the most crowded capital in Europe, was not the great eraser.

The Monday morning traffic was squeezing down the side of the Green to the West Cross roundabout, and piling lemming-like beyond it into Holland Park Avenue. The right turn lane at the roundabout was clear except for a pair of ditherers. 'Tourists!' Slider said, gave them a couple of bloops and swung round into Holland

9

Road. A moment later Atherton roused himself from his torpor to say, 'Here's Sinclair Road. So where's this crescent?'

It was misnamed – not a crescent at all, but a little snip of a straight road leading off Masbro Road at an angle. They had to leave the car in the only space left in Masbro Road and walk the rest. It was bitterly cold, despite the sunshine. The icy wind was coming down direct from the north, which accounted for the searing clarity of the sky, but it meant there was nothing between the Arctic floes and Slider's skin except some wholly inadequate clothing.

Seduced by the sun, Atherton hadn't worn an overcoat either. He shivered beside Slider like a fastidious cat. PCs Renker and Gostyn, on duty at the barrier closing off the crescent, were bundled into multiple layers, and stood massively impervious to the wind-chill factor – as weather forecasters so blithely called it these days. They smirked a little as they moved the barrier to let them through. Beyond it, there were unit cars and the forensic waggon blocking the road, and other uniforms keeping the curious residents and the press back from the blue-and-white tape which made a clear space in front of the house.

The sight of the house made Slider forget the cold for a moment. While the other side of the street consisted of a perfectly standard row of 1840s artisan cottages, their destination was one of a terrace of four Regency villas, harmonious in proportion, exquisite in detail, white-stuccoed, with the original fanlighted doors, and a little wrought-iron balcony at each first-floor window. 'It's a gem,' he said, pausing in admiration.

'Unexpected,' said Atherton, who had had to start noticing architecture since he had been working with Slider.

'They're earlier than anything else around here,' Slider said. 'They must have been here first – when Shepherd's Bush was still a country village. They'd have had a view over the fields in those days.'

'Must be worth a fortune. I had a look at a cottage like one of *those*,' Atherton said, jerking his hand over his shoulder, 'for Emily and me, but they were going for nearly seven hundred thou, and they're just two-up, two-down.'

'I think we can surmise that our victim is a man of means,' Slider concluded.

'Well, thank God for that. Maybe we won't need the industrial strength cologne after all.'

Detective Constable Kathleen 'Norma' Swilley, returned at last from maternity leave, was co-ordinating the troops on the scene. She had arrived back just in time to replace Hart, who had passed her sergeant's exam and secured a posting to Fulham – a good promotion, though she went with many a wistful backward look. 'You're fam'ly,' she had informed Slider's firm tearfully at the leaving do, and had insisted on kissing every member of it full on the mouth – even McLaren, which was quite a feat. She'd had to compete with a vegetable samosa. McLaren never saw the point in wasting his lips on anything other than eating, which was perhaps why

11

he hadn't had a date since the Thatcher administration.

Swilley – whose sobriquet, bestowed for her considerable machismo as a policeman, seemed rather inappropriate now she was a mother – was sensibly wearing a trouser suit over a roll-neck sweater, and a big, thick overcoat: cream wool, wrap-around and belted, Diana Rigg style. She looked warm and delicious. Well, Slider thought she looked warm, and Atherton, slightly wistfully, thought she looked delicious. Swilley had been his one notable failure in his pre-Emily career as a hound.

Connolly, the newest member of Slider's team, was talking to the next-door neighbours at Number 5, a well-dressed elderly couple, so tiny and immaculate they could have earned spare cash standing around on wedding cakes. They huddled in their doorway as though sheltering from a storm.

'Deceased's name is David Rogers, guv,' Swilley reported. 'He's a doctor, according to the neighbours. That's Mr and Mrs Firman.' She gestured discreetly towards the elderly couple. 'Lives alone – divorced or maybe single, they're not sure – but has girlfriends round. Neighbours in Number 1 and 7 are young couples, but they're out at work. No one at home in Number 7, and all there is in Number 1 is the nanny. Fathom's in there having a go at her, but I don't think he'll get much change out of her. She doesn't speak much English.'

'Who's inside?' said Slider.

'Forensics and the photographers. Doc

12

Cameron's not arrived yet. The local doctor pronounced, then had it away on his toes. He looked nearly green. Probably never seen a gunshot wound before.'

'They are reassuringly rare,' Slider said.

'Well, it wasn't pretty,' said Swilley, who had seen her share of nasty sights. 'Shot in the head.'

'Suicide?' Atherton queried. If so, they could get out of this icy wind double quick and back to the nice warm station.

'Not unless he was a contortionist. Also—'

Connolly joined them at that moment and said, 'Are we going in, so?'

Slider eyed her. 'What's this "we"?'

'I've never seen a gunshot wound. Wouldn't it be grand experience for me?' she said innocently. 'I've got everything we're going to get outta the owl ones. Not that they know much. Didn't hear the shot – deaf as Uncle's donkey. They didn't know there was anything going on at all until the girl dropped in.'

'The girl?'

'The girl outta Rogers's house.'

'There was a *witness*?' Atherton said. 'Nice of you to mention it.'

'I was just about to,' Swilley said, 'when I was interrupted.'

'Where is she?' Slider asked.

'At the hospital,' Connolly answered. 'She jumped out the window or fell offa the balcony – they don't know which. Landed in that bush outside their front window.' It was a large, clipped bay, which had been flame shaped, but was now hit-by-a-heavy-body shaped. 'She

13

literally dropped in.' Connolly grinned. 'Frit the life outta them, banging on the window. She was in bits, sobbing with fright and babbling about your man being dead. So the owl ones took her in, made some tea—'

'Ah, yes, tea. I'm glad they got their priorities right,' Atherton said.

'—and phoned for the peelers and the ambulance. Well, they didn't have a key, and the girl was in a dressing gown so she hadn't one either, so there wasn't much else they could do. Anyway, the ambulance got here first and took her to Charing Cross.'

'Was she conscious?'

'Oh yeah. I don't think she was bad hurt, from what they said. But she was in rag order from the shock, you know?'

'We'll have to interview her ASAP,' Slider said. 'She could be a suspect or an accomplice. You'd better ring the factory, get them to send someone to sit with her,' he said to Atherton. 'She shouldn't be left alone. I might as well have a quick look at the scene now I'm here. There's Freddie arriving, if I'm not much mistaken,' he added, seeing a grey Jaguar XJ6 pull up beyond the barrier.

It was indeed Freddie Cameron, the forensic pathologist, well bundled-up in a camel cashmere overcoat and navy scarf, his face looking lean and brown from his 'summer' holiday in California. He never went away in June, July or August because that's when his garden was at its best. He had an – to Slider – incomprehensible passion for dahlias.

'You'd better go back to the Firmans,' Slider said, breaking Connolly's heart. 'Since you've got a relationship with them. Get their statement down while it's still fresh in their minds. Anything they saw or heard, however trivial. Everything the girl said. And find out everything they know about the victim – where does he work, what are his interests, who does he see, is he in financial or woman trouble?'

'Righty-oh, sir,' Connolly said glumly.

'You'll see all you'll want to see in the photographs,' Slider reassured her. 'It won't be pretty.'

'I need to see it for myself, but,' Connolly grumbled. 'How'll I learn?'

Slider turned away. 'Freddie! Good holiday? You're looking brown.'

'My dear boy, this is rust! They're having freak rainstorms over there. It was just like home.'

'Not beach weather, then?'

'I went whale watching, and Martha read seven books.' Cameron paused a moment to consider the memory. 'Not all at once, you understand. Sequentially.'

While Cameron went in, Slider had a word with PC Dave Bright, who had been the first officer on the scene, and was now keeping the log at the door. He was the citizen's dream copper, big and burly, unflappably good-tempered, but with a core of steel that made villains think twice about lipping him.

'Had to break the door in,' he told Slider, with a gesture towards the splintered frame. 'The neighbours didn't have a spare key. Said they

15

weren't that friendly with the man.'

'It hadn't been tampered with already?'

'No, sir. Looked perfectly all right. But it was only on the Yale – not deadlocked.'

'So the killer didn't break in,' Slider said.

'No, sir. I did a quick check before I called it in, and there was no sign of a break-in. All the doors and windows at the back were locked. Upstairs windows were locked except the French windows of the main bedroom, but that was where the young lady went out, apparently.'

'All locked up, even though he was at home. A careful citizen.'

'Yes, sir. So maybe he let chummy in, and chummy let himself out the same way.'

'What time was this?'

'Working it back, sir, it must have been about half past six or thereabouts. The 999 call came in at a quarter to seven, and I got here just after seven.'

'On your own?' Atherton said. 'To a firearms shout?'

'There wasn't any mention of shooting,' Bright said. 'Whether it was the young lady or the old people who weren't clear, I don't know. All I was told was that there was a suspicion of foul play and no one had a key. As it was, the victim was there alone and anyone else was long gone. So it worked out all right,' he said with a shrug.

'Six thirty in the morning,' Atherton said to Slider as they clothed up. 'And on a weekday. Most people would be busy getting dressed or in the shower. Except for the high-flyers at numbers one and four, who'd have left for

16

work at six.'

'You're supposing they're high-flyers.'

'Must be. Do you know what the mortgage payments would be on a house like this?'

'It was a good time to choose,' Slider said. 'No one passing by to see anyone arriving or leaving.'

'Even if anyone saw, they wouldn't notice. Who notices someone coming out of a house, unless they're acting suspiciously?'

'Or covered in blood,' Slider said. But he wasn't hopeful. There wasn't so much as a drip on the doorstep or the least smear on the door frame. Besides, shooting was not the murder method of choice for crimes of passion; which, together with the lack of a break-in, made it look like something more deliberate – and the deliberate didn't dabble in their victim's fluid emissions. Still, he checked himself, there was no sense in ruling things out beforehand. As he always told his firm, facts first, theories afterwards.

Deceased was in the doorway between the hall and the sitting-room on the right, lying face down, which was probably just as well because he had been shot in the back of the head. He looked to be about five ten, and was dressed in dark trousers, white shirt, shoes and socks.

'So he wasn't woken by someone ringing the bell,' Slider said. 'He was up and dressed already.'

'Nice shoes,' said Atherton. 'Italian. See the feather stamped on the sole? That's Amedeo

17

Testoni. Knock you back twelve hundred a pair. I like a man who spends on his footwear.'

'As against which he's wearing a gold ring, and has diamond cufflinks,' said Slider, who had a thing about men wearing jewellery. 'I don't think you could have been friends.'

Not much else could be told about the victim, except that what could be seen of his hair was thick and dark and shiny. There was a messy tangle of blood and shattered bone which marked the entry wound, blood pooling under the head, and an unspeakable porridge of brain, blood and tissue on the carpet ahead of him, in the direction the bullet had taken. Slider averted his eyes for a moment while he swallowed and took a settling deep breath.

'I'll bet that was a hundred-pound haircut,' Atherton mourned. 'What a waste!' They all had their different ways of coping.

Freddie Cameron, kneeling beside the body, looked up. 'I take it you're not interested in time of death?'

'Unless it's not compatible with all the high-jinks at six thirty,' said Slider.

'Six thirty's all right, from the warmth of the body and the condition of the blood. So, what can I tell you? He was shot in the back of the head, as you see. A single shot at close range, probably no more than eight inches away – you see the gas-rebound splitting, and the localized scorching. He was upright at the time, as you'll see from the blood and tissue distribution. The bullet will be somewhere over there, probably embedded in the wall.'

'He's not far from the front door,' Slider observed. 'He could have let the person in, and then they shot him as he led the way into the sitting-room.'

'That's your province, not mine,' Freddie said. 'Sounds depressingly professional.'

'*Could* be a vengeful lover or husband,' Slider said, keeping an open mind. 'If it was someone he knew well enough to let in...'

'Well, either way, I'd say it was a 9mm or .38 pistol wot dunnit,' Freddie said. 'The 9mm is the most commonly used handgun this side of the Atlantic, and consequently the most numerous and easiest to get hold of.'

'There's lotsa blood,' Atherton observed.

'He was lotsa hurt,' Freddie said. 'A high velocity bullet causing complete ejection of the brain will have destroyed most of his face. I hope identification isn't going to be a problem?'

'We're assuming he's the householder,' Slider said. 'A Doctor David Rogers.'

'Don't think I know him,' Freddie said. 'I'll take the fingerprints for you, anyway, just in case. There probably won't be much chance of comparing dental records. I'm ready to turn him over now – where's the photographer?'

Slider had no wish to see this part. 'I'll have a quick look round, get the lie of the place, see if there's a photograph of the good doctor,' he said. 'Call me if there's anything significant.'

The sitting-room was expensively furnished, with no sign of any interference. There were modern paintings on the wall, a large flat-screen television, DVD and sound equipment, silver

19

candlesticks and an antique clock on the mantel, all untouched. Not a standard burglary, then. Slider noted a leather-topped kneehole desk in one fireplace alcove – it had the air of a decorative feature, but it could be the place to look for personal papers, perhaps. The fingerprints team were busy dusting everything and another forensic pair were on their knees marking all the blood and tissue spatters, so Slider did not go in. He could see all he wanted from here, for now. What struck him most was that the antique furniture looked like repro. The buttoned leather sofa and armchairs were modern, too. Everything was new-looking, immaculate, and curiously lifeless, like the lounge section of an expensive hotel suite. It only wanted an oversized flower arrangement and a leather-bound room-service menu. There was no personal clutter lying around, either. It was a room in which it was impossible to imagine anyone doing anything other than having a large whisky and watching the television for ten minutes before going to bed. Well, perhaps that was all the doctor had done. Didn't they all work impossible hours, these consultants? He was assuming he was a consultant, to afford a house like this.

Bob Bailey, the Crime Scene Manager, conducted them upstairs and showed them the master bedroom, again furnished in modern luxury style with a deep-pile carpet and concealed lighting. The super-king-sized bed had the covers thrown back, and there were dark-blue silk pyjamas carelessly dropped on the floor at one side. The French windows on to the

20

balcony stood open, the wind blowing the voile curtains about like an advert for Fry's Turkish Delight. On the balcony were two lollipop bay trees in silver-painted pots, one at either end. Apart from the bed there was an empire chaise longue and two matching chairs in striped silk, and two Louis XV bow fronted chests of drawers – all repro. And an unnecessary number of mirrors.

'Cheerfully vulgar,' Atherton remarked. 'It's what our Aussie cousins would call a sheila-trap.'

Bob Bailey gestured to the two doors, one either side of the bed, and said, 'Bathroom through there and dressing-room through there. I'd rather you didn't go in. We're still finger-printing. There's nothing much to see except that the drawers in the dressing-room are all pulled out, same as in here.'

All the drawers in the bedside cabinets and the chests were open – an expert opens the bottom one first and leaves it open to save time – but there was no evidence of rifling, nothing thrown out on the floor.

'Looks as though whoever it was was looking for something specific,' Slider said.

'We've got a nice foot imprint or two,' Bailey said, gesturing to the marked places on the floor. 'Benefit of a thick carpet like this. Bigger than the victim's, so let's assume they're chummy's.'

'Anything in the bathroom? Bathroom cabinet?'

'Door closed and no sign of disturbance,' said Bailey. 'We'll collect the contents and send them

21

to you, in case they're significant, but it doesn't look as though drugs were the object. Otherwise – damp towels, wet shower-tray, damp toothbrush. All the normal signs of getting ready in the morning.'

The other room on this floor was set up as a study, with a desk bearing a computer. The drawers of the desk were also standing open, but again, there was no sign of rifling. And on the top floor were two more bedrooms and a bathroom, minimally furnished and untouched.

'Don't think he even went up there,' said Bailey. 'No footmarks at all on the stairs – just hoover tracks. Looks as if no one's been up there since the cleaner last called.'

'Interesting,' said Slider. 'They were looking for something they were sure couldn't be upstairs.'

'Or downstairs,' Bailey said. 'The desk drawers in the sitting-room were closed.'

'Maybe they were disturbed before they had to chance to look further,' Atherton said. 'Who's to say they knew what rooms were up there?'

'Well, thanks, Bob,' Slider said. 'Let me know when we can come back for a closer look. What I really want most urgently is a photograph of the good doctor, since we're not likely to get a mugshot.'

'No difficulty there,' Bailey said. He gestured towards one of the chests, where there was an assembly of photographs in matching silver frames. 'Most of them are of the same man so I'm guessing it's him.'

'I guess too. The sort of person to have

22

matching silver frames would be bound to keep lots of pictures of himself around,' Atherton said. 'I bet he had a monogrammed wallet as well.'

Bailey grinned. 'How did you know? In his jacket, hanging on the dumb valet in the dressing-room. I'll let you have it as soon as we're done fingerprinting, but there's money and credit cards in it – doesn't look as though it's been disturbed.'

'A very selective intruder,' Slider said.

Bailey brought him some of the photographs, and he chose one of a man wearing nothing but swimming trunks standing in the sunshine on a dock somewhere, smiling directly at the camera, with a motor yacht moored up just behind him. He was very tanned, with a hairless chest, and not in bad shape, reasonably muscled arms, just a little sly bulging to either side above the elastic of the trunks. Slider chose it because he was full-face and clear. He picked another of the same man with a woman. In this one he was in white dinner jacket. The woman was in a clinging white evening dress with more décolletage than was *strictly* proper, unless she was hoping the good doctor was about to give her a thorough physical. From the way she was hanging on to his arm and gazing at him, perhaps she was.

'You keep calling him the good doctor,' Atherton said. 'From the look of Doris here he's more the original Dirty Doctor.'

Both had champagne glasses in their free hands, and the edge of a table covered in plates of fiddly food could be seen to one side. The background was a terrace at night, with a string

23

of fancy lamps overhead, and the dots of light in the darkness behind them could have been any major city in the world, seen from a penthouse terrace. Corporate party of some kind, Slider was willing to bet, from their cheesy grins and the canapés.

Bailey removed them from the frames and handed them over, and as Slider was turning to go, said, 'Oh! I nearly forgot! You're going to love me for this.' With a rabbit-and-hat air, he brought out from his pocket an evidence bag containing a mobile phone, and held it out to Slider with a grin. 'Also in his jacket, in the dressing-room. I know how you love following up numbers.'

'Terrific,' Slider said. 'Just what I wanted. If I weren't wearing a mask I'd kiss you.'

'I'm not that easy,' said Bailey.

Slider left Atherton on site, and took Connolly with him to the hospital, a sort of consolation prize for having denied her the corpse. Besides, it was always as well to have a female on hand when interviewing a female. He scuttled in hunched mode through the icy wind to the car, and Connolly, who had been strolling in her warm tweed Withnail coat, had to run to keep up with him, a panther pursuing a crab.

'What's the girl's name – do we know?' he asked her as they turned out of Hofland Crescent into Masbro Road, realizing belatedly that he had never heard it mentioned.

'Katrina Old. The ambulance paras asked her, and that's what the owl ones remember – though they were in flitters, so they may have got it wrong.'

In the car, Connolly picked up the photo of the man with the girl. 'That dress leaves everything to be desired. So this is your man Rogers?' She studied the face. A bit Pierce Brosnan, if you squinted: forties, handsome, perma-tanned, going a bit soft; pleased with himself; expensive haircut just too young for him – unlike the female on his arm, who was a lot too young for him. 'Well,' she said at last, 'hasn't *he* the face you'd never tire of slapping?'

Slider smiled to himself, turning into Blythe Road. He liked the way Connolly talked. 'Little Katrina doesn't think so,' he said, nodding at the photograph.

'Plastic Mary here? Is that her, so?'

'Dunno. I'm assuming.'

Connolly studied the exposed cleavage again. 'Convent girl, obviously,' she murmured.

The rush-hour traffic had done its thing and he got through to Charing Cross hospital fairly easily. The stained concrete building, built in the worst of the brutalist style of the seventies, was depressing. The Victorians, he reflected, at least realized that illness is ugly enough anyway, and added curlicues and turrets and fancy brickwork to their hospitals for distraction.

They found the witness in a private room being watched over by PC Lawrence, a slight girl with transparent skin and the kind of thin fair hair that always slips out of its moorings. She looked to Slider altogether too frail to be a copper, but you couldn't say that kind of thing now. At least

25

Connolly, though not tall, had a muscular look about her and a sharp determination in her face. She and Lawrence had been friends in uniform. 'Howya, Jillie,' she greeted her.

''Lo, Reets,' Lawrence replied laconically, lounging in her chair; then, seeing Slider, stood up sharply and said, 'Sir,' while a disastrously visible blush coursed through her see-through face. How had she ever got through Hendon, Slider wondered despairingly.

The witness's name was in fact Catriona Aude; she was twenty-seven and lived in a shared flat in Putney. And she was not the blonde in the photograph. It showed a coarsening of the fibres, Slider thought, to display one woman's photograph in your bedroom when you were furgling another. Or as Connolly put it indignantly, 'He'd sicken you!'

'Miss Aude,' said Slider, 'I am Detective Inspector Slider of Shepherd's Bush police, and this is Detective Constable Connolly. Are you feeling up to answering a few questions?'

As Lawrence could have warned them – and in fact she did mention it afterwards – the difficulty was to stop her talking. They had given her a painkiller and something to calm her down, and for some physiological reason the combination had made her loquacious.

'Oh no, I'm fine, I mean, I wasn't really hurt, just a few bruises and I twisted my ankle when I landed but that's all right now and my hands are a bit sore from the railings, the paint's kind of flaky and sharp and I had to hang on for ages, I thought I was going to fall but I sort of froze,

26

y'know? and then I couldn't let go and my arms were nearly coming out of their sockets, I can't tell you how much it hurt, I thought he was going to kill me, I thought I was going to die.' Suddenly she set her fingers to her face and dragged it downwards into a Greek mask of tragedy, and behind them moaned, 'Oh God. Oh God. Oh God. He's dead, isn't he?'

When not pulling her eyes down in imitation of a bloodhound, she was an attractive young woman, with brown eyes and long, thick brown hair with purple highlights, and the kind of spectacular frontal development that seemed to mark a definite taste on the part of the deceased doctor. She had a suspiciously even tan, and the remains of last night's eye make-up had been spread around by sleep and perhaps the sweat of fear, but not, it seemed, by tears.

'I can't cry,' she confided. 'I want to cry, I really want to cry, but I can't. I dunno why.'

'It'll be the pills they gave you,' Connolly said comfortingly, and the young woman turned to her so readily that Slider took a back seat and let Connolly get on with it.

'Really?'

'Don't worry, you'll cry all right when they wear off. But it's good you can't cry now, because we need you to be calm, so's you can tell us everything that happened. Every little thing you can remember. Are you up for that, Catriona?'

'Cat. Everyone calls me Cat.'

'Cat, so. Are you able for it? Because it's very, very important you tell us everything while it's

27

fresh in your mind.'

Cat nodded helpfully. 'I know. So you can catch him. I've seen the cop shows on the telly. But what if he comes back for me?'

'The murderer? Do you know him?'

'No. I mean I never saw him, not his face. But what if he finds out who I am and comes for me?'

'Don't worry a thing, we'll mind you,' Connolly said with huge, warm assurance. Even Slider felt himself relaxing. This girl was *good*. 'Just start at the beginning and tell us all about you and Dr Rogers.'

'David.'

'Sure, David.'

'I love that name, David, don't you? It's so upper. David Rogers. And it really suits him. He's a real gentleman, d'you know what I mean? Like, lovely manners, opening doors and all that sort of thing.'

'A real gent,' Connolly said, thinking of *noblesse oblige* and the openly-displayed photo of the blonde. I bet he's so posh he farts Paco Rabanne, she thought. Slider handed her the photo of the man by the boat, and gave her a nudging look. Right. Better get it over at the start. 'Before we start, would you just have a look at this photo and tell me if it's David, so we know we're talking about the same person?'

Cat took it, looked, and her face screwed up as if a gnat had flown up her nose, though she remained dry thanks to the chemicals in her blood. But she started moaning, 'David. Oh David. David. Oh God. Oh David,' and it looked as though it would be a while before she was finished with the mantra. Slider settled in to wait it out, and quelled Connolly's impatient movement with a look. You didn't get to see the badger unless you were prepared to put in the time outside the hole.

TWO

Witless for the Prosecution

Cat Aude met David Rogers at Jiffies Club in Notting Hill.

'You go there often?' asked Connolly.

'I work there.'

'You're a stripper?'

Cat was offended. 'I'm a *dancer*. It's a different thing altogether.'

'A pole dancer?'

'I suppose you think that's easy. Well, it's not. You have to be ballet-trained to do it properly. Anyway, I'm a featured artist, I'll have you know. I have my own spot, and my own music and everything.'

'I'm sorry,' said Connolly humbly.

Slider gave her a tiny nod of approval. This early on it was right to placate the girl. But he knew and Connolly knew – and presumably Cat Aude knew, featured dancer or not – that Jiffies was an expensive strip club where well-to-do men could go and look at titties without spoiling their reputation either for respectability or cool. There was a dress code (for the customers), the drinks were wildly expensive, and women were not allowed in free. It was all very reassuring. But it was the knockers they went for, not the ballet.

'I'm Ceecee St Clair,' the stripper went on. 'That's my professional name. I do two sets twice a week. It's not my main job. I work for a publisher days, but you can't afford rent in London on what they pay you, so I do Jiffies extra. The pay's all right and you get nice tips as well. I could do more than two nights if I wanted but I don't want to overexpose myself.' Connolly managed to suppress a snort at that point. 'I'm going to be an actress, you see,' Ceecee St Clair concluded. 'That's why I use a professional name, to save my real name for acting. I'm going to be a serious actress, stage first and then go into movies when I've learnt my craft. You see, all my life I've dreamed—'

Slider didn't want to get lost in the byways of the Judy Garland Story, and interrupted gently. 'So how did you meet David Rogers?'

She didn't seem to mind being redirected. 'It was a couple of months ago. Between my sets I'm supposed to put on a nice dress and go out and talk to any customers who're on their own. Put them at ease, sort of. Make sure they buy drinks. There's no funny business,' she added sharply, 'so don't you think it. The management are very strict about that.'

'Of course,' said Slider graciously, as though

the thought had never crossed his mind.

'Well, I'd seen David in there a few times,' she went on, mollified. 'He brought other men in – clients of his, I suppose. Lots of blokes did that. Usually it was foreigners they brought – Arabs and Chinese mostly. Entertaining them to get their business – drinks, nice meal, and a visit to a club. Anyway, this night, David came in alone. He was at a table on his own and he sort of caught my eye and nodded to me so I went over. He bought a bottle of champagne straight off – nothing mean about him – and we sat chatting, and I thought he was really nice, charming, you know, and well spoken. And lovely manners. When I had to go he stood up when I left the table. I mean, you can't buy manners like that. And he was a fantastic listener.'

He'd need to be, Slider thought, but he didn't say it.

'I always wanted to go out with a doctor,' Cat concluded.

'He told you he was a doctor?' Janey Mackers, Connolly thought, could this bloke be any more obvious?

'First thing,' she said proudly. 'Said he was a doctor, but not NHS. Private medicine, that's what he said. A consultant.'

'What in?' Slider asked.

'Excuse me?'

'What branch of medicine was he a consultant in?'

'I told you,' she said. 'Private medicine.' Slider let it go. 'So when I had to go back for my second set he asked if I would join him for

31

supper when I got off, and it went on from there. He took me to another club for supper – like I said, nice manners, he knew I wouldn't want to eat where I worked. And everything was the best – champagne, whatever I wanted off the menu, tipped the doorman, taxis everywhere. And it was cash for everything. I like that in a man – no fiddling about with credit cards. Always paid in cash, David.' A moist sigh.

'And after the supper?' Connolly prompted.

'We went back to his place. Beautiful house – I could see he must be rolling in it. Full of lovely antiques and stuff. Nice clothes, all designer labels. The next day he said he'd like to see me again and I said yes.'

'Was he married?' Connolly asked.

'Excuse me! What do you take me for? Of course he wasn't married.'

'He told you that, did he?'

Cat fixed her with a flat stare. 'There's no woman's stuff in that house – not in the bedroom or the bathroom. There was no woman living there, I could see that right away.'

Fair point, Slider thought. She had more intelligence than he had credited her with. 'We need to know, you see,' he said to take the sting out of it, 'who his next of kin was. Did he mention any relatives?'

'We didn't talk about that sort of thing. Well, to be honest, we didn't do that much talking.'

'So you've been seeing him for a couple of months?' Connolly picked up after a beat.

'Yes,' she said; but then some impulse of honesty made her add, 'Well, twice a week. On

32

my Jiffies nights. He comes in for my last set and we go out for a meal and then back to his place.' She seemed to think this sounded inadequate, and added defiantly, 'But we were going to see more of each other. We were going to go away for a weekend to really get to know each other – that's what he said – only we hadn't fixed on the date yet.' Her face crumpled. 'Now I suppose it'll never happen.'

You suppose? Connolly thought. *Unless you're into necrophilia...*

'Did he tell you anything about his work?' Slider asked, to distract her.

'Not really. I wasn't that interested, tell you the truth. Doctor stuff gives me the creeps.'

'Then why did you always want to go out with a doctor?' Connolly couldn't help asking.

'Because they're professionals, not just blokes with a job. And they have scads of money. He was really generous – bought me lovely presents. Always had something for me when we met – chocolates, smellies, lovely undies. He bought me this watch.' She extended her arm. 'I never take it off. Those are real diamonds. And he paid cash for it, too. That's how well off he was.'

'It's grand,' Connolly said, with a ring of authenticity in her voice. It *was* a nice watch.

'But it wasn't just the money. Professionals know important people. I thought he'd be able to introduce me to them, help my career.'

'And did he?'

'Well, not *yet*,' she said impatiently. 'I hadn't been going out with him that long. But he was going to. He said he thought I'd make a brilliant

33

actress. Said he knew loads of high-up people – professionally, I mean. He was going to help me get an agent. And he was going to take me to this big promotional party thing, at this hospital, so I could meet the right people and be seen. Oh, yeah, wait – I remember now! He said he worked at this hospital in Stansted. That's where this party was going to be. With all celebrities and that.'

'Stansted?' Slider queried. 'Did he say the name of the hospital?'

'I can't remember. I don't think so.'

'And he never said what sort of medicine he practised? Neurology, orthopaedics, whatever?'

'No. I never asked.'

Never mind. It would be among his papers, Slider thought. 'Would you like to tell me about this morning?' he asked gently, and at once an alarmed look came to her eyes, and she leaned back against the pillows and twisted the fold of the sheet between her fingers.

'This morning. Yes. Well. He got up early, said he had to go in to work. Five o'clock! I mean, we hadn't long been asleep, and he gets up at five. Fair go, he says to me I can sleep a bit longer, but I was awake anyway. No, wait – he had a phone call. That's what woke me up. The phone went off about ten to five, he listens a minute, rings off, and goes into his dressing-room and rings someone on his mobile. I mean, what's that all about?'

'Did you hear any of the conversation?' Connolly asked.

'What d'you think I am? I don't earwig.'

34

'It might be very important,' Slider suggested. 'I didn't really hear anything,' she said, mollified. 'It was just like hello, yes, no, all right – that sort of thing. But when he came back into the bedroom he looked sort of worried, and said he had to go in to work. He said I could sleep a bit longer while he got ready – I never knew a bloke take so long getting washed and dressed and everything. I mean, I'm quicker, putting on a full face! But I have to say he's always beautifully turned out. Immaculate. Every hair just right. Anyway, he says I've got to leave when he does. He's never left me in the house without him. He said the burglar alarm was too complicated for me to set.'

Modern burglar alarms weren't complicated to set, Slider thought. More likely it was just natural caution. There were many reasons for not leaving a girl you'd only known a few weeks alone in your pad.

'So what happened next?' he prompted her.

'Well, he'd done all his bathroom stuff and he was getting dressed. I took the chance to get in the bathroom for a pee, and when I came out he was in trousers and shirt and picking out a tie, and he says to me I'd better get dressed because he'll be going soon. Well, I was just in this bathrobe he lends me.' She looked across at it, lying on the back of the chair in the corner of the room – dark blue velvet towelling, thick and plushy – and her lips trembled at this reminder of him.

'Did he say where he was going?' Slider asked quickly, to keep up her momentum.

35

'No, he just said to work. The hospital, I suppose. Anyway, then there's this ring at the doorbell.'

'Do you know what time that was?'

'I dunno, but it must have been about a quarter past six, because he'd said he was leaving at half past and he was all but ready.'

'How did he react when the bell went?' Connolly asked.

'Dunno, really.' She frowned in thought. 'He didn't say anything, just went downstairs.'

'Do you think he was expecting it?'

'Maybe. He wasn't that surprised, really.'

'He wasn't anxious, or afraid?'

'I dunno. I don't think so. Well, like I said, he'd been a bit worried since the phone call, but not, like, sweating it. Just – thoughtful, sort of. Anyway, so he goes downstairs and I hear him opening the front door, and talking to someone. I couldn't make out what they were saying. I'd gone to the door of the bedroom, but I could just hear, like, the murmur of voices. And then – and then—' She had come to the hard part. Her eyes were wide and staring. 'I heard this gunshot.'

'How did you know that's what it was?' Slider asked.

'I dunno really. I just knew. I watch a lot of cop shows on the telly,' she explained. 'It was a gunshot. With a silencer.'

'Just one shot?'

She nodded. 'And then a sort of thump, like someone falling down. I knew it was David. I knew someone'd shot him. I started shaking all over. I wanted to go downstairs to him, but when

I got to the top of the stairs I see this sort of shadow move and I knew the killer was still there. And then I realized if he knew I was in the house he'd come after me next. So I ran back in the bedroom, and I see his mobile, where he'd left it on the bedside table, and I grabs it to ring 999, but then I hear the bannister creak and I know this man's coming upstairs. God, I was scared! I was gonna hide in the bathroom but I realize he'll come in there looking for me and I'd be trapped. I could lock the door but if he's a big bloke he could kick it open. Then I think of the balcony. The door was open – he always opens it when he gets up, to air the room, he says. If I get out there I can climb over the railings and, like, let myself down by my arms and then drop the last bit. It's not gonna be that far to drop, like six feet or something.'

She gulped for air, her hands still now, but gripping the sheet so hard her knuckles were white. There was a sheen of sweat on her face.

'I could hear his feet on the stairs so I get out on the balcony. There's this stupid plant in a pot and I have to get past it. I climb over the railings at the side. I'm still crouching there, trying to sort me feet out when he comes into the bed-room.'

'You saw him?'

'Just, like, this shape in the doorway. He comes into the room. I could hear him opening drawers, looking for something. I hear him go in the bath-room and come out again. Then I think: if he comes to the balcony door he'll see me. I thought I was going to die. I can't tell you – it was like I

37

could *feel* that bullet going into me. So I let myself down quick on my arms. God, it hurt, like having my arms pulled out. It looks easy when they do it in the films. And then he was at the balcony door and I sort of froze.'

'Why didn't you drop and make a run for it?' Connolly asked.

'I was too scared. All I could think was keep still, girl, keep quiet, maybe he won't find you. If he'd come out on the balcony he'd have seen me, but he just stood at the door, and that stupid plant hid my hands, hanging on to the railings. And then this pigeon flew down on the railings, making this noise with its wings. I nearly screamed, it frit me so much. The pigeon sees him and flies off, and I hear this beep, like an alarm on a watch. And he goes. I'm gonna let go then and drop, but me hands have kind of frozen up, and I can't make them let go. And I'm nearly crying with fright now because he's come out of the front door, and if he looks up he'll see me. But he walks off the other way, and when he turns the corner my hands give up on their own and I fell down into this bush.'

She stopped abruptly, and tried to reach out for the glass of water on the cabinet beside her, but her hands were shaking too much. Connolly got up and did the honours, and gave her a tissue to wipe the sweat from her face.

'You're doing really well,' Slider said. 'Take a minute to catch your breath.'

'You were really brave,' Connolly cooed to her, proffering the water again. 'Fantastic, really.'

Cat turned her eyes up at her. 'You think so?'

she whispered. 'You were brilliant. I could never be that brave. I'd fall apart.' Slider thought this an unwise thing for a police officer to say, but it seemed to do the trick, and Cat took a steadier breath and seem ready to go on.

'So let me help you along for the last bit,' Connolly said when she resumed her seat. 'You knocked on next door's window...?'

'I could see them behind the glass, looking out. They must have heard me fall in the bush. I kind of staggered over and banged on it and said something – I can't remember what. They looked shit scared. But they let me in. I can't remember much after that. I kind of went to pieces.'

'And no wonder. You'd done so well,' Connolly said.

'Just one more little bit,' Slider said, 'and then we'll let you rest. About this man. What can you tell me about him? Did you know him?'

'I never saw his face.'

'Had you ever met any of the doctor's friends or work colleagues?'

'No. It was always just him and me.'

'So, tell me what you did see of the killer.'

'Just the shape of him across the room. And then when I was hanging there, he came to the balcony door, and I saw, like, his feet, between the pot and the wall.'

'What kind of shoes was he wearing?'

'I dunno,' she said, seeming dazed. Then, 'Work boots. Yeah, he had, like, work boots on. And dark-blue trousers. Not jeans. Like, Chinos.'

'Good, very good,' said Slider. 'Now, when you saw him by the bedroom door, just the shape of him, how tall do you think he was?'

'I dunno. I think he was tall. And, like, big. In the shoulders, I mean.' She paused, thinking. 'And when he was walking away down the road, he had a dark top on, like a bomber jacket. And dark hair.'

'You've done very well,' Slider said. 'You've helped us a lot. And you were very brave.'

She accepted the praise this time without pleasure. She looked at him blankly out of a blank face. 'It doesn't make any difference,' she said. 'David's dead. I never knew anyone get killed before. Especially not like that. I can't get my head round it.'

'You couldn't have helped him,' Slider said.

The pills must have been wearing off: tears began to gather in her eyes. 'But who would do a thing like that? I mean, he's a *doctor*. Who would kill a *doctor*?'

'That's what we mean to find out,' Slider said.

'I'm surprised at her resourcefulness,' Slider said, when they were outside again in the chilly sunshine. 'I imagine most people would have panicked and run into the bathroom and been trapped, but she managed to think her way through that, despite being afraid for her life.'

'Fair play to her,' Connolly said. 'She was dumb enough about dating the doctor. Sex twice a week for the price of a meal! And phony promises to help her career. Holy God, she'd want to cop on to herself. Can you imagine her

40

an actress?'

'Stranger things have happened.'

'Like?'

'Who would have bet ballroom dancing would become top-billing TV?'

'Oh, right. I'll give you that one.'

'But given that she'd only know him a few weeks, we can't discount the possibility that she's a plant—'

'Yeah, from the neck up!'

'—or an accomplice. That she knows more about the killing than she's saying. She came across as genuine, but we'll need to investigate her enough to cross her off. Since you liked her so much, I'll put you on to that.'

'Thanks, boss,' Connolly said, with commendable restraint.

'And we can't discount that it was a crime of passion.'

'It sounds more like a hit man.'

'Disgruntled spouses and lovers have been known to hire them. And actually,' he corrected himself, 'we don't know that it *was* a hit man.'

'A gun with a silencer?'

'But we only have Miss Aude's word for the silencer.'

'Wouldn't the next-doors have heard if it wasn't silenced?'

'They're solidly built, those houses. And you said the Firmans were deaf.'

'Deaf-ish,' she qualified, for the sake of the theory.

'Besides, it's astonishing,' he concluded from the depth of a long experience, 'what people

41

don't see and hear, even when it's under their eyes and ears.'

Porson was surging restlessly about his office, like an electron searching for its nucleus. Given the amount of motion relative to the observer, you'd have expected him to generate a magnetic field.

'So we're looking for a tall bloke with dark hair, and that's it? Talk about a needle in a wood-pile! You're looking for the weapon?'

'Dustbins and front gardens. But I doubt we'll find it. From the sound of it the killer was very calm and collected, so he's not likely to have chucked the gun away in a panic.'

'Probably a rental, anyway,' Porson grunted. 'I hate gun crime.'

'I don't think going after the man or the gun will yield anything,' Slider said. 'We know the victim knew the killer—'

'We do?' Porson said sharply.

'Why else would he have let him in?'

'Any number of reasons,' Porson said, though he didn't offer any. 'I don't like to see you jump-ing to collusions. All the same,' he added after a beat, 'you're probably right. Which raises some interesting questions.'

Yes,' said Slider. 'It looks like a professional hit, but if he knew the killer, either he has some strange friends—'

'Or some friendly enemies. What about this girl – the witness?'

'I don't think she was in on it. She seems gen-uinely shaken up, and her injuries are reassuringly slight. If she was involved, I'd have expected her to have been tied up, or roughed up, to establish her innocence. As it is, her story is quirky enough to sound genuine. And she seems really scared the killer will come back for her.'

'But he didn't know she was there,' Porson objected.

'I know. But he soon will. Even if she doesn't talk—'

'Which she will. They always do.'

'—there's the old couple, the Firmans. The press are going to be doorstepping them and we can't gag them. I've persuaded the hospital to keep Aude in until tomorrow, so that gives us time to do a quick check on her background. After that...'

Porson nodded, thinking. 'Try and persuade her to go away somewhere for a few days – parents, old aunty, whatever – and not tell anyone where she's going. I don't think she's in that much danger. If she'd seen chummy's face it'd be different, but if he's professional he won't risk offing a witness who only saw his boots. So, what's your strategy visa vee the investigation?'

'As you say, we can't follow up the man or the weapon, so we've got to find out who wanted Rogers dead. That divides into the usual categories—'

'Sex and money. My bet's on money. It smells of money to me, and this–' he tapped his considerable beak – 'doesn't often let me down. And he was getting through it all right. Clubs, champagne, big house, fancy suits.'

'All the usual suspects,' said Slider. 'It's never

43

hard to find out where it *goes*. It's where it comes from we don't know.'

Porson actually paused in his astonishment. 'He was a *doctor*,' he said. 'Blimey, even GPs trouser a hundred and fifty kay these days! Never mind specialists. There was an article in the Sunday paper about these society gynaechiatrists making two and three million a year.'

'Well, no doubt we'll find out when his papers come over,' Slider said.

'*And* who gets it now he's snuffed it. Was he married?'

'That seems to be a moot point.'

'Well *un*-moot it then, quick as you like,' Porson barked. 'What are you hanging around here gossiping with me for?'

Atherton sauntered into Slider's office whistling 'I've got plenty of nuthin'.

'If that's your shorthand way of making a report,' Slider began.

'So far, nobody heard anything, nobody saw anything, and Rogers seems to have been a sweet old-fashioned type who did not have CCTV to back up his burglar alarm.' He sat down in his usual spot on the windowsill. 'My internal gypsy seer predicts we won't find the shooter, so what now?'

'We have to go round the back way. Up Motive Alley. As Mr Porson neatly summed it up, it comes down to sex or money.'

'Which are not necessarily mutually exclusive categories.'

'Sex seems the least likely. There doesn't seem
44

to have been a wife on site, and a disgruntled lover doesn't usually hire a hit man.'

'Unless the hit man *was* the disgruntled lover.'

'Don't get clever.'

'Too late. And what about revenge? Best eaten cold, as we're told. That fits in with a hit man. Furious wife brooding over her wrongs, slowly coming to the conclusion that the man's a wart and the world would be better off without him? Especially if there's an inheritance involved.'

'There was no attempt to make it look like an accident or suicide,' Slider pointed out. 'Killing him to inherit his money wouldn't work if the killing was traced back to the legatee.'

'Big *if*. I'm just saying don't rule out sex, especially as the Dirty Doctor seemed to be having a lot of it.'

'You know me,' said Slider. 'I never rule out anything. Well, let's do some background checks on Catriona Aude to begin with, so we can get her out of the way. Then we'll start on the doctor. We don't even know yet who his next of kin was. Who's in charge at the site?'

'I left Mackay on it. Norma's coming back – via the sandwich shop in Goldhawk Road.'

'Good thinking.'

'That's why I get the big money,' said Atherton.

THREE

Deliver Us from Ealing

'Aude comes up clean, guv,' Connolly said, leaning on his doorpost.

Coming back from far away, Slider hadn't made sense of her sentence at first, and his drifting mind latched on to detergent. Comes up clean? Had there been a spillage in the CID room?

'Hmm?' he said neutrally, marking time.

'She's no criminal record,' Connolly elaborated, and he fetched up to reality with a bump. 'No large chunks a jingle floating around. Owes a coupla hundred on her credit card. No big recent purchases. And she rents: shares with three others, in Putney. I know the street, guv – I looked out that way when I first came to London – and it's a bit of a kip, so she's not spending on property. She works for Tangent Publishing in Brompton Road. Editorial assistant, which means she's the office dogsbody and paid a pittance for the hope o' glory. Fifteen thousand. And that's before tax. So she has to make ends meet by stripping two nights a week.' She rolled her eyes. 'The woman's twenty-seven! She'd want to cop on to herself before it's too late.'

'Did you speak to someone at Jiffies?'

'The manager. Name a Williamson. A fine class of a man: pays the girls minimum wage and lets them keep their tips. He says no carry-on with the customers is allowed, but he doesn't know what they get up to in their free time.'

'A cautious citizen.'

'It's members only, so they get a big take at the door, and then there's the price of the drinks – which you'd want to have seen,' Connolly said. 'So they must be raking it in. Wouldn't want to get into trouble with the peelers for promoting prostitution.' She checked her notes and went on, 'Rogers was a newish member, joined last November. He gave another club – the Rochelle in Mayfair – as a reference. I checked with them. He's been a member there three years.'

'The Rochelle?' Slider queried. It was new since his Central days.

'High-end strip joint, with a casino attached. Members only. All crimson velvet and chandeliers – it'd appal you. Even the bouncers have double-barrelled names.'

'So watching strippers is not a new hobby for Rogers,' Slider mused. Could there have been something seedier in his background? Some little hobby or habit he could have been blackmailed for?

Connolly shook her head sadly. 'What is it about men and nipples?'

Slider declined the bait. 'So you think Aude's out of it?'

Connolly was flattered to be asked her opinion. 'She's not deep in debt, and she's not living on

47

the pig's back. Her story checks out, and I can't find any medical connection. And flat-sharing'd make it hard to get up to any carry-on without getting caught out.'

'All right. I don't want to waste any more time on her if she's just an accidental bystander. But we'll need to keep tabs on her, in case we have more questions. Has she got family?'

'She has parents, according to HR at Tangent. They're her next of kin. They live in Guildford.'

'That'll do. See if she can go and stay with them for a few days when she comes out of hospital tomorrow. I know Mike Polman at Guildford. He owes me a favour. I'll ask him to keep an eye on the house. She ought to be safe enough there.'

It was late when McLaren stuck his head round the door to say, 'The first of the papers have come in from the house, guv.'

'Right,' said Slider, glancing at his watch. 'Let's have a quick look.' So far, from the site they had culled a big zero. The street search had produced no gun or discarded clothing, and the canvass had drawn a blank. Nothing for which to pull an all-nighter. He might as well send them all home and save the overtime for another day.

He didn't expect great things of the first bag, but there was treasure of a sort: the doctor's birth, marriage and divorce certificates, tidily together in one envelope, taken from the top desk drawer.

'Born fourth of June 1962 in Greasley in Nottingham,' Atherton read out over Connolly's shoulder. 'Father's down as clerk, insurance office. Humble beginnings for the Dirty Doctor.'

'He was married in June 1988 to Amanda Jane Knox-Sturgess of The Lodge, Quickmoor Lane, Sarratt,' Connolly continued. 'Where's that?'

'Hertfordshire,' said Atherton. 'Carrot country.'

'Ah, she's a culchie, so!' Connolly said innocently.

'It's a very expensive village,' said Slider corrected. 'The local church is one they used in *Four Weddings and a Funeral*. Waiting list from here to maternity. Lots of money around. Old families. County types. Plus, these days, commuting masters of the universe.'

'Her father's down as a solicitor,' Atherton said. 'That plus "The Lodge" suggests money all right.'

'Definite step up for the lad from Greaseborough,' McLaren commented.

'Greasely,' Slider said. 'Very different place.'

'Come on, guv,' McLaren objected. 'It's all "oop north" to us.'

'Here, the doctor's address book.' Slider threw it to him. 'See if you can find the ex-wife in it.'

'Shame the marriage didn't last,' Connolly commented, opening the Decree Absolute. 'They were divorced in September 1999.'

'Eleven years isn't bad in these debased times,' Atherton said. 'No other marriage certificates in the envelope. Can we assume he's been fancy-free for the last ten years?'

'Maybe the ex-wife will know,' Slider said. 'If there were children, she would probably have kept in touch. I'm hoping she'll be able to tell us who the next of kin is, anyway.'

McLaren said, 'Guv, there's an address and phone number in here under A for Amanda, no surname. Grange Road, Ealing.'

'Look it up, get a surname,' said Slider.

'Where's Grange Road?' Atherton asked. He didn't know Ealing as well as Slider did.

'On the Common.'

'Common? Bit of a comedown from a lodge in Sarratt.'

McLaren, at his own desk, was not long in finding the property on the electoral register. 'The name's Sturgess, guv, no Knox and no hyphen.'

'So she's reverted, and simplified,' Atherton said. 'What does that tell us?'

Slider gave him a look. 'That she's called Amanda Sturgess. Don't strain yourself.'

McLaren went on. 'Also listed at the property is a Robin Frith.' He looked up. 'Either she's letting a room, or she's shacking up.'

'Either way, definitely letting herself slip,' said Atherton. 'Not the conduct we expect from the best people.'

'Ex wives can be bitter,' Slider said, ignoring him. 'Apart from the next-of-kin issue, she could be a suspect. We'll have to visit her.'

Connolly was eager. 'Oh guv, can I go?'

Slider looked at his watch again. 'It's after quitting time. I'll go myself. Anyway, it's out in my direction.'

'I'll come with you,' Atherton said. He caught Slider's look. 'What? It's all right, I don't expect overtime. Emily's not back until tomorrow so I've got nothing to go home for.'

'Play your cards right and you might get invited to supper,' Slider said.

The house was a two-storey Victorian semi-detached – which description did not come near to expressing the size of it. Red brick and white stone edgings, enormous sash windows, a bay window on the ground floor; a small window in the tall, pointed gable indicated there would be servants' rooms in the attic. Counting them, it would be a five- or six-bedroom house. And from the state of the outsides Slider could tell that all the houses along here had been refurbished. Given the proximity to Ealing Common they would be very expensive. Not so much of a comedown after all.

The woman who came to the door could only be Amanda Knox-Sturgess. Slider had subconsciously been expecting Penelope Keith from *The Good Life*, and she didn't disappoint him. She was tall – too tall for a woman, probably five-eleven – with a long and prominent nose and not too much chin. Oddly, she still managed to look reasonably attractive despite these handicaps, and Slider put that down to her immaculate turnout. Her hair was brown and subtly highlighted, in a smooth short bob, held back by an Alice band; her make-up was perfect; and she wore a navy skirt, blue-and-white striped shirt, low-heeled court shoes, large false pearl earrings and a string of large pearl beads.

That she was not glad to be disturbed was

immediately apparent.

'Yes?' she snapped, her face fixed in an expression of impenetrable *hauteur*.

'Amanda Sturgess?' Slider asked politely.

Her expression changed to one of suspicion and dislike. Her eyes flicked to Atherton, rapidly assessing his suit; and, strangely, this seemed to deepen her aversion. 'If you're from the Bible College, you're wasting your time. My religion is *not* open to discussion.'

Slider winced. Oh, poor Atherton, he thought. The Hugo Boss wouldn't be getting another outing any time soon. 'We're police officers, madam,' he said, showing his brief, before she could slam the door. She inspected it without touching it; Atherton's did not merit even a glance. 'I'm sorry to trouble you but we'd like to speak with you. May we come in for a moment?'

Atherton noticed that, as well as using his most deferential tone, he had allowed a very slight hint of a country accent to creep in. He had used this before, to disarm 'county' types, but Atherton was never sure if it was deliberate or instinctive.

Perhaps Sarratt didn't count as 'county'. There was no thaw. 'What about?' she demanded.

'I'd rather not talk about it on the doorstep, madam.' Slider, gently persuasive.

'Tell me what it's about, or I shall close the door.' Amanda Sturgess, magnificently unpersuaded.

'It's about your former husband, David Rogers.'

For a moment something flickered through her

52

eyes that might have been alarm, but then there followed overt and sighing exasperation. Overdone? 'What's he been up to now?' Interesting, Slider thought. He'd been up to things before? 'As you point out,' she went on, 'he is my *ex*-husband. I know nothing about his present exploits. I can't help you.'

'We're hoping you can help us with some background information,' Slider said, and threw in another 'madam' for good measure. He had dropped the slight burr now, Atherton noted. Smart and workmanlike was the way to go with this dame. 'We shan't keep you long.'

He could do as good an unyielding as her any day, and did it now. Unwillingly, she let them in. The house had been refurbished to a high standard of what passed these days for luxury – that is, all the floors had been stripped and polished and left bare, the walls were painted white, the furniture was modern and minimal, and an extravagant number of walls had been knocked out, so that the downstairs into which they were led formed a vast L shape with the sitting-room, the short leg, leading through to a kitchen-diner that stretched across the whole back of the house, and had glass doors across most of the width. Slider guessed they would be both sliding and folding, so that in summer almost the entire back of the house could be opened on to the patio. If ever the weather was hot enough. For the rest of the year, it seemed to him, the set-up would be pointedly un-cosy. It struck him that the current fashion for vast open spaces inside houses was an import from a country with a very different climate. But of course, the Amanda Knox-Sturgesses of this world had never set great store by comfort.

Her heels clacked aggressively on the bare boards; Slider's and Atherton's police rubber soles were soundless behind her. No cat or dog came to greet them; the air smelled only of pot-pourri, not supper; there was no visible food pre-paration going on in the kitchen; and the sunless rooms were chilly. It was not Slider's idea of a home; but he was a farm boy from the sticks, so what did he know?

She turned to face them at the point where the sitting-room turned into the dining end of the kitchen and, menacingly tall under the RSJ, said, 'Very well. Please be brief. What has David done now?'

No please-sit-down, no cuppa. There was nothing for it: Slider said, 'I'm sorry to have to tell you that he's dead.'

He was watching her face, and it went station-ary with shock; though again he felt there was a flicker of something – guilt or fear? – before she regained her icy mask. 'I suppose he crashed his car. He always was a careless driver,' she said as if indifferently, but she was not unaffected. Her eyes seemed blank, and her voice was by the tiniest degree not steady. She sat abruptly in the nearest armchair. Thus licensed, Slider and Atherton sat too.

'One of the things we hoped you might be able to tell us,' Slider said, sidestepping the car crash thing, 'was, who is his next of kin? He seems to have been living alone. Did he remarry after your divorce?'

'Neither of us remarried,' she said, a little absently, surveying some inner landscape.

'So you did keep in touch with him,' Slider said. She looked up sharply. 'If you knew he hadn't remarried, you must have had some contact with him.'

'We sent birthday and Christmas cards. And occasionally we spoke on the phone – about once a year. He would have told me if he was getting married. But that's all. I haven't seen him in years, and I know nothing about his present life.'

'Are his parents alive?' Slider asked, pursuing the next-of-kin line.

'No. His father died in nineteen-eighty-eight and his mother in ninety-four. They were quite elderly when they had him.'

'Brothers and sisters?'

'He was an only child. And his parents were only children as well. He had a quite remarkable lack of relatives. It made his side of the church look very empty at our wedding.'

An extraneous comment! Slider was glad of this evidence of softening. 'At Holy Cross?' he suggested beguilingly.

'You know Sarratt?' she asked, but not warmly – almost suspiciously, as if she suspected he was sucking up to her.

Which he was, of course, though she wasn't supposed to know it. 'I know that part of the world. It's a lovely church. And you and David didn't have any children?' Somehow he knew that: there was nothing maternal about her shape or her manner.

'No,' she said shortly, and in such a voice that it was impossible to pursue the subject.

'Then it looks as though you are the nearest thing he had to next of kin,' Slider concluded.

'I am his *ex*-wife,' she reminded him again, sharply. 'I am not responsible for anything to do with him.'

'Not legally, of course,' Slider said, as though there was another kind of responsibility. She eyed him and opened her mouth to retort but he got in first – soothingly. 'I was just wondering whether there was anyone else who needed to be told about his death.'

'*And* you were wondering who's going to pay for the funeral, I suppose,' she suggested tartly.

'Oh, I dare say there'll be enough in his estate to cover that. He seems to have been living in comfort.'

This seemed to interest her. 'You've found money?'

'I didn't mean that – just that his style of living suggests he was comfortably-off.'

She looked down at her hands and then up again. 'I thought perhaps he had got into financial trouble and committed suicide.'

'It wasn't suicide,' Slider said.

She surveyed his face keenly. 'You're sure of that? David wasn't a very – *resolute* person. Liable to look for the easy way out when things – set him back. Not a striver against misfortune.'

Why was she keen to sell them on suicide, Slider wondered. 'He didn't kill himself,' he said.

'Sometimes these things can be made to look

like an accident,' she said, and then hurried on, as though she had come to a decision. 'You needn't worry about the funeral. I'll make all the arrangements, if that helps. I don't suppose there's anyone else who—'

'Cares for him?' he suggested gently.

'I don't care for him,' she said. 'I did once, but that was a long time ago. However, there is such a thing as common decency.'

She hadn't looked at Atherton since they'd sat down. She had forgotten him. And he could see she was ready to talk to Slider. He wondered again how Slider did it. Animal magic – pheromones – mesmerism? Something.

'He was an attractive man,' Slider suggested.

'You don't know how attractive.' She stopped abruptly as something occurred to her. 'You haven't said yet how he died. *Was* it a car crash?'

Slider held her eyes. They were not blue, as he had first thought, but greenish-grey. Unusual, but not very – what was the word? – *sympathique*, in the French sense. Better suited to expressing *froideur* than warmth. 'I'm sorry to tell you that he was murdered.'

For the first time she lost her composure. Colour drained from her face, and she looked suddenly older. Her lips rehearsed some words she didn't speak. At last she got a grip. 'How can you be sure?'

'He was shot in the back of the head,' Slider said.

The words were as brutal as the shot itself.

'Oh my God,' she said, staring at him as if he had slapped her. She put both her hands to her

57

mouth. But evidently her mind was still working. After a moment she said from behind them, 'Was it over some woman?'

'That's what we have to find out,' Slider said, 'and it means going into his background, which is why I hoped you would be able to help us. The more we know about him, the better chance we have of finding who did this.'

'There'll be a woman at the bottom of it,' she said, and now there was a hint of bitterness in her tone. 'There always was. That's what killed our marriage – women. He couldn't resist them. And they couldn't resist him. To some extent he wasn't to blame. They threw themselves at him. He was so handsome, so charming. He had a way of making you feel you were the only person in the world who mattered. And of course it was sincere – at the time. It took me years to under-stand that. He wasn't pretending. It was just that he made every woman feel like that.'

'It must have been a useful thing for a doctor.'

She didn't take it amiss. 'Yes. The ultimate bedside manner. He ought to have been a psy-chiatrist. Or even a dentist. Women would have flocked to him.'

'What was his field?'

She seemed slightly put out by the question. 'Urology,' she said flatly.

'Not glamorous,' Slider sympathized. But lucrative – and more male patients than female, he reflected. She should have been glad about that. 'Was he ambitious?' he asked. 'I suppose he must have been to get as far as he did. He came from quite humble beginnings, didn't he?'

She studied him a moment, as if to weigh the implications of his question, and then, oddly, glanced at Atherton. He took the cue. 'On his birth certificate, it said his father was an insurance clerk.'

She nodded, as if that explained it. 'He grew up in a terraced workman's cottage. Two up, two down. He used to make jokes about D.H. Lawrence, but it wasn't quite that bad. Greasely's quite a pretty, country place. And his parents were respectable working people, very keen for him to get on. He went to the grammar school, and got a grant to go to university. Which is where I met him.'

Slider had not pictured her a student; and he became aware that he had noticed subliminally that there was not a single book on display in the immaculate sitting-room. On the shelves in the chimney alcove there were only ornaments. 'Which one?' he asked.

'Edinburgh. He wanted to go to London but couldn't get in. I chose Edinburgh to get as far away from home as possible. So we were both rather lost sheep.'

'What did you study?' Atherton asked, mainly to keep her going, but also out of curiosity. He couldn't see her as a scholar, either.

'Philosophy,' she said, surprising them both. English – the easy option – was what they would have betted. 'Daddy said it was a waste of time, because it couldn't lead to a career. And Mummy didn't want me to have a career anyway, so she didn't want me to go to university at all. Least of all Edinburgh. She was afraid I'd meet someone

59

unsuitable there. Which I did, in her sense. So they were both right.'

'And you were attracted to David right away?' Slider asked.

'I admired him for the way he'd got over his disadvantages and moved himself into a different world. Without being resentful. There were other working-class students, of course, but they tended to be – what's that word they use nowadays?'

'Chippy?' Atherton suggested.

'Oh yes. There were a lot of chippy people around back then. But David wasn't the least like that. He loved the fact that I came from a privileged home. He made me feel it was something to be proud of. So we – clung together, I suppose. And then – well, he *was* tremendously attractive. Thick, black hair, blue eyes, wonderfully athletic. And that charm of his...'

'You fell in love,' Slider suggested. She assented by a slight nod. 'But you didn't get married for quite some time.'

She sharpened. 'You seem to know an awful lot about me.'

'I'm sorry,' Slider said. 'We found the marriage certificate, you see, so we know the date.'

She sighed. 'There was a lot of opposition at home. Mummy was horrified because he wasn't "one of us". Daddy insisted David must prove himself before we could get married. They hoped I'd meet someone else if they made me wait.' Her mouth hardened as she said it. 'For five years they threw eligible men of the "right" sort at me, made me go to every dance and party,

60

tried to pretend David was just one of the field. It wasn't until he was a senior houseman, and Bernard Webber got him a registrar slot, that they gave in.'

Interesting, Slider thought. She would have been of age on leaving university, and could have married him then, but it did not seem to have occurred to her to do it without permission. Or was it a matter of money? It wasn't in his remit to ask, though he'd have liked to.

'We got married,' she went on, 'and he proved them wrong – as far as career and income went. Mummy always looked down her nose at him rather, but Daddy respected him for what he achieved. I always kept the women thing away from them, until the end. But they wouldn't have cared about that, anyway, as long as there wasn't a scandal. They would have told me not to make a fuss. And I didn't, for a long time. But in the end, it just wore me down.' She met Slider's eyes. 'You don't know what it's like. The constant, constant—' Her eyes glittered with unshed tears. 'The lies. The excuses. The "conferences". The "medical emergencies". The tawdriness of it all! The way those girls behaved – no restraint. No self-respect. Notes left in his pockets. Telephone calls – the ones where they hang up when I answer and the ones where they pretend to be calling from work. The ones who sat in their cars outside the house hoping to catch a glimpse of him. The ones who were friendly to me at functions to show there was nothing going on and the ones who glared furiously at me across the room. The ones who showed up at the house in tears. The ones who thought he would marry them. They didn't understand the first thing about him. He would never have left me. And I'd have put up with it, if it was just an occasional thing, if it was kept out of sight. But it just – never – stopped.'

She looked around her helplessly, and Atherton, divining her problem, jumped up and brought the box of tissues to her from the coffee table. She looked at him properly for the first time as she took one and said, 'Thanks.' He thought she might have been quite attractive if she ever smiled.

'It must have been very hard for you,' Slider said when she had dried her eyes and discreetly blown her nose.

'It was. I did care for him, you see, and in a way he couldn't help it. He was just made that way. He loved sex, and he couldn't resist when it was offered. And of course a doctor gets offered lots of it. He was a very uncomplicated person, really. But I just couldn't go on. He cried when he moved out. I hated that. We sold the house – we had a lovely place in Chipperfield – and the London flat, and divided the money, and I bought this house.'

'Did he pay you maintenance?'

'No. I told you, we shared the capital. I didn't want anything else from him. I wanted to cut him out of my life, and that's what I did. Made my own life, concentrated on my own career.'

'Which is?' Slider asked.

'I co-own an employment agency – Sturgess and Beale, in Chiswick. We specialize in placing disabled people.'

It was a bit of a conversation-stopper. 'That must be very – rewarding,' Slider managed.

'It is,' she said, back in control and blanking them out again. 'Since then, as I say, I have had nothing to do with David, beyond the occasional phone call. I can't even recall when the last one was. Last year some time. So I don't know what he's been getting up to.'

'Do you know where he's been working recently?'

'No,' she said. 'I have no idea how he supports himself. He could be a taxi driver for all I know.'

'Has he ever suggested to you that he had money worries?'

'No. I imagine he does all right, since he's still living in that house in Shepherd's Bush. I know that cost quite a bit when he bought it. But he wouldn't ask me for money anyway. He'd get short shrift if he did! When I think of what he made me give up ... I loved our life – the parties, the holidays – living in the country – our lovely house. And it's come to this.' She looked around her bitterly. 'A semi-detached in Ealing. That's all I have to show for all those years.'

What was so bad about that? Slider thought. It was a pretty nice house. He made a noncommittal noise.

She looked at him. 'And now he's dead. Shot. He shamed me, but I wouldn't have wanted it to come to that. You'll find there's a woman at the bottom of it. Some jealous woman or some angry husband. I suppose he's gone out in a blaze of glory, in a way. I don't know if that isn't an

63

ending he'd have approved of.'

They were interrupted at that moment by the sound of a key in the front door, and her faced snapped back instantly into *hauteur*, salted with a hint of annoyance. She rose to her feet, forcing Slider, who'd been brought up that way, to stand as well. A man came in from the hall: a lean, well-built man – though a couple of inches shorter than her – in his forties, with a deeply weather-tanned face, unruly dark hair and bright-blue eyes. He was wearing a donkey-jacket over a navy guernsey, heavy cord trousers and mud-stained work boots.

'Oh,' he said. 'Sorry. I didn't know you had visitors.' His accent, while not as cut-glass as Amanda's, was quite pure – a surprise, given his clothing, and hands which had seen manual labour in the recent past. He saw Atherton looking at them and put them behind his back.

'These gentlemen are just leaving,' Amanda said. There was a pink spot – of annoyance or embarrassment, or both – in her cheek. Slider stood his ground sturdily and smiled enquiringly until she was forced to say, 'Robin Frith, an old friend of mine. These gentlemen are police officers. It seems David's had an accident.'

She gave him a glare that would have turned Medusa to stone, and a flick of the head which made him say, 'Well, I won't interrupt,' and absent himself hastily.

Slider could hear him going upstairs; and Amanda's body language was urging them towards the door.

'I mustn't keep you,' she said. 'I'm sorry I'm

not able to tell you anything useful.'

'Oh, you've been very helpful, thank you,' Slider said, but more to give her something to think about than because it was true.

'Odd,' Atherton said when they had left. 'Don't you think it was odd?'

'What, specifically? She's an unusual woman.'

'Her attitude to David Rogers, for a start.'

'In particular?' said Slider.

'Well, she's driven by his womanizing into divorcing him, but she doesn't make him pay alimony. It shows an unhealthy lack of desire for vengeance.'

'Unless she's trying to make it *seem* that she has no desire for vengeance. Or for his money.'

'You think she could be guilty?'

'Anyone could be guilty. I'm sure she's not telling us everything.'

'What she said did seem inconsistent,' Atherton agreed. 'She complains about her lifestyle but didn't want his money. She's confident he'd tell her if he got married, but says she doesn't know where he's been working. I think that there was more contact between them than she's letting on.'

'Probably. But why hide it?' Slider said.

'Because she's guilty?'

'I don't know,' Slider mused. 'She obviously still had feelings for him. A mixture of sentiment and bitterness. And she really seemed shocked by his death.'

'Could be shock that we'd come to her so soon. And you admit the bitterness.'

'Hmm. But they've been divorced for ten years. Wouldn't she need a more recent motive to want to do away with him?'

'She seemed to be deliberately distancing herself from him and his money,' Atherton said. 'But wouldn't it be interesting if it turned out he'd left everything to her? That would answer a lot of questions. "He shamed me but I've had the last laugh." Revenge eaten cold and so on.'

'I wonder what she is living on? This agency of hers? I suppose we'll have to check if it's pukka.'

'It would be a brilliant front if it wasn't,' Atherton said. 'So utterly worthy you'd feel like a complete shit asking questions. And she obviously didn't want to talk about it.'

'But equally, if she's a genuine philanthropist she wouldn't want to talk about it. That would be blowing her own trumpet.'

'You always have to see both sides, don't you? Well, and what about old Mellors coming in? Did she blush! Old friend, indeed – and he went straight upstairs. She's shacking up with him.'

'Quite possibly.'

'It looks as if she has a bit of a thing for horny-handed sons of the soil. OK–' he forestalled Slider – 'Rogers was a doctor, but he started out with coal dust in his hair.'

'Greasely, not Greaseborough,' Slider said, for the second time of what he was afraid would be many. 'Different sort of place entirely.'

'Still, she seems to like sinning below her station.'

'Did you catch the smell from Frith when he

came in?' Slider pondered.

'We don't all have a hooter like yours. What was it?'

'Horses.'

Atherton didn't know what to make of that bit of information. They had reached the car. The gritty wind, rollicking unchecked across Ealing Common, slapped a greasy sandwich paper against the side window, just missing his sleeve. He peeled it off with flinching fingertips. The homeward-bound traffic was pouring across the junction into Hanger Lane and backing up, like water pouring into a jar. Dusk had come, and it wasn't any warmer, and he still didn't have an overcoat on. He shivered, and his mind turned naturally to crackling fires, old oak beams, naff crimson carpets and the sultry gleam of horse-brasses.

'Fancy a pint?' he asked.

'I thought you'd never ask,' Slider said, unlocking the door.

FOUR

They Tuck You Up, Your Mum and Dad

As Slider was trying to get his key into the lock, the door opened, and his father smiled a welcome at him.

'Joanna not home yet?' he divined.

'She's on her way,' Dad said. She had been doing a concert in Norwich, a repeat of the one in Harrogate. 'She rang from her mobile – said they were stopping in The Red House for a pint.'

Slider nodded. He understood how they had to 'come down' from a performance; and also that in a freelance world it was the clubbable people who got the jobs, all other things being equal.

'She'll only have the one,' his father went on. Slider was amused that he should defend her. Or was he reassuring him? In the early days he had worried all the time when she was out on her own in her car. Not that she wasn't a good driver – she was excellent – but she carried so much of his love with her it made him vulnerable. And he was a policeman – he knew what road accidents looked like.

'I know,' he said.

Dad looked past him at Atherton. 'Hello, Jim. You another orphan? Emily's away, isn't she?'

68

'Covering the Irish elections.'

'I was always the same when Bill's mother was at the WI. Home's not home without the woman. Well, come in, don't stand on the doorstep. You both look cold. I thought this morning Bill should have taken a coat. And I see you're no better, Jim. Can't trust March sunshine, you know. I lit the fire.' He looked from one to the other. 'Have you eaten?'

'Lunch,' Slider said, remembering with an effort. It seemed so long ago.

'Sandwich, I dare say,' Dad said. 'You want something hot this weather. I made a bit of stew and there's plenty left. It's in the slow oven, just in case. You go in to the fire and get warm and I'll serve it up.'

'All serene upstairs?' Slider called after him as he went away.

'All serene,' Dad said, looking back. 'I give my boy his supper, we had a little play together, then bath and bed, one story, and he was off like a lamb. There's nothing like routine, if you want a happy child. You were just the same. Never had an ounce of trouble with you, bedtimes.'

He was gone. 'He must like it here,' Atherton said, following Slider down the passage. 'I've never known him so chatty.'

'I feel guilty because he does so much,' Slider said. 'He's taken care of the baby all day and into this evening, and then he's made supper as well.'

'He enjoys it,' Atherton said, with the wisdom of not being involved.

'And he gave up his home and his garden and everything. The garden here's a fraction the

69

size.'

'Flagellate away,' Atherton said. 'I know you need it. Just remember he was all alone, day after day, stuck out there in the middle of nowhere—'

'Essex,' Slider corrected.

'Same thing – hardly seeing a soul.'

'Oh, thanks. Now I feel guilty about neglecting him before. Make yourself comfortable. I'm just going to pop up and see George.'

He trod up the still-uncarpeted stairs, trying not to echo like a mastodon in a drill hall. The house did not yet feel like home, but his senses were soothed by the Edwardian proportions, and the fine detailing which, miraculously, had not been ripped out in the dread days of the seventies' home improvement. The house had been quite a stroke of luck, for even with all Dad's money it was not easy to find a place with a separate flat or 'granny annexe' attached, in the right place and at the right price. It had been a probate sale: an old lady who had lived there most of her married life and died alone, with only a son in New Zealand who wanted the money rather than the property. The separate quarters were in an extension added in the eighties to be let separately and create an income, but which latterly had been occupied by the old lady's companion-stroke-housekeeper.

It needed a certain amount of updating and decorating, but they couldn't afford to do that yet. They couldn't even afford properly to furnish it. It was so much bigger than Joanna's one-bedroom flat, where he had been living with her; and the family furniture from his marriage with Irene had been disposed of long ago. So there was too little in it yet to make it cosy. But they had done their best with the sitting-room, buying a Turkish-style carpet to cover the bare floorboards, opening up the fireplace and arranging Joanna's saggy old sofa and two disreputable armchairs around it.

Dad had his own furniture in his own quarters, of course, and he'd given them one or two pieces that wouldn't fit in; and he had found a wonderful second-hand furniture store where they sold 'Utility' furniture from the forties. The style of it was out of fashion, which was why it was cheap, but it was well made and of solid wood, and only wanted 'a bit of buffing up' as Dad called it. A solid oak extendable dining table, bought for ten pounds, rubbed down, stained and varnished, was a handsomer thing than any skimpy Ikea make-do, and a fraction of the price.

Mr Slider had done everything he could to make Bill and Joanna comfortable. As well as looking after George while they were at work he had turned his quiet, capable hands to a spot of repairing and decorating, as if *he* had to be grateful to *them*, rather than vice versa.

In the baby's room, Slider's latest son was asleep in his cot. By the small light from the hall through the open door, he could see his rosy face, the faint sheen of moisture on the delicate eyelids, the gently parted lips, the madly ruffled hair. George didn't sleep curled up like his other children at that age: he was sprawled on his back, arms outflung, legs straight, fists lightly clenched, as though prepared to go three rounds with sleep before it got him. He hated to miss anything. He had thrown the covers off in his energetic struggle against unconsciousness. It was cold in the room. Slider lifted them gently back over the boy; and had a sudden flash of waking once in his own childhood to find his father doing the same thing. Ah, the massive continuity of fatherhood!

Downstairs again, the sitting-room was deliciously warm from the fire, which was at the red and glowing stage. Slider put on some more smokeless fuel and roused it up with a poker, and he and Atherton stood over it, warming their hands. Slider was remembering an exchange he had had with his father a week or so ago. He had got back from work one evening when Joanna was out and Dad was babysitting, and had found that after digging the garden all morning to plant vegetables for them all to eat, Mr Slider had spent the rest of the day painting the dining-room. In his guilt over the exhausting work rate – the old man was all of seven stone ringing wet – Slider had said, 'Really, Dad, you don't need to do all this stuff for us.'

And after a beat of silence Mr Slider had said, 'All right, son. I'm sorry. I won't interfere any more.'

He hadn't been being a martyr, either. Slider had cried, 'I didn't mean that! I *don't* think you're interfering. I never said—'

'I know you didn't.' Mr Slider had looked at him carefully. 'Look, son, the last thing I want is to be a nuisance to you and Jo. I know how awkward it can be to have someone hanging

72

around when you want to be private.'

'How can you say that? We're so grateful for all you do for us—'

'Ah, that's just it, don't you see?' Mr Slider had said, with a gleam of humour. 'Being grateful, you can't tell me to sling my hook. But I don't want you to be grateful to me. I like to be nearer you, and to have little things to do – you know I don't like to be idle – and I like taking care of my little lad. So I just want you to be honest and tell me if you're seeing too much of me. You won't hurt my feelings, I promise you that. I've got my own comfortable place to go to, and I'm used to being on my own, so you needn't worry. Promise you'll be honest with me.'

They had looked at each other for a moment: level blue eyes, in faces made from the same fabric; one under brown and one under grey hair, but hair that grew the same way. And Slider knew that it would never be possible to say, 'Dad, we want to be alone. Could you go, please.' And he knew, moreover, that his father knew that too. They were caught in a benign leg-trap of mutual love, respect and kindliness, and any such promise was worthless. Worst of all was that he really *liked* having the old man around, and he knew Joanna felt the same, and he was afraid that his father might not know that, and believe he was only being tolerated. But between men, and particularly between father and son, there weren't sufficient words for this sort of thing. All you could do was hope the love underneath was sensed. 'I promise,' Slider had said.

Atherton turned to toast his other side. He had known Slider a long time, and could guess some of his thought patterns. 'For what it's worth,' he said, 'I think you've got a brilliant set-up here.'

Slider looked at him, and read all the things which, again, being men, they weren't going to say to each other. So he said instead, 'I'm going to have a malt. Ancnoc. Fancy one?'

Atherton grinned. 'Better make it three.'

When he had poured them, Slider sat down with his, shoved his shoes off and wriggled his besocked toes towards the flames. A whiff of Dad's rich and delicious stew scented the air. His colleague who was also his friend was enjoying fire and malt with him. Little George was asleep upstairs, and any minute Joanna would be coming home. Sometimes he wondered what he had done to deserve such multiple blisses. It more than made up for the things he faced at work: the smell of blood, the horror-porridge on the carpet, the man with no face, the stupidity and wickedness of murder. He turned his mind resolutely from those things. Sufficient unto the day was the evil thereof.

'I'd like some music,' he said, 'but I'm too comfortable to get up and put a disc on.'

'Me too,' Atherton said. He thought a moment. 'Would you like me to hum?'

'Nah,' said Slider slothfully. 'Dad'll be back in a minute. We'll make him do it.'

There had been nothing in the papers the first day except, 'Man found shot dead in Shepherd's Bush', and the evening local television news had

74

had little more, only some distance shots of the road and the house and the barrier tape, and some white-clad forensic bods coming out past the doorkeeper constable. The victim had not been named, went the commentary, but the police confirmed that they suspected foul play. With no name or even description of the perpetrator there was nothing else to put out.

But by the next day the press had got hold of the Firmans, and the story of the girl dropping off the balcony was too good to leave alone. Fortunately the old people had still got the name wrong – they had given it as Katrina Old – and so far the hospital was maintaining discretion.

'So we've got a bit of time left,' Porson said to Slider first thing, his hands clasped around a mug of tea, inhaling the steam as though for medicinal purposes. His tremendous eyebrows, so bushy they looked like an advertisement for Miracle Grow – the sort where a small child stands next to a chrysanthemum bloom as big as her head – were drawn down to bask in the fragrant vapours, and he peered out at Slider from under them. 'We have to decide whether to put Rogers's name out,' he went on. 'Will it stand us any good? Are we wanting anyone to come forward? What about next of kin?'

'He doesn't seem to have had any,' Slider said. 'The ex-wife says there were no children, his parents are dead, and he didn't have any brother and sisters or uncles and aunts.'

'Very tidy of him,' Porson commented, sucking in tea with a noise like a horse at a trough. 'Hot,' he explained. 'Got any suspects?'

'The only connection we have so far is the ex-wife,' Slider said, 'but I've no reason to suspect her. She does seem to have a man living with her, so it's possible he's involved. Or it could have been a contract killing.'

Porson made a restless movement. 'Don't like the idea of contract killers. Hardest thing in the world to prove. You're on the back foot all the way. Still, if that's what it is, you can't disignore the facts.'

'We have precious few of those,' Slider admitted.

'Then maybe we should put the name out. Poke a stick down the hole, see what comes out. You might stir up a whole new kettle of worms.'

'On the other hand, putting out his name may expose Catriona Aude,' Slider said. 'Her friends may know she was going out with him and make the connection. And the strip club does know there was a relationship.'

'Getting her jugs out for a living, she's no shrinking violet,' Porson objected.

'She's afraid the killer may come back for her.'

'Unlikely,' Porson decided.

'Still, she's all the witness we have. We have to do our best for her,' Slider urged.

'I suppose so,' Porson sighed. 'I'll make a press statement that the witness didn't actually *see* the intruder, only heard him. Makes us look behind the curve, but there's no harm in putting the killer off his guard. Speaking of which,' he went on sternly, 'what *about* the killer?'

'We're still combing the streets and canvassing the neighbours, but without even a description to go on, we've nothing to canvass with. No point in leaflets or posters. We're trawling records for a similar MO, but there's not much to go on there, either – a single shot to the back of the head.'

'Sounds like the bloody KGB. Ballistics?'

'Report's not back yet. I expect it today.'

'Fingermarks?'

'Rogers's and the girl's. The killer was professional enough not to leave any. But the fact remains that Rogers let him in, so it looks as though he knew him.'

'Could've been a meter reader,' Porson pointed out.

'Rogers seemed to have been leading him into the sitting-room.'

'TV repair man.'

'Early in the day for either of those. I suppose the killer *could* have made some excuse to get admittance – people are very gullible when it comes to inspectors with official-sounding business. But there's no apparent robbery, so if Rogers didn't know him, we're back with the contract killer. And either way, unless ballistics gives us a lead, I can't see what I can do except go after the motive – dig into Rogers's background and find out what he was up to lately.'

'Well, *find* out,' Porson snapped. 'Time and tide gather no moss. Get on with it.'

'Yes, sir,' Slider said, turning away.

'And remember,' Porson added more kindly as he left, 'if you need anything, my door is always here.'

* * *

Swilley waylaid him in the corridor. 'Guv, I wanted to ask you—'

'What's happening with the Aude female?' he forestalled her. 'What time are they letting her out?'

'That's what I was going to say. They're letting her go after morning rounds, and she's going to her mum and dad's in Guildford.'

'Right. I'll get on to Mike Polman and give him the word. Arrange an escort for her – I don't want her to travel alone, and I want to be sure that's where she goes.'

'I was going to ask you if you wanted me to go with her,' Swilley said. 'Thing is, she needs some clothes – she's only got that bathrobe at the hospital. Forensic's got her glad rags, and they're a bit saucy for daywear anyway. She needs something from home – from her flat. It occurred to me I could go and get what she needs—'

'And have a look round her room while you're there, in case there's anything of interest? Smart thinking.'

'Thanks, guv.'

'You might see if you can have a word with her flatmates, too, if you can track them down. Don't tell them where she's going, just in case. Tell them she's being taken care of and that they shouldn't try to contact her for a few days. See if you can find out what they know about her and Rogers, and anything else she was involved in. Without giving anything away, of course.'

'Right, guv.'

'Take Asher with you to the flat, and let her

take the clothes back to Aude and escort her to Guildford, while you go after the flatmates. I can't spare you for babysitting. Get back as quick as you can. I think Aude's a dead end and there are better things you can be doing, but we need to be sure. Use your instincts around the flat and the flatmates and don't waste time on it if you think there's nothing doing.'

'Guv, there's no hospital in Stansted,' Mackay said. 'The nearest are the Princess Alexandra in Harlow, the Herts and Essex in Bishop's Stortford, and the Broomfield near Chelmsford. I've checked, and no David Rogers works in any of them. I've gone as far out as Stevenage, Brentwood and Roydon, and I've checked all the private hospitals and clinics – even a veterinary hospital that came up, just in case – but no one's ever heard of him. D'you want me to widen the search?'

Mackay was the thorough one. Slider shook his head. 'No, leave it now. Either the Aude girl got it wrong, or he lied to her. We'll probably find something in his papers.' More bags had been delivered from the site.

'About those papers,' said the Mancunian Hollis, looming over from his desk to join the conversation, tall and thin and shiny at the top like a bendy lamp-post. 'It strikes me that there's not nearly enough of them. Bob Bailey says we've got the lot now, but where's all the personal stuff? You know, photographs, old letters, keepsakes, stuff from his childhood – old school reports, swimming certificates – things from his

79

mum and dad. There's none of that sort o' tackle. Just the basic necessities. It's almost like he was living in a hotel.'

'The place did have that look about it,' Slider said, remembering the artificial tidiness of the house.

'Maybe his ex-wife took it all when they split,' Mackay suggested.

'I don't think so. I've seen her, and I can't imagine her cherishing his clutter,' Slider said.

'He might just have been a very tidy person,' Atherton said. 'Not everybody clings to their bits and bobs. Maybe he chucked out all his child-hood stuff when his parents died, then got rid of everything else when Mrs R evicted him from paradise.'

'Or maybe he's got another pad we don't know about,' Hollis persisted.

'You think there's an attic in his picture?' Atherton suggested.

'Eh?'

'You think he was leading a double life?' Slider translated.

'Not necessarily, guv. But it might be the Hofland house is his town pad, and he's got another house in the country. He might have a wife tucked away there for all we know.'

'You're getting into the realms of speculation now,' Slider said. 'The fancy stuff. The Christmas and Easter menus. Let's stick to what we *do* know.'

'Which isn't much,' said Atherton. 'It starts with Amanda Sturgess, and stops there as well.'

'She could be a tasty suspect,' Mackay said.

80

'Wronged wife, pissed off with his womanizing, set on revenge—'

'After being divorced ten years? Have sense,' Connolly objected from her desk. 'She's a life of her own now. Why would she want to kill him?'

'Revenge, and money,' Mackay said. 'The two best motives.'

'We don't know there's any money,' Connolly said.

'Well, anyway, using a contract killer is good for it being her. It's cold, and it's arm's length.'

'We don't know it was a contract killer. What about Frith?' Hollis put in. 'She's living with him. Maybe she used him.'

'Aude said the killer was tall,' said Atherton, 'and Frith isn't.'

'What's tall? And how could she tell, hanging off the balcony at floor level?' Hollis said. 'She said the killer had dark hair, and Frith has dark hair. And you said he had work boots on.'

'Let's not run away with ourselves,' Slider said. 'Amanda Sturgess came across to me as a determined and well-organized person who could carry through any project she put her mind to, but we haven't the slightest reason to suppose she wanted Rogers dead, so let's just clear as we go, shall we? Mackay, you can look into this agency of hers, see if it's genuine. Connolly, I want you to look into Robin Frith.'

'The dyslexic's Colin Firth,' Atherton said.

'Is she getting the ride off him?' Connolly asked.

'He could be the lodger, her long-lost cousin or one of her ex-clients, for anything we know,'

81

Slider said. 'That's why you have to look into him. What else have we got?'

There was a bit of a deadly silence.

'Then get on with this lot,' Slider said, waving at the bags of Rogers's effects, and took himself off to his office to make phone calls.

Dennis Markham, the ballistics man, rang. 'I'm sending over the report to you,' he told Slider, 'but I thought I'd tell you what it says.'

'I'm not going to like it, am I?' Slider guessed from the sympathy in his tone.

'Sorry, mate. Wish it was better news. We've got a match with a weapon used in a non-fatal shooting three years ago, a post-office robbery gone wrong in Lewisham. The gun – a .38 revolver – seems to have been let off by accident. The evidence of the postmaster was that three masked men came in brandishing the shooter and shouting for the money. He hit the alarm, the one with the gun let off a shot into the ceiling, and they panicked and ran for it. Didn't get a penny. Local police had a fair idea who it was, but they couldn't get the evidence against them, so nothing happened, except that the suspected lads made themselves scarce. So you see?'

'Yes, I see,' said Slider. 'It sounds like a rental.'

'Got it in one,' said Markham.

'Blast.'

'Sorry about that. And given that it was used in a fatal this time, chances are it'll have been melted down by now.'

It was an unhappy fact that there was no need

for criminals to go to the trouble and danger of buying illegal firearms these days, when they could rent them by the day for an extremely reasonable fee. The dealers kept large stocks and rotated them, and if an individual weapon looked likely to be too notorious it was destroyed. There was nothing to link the firearm with its owner except the word of the criminal, and it would be a foolish criminal who dropped the dealer in it. Murder did not carry the death sentence any more, but grassing up a firearms supplier did.

'I hope you weren't depending on a lead from it,' Markham went on.

'I never expect anything but trouble and disappointment from shootings,' Slider said. 'Thank God they're rare enough in this part of the world.'

'One in the back of the head – sounds professional,' Markham sympathized.

'I don't know what the world's coming too,' Slider complained. 'What ever happened to the traditional bash on the coconut with the handy blunt instrument?'

'Beats me,' said Markham.

Atherton and Hollis had been going through the financial side together.

'According to the bank statements,' Atherton said, laying them in front of Slider on his desk, 'he has a regular monthly income, paid direct into his account, from something called Windhover. Here, you see – and here. Fifteen thousand every month.'

'Which sounds like a salary,' Hollis said. '

blew through his scrawny moustache in disgust. 'Hundred and eighty kay a year? Nice work if you can get it.'

'But it's not a huge amount for a top consultant,' Atherton objected. 'A GP can make that much. It's not nearly enough for our fancy-dan Dirty Doctor.'

'Maybe it's not his only income,' said Slider.

'There's nothing else incoming in the statements,' said Atherton.

'O' course,' said Hollis, 'we don't know that this is his only bank account. If he did have another house somewhere—'

'You haven't found any documents to suggest he had?'

'Well, not so far. But like I said, there just doesn't seem enough stuff here, to me. And we haven't found anything like a contract of employment, or any correspondence with this Windhover.'

'What is it, anyway?' Slider asked.

'Don't know yet, guv,' said Hollis. 'The bank's being a bit sticky. You know what they're like.'

'We might need Mr Porson to lean on them,' Atherton said.

Slider was running a finger down the statements. 'Regular outgoings,' he commented. 'This one, three thousand and change, must be the mortgage.' He calculated in his head. 'That's not enough, though.'

'Could have put in cash.'

'It would have had to be a lot of cash,' Slider said. 'Utilities bills, council tax. What's this one, five thousand exactly?'

'Automatic transfer into a savings account with the same bank,' Atherton said. 'We've found a statement for that. There's about four hundred thousand in it. That's about six years' worth, plus interest.'

'Credit cards, two,' Slider noted.

'Paid off in full every month by direct debit. And here's the thing – there's not a whole hell of a lot on them. Clothes, petrol, drinks and meals, but in moderate amounts. It's not exactly the lifestyle of the rich and shameless.'

'Adding it all together–' Hollis took over – 'it leaves him with a small surplus each month – which fluctuates only by a little – and a growing savings account which he doesn't seem to draw on. Which doesn't make sense to me. It's all too tidy.'

'There *must* be some more money some-where,' Atherton said. 'I'm starting to think Colin must be right–' with a glance at Hollis – 'and there *is* another house somewhere.'

'Don't get carried away,' Slider admonished. 'You only think there's some more *paperwork* somewhere. He could have had a safety deposit box.'

'Not at this bank. We asked.'

'Or something hidden in the house. Have all the papers come over now?'

'Yes, guv,' Hollis said. 'Bob Bailey says he should have finished this afternoon, but he's emptied all the drawers and cupboards.'

'Hmm. Well, you'd better find out who this Windhover is and what they were paying him for. And while the four hundred thousand might not be a Blair-type fortune, it'd be nice to know who comes in for it. You haven't found a will?'

'It'll be with all that other paperwork,' Atherton said, 'in that hidden cupboard we haven't found. Behind the secret panel in the library.'

FIVE

Frith Element

There is a certain amount of luck in police work – not so much in finding things, but in finding them early on in the search rather than late. Connolly, charged with finding out about Robin Frith, had begun by looking up the last census for Amanda Sturgess's house at Ealing Common, and had found Frith listed there, all present and correct, in 2001. That was only a bit more than a year after the divorce. Quick work. Was your woman maybe doing the nasty with Frith all along, while blaming the Dirty Doctor for not being able to keep his lad in his pants?

Even more interesting was that Frith's profession in 2001 was listed as riding instructor. Given the Guv's description of Amanda as a sort of rich man's Margo Leadbetter, it was either dopey or dotey – she wasn't sure which – that she should have been shacking up with the stable boy, so to speak. A bit of Lady Constance and Mellors in that carry-on. Of course, that *was* nine years ago, so he might have moved on to a different profession by now. But then she remembered that Atherton had said the Guv had smelled horses when Frith came in, and given the reputation of the Guv's nose, maybe he was still at it. Riding instructor? You wouldn't make a lot of jingle at that. Maybe he was just the lodger after all. Stranger things had happened.

Of course, he might just be riding for a hobby; but if he was still teaching Thelwell kids to fall off ponies, where was the stable? Hyde Park? Richmond Park? Somewhere out west of London, Uxbridge, Denham, whatever? The field was huge. She started west of Ealing and worked a sort of arc northwards round London, but got no nibbles. It was when she had got as far as Harefield that the word Sarratt on the map caught her eye. Amanda had said Frith was an old friend. She came from Sarratt. And Sarratt was a country place where they'd just as like have horses. Give it a try. What harm?

She found the right place at the first attempt: a stable just outside Sarratt called Hillbrow Equestrian Centre. She knew it was the right place because right there on the website at the top under the title it said, 'Proprietor: Robin Frith BHSI.' What did BHSI stand for, she wondered. Big Hairy Sappy Ijit, maybe. It was a grand class of a place: swanky-looking stables with a clock-tower yoke in the middle of the roof. Indoor manège, all-weather outdoor school, cross-country course. Offered tuition in cross-country, dressage and showjumping, as well as basic lessons. Also did livery. Young horses trained. Children a

speciality, hacks in the beautiful Chiltern countryside, blah blah blah. Maybe with all that going
on, he *was* making some money, he wasn't just a
no-hoper after all.

'I used to ride when I was a kid,' she told Slider
when she took it to him. 'Summer hollyers in
Connemara and Kerry. And not just beach ponies
– I went in for gymkhanas, even did a bit of
cross-country once. So I can talk the talk, guv. If
I went to this place saying I wanted to take it up
again, sure I could find out something about the
boss.' To his apparently doubtful look she added,
'Most of the people who work at stables are
females. If your man Frith is a bit of a Bob,
they'll all be secretly in love with him. They'll
be gagging to talk about him to someone.'

'I don't doubt you could get them to talk,'
Slider said. 'I'm just wondering if it's the best
use of your time.'

'Well, guv, the ex-wife's the only connection
we have, and we know the deed was done by a
man. If they've been shacked up such a long
time and she did want the doctor done, who's she
going to turn to? And you did say he'd dark hair
and was wearing work boots, and that's all we
know about the killer.'

'All true.' Slider sighed. 'Well, we don't have
such a hell of a lot of leads, so you might as well
find out what you can.'

'Thanks, guv.' She turned away eagerly, and he
called after her.

'But remember it *is* a village, where gossip
spreads like wildfire, so don't go giving anyone
the idea that Frith is a suspect, OK?'

'You can trust me, guv. I've just got a feeling there's something queer about the set-up, Lady Connie and the gamekeeper, and him moving in so quick after the divorce. There's a story there.'

'I'm all for stories,' Slider said. 'As long as they lead us somewhere.'

From the way Fathom bounced into Slider's room, bringing with him the faint fragrance of sweat mingled with Obsession for Men, it was obvious he had not come simply to chalk up another NTR from the Front.

'Guv, I think I've got something!'

'All right, I'm buying. In fact, I'll have two.'

'Come again?' The large, excitable lad was not very quick on his mental toes.

Slider waved it away. 'What have you got?' He enunciated clearly for the hard of thinking.

Fathom presented a video cassette. 'CCTV,' he said proudly. 'Well, you know the Aude female said when she was hanging off the balcony, she saw the perp go down the end of Hofland and turn left?'

'Yes, into Masbro Road. But don't call him "the perp". You're not on *CSI*.'

'Sorry, guv. Well, I was on the canvass and I'm going down Masbro in the same direction – like as if I'd turned left out of Hofland – and I get this feeling someone's looking at me. You know what I mean. I looks round and I see this security camera. It takes a minute to register—'

'I'm sure it did,' Slider murmured.

'There's this school down the end of the road.'

'Yes, Masbro Primary.'

89

'Well, the camera's in the school yard, high up on a pole. I s'pose they've all got security problems these days. But I reckon if this one's aimed at the school-yard walls, maybe there might be a bit of the street in it as well. So I goes in and talks to the school seckertree, and she lets me have a look at the tapes. And this is Mundy's.'

'Stop hanging it out,' Slider said. 'Can you see anything?'

'Yes, guv. That's what I'm telling you.'

Slider grabbed the tape and walked rapidly through the CID room to the cubby where they kept the viewing equipment, gathering a little trail of his firm as he went. It was the usual sort of security video, grey and grainy, with the date and time in the corner. The view was the brick wall dividing the school yard from the street, with the iron gate in the middle of it; but true enough, the camera had been set high enough to see over the wall as well, and a section of the street, heavily parked on both sides, was visible, with the junction with Hofland Crescent in the distance.

Using the time cue, Slider ran it forward to six fifteen. There were few people about, just the occasional man or woman walking jerkily down the street on their way to the tube, and the odd car passing. The cue ran on towards six twenty.

'There!'said Fathom. He had the benefit of having viewed the tape a few times already. The rest of them squinched up their eyes and prayed. A small figure had appeared in the distance, apparently leaping out of nowhere, because of the way these tapes took exposures with breaks in-between. As he jerked towards the camera, it could be seen that he was wearing dark trousers and a blouson-type top.

Right place and roughly the right time. It *could* be their man. Slider wasn't getting excited yet. He almost did when the figure reached under his jacket – were they going to see him dump the gun? – but what he got out was something small enough to conceal in his palm. Next minute, it became obvious what it was, for the man squeezed between two parked cars into the road, then passed along the offside of the front one and bent to aim the key and plip the door open. He got in, backed and filled a bit to get an angle, and drove away in the direction he had been walking, the bulk of the car disappearing below the line of the school wall and out of shot.

The breathless silence was broken.

'We got something at last.'

'Good on yer, Fathom.'

'Brill, Jezza!'

'It could be our man.'

'Can you see the number?'

Slider, ever cautious, said, 'We can't be *sure* it's him.'

'There aren't that many people around,' Atherton said. 'And he must have come out from Hofland – you could see he didn't come from further down the road.'

'Guv, there's something else,' Fathom said eagerly. 'If you go back a bit further, you can see him arrive. He had to park there, it was the only space. He's trying to look normal, he just takes the space, and walks, not hurrying I mean, up the road and disappears down Hofland. But here's the thing – he arrives about ten past six, and no one else arrives at that time. So it's gotter be him, hasn't it?'

Slider ran the tape back further and watched for himself.

The man sat in the car a few minutes before he got out, but they couldn't see what he was doing. 'What's he up to?' Swilley complained.

'Psyching himself for the deed? Putting on gloves?' Atherton offered.

'He'd made the appointment for six fifteen,' Hollis observed, 'and he wanted to be on time.'

'What the hell did it matter?' Atherton complained. 'Who was going to argue about a minute either way?'

'I s'pose he's just efficient.'

'Bloody 'ell, that's creepy,' said McLaren. He watched the man reappear, returning from Hofland Crescent. 'You can't see his face properly,' he complained. 'He's got his head down. Do you reckon he knew the camera was there?'

'No,' said Atherton. 'He wouldn't have parked there if he had.'

'Nowhere else to park,' Swilley pointed out.

'He was early enough to have parked further off.'

'It was cold,' Slider reminded them, still watching the tape. 'And windy. He's hunched into his collar, that's all.'

'And he wasn't very long. Was there time for him to be the murderer?' Swilley asked, worried.

'It doesn't take long to shoot someone,' Slider

said. 'Also, Miss Aude said that while she was hanging off the balcony, she heard some kind of beeper go off. I'm wondering if this man set himself a specific time-limit to do his search after shooting Rogers – say, two minutes – to make sure he was away before anyone came.'

'But no one heard anything,' Fathom complained.

'He couldn't know they wouldn't,' Slider said. 'If someone had heard the gunshot and called the police, the response would have been rapid. Also there might have been hidden alarms he knew nothing about. This man was so precise he sat in his car to make sure he arrived exactly on time. Setting himself a time limit on his search fits in with that.'

'That's true,' Atherton said. 'And we don't know yet what it was he was searching for.'

'Or if he found it,' Swilley concluded.

'Damn, with all this talking I missed it,' Slider said, and ran the tape back, then forward again, watching the man walk towards the camera. 'Ah,' he said, with immense satisfaction, 'this was the bit I wanted. I thought I was right.' He waited until the figure squeezed between the two cars again and froze the image. 'Look.'

They looked in silence. It was McLaren who got it. 'He's put his hand on the bonnet, the plonker.'

There it was, the pale starfish outlined on the dark metal of the bonnet of the car parked behind his own. An instinctive movement to balance himself as he squeezed through the inadequate space. And after he had driven away, the parked car's number was quite clearly visible.

'Chances are it's a resident's car,' Slider said, 'and if they haven't washed it since then—'

'Cars get washed on Sundays,' Fathom said hopefully.

'And he wasn't wearing surgical gloves,' Slider added, and a few crests fell.

'And, of course, we still have to find him,' Atherton pointed out.

'But if we do,' said McLaren.

'And we get a print off the bonnet,' said Hollis.

'We'd have a piece of concrete evidence against him,' Slider finished. 'Let's get this tape to the lab, get it enhanced, see if we can get the number of his car, and get some stills made.'

Everyone was more cheerful. 'It's a breakthrough,' McLaren said. 'Good on yer, Jezza!' and slapped Fathom so hard on the back his teeth clicked together.

'It *may* be,' Slider said. But he couldn't be churlish with the lad, who, to be fair, didn't sparkle all that often. 'Well done, Fathom.'

Connolly, unaware of all the excitement she was missing, had made her way out to Sarratt, shocked to discover how far away it was and how long it took her to get there. Your man Frith'd want to find a job nearer, she thought, or make Lady Constance move back home: it was a hell of a commute.

She found the stables without difficulty, and saw at once it was a superior establishment, not just from the grandness of the buildings, but the quality of the horses' heads looking out over the doors. Like most stables it seemed deserted, though a chained dog emerged from a kennel at one end of the yard and barked in a bored fashion, wagging at the other end without much hope that this incursion would lead to a nice walk, any more than any previous one had.

Connolly walked over to what she surmised was the office, and found that abandoned too. As well as the usual pegboard covered with rosettes, there were a lot of photographs on the wall, of triumphal moments for the stable, she supposed. A child on a palomino pony receiving a cup – presumably for showing, given the exaggerated backward seat. An old black-and-white glossy of a dark young man on a big horse soaring over a show jump. Press photo, she reckoned: an amateur would be lucky to get an action shot like that. A young woman in a crash cap bending from the saddle to receive a rosette from a woman in powder-blue coat and hat and unsuitable shoes: cross-country, to judge by the mud liberally coating the horse's legs and splashed on the girl's beaming face. A dark-haired man, also mud spattered, on his own two feet, holding the reins of a steaming horse and smiling into the camera, his hair blown by a winter wind. A faint similarity suggested this was the same man as the earlier showjumper; and there were two other photos of him as well, receiving prizes. If this was your man Frith, Connolly thought, he was definitely ridey. No wonder Lady Connie wanted him. And fair play to her, she must have something herself, if he was still with her after nine years. Either she was hot stuff in the scratcher, or she had some other hold on him, because a hunky Bob like him, surrounded by horse-mad girls, would never be short of something to sling his leg over, and she wasn't talking about the horses.

A shadow came over the doorway and she turned to see a young woman in breeches, boots and a thick sweater, with a weather-reddened face and the usual scraggly blonde hair, dragged back into a thin tail, who asked, 'Can I help you?'

Connolly did her bit. 'Hi. Yeah – I used to ride a lot, but I haven't done it for a few years and I want to get back into it. I was thinking of getting my own horse, but I thought maybe a few lessons first'd be a good idea, to get me back in the way of it. It's cross-country I'm really interested in. I understand you do training, too – the horse and the rider?'

'Oh yes, we've coached some of the Olympic team here,' she said proudly.

'Is that right?' Connolly sounded impressed. 'It is you that's the coach?'

'Well, I do a bit, but it's really Robin. He's brilliant. He's won Badminton twice himself.' Her eyes took on a dedicated look as they drifted towards the photograph with the windswept hair. 'That's him with Top Gun – you must have heard of *him*.'

'Wow, yeah,' Connolly said fervently. 'Great horse. But Badminton's as much about the rider, sure it is?'

'Yeah, and Robin's the best.' The girl warmed to a fellow enthusiast. 'I'm Andy Bamford, by

96

the way. You're from Ireland, aren't you? Is that where you rode?'

It's as easy as that, Connolly thought. She was almost disappointed that it was not more of a challenge.

'I'd worried I might have trouble getting people to talk,' she told Slider when she got back, 'but the trouble was getting them to stop.'

Frith himself, it turned out, was out all day, taking a horse that had a sprain to a specialist hydrotherapy facility; which was a blessing in a way because it left the field open for Andy Bamford to talk about him. The rapport with her was established so rapidly that she accepted the invitation from Connolly to go for a jar when her lunch break arrived shortly afterwards, leaving another groom – younger and rather miffed-looking – in charge. Following Andy's battered, mud-and-rust streaked Fiesta, with tangled hemp halters and terminally sick plastic buckets rattling about in the back, Connolly drove to The Cock in Sarratt, and over toasted cheese sandwiches and a half of shandy, she got a full dose from Bamford of how wonderful Robin Frith really was.

'She's pure dotey on him, but I did get one thing out of all the drivel,' Connolly said, 'which was that he's only been at Hillbrow since October ninety-eight, when he bought the place. It was a bit of a kip until then. The previous owners had let it run down, and he was the one that built it up to the piece o' glory it is now. Before that he was working at another stables across the other side of Sarratt, place called Chipperfield—'

'Which was where Amanda Sturgess said she and Rogers had their house,' Slider remembered.

'Is that so?' said Connolly. 'Well, that makes it interesting. Anyway, he'd been working at this stables, training horses, and competing himself, and then Hillbrow came on the market and he saw a chance to set up his own place and do it his own way. He'd his prize money saved, and he sold his house and used the money from that, but here's the thing, guv – Andy says he also took on a partner, who put the rest of the cash up, but nobody knows who it is. He keeps it a secret, and it's only his name on the headed paper, but Andy reckons it's one of his sponsors who wants to keep his name out of the limelight.'

'I thought the limelight was the whole point of sponsorship.'

Connolly shrugged. 'She thinks it's an eccentric millionaire, the looper! She didn't like my suggestion at all, that it was a married woman he was having an affair with. Assured me *her* Robin wasn't like that.'

'You're thinking it was Amanda put the money up,' said Slider.

'It crossed me mind. But there's more. This one had to go back to work, but she'd said earlier that the Friths were an old Sarratt family. I said I'd settle the bill, and when she was gone I had a crack with the barman. I made out I was interested in local history and – well, long story short, he said I should have a word with this barmaid Maureen Hodges at The Boot, who knew every-

98

thing about the place. So I went over there, got meself a jar, got into it with this Maureen, and struck gold.'

'How did you open the subject?'

'Oh, I didn't need to. It turned out she had an Irish granny from Clare, and I let on my granddad was from the same place—'

'That's a coincidence.'

'Well, he wasn't. He was from Raheny, but what did she know? Anyway, after that she felt we were practically cousins, and it didn't matter what I asked, she'd tell me, no charge. Janey, she was a babbling brook! But she knew all about the Friths and the Sturgesses.'

There'd been Friths in Sarratt since Moses was a lad, it turned out. The Sturgesses were comparative newcomers, arriving in the eighteenth century, but they were very well thought of. The Friths were farmers; the Sturgesses had private money, and as well as patronage had supplied two rectors over the period, and had built the village hall. The Knox bit had only recently arrived: Amanda's mother had been a Knox and had wanted it tacked on, but local people sturdily rejected that piece of showmanship and refused to use more than Sturgess – which was perhaps why Amanda had reverted after the divorce.

Maureen had attended the local school with both Robin and Amanda, through infant and primary stages. After that she had gone to the local secondary, Amanda had gone private to St Mary's girls' school, and Robin had gone to Sarratt Grammar for Boys; but they'd still met up after school, at various local do's and friends' parties. As they grew older the social differences between them made themselves apparent: Robin's family were well-to-do, Amanda's a cut above that. Maureen's father was only a shop-keeper, so she gradually drifted into her own set, and she left school at sixteen while the other two went on to the sixth form. But they all remained friendly, on village terms, and Maureen was witness to how things panned out.

'She said it was always Robin and Amanda,' Connolly told Slider, 'from the nursery up. They did everything together. Everyone thought they would get married when they grew up. Well, these childhood romances don't often work out, but the two of them just seemed to get closer. Then apparently when they were sixth form age, Robin threw a spanner in the works, saying he wanted to work with horses. Well, he'd always ridden – so had she – but to her it was just a hobby. She said he was an eejit – he'd never make any money at it, it was a waste of his brains. He said it was all he'd ever wanted. Eventually they had a big row about it. Maureen said Amanda gave out it was a menial job, working with animals, and he was better than that, and he took offence because his family were farmers and he thought she was looking down on them. So it was the big split, and she went off to university, while he went to do a horse management course at this posh residential place in Sussex.'

'She said she went to Edinburgh to get as far away from her family as possible,' Slider said. 'But this story makes sense of that, too. And it would mean she was vulnerable to Rogers when she met him there.'

'On the rebound?' Connolly said. 'Right. And him having the ambition to be a doctor – she'd have approved of that.'

'What did Robin's parents think about his career?'

'They didn't mind. There was another son, the older boy, to take over the farm, so Robin had to fare for himself somehow, and wanting to work with animals seemed normal to them. Maureen said she'd always though he'd become a vet, because he was so good with animals – could do anything with them, dogs never bit him and so on – but he just wanted to ride and train horses. Well, by the time Amanda came back from university, he'd got himself taken on at this stables in Chipperfield – which was quite a high-powered establishment from what Maureen said – and was competing and winning cups and all that carry-on, so he was happy enough. But your woman didn't see it that way.'

'I was under the impression that Amanda came back from Edinburgh already committed to Rogers,' Slider said. 'In love and wanting to marry, only the parents disapproved.'

'Yes, sir, I read your notes. But Maureen tells a different story. She says Amanda came back with the doctor in tow all right, but she still wanted to take up with Robin again. Rogers was a fallback, just in case. She tried to get Robin to stop messing about with horses and better himself, but he wouldn't. Maureen says he's one of these quiet types that you think are a pushover but they're stubborn as a donkey when they make their mind up. And in the end he wouldn't do what she wanted, while the doctor did get on, so she married him instead.'

'That sounds rather cold and calculating,' Slider commented.

'Well, sir, we've only Maureen's word for it that it was that way, but the facts fit. And then she and Rogers buy a house in Chipperfield – that's another one. And here's the really interesting bit: she gets divorced, and no sooner does the Dirty Doctor move out, but your woman puts up the money for Robin to buy Hillbrow and get it in order.'

'Ah, so she *was* the secret benefactor,' Slider said. 'You could have mentioned that when the subject first arose.'

'And spoil the story?' Connolly protested. 'Isn't it better this way? Anyway, the benefaction – is that the word? – is supposed to be secret, which is why she doesn't appear on the website or the stationery. But of course Maureen knows the protagonists. In fact, given it's a village, I should think everyone in Sarratt knows the secret. It's probably only outsiders like the employees who're kept in the dark.'

'Does Maureen know Robin's living with Amanda?'

'No, sir. She said he sold his house to buy the stables and took a flat somewhere in Watford. And I asked her if she knew where Amanda lived and she said somewhere in London. She didn't know more than that. She'd lost touch with her since the divorce and Amanda never came to

102

Sarratt any more so she hadn't seen her in years.'

'So they managed to keep that part secret,' Slider mused. 'Though we still don't know whether they are living together, or whether he's just lodging with her for convenience's sake.'

Connolly eyed him as if he were mad. 'Sir, she wanted to marry Robin all along. No sooner does she finish with the doc than she funds his new business and he moves in with her. It looks black and white to me.'

'It *is* very persuasive,' Slider agreed. 'But is there anything in this to suggest either of them would want Rogers dead? As far as I can see, he's out of the picture. They're divorced, and she could have married Robin ten times over if she wanted to. I can't see any motive there.'

She looked disappointed. 'Well, guv, now you mention it, neither can I. But that's not to say there isn't one. And she's all we've got.'

'So far,' said Slider. He drummed his fingers on the desk, thinking. Amanda Sturgess had still seemed very bitter towards Rogers, even after all these years and having got, apparently, the man she wanted in the end. 'Revenge?' he said aloud. She had said there would be a woman at the bottom of it. Had she been being clever at their expense? It was a common failing in killers who had planned the killing – they longed to boast, particularly to the police. There was no fun in it if no one ever knew how clever they had been.

'Or money,' Connolly said, watching him hopefully like a bird eyeing a worm hole. 'There's got to be money in this somewhere.'

Slider shook his head. 'Even if, long shot,

Amanda was behind the murder, we don't know that she'd get Frith to do it, rather than a professional. She might keep him entirely in the dark.'

'But given everything he owes her...'

'It still isn't enough to ask someone to do murder for you.'

'Unless he hates Rogers as well.'

'Even so, if he's as soft as you've been making out—'

'Oh, I don't think he can be soft,' Connolly said. 'Maybe a pushover in the love stakes, but he's won Badminton twice, and you don't get to do that being a softie. And when Maureen was talking about how good he is with animals, she told how once they were walking home from school, the three of them, and a car going past them hit a pheasant. The poor beast was flapping around, and Robin – they were all about ten at the time – picked it up and broke its neck, just like that.'

'Anyone would do the same,' said Slider, who was a country boy himself.

'I'm from Dublin,' said Connolly. 'I'd have taken it to the vet.'

SIX

Route of all Evil

Freddie Cameron rang last thing. 'To let you know I've taken the fingerprints and I'm sending them over to you. Just in case there's any doubt about the corpse being the corpse.'

'We're sure it is, but thanks anyway.'

'A little surer never hurts,' Freddie said. 'There are no scars or interesting marks on the body, and I'm afraid there's nothing of the face left. Hardly any of the teeth, either, just a couple of molars – not enough to match for dental work. Not sure really how you would make formal identification.'

'From what we know about him so far, there may be several young ladies who could recognize one part of him.'

'Hmm. Identification *per pinem*. Wonder how that would go down in the coroner's court.'

Slider winced. 'Unfortunate choice of word in the circumstances – "go down".'

'You're obviously feeling frisky, old chum. Case going well?'

'As smoothly as a hippo through a hand-operated mangle.'

'Ah. Situation normal, then. I take it you're not

worried about tox screens and other such arcana?'

'At the moment I'm working on the premise that it was the gunshot that killed him.'

'It didn't do him any good, that's for sure. Well, let me know if there's anything else I can do for you.'

'Doctor to doctor, you could tell me where he was working, if you wouldn't mind. He's not on any GP register. The witness said he worked at a hospital in Stansted but there's no such place. And his salary seems to have come from something called Windhover, which we can't identify so far. Ever heard of it?'

'Windhover? Nope. Though there is something faintly familiar about the name David Rogers, which I haven't been able to pin down in the old cerebellum.'

'You think you've heard of him before?'

'Could be. On the other hand, it's a very ordinary name, isn't it? There could be any number of David Rogerses. Or Roger Davises. Roger Davidson,' he tried out, speculatively. 'David Rogerson. Rabid Dodgerson. It could be anything, really. Or I could have dreamt it.'

'Thanks, Freddie,' Slider said warmly. 'I knew I could count on you.'

Porson came to the meeting the next afternoon, carrying a mug of tea on top of which was balanced a plate bearing a Chelsea bun. The troops parted deferentially for him, but he eased his way to the back of the room and perched on a desk. 'Carry on,' he said. 'I'm not here. I'm a

106

fly on the wheel.'

Slider nodded to Hollis, who went through the basic facts of the case so far: the shout, Catriona Aude, the Firmans, the school's CCTV, the gun's provenance. Then Slider took over.

'We're assuming, for working purposes, that deceased was in fact David Rogers and that death was in fact caused by the single gunshot at close range to the back of the skull. There's no reason at the moment to doubt either of these basics, so let's not complicate an already difficult case. Swilley, what did you find out about Aude and her flatmates?'

'Nothing suspicious, guv,' Swilley said. 'She shares a flat with two blokes and another female. She pays the least and gets the smallest room, and it's a bit of a pit: clothes, make-up, sounds, magazines – never seen so much shite. She wouldn't want a cleaner, she'd want a curator. But there's nothing sinister in there. The flatmates seem decent, normal types. They've all got steady jobs, no big debts, no big spending habits. No obvious drug use. The four of them do the usual things – go to pubs, go clubbing, watch telly, have friends round. The two men have got semi-permanent girlfriends. The female and Aude were playing the field – looking for The One, according to the other female. I got plenty about that. Usual rant about how impossible it was to find a bloke who'll commit these days.'

'She was telling the wrong person,' Atherton said. 'Look how often you turned me down.'

Swilley ignored him. 'It sounds as if Aude was the more desperate of the two. Always getting

107

off with unsuitable blokes. One-night stands. Nothing lasting more than a couple of months at best. They were quite excited about Rogers. Pleased for her. He was a bit out of her usual class: money, nice manners, and the fact he wasn't married was a real bonus. She told her flatmates he was a consultant at a hospital, but that was about all. They said he was generous with his money – took her to posh restaurants, gave her a couple of nice presents. Anyway,' she concluded, 'I can't see she was in on it, guv. The impression was she was really stuck on him. Apparently she thought the relationship was going places, talking about something permanent down the line. Talk about the triumph of hope over experience.'

'So you think she was just in the wrong place at the wrong time?' said Slider. 'OK, we'll put her to one side. The only other contact we've got at the moment is Rogers's ex-wife.' He ran through the interview with Amanda Sturgess and related Connolly's story about the relationship between her and Frith. 'Whether the barmaid Maureen is right or not, there is obviously more to it than Amanda told us. The divorce seems to have been acrimonious – on her part, at least. She didn't mention anything about Frith or helping him to buy the stables, and while there's no reason she should have, she did seem anxious for us not to speak to him when he came in. Who's been looking into this agency of hers?'

'Me, guv,' said Mackay. 'It's pukka, all right. Does good work. Big employers these days have got to take on a certain number of disabled by law, but there's nothing token about it. It's got a good name with the disabled charities and lobby groups I contacted.'

'Who's the Beale of "Sturgess and Beale"?' he asked.

'She's a Nora Beale, married, lives in Ealing, used to work for an ordinary employment agency, got a disabled son, decided a specialist agency was needed. Met Amanda at some social do when Amanda first moved there. Her and Amanda set up the agency together and they do all the work, bar one girl who does the clerical.'

'Which makes our Mandy thoroughly worthy and out of the frame for First Murderer,' Atherton said, but discontentedly.

'We still don't know what Rogers was doing for a living,' said Slider. 'What about this Windhover? Have you found out any more about it?'

Atherton answered. 'It's the Windhover Trust, in full, and it's a part of something called the Geneva Medical Support and Research Foundation. The British arm, if you like. It has an address in SW1 but it's only an accommodation address. Everything is forwarded from there to the parent organization in Geneva, and we have not been able to find out anything more about that, except that it's supposed to be non-profit making. The website is outstandingly unhelpful, with little more than an address and a mission statement, and the authorities won't play ball. You know what the Swiss are like. They didn't stay out of the EU to answer questions to the likes of us. There is something called The Windhover Outreach, which does vaccinations in

Africa, but whether that's part of the same thing I haven't been able to find out yet. And what they were paying David Rogers a hundred and eighty kay a year for is anyone's guess.'

'It's not a huge amount,' Slider said. 'And yet he must have been giving them some value in return for it.'

'Advice. Expertise,' Hollis hazarded. 'Maybe he was a consultant in that sense – like a business consultant.'

'Certainly possible,' said Slider.

'And yet,' said Atherton, 'he doesn't seem to have been living on it, or not entirely.'

'Consultants don't usually consult only for one company,' Slider said.

'No, but anyone else he was working for was not paying him a salary into his bank account,' Atherton pointed out.

Porson stirred restively. 'This is all airy-fairy stuff,' he objected, forgetting his temporary membership of the diptera muscidae family. 'It's hard evidence butters the parsnips. What about that CCTV tape? What did you get off that?'

Hollis answered. 'We got the number of the parked car, sir. Right enough it went back to a resident of Masbro Road, a John Fletcher. We caught him at home last night and got some lifts off the bonnet. Luckily he'd not cleaned it for a while, and even luckier that's not a place people put their hands a lot. We took his fingerprints for elimination purposes, anyway. But there was a good set of four fingers and a palm in the middle of the bonnet, matching where we saw the suspect on the CCTV put his hand to balance

110

himself. He must have took off his gloves when he left the house.'

'It's the old saying, they always make one mistake,' Porson pronounced with satisfaction. 'Hoist with his own canard. Have you run the prints?'

'Yes, sir,' Slider answered. 'There's no match in the records.'

'Ah well, can't have everything, I suppose,' said Porson, evidently disappointed. 'But at least when you do get a suspect—'

'We'll have something to nail him with,' Slider concluded. 'It'd be a nice short cut if the prints matched Frith, but he has no criminal record, and at the moment we don't have enough to ask him to give a sample.'

Porson grunted in acknowledgement of the point, drained his tea mug, and said, 'All right, what about the other car? The suspect's?'

'It's a BMW seven-series. Black. The best we could do after the lab had enhanced the pictures was a partial number, missing the last digit and with some doubt as to whether one number was a three or an eight. It gives us quite a lot of cars to check. We're working on that. And we've also put the possible variations into the ANPR at Hendon, see if we get a ping.'

The Automatic Number Plate Recognition system was the computerized record of the millions of photographs a day taken by a network of cameras, some of them part of the congestion charge set-up, others placed on motorways, at road junctions, outside petrol stations, important buildings and so on. Very few members of the public knew about the system, which Slider thought was probably just as well, as there were certainly civil rights implications about the level of surveillance to which the general public was being submitted without its consent. But the images were so well defined that the registration numbers were able to be processed automatically by the central computer. Enter a number, and if that car had passed any of the cameras it would be 'pinged' and its route could be tracked. In many cases, the faces of the front seat occupants could also be clearly identified.

'All right.' Porson nodded. 'Well, let me know if anything comes of that. Do we know what car Frith drives?'

'Haven't found that out yet,' Slider said.

Porson didn't need to say the obvious. 'What else? Have you got Rogers's phone dump yet?'

'Yes, sir,' Hollis answered. 'Seems to be all social. Restaurants, clubs. Garage where he got his car serviced. A lot of women – most of 'em appearing in his address book. He doesn't seem to have had any men friends. Dunno if that's strange or not. Nothing work related. Hasn't rung the only number we have for Windhover, nor any other medical establishment. And he didn't make any calls on the morning he died.'

'Wait a minute,' Slider said. 'Aude said he got a phone call early in the morning, and went into his dressing-room and rang someone on his mobile.'

'Yes, guv,' Hollis said. 'She must have been mistaken.'

'She said she heard him talking.'

'Must have been talking to himself, then. Or she was dreaming. The fact is there's no call logged on either his mobile or his landline.'

'She was in flitters after what happened,' Connolly pointed out. 'Wouldn't be strange if she got herself all mixed up. Coulda been another day the phone call bit happened.'

'I suppose that must have been it,' Slider said. 'What about his landline?'

'Nothing of interest there, except that he made quite a lot of calls to his ex-wife.'

'She told me she hardly ever spoke to him,' Slider objected.

Hollis nodded. 'Definite porky, that.' He took up another piece of paper. 'He's rung her four times in the last three weeks, the last call a week before he was killed, lasting eighteen minutes. You wouldn't forget a call like that.'

'She may just have panicked, given he was murdered, and tried to distance herself from him,' Slider said. People did things like that all the time. 'It probably had nothing to do with anything. Still, I'd like to know what they talked about.'

'I like it when people lie,' Porson said, rubbing his hands. 'Gives you a reason to ask more questions. Find out what car this Frith character drives. And I could stand to know where he was on Monday morning. Given he's the nearest thing you've got to a suspect.'

'Yes, sir,' said Slider. 'Provided we can find out without being obvious. He's not a suspect until we know he's done something suspicious.'

'Can't find out if he's been suspicious until you

113

ask. Which came first, the chicken or the road? Well, keep at it. I've got to go and tell Mr Wetherspoon where we are.'

That'd be up the junction without a paddle, Slider thought. It's a long road that gathers no moss.

Connolly's work in setting up a rapport with Andy Bamford reaped its reward, saving her another trip to Sarratt. She rang her 'for a chat' and found her new friend only too eager, though she was obliged to book the first of a course of lessons to allay possible suspicion that she was time-wasting. Still, she could always cancel later. In the course of the ensuing bunny, Connolly had as much difficulty in easing Andy round to the subject of Robin Frith as in getting a compass to point north. After considerable discussion of the horse he had taken for hydrotherapy and how good he was with animals and how much he cared for them – 'They're not just a way to make money to him, like a lot of trainers I could mention,' – and his prospects of having another winner at Badminton this year, Connolly said eagerly that she was really keen to meet him, asked wistfully if he would be taking her lesson, and added, 'Oh, d'you know, I think maybe I saw him when I was going through the village the other day. Early Monday morning. I bet he comes in really early, doesn't he?'

'Yeah. He's here by seven most mornings.'

'It could have been him, then. Does he drive a black BMW – a seven series?'

Andy laughed. 'A Beamer? No, he's got a four-

114

by-four, a Mitsubishi Shogun. He wouldn't have room in an ordinary car for all the stuff he carries – tack and rugs and everything. And it has to pull a trailer. It is black, though.'

'Oh,' said Connolly, sounding disappointed. 'I was sure it was him. It was a dead handsome man in a black BMW. Maybe he has an ordinary car as well? I could swear I saw it going into your stables.'

'Well, he might have another car, I don't know, but I've never known him bring it here,' Andy said. 'He always comes in the Shogun. Anyway, he wasn't in early Monday morning, so that can't have been him. He had an appointment at Archers, the feed merchant in Hemel, at eleven and he said it wasn't worth coming in first. He said he'd work from home and go straight there, so he didn't come in until the afternoon.'

'So it doesn't get us any further forward with the car,' Connolly said to Slider. 'He might or might not have a Beamer. And anyway, guv, it occurs to me any murderer might hire, borrow or steal a car rather than use his own, when he's going to a murder.'

'That thought had occurred to me, too,' Slider reassured her. 'We have to cover the bases.'

'Right, guv. But if the feed merchant's his alibi, that's easy enough to check.' She looked at him hopefully.

Slider thought a moment. If Frith had been at the stables, all present and correct, at the appropriate time, he would happily have dropped him, having no real reason to suspect him of anything.

But by his own rule of clearing as you went, he ought at least to make sure the man was accounted for. 'OK,' he said. 'Check it out. Discreetly.'

'Sure, they'll never know I've been there,' she assured him. 'I'll be in and out like Jimmy the Dip in a punter's pocket.'

Slider had just got back to his office when Joanna rang. 'Is it any use asking you about having the children over at the weekend?' she asked. 'Irene just rang. She and Ernie want to go to a bridge rally thing at Aylesbury, organized by Rotary. Sooner them than me.'

'I'm with you on that one,' Slider said, settling in behind his desk. The cup of tea someone had brought him before he was interrupted had got tepid. He didn't like tea unless it was almost too hot to drink. He pushed it sadly away.

'Well, she sounded really keen. Did you never play together?'

'Oh, once or twice. I don't mind it as a game, but I can't treat it like a religion, like these real bridge enthusiasts. But Irene liked it as a way to meet what she called nice people.'

'Aren't we nice people?' Joanna said indignantly.

'I'm a policeman, and you're a policeman's wife. Of course we're not nice.'

'I'm a musician.'

'Comes out the same. Irene never approved of anyone who worked unsocial hours. I think ideally she'd have liked to marry a solicitor – office hours, nice suits and plenty of money.'

Joanna laughed, but a little reproachfully. 'She can't really be that shallow. You loved her once.'

'I'm sorry. I did, of course. And she has many good qualities. I just never brought out the best in her. Dad always used to say there was only one reason marriages broke up – you weren't suited to each other.' Hollis appeared in the doorway, with Atherton behind him. 'I'll have to go. Someone wants me.'

'I certainly do,' Joanna said seductively. 'And just as soon as you get home I'm going to get you out of those wet clothes and into a hot bath, young man.'

He grinned, feeling his automatic twitch of reaction to her. Even after all this time ... Ain't love grand? 'Stop it, people are watching,' he said. 'What was it you phoned me for?'

'This weekend. Having the children.'

'Oh yes. Of course, by all means, but you know I can't promise I'll be there. But if you're willing. And around.'

'I'm around except for Saturday night – repeat of Friday's concert. But your dad can babysit.'

'Thank God for Dad,' Slider said.

'I'll second that,' said Joanna.

'Guv, we've got to the end of the possibilities on that reg number,' Hollis said, the list in his hand. 'We struck off all the 03s to start with. McLaren says that car on the CCTV couldn't be that old. It's got the all-in-one intake grille, and that didn't come in until 2008.' He looked at Slider, who got the significance.

'Right.' He nodded.

'McLaren might be a pain–' Atherton put it into words – 'but he does know about cars.'

'So that cut it down a good bit,' Hollis went on. 'Then we ran the possible 08 numbers that were issued to BMWs, and there weren't many of those.' He looked down at his list. 'Just six, in fact. We've checked them out and they're all accounted for. D'you want me to go over them with you?'

'No, I trust you. So what does that leave us with?'

Hollis picked it up. 'There was one car, with the last letter a W. It was an Astra, not a BMW, but it was in an RTA a couple o' months ago and written off. Went to a scrapyard in Stanmore – Embry's.'

It was a well-known ploy. Just as those wanting a false identity trawled churchyards for names of people who died in infancy but would have been the right age had they lived, so those wanting false number plates trawled scrapyards for dead cars of the right vintage.

'It's worth looking into,' Slider said. 'Let's put that number through the ANPR. If we get a ping on a dead one, we'll know we're in business.'

'Might get a picture of the driver, too,' Atherton said. 'Wouldn't that be nice?'

'It would be wonderful,' Slider said, 'if it were Robin Frith. But if it's a complete stranger...'

'Anyone can hire a professional killer.'

'Yes, but tracing him back to the one with the motive is the good trick,' Slider concluded.

The ANPR did its thing and the number of the

scrapped car duly came up, striking joy into all hearts.

'What you might call,' Slider said, looking round at the happy faces, 'a motorized transport.' Given that the carcass belonging to the number was mouldering in its unmarked grave, it was the strongest indication that they were on the right lines.

'The first ping is at the West Cross roundabout,' Atherton enthused, 'a few hundred yards from Masbro Road and the obvious way out of Shepherd's Bush for anyone trying to get far, far away in as short a time as possible.'

The computer picked it up on the A40 at Hanger Lane, and then at Henley's Corner on the North Circular, turning on to the M1. At Five Ways Corner, where the M1 and the A41 join, it was seen again, and at Apex Corner it was on the A41. The final ping caught it at the roundabout where the A410 joins the A41.

'Nothing after that,' Hollis said, 'so it didn't stay on the A41, or it would've been caught at the next roundabout, which is the M1 Junction 4.'

'If he'd wanted to be on the M1 he wouldn't've come off at Five Ways,' McLaren pointed out.

'So the assumption is he came off on to the A410, and since the car – or at least the number plate – doesn't appear again, he must have gone to ground somewhere near there,' said Slider.

'The number hasn't been noted anywhere since,' Atherton confirmed. 'Though we asked Hendon to keep a look out, in case it moves again.'

'And by a strange and yet delightful coincidence, the first place on the A410 is Stanmore,' said Slider. 'Ladies and germs, I think we have our getaway car.'

'Now all we have to do is find the driver,' Atherton said. 'It's a pity the computer didn't give us a good look at him.'

'This is the best photo,' Hollis said, 'when he were stopped at traffic lights on the A410 roundabout, but it's not clear. You can see it's a man, dark-haired, with a dark top on.'

'It *could* be Frith,' Atherton said, leaning over the print. 'Can't tell for certain. He's tall enough, and he's got enough hair.'

Slider also looked. 'Frith was very tanned. Doesn't this man look a bit pale?'

'Just the way the light works,' Atherton said. 'You can't tell if he's tanned or not. The more I look at it, the more it looks like Frith to me.'

'Hmm,' said Slider. 'Not certain enough. Pity. We need to get Frith's fingerprints to rule him definitely in or out. Unless Connolly establishes an alibi for him, I'm getting close to the point where I think we'll have to pay another visit to Ealing Common – loath as I am to upset them needlessly – just so we don't keep chasing our tails. But first let's have a look at the scrapyard, take this photo, such as it is, along, see if someone who looks like this was hanging around there recently.'

'Send McLaren,' Atherton suggested. 'He can talk cars for hours.'

Slider looked at his watch. 'Too late tonight.

They'd be shut by the time he got there. It'll have to be tomorrow morning.'

Connolly was back from Hemel Hempstead, looking pleased with herself. Slider, Hollis and Atherton were still in the factory, Slider toiling over the paperwork, Hollis filling in rotodex cards and Atherton still trawling for information on either Windhover or the Geneva Foundation. The latter two followed her to Slider's office to hear her report.

'Archers is a big place, guv. I don't know why, but I was expecting some little High Street seed merchant, pet shop sort o' yoke. But it's got a forty-foot frontage, and they've a grand big yard at the back for lorries, and a warehouse beyond like a barn. Me heart sank when I saw it, thinking it would be all impersonal; but they knew who Robin Frith was all right. There was this nice owl me-dad sort o' feller – grey hair and specs – in a brown overall who turned out to be Mr Archer himself. I told him Robin Frith had recommended me to come there, and his face kind o' lit up as if I'd mentioned his favourite nephew. Then it turns out he's known Frith all his life, used to see him compete in juvenile classes when he was at Merridee's – that's the Chipperfield stable. His daughter was about the same age – Mr Archer's – and they used to ride in the same competitions. It was gas, the way he was telling me all this! And when Frith bought Hillbrow he took his whole feed and straw order to Archers, so you can see why they like him.'

'What reason did you give for asking about

Frith?' Slider wanted to know.

'I said I was buying a horse and wanted to get an idea of feed and bedding costs, and that Frith had said Archers would treat me fair,' Connolly answered. 'But the way it was, I didn't need an excuse. Mr Archer was only too happy to chat. He had me ear bent the moment I said the name Frith.'

It was Connolly herself, Slider thought. It couldn't be coincidence that she kept falling in with people ready to tell her their entire life story without provocation. She was a real asset to the Department.

'So anyway,' Connolly went on, 'I said I'd spoken to Frith on Sunday and that he'd said he was coming in to Archers on Monday and would tell them to expect me. But Mr Archer says Frith didn't come in on Monday at all. So I say, maybe I got the day wrong. And he says Robin Frith hasn't been to the shop in months. There's no need, they know what he wants and he just rings an order through. I ask if he's quite sure he didn't come in, maybe someone else spoke to him, so he asks around and everyone agrees, Frith didn't come in on Monday, and it would be a bit of an event if he did show up in person so they'd be sure to notice. Then the owl feller looks a bit worried and asks why I'm asking, and I shrug it off and say I must have misunderstood, but anyway I'll definitely be coming to Archers for me feed, and that cheers him up and he forgets all about it.

'So then when I get outside I ring your woman Andy to check with her that it was definitely

Archers Frith said he was going to, because I'm there now, looking into feed for the horse I'm going to buy, and I want to be sure it's the right place. So she says yes, it was definitely Archers, and he definitely said he'd be late in on Monday on account of going there first, straight from home. She knows it was Archers because he said Fred Archer had got some new kind of horse nuts in that he wanted to show him, that were going to be better and cheaper than his usual. And anyway, she says, that's the only merchant he uses, and he goes in there every six or eight weeks to discuss things with Archer himself.'

She beamed around at them.

'Beautiful,' said Atherton.

'It was grand,' she agreed. 'It has your man's alibi destroyed. Did he think no one would check up, the eejit?'

'Criminals *are* idiots,' Atherton asserted. 'This calls for a drink.' He looked at his watch. 'Time to pack up, anyway. Who's for a pint?'

'I'm your man,' Connolly said. 'Me mouth's as dry as a nun's growler.'

'I don't even want to think what that means,' Atherton said. 'Colin? Guv?'

'I've still got some stuff to finish,' Hollis said.

Slider shook his head. 'Go with my blessing, children. I've got thinking to do.'

Thinking, among other things, that while Frith's alibi had turned out to be laughably in-adequate, a man didn't need an alibi at all if he wasn't doing anything wrong. Amanda had been less than honest with Slider, and now Frith had shown he was hiding something. They had

123

become more interesting to him, not less – proving the truth of the old saying, that honesty was the best policy.

SEVEN

Fingers in Pies

Slider was packing up to go home when Freddie Cameron rang again. 'Are you still there?'

'Apparently,' Slider said gravely. 'Was that all you rang to find out?'

'Don't get snippy with me, my lad, or I shan't tell you what just occurred to me.'

'Go on, then. I'll buy it.'

'I have a strong feeling that the reason I thought I knew the name David Rogers was that he was involved in a scandal some time back. Normally I don't pay attention to scurrilous gossip, but when it's a doctor that's involved, the old antennae tend to twitch all on their own.'

'Scurrilous, eh?'

'If it was the same man. Something about furgling a female patient.'

'That sounds like Rogers, from what we know of him. Could have furgled for England.'

'Now, I'm not certain, mind,' Freddie warned. 'As I said, it's a pretty common name. But worth checking on?'

'Certainly. Thanks Freddie. Any idea *when* it happened?'

'Sorry, old horse. A longish time, anyway. But it was in all the papers. Bit of a cause celeb at the time. You ought to be able to track it down. If it was him. And not Roger David or any of the other combinations.'

'Right.'

A few minutes later, when he switched off his light, he saw there was still a light in the CID office next door, so he went out that way, and found Hollis still there, office-managering away at his desk. He looked up. 'I'm just about finished, guv. Putting a coupla last things to bed.'

'Fine. I'm just going home myself.' Slider told him what Freddie Cameron had said. 'The quickest way to get a handle on it might be to put Rogers's fingerprints through the system. There may have been a criminal investigation at the time. If not, then it will mean trawling newspapers or going through the BMA, which will take a lot longer.' These professional bodies were always reluctant to part with information, especially if the business had been hushed up. And if Rogers was still doctoring, it must have been. But if there had been a case, even if it had been dropped, his fingerprints would still be on record.

'I'll get on to it, guv,' Hollis said.

'No need to worry now. Tomorrow will do. Rogers isn't going anywhere.'

And neither, Slider thought as he headed down the stairs to his car, was the case.

* * *

McLaren and Fathom went together to Embry's scrapyard, in case of trouble, and they went early, in the hope of getting the owners to themselves. Stanmore was at the outer edge of London: the A410 – which bore various names along its length but was called the Uxbridge Road at that point – was like a boundary line, with near solid suburban street development below it, and countryside above. Here, on the map, lanes petered out like streams running into sand, and buried their ends in farms, woods, public open spaces, sports fields and the like. So there was plenty of room for a large scrapyard to be hidden behind a fringe of poplar trees – probably put in at the urging of the locals, because a scrapyard was not the most beautiful thing to have on your horizon.

As well as the trees, Embry's yard was fenced around with twenty-foot high steel railings topped with razor wire. Behind lay an automotive Goodwin Sands. The wrecks, once gleaming with new paint and the hopes and desires of their owners, lay sadly rusting in rows and stacked rudely on top of each other, awaiting the stripping of their useful parts and the final appointment with the crusher on the far side. Appropriately, a crow perched on top of the crane was yarking in a desolate, Edgar Allen Poe sort of way as McLaren and Fathom got out of their car. Both being geezers to the core they did not notice the sad poetry of the place, and the only comment voiced was Fathom's: 'Wonder if I could get a dynamo here for me Dad's old MG?'

Dogs began barking as they walked towards the hut which housed the office. One was a Rottweiler chained to a kennel at one end of the hut; the other was a Dobermann on a chain held by the man who emerged from the office, and stood just outside waiting for them. He was squat and neckless, with a boxer's arms and shoulders, a squashed nose and pitiful ears. His brow was low, and made lower by his ferocious scowl, and he had an old scar down one cheek which had puckered slightly and pulled up one corner of his mouth into what looked like a cynical smile. All in all, a face a little girl wouldn't want to kiss goodnight. The eyes under the scowl were cold and grey as lead, and they clocked McLaren and Fathom effortlessly as coppers.

'What do you lot want?' he asked, as unfriendly as his dog, which had given up barking for snarling.

'Just a little chat,' McLaren said. 'You Embry?'

'What's it to you?'

'Come to do you a favour.'

Embry snorted. 'Be the day!'

'Reckon you've had a bit of trouble with theft.'

'I ain't reported nothing. Where are you from? You ain't locals.'

'Reckon you *have* had a theft,' McLaren insisted. Fathom was wandering away a few steps, looking around, which was giving Embry trouble keeping his eyes on the two of them at once. 'Matter of a number plate. Comes back to a wrote-off Astra you got here.'

'My business is legit, 'undred per cent,' Embry

said. 'Had your lot crawling all over the place at the start, making sure of that. And tell your mate not to go wandering off. These ain't the only two dogs I got.'

'Well, if the number plate weren't stolen, you sold it,' McLaren said. 'And that means you been a naughty boy.'

Embry's stance shifted very slightly. 'I got scads a people coming in here looking for spares. I sell 'em legitimate. Bound to be the odd nut and bolt took on the side. Can't watch every bastard all the time.'

'That's why you got all these cameras, ain't it, mate?' McLaren said, gesturing round to the four CCTV cameras mounted on poles in the four corners of the yard.

'They don't work. Just for show – try an' scare some of the thieving fuckers off.' He looked aggrieved. 'And a fat lot o' use you lot are. Had an OHC off a Porsche nicked last week. You know what that's worth? Fuck knows how he got it out without me seeing. Know who it was but I can't prove it. No point telling you lot. You don't do anything when I do report a theft. Useless bunch o' tossers, ain't you?'

'Oh, now, you've hurt my feelings,' McLaren said. 'I come here to do you a favour. Might not feel like being so kind now.'

'Favour! That'll be the day.'

'This Astra. We'd like to have a look at it.' He held out a copy of the scrappage form.

Embry's granite face did not flicker. 'Have to look it up. Can't remember every wreck in the place.'

They followed him into the office, where McLaren noted another security camera, up near the ceiling in the corner, covering the door and the wooden counter. The red monitor light on its base came on as they walked in, indicating it was either motion- or heat-sensitive. As Embry had his back to them, going to a filing cabinet, McLaren nudged Fathom and drew his attention to it.

Embry drew out a folder, opened it on the counter, and ran a finger down a column, comparing with the piece of paper. His finger stopped and he looked up.

'Gone,' he said. 'Went in the crusher Monday.'

'How convenient,' McLaren said. 'And what about the plates?'

Embry scowled. 'They'd a been on it. Crush the 'ole lot together.'

'Then how do you account for 'em being clocked on a BMW in Shepherd's Bush Monday morning?'

'How the fuck should I know?'

'We know you sold them plates.'

'I don't sell number plates,' Embry said, calling their bluff.

'Rented 'em, same thing. Either way, they come out of here and come back in here, ended in the crusher. Car was tracked all the way. So you can make it easy on yourself or you can make it hard.'

Embry said nothing, but he looked at McLaren a touch more receptively. The Dobermann had stopped snarling, and was sitting down, looking warily from face to face. Now it sneezed, rubbed its nose on its wrist, and sighed.

McLaren got out the print taken from the A410 roundabout camera. 'Seen this man before?' he asked.

Embry took the print and, while his face had probably never been one designed for showing emotions, and life had only made it less so, McLaren was sure that awareness flicked through it for a split second. Embry recognized the man all right – McLaren was sure of it.

'Don't know him,' Embry said, pushing the print back at him. 'What's he done, anyway?'

'Murder.'

The tight face flinched, and he must have tensed, because the dog was up again and snarling. Embry jerked the chain to shut it up. 'Bastard,' he said, but it was not apparent whether he was referring to the dog or not. 'I don't know him,' he said again, 'but he might have been here. Might have nicked them plates. Like I said, I can't watch everyone all the time.'

'But the plates were on the car when you crushed it, so he must've brought 'em back. Tidy sort of thief, that.'

'Look, whadder you *want*?' Embry said irritably.

'A look at your CCTV tapes'll do for a start.'

'I told you, they don't work.'

'This one does, though,' McLaren said, pointing upwards. 'Wouldn't leave yourself without a bit of backup, not a cautious bloke like you. And chummy here'll be on it. We need a better picture of him. Give us the tapes, and we may forget about you selling number plates illegal. Or we

130

can shut you down and take 'em anyway. Up to you.'

'You got nothing on me,' Embry said scornfully. 'Stuff gets stolen. Not my fault.'

McLaren leaned forward slightly, fixing Embry with his eyes. 'You don't wanner get us interested in you, mate. There's worse things than number plates to have coming back on you. If we start taking you apart you never know what we'll find. Be a sensible boy and give us the tapes so we go away happy.'

Hollis came in to Slider's office with the air of excitement detectives get when they've had a breakthrough. His gooseberry eyes were bulging, and he brushed at his terrible moustache with the back of his forefinger as though preparing it for the cameras. Not than anything short of the ultimate sanction would do anything to make that pathetic soup-strainer look any better. Hollis was a nice bloke, Slider often reflected, but he simply had no talent at growing hair.

'Got him, guv,' he said. 'He's in the records all right.'

'Rogers?'

'The Dirty Doctor,' Hollis said, accepting Atherton's sobriquet for him. 'Fingerprints came up positive. It was a while back, though – June 1998. Long story short, he was accused of sexually assaulting a female patient while she was under sedation. Happened at a fancy Harley Street place him and two other doctors were sharing. Had his hand up her skirt. But it never went to court. She settled for compensation and

131

withdrew the charge.'

'Well, well. The naughty lad,' Slider said. 'Freddie was right. He said there was a scandal around Rogers.'

'I looked up the newspapers from the time, and it did get in, though there weren't that much, only in the tabloids, and they were big on innuendo and headlines and not much text,' Hollis said. 'Which is always the clue they've not got much. And it died down pretty quick – I suppose when the woman dropped out.'

But as Freddie had said, when it was one of your own, you noticed.

'Was he struck off?'

'I haven't found that out yet. You know what the General Medical Council are like. I'm trying to get on to someone but they're not ringing me back.'

'Keep trying.'

'Aye, guv. But you know, it could have been a false accusation. Happens all the time. Woman wants to make money, it's the easiest way.'

Slider nodded. It happened to policemen, too. And rather than have to fight it through the courts, with all the disastrous publicity, establishments tended to prefer to settle.

'Or she might have made a genuine mistake,' Slider said. 'If she was groggy or drifting in and out of consciousness—'

'Doesn't look as if the practice put up much of a fight,' Hollis said, 'so I reckon there was something in it. Anyway, I'll keep on at the GMC and try and get to bottom of it. So t' speak.'

'Thank you, I'll do the jokes,' Slider said. He

frowned. 'June 1998? And the Rogerses were divorced in September 1999. I wonder if this was the proverbial last straw?'

'Amanda Sturgess never said anything about it, did she?'

'No,' said Slider. 'She did say he had shamed her, but only that he'd had a lot of women. Nothing about his being accused and arrested. I wonder whether that was just natural modesty—'

'Or she didn't want you to know she had a bloody good reason to hate him,' Hollis said, finishing the sentence.

'But it's always the same objection,' Slider concluded with dissatisfaction. 'Why would she wait all this time if it was revenge she wanted?'

Hollis shrugged. 'Maybe you need to ask her. Oh, and another thing, guv – it says in the papers Rogers was a plastic surgeon. But we've got him down as urology.'

'That's what Amanda Sturgess told us,' said Slider. What with that, the unadmitted telephone calls, and Frith's lie about his whereabouts on Monday, the Sturgess *équipe* was definitely due for another visit, Slider thought.

The Sturgess and Beale agency was an office above a travel shop on the Chiswick High Road, more or less opposite the common – a good, central position that would probably command a steepish rent. 'Although possibly the landlord may give it a favourable rate because it's a charity,' Slider said, as Atherton scanned the roadside for somewhere to park.

'Bless your Pollyanna heart,' Atherton said.

'Landlords don't think like that. They'd have to hand back the badge if they did something kind.' He saw a space and drew up parallel to the car in front of it. 'But there's no reason the agency shouldn't have wealthy donors. Oh, get off my tail, you halfwit!' he bellowed into the rear view mirror. 'Can't you see I'm parking?' He jerked a hand out of the window and furiously beckoned past the car that was jammed up behind him. It was a souped-up black Mazda 3 Sport with a driver who looked about fifteen and had his windows wound down so that the whole world could share his CD choice. 'Get you next time,' Atherton said. 'And if I listened to music like that, I wouldn't want anyone else to know about it.'

They walked back to the travel shop. The door for the upstairs lay between it and the next shop: a genuine old Victorian door that matched the age of the building, handsomely painted in fresh red gloss, with a big brass dead-knob in the centre. There was a brass nameplate on the return of the wall: *Sturgess and Beale Agency, Employment Solutions for the Differently Abled.*

'Classy,' said Atherton.

Below that was another plate saying: *Disabled access and lift to the rear, or please ring for assistance.* Below again was the bell, a large brass mounting around a white porcelain button with PRESS enamelled in the centre in black. 'All right for the press; where do the rest of us ring?' Atherton complained.

'I think we'll just go up,' Slider said. The door was on the latch and pushed open. Inside was a narrow hallway with green marble-effect lino tiles and a steep staircase going up; the passage went past them right through to a glazed back door and the lift. The walls were painted cream and pale green and there were sunken halogen lights in the ceiling. All very fresh and attractive. They climbed to the first floor, where the lift came out on the landing, and walls had been moved to make manoeuvring room for a wheel-chair. The doorways were extra wide, and there were polished wooden handrails everywhere. 'I bet the lino tiles are non-slip, too,' Atherton said. 'They've thought of everything.'

'I should hope so,' said Slider.

Through the first open door, they passed into an office, light and airy, well lit, with plenty of floor space. There were three desks, one bearing a printer and copier and stacks of forms and leaf-lets. The other two had computers and tele-phones and the usual office accoutrements. Behind one sat a slight young woman, very fair and pale, who appeared to be suffering from a heavy cold – her eyes and the end of her nose were red and swollen – clattering away full-speed on the keyboard. At the other was a woman in her fifties, rather shapeless-looking, with a mass of greying frizzy hair spreading out and past her shoulders, oversized tortoiseshell glasses slipping to the end of her nose, and an expression of tense concentration on her face as she picked two-fingered at the keys. Through a further wide and open door was a glimpse of a second office, the one which had the windows on to the street. The desk was out of sight to the left,

135

but a youngish man in a wheelchair could be seen, his attention on the occupant of the desk. Slider could distinguish the cut-glass tones of Amanda Sturgess coming from within.

'Can I help you?' said the shapeless woman.

'Detective Inspector Slider and Detective Sergeant Atherton,' Slider said. 'To see Amanda Sturgess.'

'Oh,' said the woman, looking alarmed. She stood up jerkily, knocking over a pot of pencils and biros on the desk. 'I'm afraid she's not available.' A pencil rolled off the table and she stooped awkwardly to retrieve it. She was about five foot four and extremely fat, and was wearing a waistless print dress which reached her ankles, like a floral tent. She pushed her large glasses up her nose and they slid straight back down, as arrogantly as the Queen Mary down the slipway. 'Can I help at all? I'm Nora Beale. Ms Sturgess's partner.' She came round the end of the desk and took a step towards them, and dithered, as if wondering whether to offer to shake hands or not. The outer edge of her hip knocked a small pile of papers to the ground. 'Oh!' she said again, and made to retrieve them, but Atherton got in first, stooping like a hawk, gathering them in one pass of his long fingers and presenting them to her. She almost snatched them from him, looking at him in confused annoyance. 'They're confidential,' she objected, and pushed her glasses up again. 'Were you enquiring about employing a differently abled person? I have a leaflet covering the legal requirements, if you aren't sure about them.'

136

Unseen within the inner room, a hand closed the door.

Slider raised his hand slightly, to prevent the woman attempting to get across the room to the leaflet table, which he thought in her state of nervousness would leave a trail of havoc. The young woman had ceased typing and was watching the scene. 'No, thank you. I need to speak to Mrs Sturgess about a personal matter.'

'It's *Ms* Sturgess,' Beale corrected, with more force than anything she had said so far. 'And I'm afraid it's quite impossible to speak to her. She has someone with her. One of our clients.'

'Yes, so I saw,' Slider said. 'I'm afraid it is rather urgent, however. Would you please tell her we are here?'

'I can't disturb her when she's with a *client*,' she objected, outraged. 'Our clients are very vulnerable, and must be given every consideration. You'll have to come back some other time. It's best to make an appointment, you know. Ms Sturgess is always *very busy*.' Her face was mottling, though whether with fear or anger, Slider couldn't tell. Her devotion to Amanda Sturgess was obvious, but from the little he had seen, it was not so obvious why Amanda would keep her about the place.

'I quite understand,' he said soothingly, 'but I must ask you to interrupt her and tell her we are here. We'll wait while she winds up the interview.'

Ms Beale made various disapproving, tutting noises, but she blundered back round her desk and rang through to the other office, turning away and covering her mouth while she muttered her message. When she had put the phone down again she went back to her hunt-and-peck typing without a word to the two intruders, though judging from the amount of backspacing she was doing, she was too upset to be making a good job of it. It was the younger woman who said, 'Would you like to sit down?' and gestured towards some chairs on her side of the room. Slider smiled at her and politely declined. He was not going to be passively seated and let them think the waiting was all right.

It was eight minutes before the inner door opened and the man in the wheelchair appeared, with Amanda Sturgess behind him. She ignored the visitors with glacial completeness as she escorted him out, talking to him the while, all the way to the lift. Only on her return did she give Slider a cold glance and say, 'You may come in,' and then stalked past them into her sanctum.

They followed her in and closed the door, and she faced them, standing, across her desk and got the first punch in. 'If you wish to speak to me in future you *must* make an appointment. I do *not* appreciate your turning up here unannounced, embarrassing me, annoying my staff and upsetting the clients. You must understand that our clients are extremely vulnerable people, and I cannot have disturbing influences putting them at risk.'

Slider took it straight back to her. 'And you must understand that I do not appreciate being lied to. It makes me feel very disturbed, and when I get disturbed I tend to come and disturb

138

others.'

She was shocked by his use of her own words. Her eyes widened and she reddened angrily. 'How *dare* you be facetious?' she cried. 'Don't you grasp the importance of our work here? We are a *charity*! We deal with *disabled people*!'

'It's not your business I'm interested in, it's you personally. And you need to grasp that I am investigating a murder, and that hindering an investigation is an imprisonable offence.'

Atherton thought his boss was going in a bit hard, but it seemed he had the measure of her. She shut her mouth with a snap and sat down abruptly, and when she spoke again a moment later her tone was different, quieter.

'But I'm *not*. I *wouldn't*. Obviously I want to help you if I can, in any way possible, but I don't see what I can do. I don't know anything about it. You can't really suppose that I do.' She looked at him with furious appeal.

'What I may or may not suppose is beside the point,' Slider said. 'I deal in facts, and the fact is that you have lied to me, and I don't like it. Lies make me restless. I have to know what's behind them.'

'I *didn't* lie to you,' she said indignantly, but there was a consciousness in her eyes, and a wariness. Atherton noted it with interest. She was wondering which lies had been uncovered, he thought – which argued that there had been several of them.

'There are lies of commission, and lies of omission,' Slider said. 'Perhaps a purist might ease their conscience over the latter, but there's no excuse for the former. You told me that you hadn't spoken to your former husband for months, and that you only spoke to him about once a year anyway. But we know that you have spoken to him frequently in the last few weeks. And that you had a long telephone conversation with him only a week before his death.'

And suddenly she was quite calm again. She straightened her shoulders, laid her hands before her on the desk, and said, as if it were a normal interview and she was in control of it, 'The telephone conversations had nothing to do with your investigation, and my not telling you of them has not hampered you in any way. Really, these are very trivial matters to come trampling in here threatening me about. I have a mind to make an official complaint about your behaviour, Inspector Slider. You may not be aware that the Chief Constable of Hertfordshire is a very great personal friend of mine.'

'I'm afraid he does not have any authority over me,' Slider gave her back calmly. If she was threatening him, she must have something to hide, which only spurred him on. 'The Metropolitan Police report directly to the Home Secretary.'

She smiled unpleasantly. 'Please don't suppose that I have never met *him*, either. Is that it?'

'You told us your husband's specialty was urology, but in fact he was in plastic surgery.'

That caused her a little flicker, but she came back smoothly. 'He *began* in urology, but he changed to plastics when an opportunity came up. Again, it had nothing to do with your investi-

140

gation. And what are these so-called sins of omission? Equally trivial, I have no doubt.'

This was not the way round Slider wanted to do the interview, but he had not managed to shake her sufficiently. 'You didn't tell us that your husband had been arrested for indecent assault.'

'My ex-husband. No, why should I? It was a long time ago. It's none of my business now, and none of yours either.'

'I'd like to know something about it.'

'Look it up in the papers. I'm sure it's all there. It is not something I wish to talk about.'

'Was that why you got divorced?'

'Really, I *will* not answer questions about my private life. It was more than ten years ago. It has nothing to do with anything in the present, and I refuse to satisfy your prurient and idle curiosity. You should be concentrating on finding out who killed David, not harassing responsible citizens and interfering with their work. If that is all you have to say I must ask you to leave. I am too busy for this nonsense.'

Slider studied her for a moment and she held his look unflinchingly. Quietly, he tried, 'You didn't tell us that you had put a large amount of money into Hillbrow Equestrian Centre.'

Now that was interesting. That one, which ought to have received only a puzzled 'what's that got to do with anything?', actually made her blink. You could see her trying to think her way through it. Finally she said, 'My financial relationship with Hillbrow is none of your business.' It was the finance that bothered her. Not passion,

141

but money? There was definitely something to be found out, and he meant to find it.

'Where was Mr Frith on Monday morning?' he asked.

She was still puzzled, he could see, but she had taken comfort from this new direction. 'You had better ask him,' she said.

'I'm asking you.'

'I am not disposed to tell you,' she said grandly.

'Do you *want* to be arrested?' he asked with assumed incredulity.

'I know very well that you will not do any such thing.'

'Are you quite sure of that?'

They locked eyes across the desk, and it was Amanda who flinched. She looked away, towards the window. 'He went to work as usual.'

'At what time?'

'He generally leaves at six or six fifteen.'

'What time did he leave on Monday?'

'I think it was – six fifteen. Yes, a quarter past six.'

'Does he drive to work?'

'Yes, of course. How else could he get there?'

'What sort of car does he drive?'

'A four-by-four. A Shogun.'

'Does he have any other car?'

'No. Why would he need two?'

'But you have a car.'

'Of course. We are not joined at the hip,' she snapped, seeming annoyed by the idea that she might not need a car if he had one. 'I have a BMW 750Li.'

Atherton was too well trained to stir at that, but Slider felt his gladness. 'But in fact, Mr Frith did *not* go to work as usual on Monday. He told his staff he was working from home and going straight from there to an appointment at eleven. But the appointment was also fictitious.'

Now that *did* move her. She did not speak, only stared at Slider blankly, with some furious thinking evidently going on behind the marble front-age.

'Would you like to reconsider your statement to me?' Slider offered.

Her voice was faint and strained. 'Yes – I – made a mistake. Monday – yes – that was different. He was working from home. Some paperwork. He was still there when I left for work myself at a quarter past eight.' She rallied, composed herself, and said coldly, 'It is easy enough to mistake one day for another. My work here is important and occupies my mind to the exclusion of trivial domestic detail.'

Nice save, Slider thought. But not good enough. He switched direction in the hope of unbalancing her again. 'What did you and David Rogers talk about during that last conversation?'

It took her a second to answer. 'I don't remember,' she said, and he could see it was a lie.

'It was a long call. Nearly twenty minutes. I'm sure you must remember it.'

'I remember the *call*,' she said with faint irritability. 'I don't remember what was said. Just general chit-chat. Nothing important.'

'So you *were* on friendly terms with him,' Slider said. 'One doesn't chit-chat for twenty minutes on unimportant subjects except with people one is close to.'

She looked at him, trying to work out the implications of the statement, and did not answer.

'But you told me you were not close, that you had no idea what he was doing, that you had little contact with him.'

She shifted in her seat. 'I *don't* know what he does, and I don't want to know. And I *don't* normally have much contact with him. Just lately he has rung me a couple of times. I can't tell you why. Perhaps he was bored. Or lonely. He was a weak man, the sort who can never be satisfied with his own company. Always had to be doing something, going somewhere, meeting someone.' She seemed to be growing annoyed at the memory. 'He was weak and unreliable and irresolute, and he made my life hell–' she did not exactly pause, but the rest of the sentence came out in a very different tone, as if she had heard herself and corrected it – 'but we were married for a long time, so I suppose there was still a fondness there for him. I'm sorry he's dead. And particularly that he was killed in that shocking way.'

Outside, Atherton said, 'Well, I don't know that that gets us any further forward. Except that she has a BMW. And she gave Frith an alibi.'

'Unfortunately. If she didn't leave for work until eight fifteen he's covered,' Slider said. 'Even on the normal schedule he couldn't have left at six and been in Shepherd's Bush at ten past.'

'But if he was doing the job for her, we can't take her word,' said Atherton. 'And as there were just the two of them at home it can't be disproved. Bummer. When my love swears that she is made of truth, I do believe her, though I know she lies.'

'Eh?'

'Shakespeare.'

'The bummer, or the last bit?'

'Both. That business about the phone calls—'

'Doesn't hold water. That last phone call wasn't just chit-chat. I'd like to get hold of her phone records, see if *she* rang *him* as well, during that period. *Something* was going on; and he ended up dead. If she didn't arrange it, she knows more about it than she's telling us.'

'But getting it out of her will be the trick,' said Atherton. They paused at the kerb. 'What now?'

'Back to the factory. I still want to find out what happened with Rogers and the female patient.'

'Isn't that old history?'

'Maybe. But I have a feeling it may be important.'

'Oh, I'll go with your feelings any day,' Atherton said easily. 'If you could bottle them, you wouldn't need to train detectives, just inject them. But before we leave – there's a superlative sandwich shop just round the corner, and it is getting on for lunchtime. Shall we stock up?'

'When you say superlative,' Slider said suspiciously, 'you aren't talking grilled tofu on sundried tomato focaccia and with beetroot and courgette coleslaw, are you?'

145

EIGHT

Beauty in a Mist of Tears

Atherton's reply was lost because behind Slider's head he had seen the red door open again, and the pale young woman come out. He nudged his boss and Slider turned to see her pause, look round, spot them, hesitate, and come towards them.

'Hello. Did you want to speak to us?' Slider said kindly.

'It was my lunch break anyway, but I thought I might catch you,' she said, with a frowning, uneasy peep upwards at them – she was small as well as thin, almost a childlike figure. 'I don't know if I should – if it's important...'

'Anything you can tell us could be important,' Slider said. 'Is it about your boss?'

'Sort of. Well, it's David. I've been seeing him.'

Slider suddenly realized the signs of a heavy cold were in fact signs of weeping. 'Then I definitely think you should talk to us,' he said.

She glanced upwards at the window of the office. 'Not here,' she said. 'Amanda might look out and see us. Can we – I mean, it is my lunchtime...'

'Of course. Where would you like to go?' Slider said.

'There's a place along there – Eddie's – they do sandwiches and things,' she said.

Eddie's proved to be a wholly unreconstructed sandwich bar, with a few chrome-and-formica tables in the back of the sort that come screwed to the floor and all-in-one with their chairs. But the coffee smelled good, and the sandwiches were made to order from basic ingredients of the old-fashioned sort: ham, cheese, corned beef, liver sausage, lettuce, tomato, cucumber etc. And the coleslaw was made of cabbage.

'This is *not* the place I was talking about,' Atherton whispered as they went in.

'Oddly enough, I guessed that,' Slider murmured back.

The young woman, whose name was Angela Fraser, only picked listlessly at her food, and seemed likely at any moment to start leaking at the eyes again. Slider addressed his sandwich – he'd gone for the liver sausage, mostly to annoy Atherton, who thought it was the Devil's Truncheon – and got her started.

'So you knew David Rogers?' he offered.

She nodded. 'We'd been going out for a while.'

'Going out as in...?'

She cast her eyes down, and colour came into her cheeks for the first time. 'We were lovers,' she managed at last. It was a curiously modest phraseology, for a female who looked to be in her early thirties. 'We saw each other every week, on a Monday or Tuesday, and sometimes

147

Saturdays. Unless there was some work reason why he couldn't. Which there often was,' she admitted, sighing.

'What was his work?' Slider slipped in.

She looked surprised. 'He was a doctor,' she said in an explaining-the-bleedin'-obvious tone. 'A consultant,' she bettered it.

'At a hospital?'

'I suppose so. He never talked about his work,' she said. 'He told me he was a consultant, that was all. Well, I sort of knew that anyway, because Amanda had said so. But he never said anything else about it.'

'So you don't know what field he was in?' Atherton asked. She shook her head. 'Or what hospital?'

'No. I told you, we didn't discuss it. We had other things to talk about.' She smiled faintly. 'He was great company. And he was interested in things I was interested in, too. I mean, we talked about films and clothes and decorating and food and everything. Not just football and cars, like most of the men I've dated. He'd always notice my hair and make-up and things. He didn't think it was weak to know about stuff like that.'

'He was a metrosexual,' Atherton suggested.

She nodded, her eyes filling. 'He was great. He bought me a Dolce and Gabbana handbag. I can't *tell* you what it cost.'

'It's nice when a man is generous,' Slider said warmly. 'I suppose he was well off?'

'I suppose he must have been.' She looked dreamy, remembering. 'It was always the best, wherever we went – best seats, best restaurants, taxis everywhere, champagne. He always had loads of cash on him. He paid for everything cash – even the handbag.' Her expression sharpened suddenly. 'You're not thinking I went out with him for his money?'

'Of course not,' Slider said soothingly.

'Because it wasn't that at all,' she informed him sternly. 'He was a lovely man, sensitive and kind. He was a great listener. He always wanted to know what was on my mind, not just rushing me into bed like other men. That's what I loved him for.'

It was a good ploy, Atherton thought. If you can listen to a woman with an appearance of interest, no matter what bollocks she's talking, for long enough, she's yours. The old Dirty Doctor had doubtless developed his skills over a long period.

'So how long had you been going out?' he asked.

'Fourteen months,' she said, with a hint of pride. 'We'd started talking about taking our relationship to the next level.'

'I thought you were already lovers,' Atherton queried.

She frowned. 'I don't mean that. I mean moving in together. I've got this flat in South Acton, and he had this house in Shepherd's Bush. I never saw it – we always used my place. He said he'd never liked his house and only bought it because he had to have somewhere to lay his head, and it was a good investment. But he kept saying he wanted to see more of me, though with his work commitments he couldn't

149

manage more than twice a week, sometimes not even that, so I said maybe we should look at both selling and getting a place together, and that's where we were at when – when...' Definite filling of the eyes. Slider pulled a couple of paper napkins out of the dispenser on the table and pressed them into her hands. 'I can't believe he's gone,' she cried into her hands. 'I'll never see him again. And we were – we were – *so in love!*'

Slider exchanged a glance with Atherton while she was busy and read his cynical amusement. No doubt this poor deluded female had been due for the big drop, having brought up with Rogers the unmentionable subject of commitment, but the pain was no less real for her. Twice a week – at her flat – for Angela; twice a week – after stripping, and at his place – for Cat. How many others? How easy women made it these days, when sex was simply expected at the end of a date – particularly when they had hit the thirty barrier and were afraid of being left mateless. Hard-to-get meant you had to sit through dinner. But there was nothing wrong with Angela Fraser: she was pretty, personable, articulate. She must often ask herself, why wasn't she married? A handsome, generous doctor willing to pretend to be interested in her must have seemed like a Godsend. No wonder she thought she was in love with him – and told herself he was, with her.

She emerged from her muffling, accepted another couple of napkins, blew her nose, and said abruptly, 'When will the funeral be? I want to go.'

'I don't know,' Slider said. 'We can't release the body while the investigation is going on.' It wasn't strictly true, but at the moment they hadn't anyone to release it to; and, anyway, who knew whether Miss Fraser would end up being invited? He understood it would be important to her, seeing herself effectively as the widow, but the reality might be very different and he didn't want to get into that.

Fortunately she was bracing herself up. 'I'm sorry about crying,' she said. 'I must look a sight.'

'Not at all,' Slider said gallantly. 'Just a little pink.'

'I've been crying a lot at home,' she confessed. 'I have to try to hide it at work. Amanda would be furious if she knew I'd been seeing David. But I want to help you. Whoever did this terrible thing, they must be caught and made to suffer. Do you have any idea who it was?'

'I was hoping you might be able to give us some sort of insight into that,' Slider said earnestly. 'You obviously knew him very well. Did he have any enemies?'

'What, apart from Amanda?' Angela said with a scornful look. 'She *hated* him.'

'Why was that?'

'Because of the divorce,' she said dismissively. 'She just didn't understand him, that's what. He wouldn't have looked elsewhere if she'd been more sympathetic. I just can't imagine them married – she was so wrong for him. He was so gentle and sensitive. She's hard, and all she cares about is business.'

'I thought she cared about her clients,' Slider said. 'I mean, she's doing very worthwhile work with the agency, isn't she?'

'Oh, that's what she'd tell you,' Angela snorted. 'She loves everyone to think she's this saintly Mother Theresa sort of figure, but all she does it for is the applause. She's as hard as nails really, and the way she talks to them sometimes – telling them to stop feeling sorry for themselves, and that they can do more than they think, and they should get out and get a job and stop making a thing about their disabilities. Well, if people knew, she wouldn't get invited to all these conferences, and dinners, and opening facilities and everything. Anyway, it's me and Nora do all the work, really. She's always out "networking", as she calls it.'

'Do you know Robin Frith?' Slider asked, before she exploded with wrath.

'What, her fancy man? Yes, and how come it was all right for *her* to shack up with *him*, but not all right for poor David to find comfort in another woman's arms after the hell she put him through?'

'So you've met him – Robin Frith?' Atherton tried to get her back on track.

'Not met, exactly. I've seen him once or twice. He looks a bit of a hunk, actually – I can't think how she caught him. But I don't really know him. I think he's got his own business,' she concluded vaguely, 'but I don't know what it is. Amanda doesn't talk about him. Well, she doesn't really talk about personal stuff much. She doesn't encourage what she calls gossip in

152

the office.'

'Why do you think she would have minded you going out with David?' Atherton asked.

'Oh, because the first time I met him, he'd come into the office to see Amanda about something and she had a client with her, and he sat by my desk and started chatting to me, and we were getting on really well when she finished and came out and – well, you should have seen the look. She practically dragged him into her room, and I couldn't hear what they were saying, but you could tell from the tone she was tearing him off a strip. And when he came out he looked furious, but he sort of swallowed it down and he winked at me as he left. Then she called me in and bollocked me for talking to him, and said that I was not to use the workplace as a dating agency and she didn't pay me to flirt with men on her time and that if I wanted to make myself sexually available to aging Lotharios I should go and stand on a street corner in Soho, and she'd be happy to release me without notice if that was the summit of my ambition.' She looked from Atherton to Slider and back. 'She really said that.'

You had to admire her vocabulary, Slider thought. And if David had 'dropped in' at the office, it proved there was more contact between them than Amanda admitted. 'So she didn't want you to get to know David,' he mused. 'I wonder why.'

'Jealousy,' Angela said promptly. 'Didn't want anyone else to give him the happiness she couldn't. But she couldn't keep us apart. When I went out at lunchtime a bit later to get a sand-wich he was waiting for me in his car. Took me to Strand-on-the-Green for lunch, and it took off from there. We agreed never to let Amanda know, because he said it would make her furious and I was afraid she'd sack me if she knew. Because I could make him happy, and she'd failed. We've been together ever since. If only he hadn't been so busy, we could have seen more of each other. We could have been married by now.'

Atherton couldn't bear another helping of pink blancmange. 'What about David's friends?' he asked. 'Did you meet any of them?'

'No, not really,' she said. 'We were too wrap-ped up in each other ever to want anyone else. Our dates were too precious to water them down with other people.'

'So you don't know if he had any enemies? Any difficulties at work? Was anyone threaten-ing him? Did he have money worries?'

'No, nothing like that. I mean, he never talked about work, but he'd have said if he was in trouble. I mean, we told each other *everything*. And he had plenty of money. I've told you that.' Suddenly she frowned. 'Except – I've just remembered. He was a bit preoccupied lately.'

'Preoccupied?' Slider queried.

'A bit absent, sort of. Thinking about stuff. I'd suddenly realize he wasn't listening properly, and he'd sort of "come to" and apologize.'

'You didn't ask him what he was thinking about?'

'Well, yes, but he'd just say, "Oh, nothing, sorry," and change the subject.'

154

'How long had this "thinking" been going on?'

'About two or three weeks, I suppose. Maybe longer.'

'Can you pinpoint anything that might have started it?'

'Not really,' she said slowly, working back in her mind. 'Except – well, he used to go to this place in Suffolk.'

'What place?'

'He didn't say. You see, if we went out on a Tuesday, we'd go back to my place, but he hardly ever stayed the night because he said he had to get up really early, like crack of dawn, on Wednesdays to go to Suffolk. I just thought it was another hospital he worked at. Anyway, this Tuesday night – Tuesday before last – when he got out of bed, he came back to kiss me and said he wished he didn't have to go. I said, well don't, then, and he said he wished he never had to do that damned journey again, and for a minute he looked really—' She sought the right word. 'Really *bleak*. I thought he just meant that he wished we were living together, but I'm thinking now maybe he was talking about this Suffolk job. Because when he left he said he wasn't sure about next week because things might be changing in his life. He said, "There's a big decision to be made, and it could change everything." Well, I thought he was talking about him and me. But maybe he meant this job. Anyway, the next week we met the same as usual, but it was from then, now I think about it, that he was in this funny mood.' She looked at them anxiously. 'He was definitely worrying about something. Do you

155

think he knew what was going to happen? Was someone threatening him?' Her eyes filled again. 'I can't bear to think he had that hanging over him, and didn't tell me. He was too much of a gentleman to put something like that on me. Always wanted to protect me. But I could have taken it. I might have helped him.'

Slider handed over more napkins and said, 'Are you sure he never said anything about where he went in Suffolk? Or why he went? The name of the hospital. Did he mention a town? Or tell you about his journey? You know – "there were roadworks on the A45", or "the traffic was terrible through Saffron Walden". Anything like that?'

'No. He didn't talk about driving or traffic or dull stuff like that.'

Definitely a man in a million, Slider thought. Where two or three men are gathered together, there shall routes be discussed. How could any red-blooded male drive regularly to Suffolk and never so much as mention the Army and Navy roundabout, necessity of avoiding, the Thetford bypass, difference made by, or the little-known short cut that shaved ten minutes off the Royston to Bury leg?

He changed tack. 'You said you met him at the office. Did he often call in?'

'No, I think I've only seen him there three or four times since we opened. I suppose *she* scared him off. But he rang her up sometimes. Nora answered the phone and put the calls through to Amanda, and I'd hear her say, "It's David Rogers for you."'

'How often?'

'Oh, not often. It'd be once a month or less – except this last few weeks. Then it was a couple of times a week.'

'You didn't ever hear anything that was said?' Slider asked without hope.

She shook her head. 'They weren't long calls, and you could tell they made her mad, because she'd slam the phone down, and once I went in with some typing straight after and she had a face like thunder for a second before she hid it. I thought maybe he was trying to soften her up for him and me moving in together. But maybe—' She looked at them with pitiful and failing hope. 'I suppose it probably wasn't that? I suppose it was this trouble he was in?' Slider didn't answer. 'But why would he talk to her about it and not me about it? I thought he loved me.'

'That was a sickening spectacle,' Atherton commented when they were alone again, heading back for the car.

'I like liver sausage,' Slider said. 'And no one asked you to watch me eat it.'

'No, I was talking about that apparently normally intelligent woman deluding herself that a once or twice a week no-strings-attached bonk equates to true love and a happy-ever-after settlement. She didn't even know where the man worked or what he did, for crying out loud! She'd never met any of his friends, never been to his house, and when he said he wanted their relationship kept secret she went along with it. What a complete and utter pap-brained loser!'

'Don't sugar-coat it,' Slider advised. 'Say what you really mean.'

Atherton enumerated on his long fingers. 'So we know Amanda was talking to Rogers. That whatever it was was making her angry. That he had been worried about something lately. And then there's this Suffolk business.'

'Does it occur to you that Suffolk might just have been his excuse not to stay the night?'

'Did it occur to you? What an unkind thought.'

'On the other hand, if it was an excuse, why Suffolk? It seems a bizarre choice. He could have made it somewhere much further away, to be on the safe side. Or at least more exotic, to impress her. Catching a plane to Brussels, say – got to be at the airport at the crack, got to go home and pack a bag.'

'And what about all this apocalyptic stuff? Big decision to make and everything could change?'

'It sounds to me as if he was planning to dump her.'

'Yes, that's what I thought, too. Some rough beast of a big excuse was slouching towards Acton to be born.'

'On the other hand, he did end up dead,' Slider said, 'so there could have been something going on. I'm inclined to think Suffolk might be genuine, just because it sounds so dopey as an excuse.'

'But what was he going there for?' Atherton asked. 'On evidence so far, it was probably only another woman.'

As they came in from the yard, Nicholls popped

his head out from the front shop. 'Oh, Bill!'

'Nutty' Nicholls, the handsome Scot with the lustrous accent from the far north-west, was one of the uniformed sergeants. He had a much-loved wife and a large family of daughters, which gave him a certain vibe that had every female he encountered wanting to nestle against his heart and tell him things. He also had a fine voice and was a leading light of the Hammer-smith Police Players. His singing range was so wide that, in their latest production for charity, he had just been chosen to play Dorothy in *The Wizard of Oz*, because he could sing it better than any of the female members. That he accepted the part was a sign of his confidence in himself. Not every man was so comfortable in his sexuality he could wear a pinafore dress and a long-blonde-plaits wig when there was any chance of col-leagues seeing him. The Players only did four performances and the whole run was already a sell-out. O'Flaherty, another sergeant and Slider's old friend, had assured him that he'd heard Nutty sing 'Somewhere Over the Rain-bow' in rehearsal and 'it had me heart scalded, so it did'.

They paused, and Atherton said, 'What's a nice girl like you doing in a place like this?'

Nutty was un-phased. 'Mock away. My back's broad.'

'But I hear you have a tiny waist.'

'What is it, Nutty?' Slider intervened.

'At last, a sensible man. I will talk to you,' said Nicholls. 'There's someone waiting to see you.'

'To do with the Rogers case?'

'Name of Frith, if that means anything to you. I put him in Interview One. I gave him tea and biscuits, but he looked at me like Bambi's mother, so I think you should see him before he finishes the Hobnobs, or he might leap away into the forest.'

'Is that your next production?' Atherton asked with feigned interest.

'We're saving a part for you,' Nutty assured him seriously. 'You would do very well as Thumper. It is typecasting, really.'

Frith was on his feet when they went into the room, like someone just making up his mind to leave. Slider could smell the sweat through the aftershave – the new sweat of fear, must be, since it was not particularly warm out today, and the interview room, whose radiator hadn't worked in weeks, was positively cool.

He looked sharply at Slider and Atherton, and said, 'You're the people who came to the house, to tell Amanda.' It was not clear whether he thought that was a good or a bad thing.

'Detective Inspector Slider and Detective Sergeant Atherton,' Slider reintroduced them. 'Won't you sit down, Mr Frith. You wanted to speak to me?'

He sat, but only on the edge of the chair, as if retaining the right to leave at any moment. His eyes tracked from one of them to the other, and they were so large, and with such long lashes, that had they been dark instead of blue, Slider might have thought Nutty's comparison valid. But Frith was a big man, bigger up close, and particularly in this confined space, than he had seemed out in the high-ceilinged hall of Amanda's house: not especially tall, but muscular, and his face was lean and firm, and his shoulders were big, and his hands looked powerful. No, on second thoughts, there was nothing cervine about him. If he was nervous, it would not lead him to panic. He had twice won Badminton, and Slider knew enough about riding to know controlling half a ton of horse at speed over the toughest course in the world was not an option for the weak-minded or panicky.

Frith opened the campaign by attack. 'You've been asking questions about me,' he said. 'And I'm guessing that the woman who's been quizzing my staff and buying them drinks is one of yours. Sarratt is a small village, and in villages word gets round pretty quickly. So before you completely ruin my reputation and my business, I want to know what you mean by it.'

Slider drove the ball straight back down the wicket. 'In the course of a murder investigation, many people are asked many questions. Why should it bother you?'

'You asked my groom where I was on the morning David Rogers was murdered. That's not just any question. That's asking for an alibi, and that must mean you suspect me of something.'

'Innocent people don't need alibis,' he said blandly.

'Exactly,' said Frith with some triumph.

'Innocent people also don't tell lies to the police.' Which was not true, of course: people lied to the police all the time, about everything,

161

for no apparent reason, or for reasons so inadequate as to make them seem like perfect
imbeciles. But as Frith seemed to want to do a bit
of verbal fencing, Slider obliged him, and was
gratified to see him redden – whether with anger
or shame he didn't know, but at least it was
discomfort.

'I haven't lied to you,' Frith said, his voice
hard. 'In fact, as far as I am aware I haven't been
asked any questions, so how could I?'

'You haven't lied to *me*,' Slider agreed ami-
ably, 'but you have lied about your whereabouts
on Monday morning. You told your staff you
were going to Archers, the feed merchant, but
you weren't there. Which means you were missing all of Monday morning, a time we are naturally interested in. So if your presence here means
you have decided to come clean—'

'Come clean?' Frith said indignantly. 'I've got
nothing to come clean about! Now look, I don't
like your tone—'

Slider cut through the bluster. 'There's a
simple way to resolve this. Just tell me where
you were on Monday morning, and there's an
end to it.'

Frith maintained an angry silence, but he was
not meeting Slider's eyes any more. He seemed
to be thinking, calculating. Wondering what he
could get away with, Atherton thought.

'Look,' he said at last – the language of capitu-
lation.

'I'm looking,' Slider said when the pause grew
to long.

'All right,' said Frith, raising his eyes again.

162

'I'll tell you where I was – not that it's any of your damn business, but I can see this won't go away otherwise. But I want your word that this doesn't go any further. That – well, you won't tell anyone.'

'Anyone?'

'Amanda. That you won't tell Amanda.' His eyes shifted again. 'You see, I was with someone. Well, a woman.'

Oh, not that one, Atherton thought wearily. Had he already primed whoever-it-was to back him up, or was he just hoping?

Interesting, Slider thought: it didn't seem that Amanda had spoken to him yet about their visit this morning. That was a lucky thing. He might be able to get something out of Frith before they compared stories.

'You're seeing another woman?' he said. 'Who is it?'

Frith was looking both angry and embarrassed now. 'It's someone I've been seeing for a while. Well, Amanda and I aren't married. Her decision. She says once bitten twice shy. It's a bit insulting really – I mean, I'm not David. But I don't want to go into that. The fact of the matter is that she likes to keep her independence. She has her own job, her own friends. She always says we're not joined at the hip just because we live together. We're two separate people. So there's no earthly reason why I shouldn't see someone else. The trouble is,' he concluded with a short sigh, looking down at his big, strong hands, 'I know she wouldn't see it that way. We've known each other for a long time, and I know her pretty well.

163

If she found out there was another woman she'd go completely bananas. So I'm asking you – very strongly – not to tell her.'

'You're having an affair?' Slider said, hoping to goad him.

'It's not an affair,' Frith said indignantly. 'I keep telling you, Amanda and I aren't married. I asked her for the first time when we were both seventeen, and I've asked her God knows how many times since. But she went off and married that oaf David. And look where that got her. I could have made her happy, but she decided she wanted that – that *obvious* bastard. I know he's dead and all that, but it doesn't change what he was. And when they separated, it was *her* came looking for *me*. I said then I'd marry her when she got divorced and she ummed and ahhed about it, but once the divorce came through she said she didn't want to risk it again. This whole arrangement is her idea. She wants to keep her options open, just like she did when we were kids, always looking over her shoulder in case something better came along. I've actually heard her introduce me as her *lodger*. I'm just the stopgap. But she likes to keep a firm hold on her possessions, which means that *she's* free to look around, but *I'm* not.'

A lot of anger there, Slider thought with interest. Yet he stayed with her. Was it perhaps that the anger towards her he couldn't act on had found a displacement activity in anger towards Rogers? Amanda treated him pretty shabbily, if what he was saying was true, and he was obviously hurt and jealous that she had chosen

164

Rogers instead of him. Perhaps at some level he believed that if Rogers was really completely out of the way, i.e. dead, she might finally commit to him? But that would mean a Frith solo murder, not a Frith-effected, Amanda-designed murder. Which did not explain Amanda's lies and evasions. Or his, Slider's, conviction that she *knew something about it*.

'So let's get this straight,' he said. 'On Monday morning you left home at – what time?'

'The usual time. I always leave around six. Horses wake up early, and morning stables are the hardest work of the day. There's always a lot to do.'

'Around six? Can you be more specific?'

'Well, not really. I wasn't watching the clock. But the radio was on in the bedroom when I went in to say goodbye to Amanda – she dozes to it in bed – and they were still doing the news, so it was probably just a few minutes after six.'

'And you went – where?'

'Straight to Sue's house in Ruislip. It wasn't worth going to the stables first, because she was coming in from Dubai at six fifty-five that morning. She's a cabin attendant with BA. Well, I got to her place about a quarter to seven and she arrived about eight.'

Atherton pushed pad and pencil across to him. 'Write down her name, address and telephone number,' he said.

Frith looked alarmed. 'You can't just go and ask her! My God!'

'You mean she won't confirm your alibi?' Atherton said.

'No, I mean she's married.'

'So it *is* an affair,' said Slider.

'Well, if you want to be technical about it,' Frith said sulkily. 'It's hard enough for us as it is, what with her schedule and her husband's. He's an exhibition contractor, so he's away a lot. And we can't go to my place because I don't really *have* a place. I sold my house to buy the stables, and though there's a flat there I have to let the staff use it and live in Amanda's house because property's so expensive out there. So when Sue's coming back she rings me and if Terry's going to be away we meet at her house, and if he's not we go to this hotel. Well, it's not ideal, but she won't leave Terry, and in any case I can't leave Amanda – she's got so much money tied up in my stables, she'd make me sell up if all this came out, and then I'd be ruined.' He shook his head as if his life had suddenly passed before his eyes in all its glorious panoply. 'It's a mess,' he muttered.

No argument there, Slider thought. 'So what it comes down to,' he summed up, 'is that your alibi is that you were meeting someone, but you won't tell us who or where.'

'I know it sounds stupid,' he began.

'At least,' said Atherton.

Slider pushed his chair back. 'If you're adamant you won't tell us—'

Frith looked apprehensive, but he stuck to it. 'I *can't.*'

'Then there's nothing more to say. But I urge you to think carefully about it. Until we can eliminate you from our enquiries you remain a

166

suspect.'

'But I didn't do anything!' Frith protested.

'You can just help me on one thing.' Frith looked receptive. 'You'd known David Rogers for quite some time. What was his connection with Suffolk?'

'Suffolk?' said Frith.

'Yes – it seems he went there regularly. Did he work at a hospital there?'

'Not that I know of,' Frith said. 'But I hadn't kept up with him, so I don't really know what he did. Except—' Something seemed to occur to him. 'Maybe that was where he kept his boat?'

Slider remembered the photograph in Rogers's bedroom. 'He had a boat?'

'He'd taken up sport fishing in recent years. Bought a boat. Amanda said he was quite a bore about it.' He shrugged. 'No worse than golf bores, I suppose. These big consultants all have their rich-man's hobbies,' he concluded sourly.

'You were a bit easy on him,' Atherton complained to Slider as they trod up the stairs together. 'The blighter's taken Amanda's money and protection, yet he's banging a trolley dolly behind her back. I almost feel sorry for the Sturgess-type. But you didn't force him on his alibi. Which in any case isn't really an alibi,' he continued, 'because he says he was alone in his car from just after six until a quarter to seven, and alone in the dolly's house from a quarter to seven until eight. Virtually two hours unaccounted for. Enough time to drive to Shepherd's Bush, shoot David Rogers in the head, and drive back to Ruislip.'

'The killer didn't drive back to Ruislip. He drove to Stanmore.'

'Oh, yes. I'd forgotten.' He thought a bit. 'But that's still enough time, out to Stanmore, back to Ruislip, two hours. Easy. And even if it were an alibi, we can't check it unless he gives us the name and address.'

'Can't we?' Slider said serenely. 'How many flights from Dubai do BA have that arrived at six fifty-five on Monday morning? And how many of the cabin crew on that flight are called Sue and live in Ruislip? We get her details from BA and check with her. And if she doesn't exist, we'll nick him for obstruction.'

'You're devious,' Atherton said admiringly.

'Maybe I am, and maybe I'm not,' said Slider.

NINE

Who Dares Whinge

When they walked into the CID room, Emily was there, sitting on Norma's desk, chatting. Atherton sloped up to her and they greeted each other with studied nonchalance.

''Lo.'

'Wotcher.'

''Right?'

'Uh. You?'

168

'Young love!' Norma said sourly. 'Can you go and mate on someone else's desk?'

'You're not the same since you had that baby,' Atherton complained, and added in his Michael Caine voice, 'You gone all milkified, girl.' He turned to Emily. 'When did you get in?'

'Couple of hours ago. I came to take you out to lunch,' Emily said. 'Or have you eaten already?'

'We had a sandwich, but that was hours ago. A witness lunch. They never satisfy, somehow. You always want another an hour later.'

'Witness or sandwich?'

'Both.'

'No second lunches,' Slider decreed. 'We've got work to do.' He cleared a space on the edge of Atherton's desk, perched and said, 'Report time. Gather round.'

The troops gave him their attention. McLaren gave as much as he could spare from giving mouth-to-mouth resuscitation to a cheese and pickle sandwich. It looked as though the sandwich wasn't going to make it.

Slider went over the Frith interview and his possible, though partial, alibi. 'The good thing is that Amanda Sturgess has been provoked into giving a false alibi. She says Frith was home until she left at a quarter past eight, while he says he left at six. The bad thing is that even if the air hostess checks out, it still gives him time to have gone to Stanmore and get back to Ruislip.'

'Boss, I don't understand,' Connolly said. 'If the murderer was Frith, and his alibi's in Ruislip, why would he go to Stanmore at all?'

'To give back the number plates?' Mackay

hazarded. 'Maybe he only rented 'em.'

'Better for Embry if he didn't give 'em back,' Hollis said. 'Then he could claim they were stolen.'

'But he didn't report 'em stolen,' McLaren said. 'Didn't want to draw attention to the number.'

'I don't understand about the number plates anyway,' Connolly complained. 'Why bother with real ones? I mean, why not just make up a number?'

It was Norma who explained. 'Because you might pick a number the traffic division is looking out for. The patrol cars have on-board ANPR. The last thing you want coming away from a murder is to have the traffic cops on your tail because the number's in their computer for an uninsured driver or unpaid parking tickets. With a genuine scrapped car you can be sure nobody's looking for it.'

'And it's not that easy to get number plates made, anyway,' Hollis added. 'The suppliers and manufacturers are heavily regulated. Any hint o' wrongdoing and they'd be in a shipload of trouble.'

'I'm thinking, guv,' McLaren began, and spoke on resolutely through the woo-hoos. 'Maybe he was taking the shooter back. We know *that* was rented. The plates he could dump any time, but he'd need to get rid of the shooter right off.'

'You're thinking the armourer is in Stanmore?' Slider asked.

'I'm thinking Embry *is* the armourer. He looks well fit for it.'

'Something to take on board,' Slider said. 'Well, now, someone will have to check Frith's alibi, such as it is, which means getting hold of this Sue person. Swilley, I'd like you to do that. I trust your instincts. Get on to it as quickly as possible, before he has time to feed her any lines.'

'Right, boss.'

'How did you get on with Amanda Sturgess?' Hollis asked.

'Was that today? God, it seems like a week ago,' Slider said. 'She's still holding out, admits talking to Rogers but only recently and says it was general chit-chat. But then one of her staff, Angela Fraser, followed us out and volunteered that she was another Rogers girl.'

'That was the witness lunch,' Atherton put in.

Slider went over what Angela Fraser had said. 'It tends to confirm what we already suspected, that there must be other women out there who knew Rogers – or had been known by him. But with the two we know about, at least – Fraser and Aude – he's been playing it very cagey. Neither of them knows where he worked or what he did, beyond his being "a doctor". Aude said he worked at a hospital in Stansted, which we know wasn't true. And Fraser said he went to Suffolk once a week.'

'Suffolk?' Hollis queried.

'That's a new one,' said Mackay. 'What did he go there for?'

'Somebody has to,' said Norma, screwing up her face. She hated 'the country' with a townie's pure fervour.

'We did put it to Frith,' Slider said, 'and he suggested it may be where Rogers kept his boat. Apparently he's recently taken up sport fishing as a hobby.'

'Huh. All right for some,' said McLaren. 'Wish *I* had time for a hobby.'

There was a brief silence as everyone stared at the famously indolent McLaren. Slider, baffled, said, 'You have enough time to make your own *coal.*'

McLaren looked wounded. 'Hardly sit down, time I've finished.'

Slider left it. 'Now, two things seem to be emerging from this morning's work. One is that Amanda Sturgess had a great deal more contact with Rogers than she's admitted to. And her relationship with Frith is a complicated one. He's financially in hock to her, and resents it, and also spits venom when Rogers is mentioned.'

'Which is good for us,' Swilley said, 'if we're thinking Frith might be the murderer.'

Slider nodded. 'Also, whatever it was that Rogers did for a living, he kept it very secret.'

'That's three things,' Atherton objected.

'Glad you're still awake. With regard to the third thing,' Slider went on, 'we don't seem to be able to get a handle on it, and I have a feeling that it would help if we knew more about this trouble he got into. I get the sense that things changed then – certainly personally, but surely professionally as well. Possibly if we knew what happened we could get closer to what he's been doing lately. I want the details. The real, inside story. It's another of the things Amanda won't talk about, and anything she won't talk about naturally interests me. But it's going to take some research.'

Emily spoke up. 'Oh please, let me!'

Slider had forgotten she was there. He looked doubtful. 'It's police work.'

'Well, it isn't really, is it? Not the beginning part, anyway. Searching the archives, finding out who was there at the time, tracing them, getting them to talk about it – that's investigative journalism. It's the sort of thing I do all the time. And I'm good at it.'

'She is,' Atherton agreed. 'But what about your Irish story?'

'Done. Wrote it up last night, finished it on the journey this morning, filed it before I came here,' Emily said triumphantly. 'I have to do a piece for the Sundays, but I can fit that in easily – it's mostly rehashing. Please let me.'

'But what will you get out of it?' Slider wondered. 'I can't pay you.'

'Money isn't everything. I'm interested. I want to know what happened as well. And when it's all over – who knows, it could be a story, or grounds for an article. Nothing is ever wasted,' she concluded.

It was one of Slider's own maxims, the reason he listened so patiently to Everyman's rambles. 'You'd have made a good detective,' he said.

When the others returned to their desks he called McLaren back. 'Not you.'

McLaren looked helpful. 'Want me to get you a cuppa from the canteen?'

'No,' said Slider. 'Well, yes, actually, but that's not why I called you. Tell me about this morning – the wrecking yard.'

'Oh, yeah. Embry. He's tasty. When we got back I ran him through records and he's got a bit of form all right. Nothing for the last ten years, but that don't necessarily mean he's straight, only that he's careful.'

'What sort of form?'

'Started with TDAs, some fights, bit of stealing – mostly car parts, he was car mad – when he was in his twenties. Then he settled down until he got done for ringing. It was a big operation spread out all over North London. Reckon he was the unlucky one – he got nicked as part of a sting, and put his hands up when a lot of others got away. Took the rap for them. Did fourteen months. Since then, nothing. But he might've earned the gratitude of a lot of big players for taking the fall. And he could've made some useful contacts inside. Dunno what he's up to now. The wrecking yard looks legit, but if he's Honest John, guv, I'm Madonna's left tit.'

'Leaving celebrity mammaries out of it for the moment, what did you find out about the number plate?'

'He wasn't best pleased it'd come back to him. He didn't want to show us the CCTV tapes, but we had him cold. Applied a bit of muscle—'

'As in?'

'Just threats,' McLaren reassured him. 'You wouldn't want to try beating him up with only the two of you. Got a face like a sack a spanners and a body to match. Anyway, we brought the

174

tapes back. We got the bloke buying the plates. Embry said he didn't know him, but I reckon he did. So Fathom's looking further back, to see if he was in there before, but the tapes only go back six weeks. If the job was a long time in the planning...' He shrugged.

'But you say you got the bloke?'

'Well, sort of. It's gotta be him, right build and dark hair. But he knows the camera's there. Keeps his head down, keeps kind of rubbing his nose and scratching his eye, sort o' thing, so you can't see his face.'

'So you've come back with nothing?' Slider said impatiently.

'No, guv. There's something. I'll show you.'

'That'd be nice,' said Slider patiently. He followed McLaren to the tape room, where Fathom, looking too big for the furniture, was working his way through the back videos.

'Got the one with chummy's face, Jezza?' McLaren asked.

Fathom swapped cassettes and started fast-forwarding. McLaren, watching, excavated sandwich remains from the recesses of his mouth. Then he sucked pickle off his finger and pointed. 'There. Play it from there, Jez. Watch, guv. Just a minute – bit more – now!'

Fathom froze the frame. As the frustratingly canny customer turned away from the counter, there was a single frame of his face in profile. 'Got him!' Fathom said with quiet triumph.

'It's not Frith,' Slider said. It was a lean-faced man with thick dark hair, who could pass for Frith at a glance at a distance, but there was no

175

doubt it wasn't him. He looked older too – fifties, maybe – and harder. 'You might have mentioned this at the meeting.'

'Well, guv, it don't mean Frith's out of it,' said McLaren. 'All right, he didn't buy the plates off Embry, but he could've bought 'em off this geezer. More likely he did, really,' he argued, 'because Frith's got no record, so he probably wouldn't know where to go to get stuff. Someone puts him on to this bloke–' he stabbed at the frozen frame – 'who gets him whatever he needs. Maybe he gets him the shooter as well. He's a fixer.'

'It's a theory,' said Slider. 'But then why would Frith go to Stanmore?'

'Same reason,' McLaren said promptly. He had evidently been thinking about it. 'He's got to take the shooter and the plates back to the fixer. We don't know any other connection between Frith and Stanmore, so it makes sense it's the fixer, which we know *has* been in Embry's yard.'

Fathom said eagerly, 'Maybe Embry's still the armourer, and this bloke's the go-between. I'd swear Embry knows him. I wouldn't be surprised if he was supplying a lot of stuff out of that yard.'

'If they were working together, why would Embry CCTV him?' Slider objected.

'To make sure he'd got something on him,' McLaren said. 'Insurance, in case anything comes back to him. Which it has.'

'It's all pure speculation,' said Slider. 'However, you can take a print of this still and see if the local police know him. I don't know anyone

176

up there so you'll have to do it tactfully. And find out if they're watching Embry for anything. McLaren, that's you. Fathom, you can get on to the firearms section and see if there's anything leading back to Embry or his yard.'

As he returned to his own office, Slider was thinking that it could just be – and it was much simpler, wasn't it? – that it was Numberplate Chummy who did the murder, and not Frith at all. But that left them further from the solution than ever, because they had no idea who Numberplate Chummy was or what his connection with Rogers might have been. At least they knew Frith was acquainted with the doctor and hadn't liked him.

Swilley caught up with the trolley dolly, Sue Hardwicke, at Heathrow, coming in from another long haul flight. She turned out to be endearingly middle-aged and unglamorous, except that her make-up was so thickly applied it looked as if a sharp rap on the back of her head would make the whole lot fall off in one piece, like a Greek theatre mask. As she clicked along on her swollen ankles, towing her little black suitcase, her exhausted eyes met Swilley's blankly at first, and then as she was stopped, with faint irritation.

Swilley introduced herself and said, 'I'd like to ask you a few questions, if you wouldn't mind.'

As she stopped, the rest of the crew steamed past her, with a glance of sympathy but an evident desire not to be delayed themselves. Layovers were precious and too short anyway.

177

'What about?'

'It's concerning the death of David Rogers.'

'Who?'

'Haven't you seen the newspapers?' Swilley countered.

'Haven't had time. I've been working. Was he a passenger? Why are you asking me? Did I serve him with something? You ought to speak to the airline. We just hand the food out, you know – we don't cook it.'

'Doctor David Rogers was murdered on Monday.'

She looked alarmed at the word, and then a sort of enlightenment crossed her face, followed by caution. 'I don't know Dr Rogers. I've never met him.'

'But you do know who he is,' Swilley said. 'Does it help if I tell you that Robin Frith came in this morning to give a voluntary statement? We know about your relationship with him.'

Her rigid alertness slumped. 'Oh good God,' she muttered. 'Now what?' She eyed Swilley cautiously. 'Look, I suppose we'd better talk, but can we keep this discreet? I've got a lot to lose. I'll take you to the staff lounge, but don't tell anyone you're police, all right?'

She walked rapidly and Swilley had to hurry to keep up with her. There were keypad doors, stairs and corridors, and finally a rather bleak, window-less lounge, smelling faintly of old coffee, with the sort of mean furniture that was designed to meet a budget rather than any human need. Swilley felt sorry for Mrs Hardwicke. She had a hard-worn housewifely look about her, and no sense

178

that she was getting much pleasure out of life.

When they were settled at a table in a quiet corner, and Sue Hardwicke had a paper cup of coffee in front of her, she opened the conversation with, 'Look, I know who you mean, David Rogers. Amanda's ex. The woman Robin lives with. But I really didn't know him. You say he's been murdered?'

'Yes, early on Monday morning.'

She thought for a second. 'I was flying back from Dubai. You can check that if you want. Why would you think I had anything to do with it?'

'I don't,' Swilley said. 'But I believe you saw Robin Frith that morning. I'd like you to confirm the times.'

She looked puzzled. 'He was waiting for me at home when I got in. My husband – well, he was away. He works away a lot, same as I do.' She seemed embarrassed. 'Look, I know it's not exactly ... I mean, having an affair – it looks bad. But we both have complicated lives. Robin and me. You'd have to know the circumstances. Amanda and Terry, they don't know. Though they're not exactly snow-white lambs themselves, you know.'

Swilley was amused and, despite herself, touched. 'I'm not here to judge you, Mrs Hardwicke,' she said seriously.

'Oh, please, call me Sue. Everyone does – and I mean, absolutely everyone.'

'I just want you to tell me what time you saw Robin Frith on Monday morning.'

'Sorry, I'm a bit tired,' said Sue, and rubbed the

179

back of her neck. If she'd rubbed her face she'd have done irreparable damage. 'I can't tell you the exact time, because I didn't look, but I suppose it would have been half past seven going on eight when I got home. Robin was there already. We spent a couple of hours together and then he left after lunch and I went to sleep.'

'So you can't vouch for him for any time before eight that morning?'

She stared a moment, and then slowly began to smile. 'I'm sorry. I've been a bit slow. Must be jet-lag. You're asking me for an *alibi* for him? You can't be serious.'

'Why not?'

'Because Robin just isn't capable of murder.'

'Anyone's capable of murder in the right circumstances.'

Sue shrugged. 'Well, possibly, I don't know about that, but if you're suggesting that Robin could kill David Rogers – and why he'd want to do that I can't imagine – and then come to my house and wait for me, cook me breakfast and run my bath and talk to me as if nothing had happened – well, you're just so far out it isn't funny. He's simply not that ruthless. You don't know him. He's no tough guy. I suppose he might get into a row with someone and kill them by accident – hit them so they fell down and banged their head or something like that – but cold-bloodedly, it just couldn't happen.'

'You say he's not tough. But you have to be tough to compete at Badminton, don't you? You have to be ruthless to win there.' Swilley had this from Slider. She didn't know one end of a horse from the other, except that one end had teeth and the other made hors d'oeuvres – horse eggs, in English. 'He runs a successful business. He employs people. He coaches Olympics and trains horses. All those things suggest a very capable man.'

'He *is* capable around horses,' Sue confirmed. 'And he knows his business. And you're right, you have to be tough and brave to event at the top level. It's always puzzled me,' she said, smiling, 'how a man so brave on horseback can be such a hopeless wimp around people. Look at the way Amanda pushes him around. He'll never so much as say boo to her. She throws him into a tizzy. He spends a lot of our time together complaining about her and how awful his life is and all the things she's done in the past – and, yes, he's talked about David, too. I'm the one he tells everything to. I'm his agony aunt. I promise you, he couldn't have murdered Roger and pretended around me that nothing had happened. He'd have had to tell me. He'd have been in a blue funk about it, and I'd have asked him "what's wrong", and he'd have said "nothing" the first three times, then it would all have come out.'

Never had anyone been so transparently sincere about what they were saying. However, Swilley thought, that didn't mean she was right in her assessment. If Robin was such a pushover and so funky about Amanda, might he not have just obeyed her if she'd said she wanted David murdered? What if his fear of Amanda was worse than his fear of the law?

'You've known Robin a long time?' she said.

181

'About six years now. I met him when he was flying out with the team to the Athens Olympics. We got chatting on the plane. I had a two-day layover, and – well, the rest is history.'

'You've been lovers ever since?'

She pinked a little, but nodded. 'It isn't easy. My schedule makes it hard for any relationship. And we've both – got partners.'

'That could be changed.'

She looked suddenly very tired. 'I'd leave Terry. I would, if I had something to go to. He's – he's not an easy man. He has a temper. And it's a long time since we were – fond of each other. If Robin would commit himself I'd leave. But I can't go with nothing to go to. Terry wouldn't take it well, and I'd need support. I'd have to be going *to* someone.'

Swilley nodded. 'And Robin won't commit?'

She sighed. 'We've talked about it sometimes, but he won't leave Amanda. It's not just the money. He could get a job all right, we'd manage somehow. But he'd have to sell his horses, and that would break his heart. And it's more than that. She has a hold on him. I don't understand it. She's a stroppy cow as far as I can see, and treats him like dirt.' She sighed again. 'Maybe that's what it is. Maybe I'm too nice to him. But he'll never leave her.'

'What do you know about David Rogers? Robin's talked to you about him?'

'God, yes! I've had the whole story till I'm sick of it. How David stole Amanda from Robin, then treated her badly—'

'How, badly?'

'Oh, other women. Apparently he couldn't stop – it was like a sickness. Until Amanda got fed up with him and divorced him. Robin rushed to her side to comfort her, and she took him into her bed, but then wouldn't marry him. Oh, I had all the sob story,' she concluded wearily.

What on earth did she see in him? Swilley wondered. A man who only visits you to whinge about the woman he won't leave for you? But maybe he had a huge willy. Women could be so shallow.

'But Amanda put money into Robin's stables?' she asked.

'Yes. Robin put money in, too – sold his house and everything – but she put in more than half. So she's got him by the balls.'

'Where did she get the money?'

'The divorce settlement, I suppose. There was this mansion out in Hertfordshire she and David had, that was sold. That must have been worth millions. It all happened about that time, anyway.'

'Wasn't there some kind of scandal?' Swilley tried. 'Didn't David get into some kind of trouble about that time?'

'Trouble? You mean money trouble?'

'No, some kind of sex thing. Trouble with the police?'

'Not that I know of,' she said easily. 'Robin's never said anything about that.'

Now did that mean that Amanda had told him to keep it secret? Swilley wondered. Or that Robin had never known about it at all? But surely if they had been keeping up with each other all the time he would have known? On the other hand, how closely had they remained in touch while Amanda was married to David?

'Was Robin having an affair with Amanda?' she asked. 'While she was still married to David, I mean.'

Sue Hardwicke frowned. 'I don't know. He's never said so.'

'So what made him "rush to her side" as you put it?'

'The divorce.'

'How did he know about it?'

'Oh, I see what you're asking. Apparently, Amanda contacted him, told him that it was all over with David and that she was divorcing him, that he'd moved out and she'd filed against him for adultery.'

'So that was before the divorce was finalized?'

'Oh yes.' A bitter look crossed Sue's weary face. 'She wasn't taking any chances on being left alone. Made sure of Robin the moment David was out of the door. Made him sell his place so that he'd have to live with her. She's like a vampire octopus, that woman.'

She made Robin sell his place to buy the stables, and she put money into the stables. But if that was between the separation and the divorce, her side of the money couldn't have come from the divorce settlement. So where had it come from?

This was not a question to put to Sue Hardwicke, however. And she was looking increasingly beat. 'Well, thank you,' Swilley said. 'You have been most helpful.'

Sue roused herself. 'Is that it? Can I go now?'

'Yes, of course, and thank you.'

'You do believe me, about Robin? That he just couldn't kill anyone.'

'Yes,' Swilley said, circumspectly. 'Are you going to see him now?'

'No, Terry's home. And I'm flying out again tomorrow. I shan't see him until next week.'

Well, that was all right, Swilley thought. By next week they ought to know for sure whether they were interested in the poor woman's Colin Firth. And this, she thought as Sue stood up, swaying slightly with weariness, was the poor woman.

'We need to get some firm dates on this financial business,' Slider said, when Swilley had made her report. 'When the stables were bought, when the various houses were sold. You can get that from the property register. And you ought to be able to find out some figures from the estate agents concerned. I'd like to know exactly what happened between them, because I've had a feeling for a long time this was a money crime, not a crime of passion.'

'People get passionate about money,' Swilley said.

'True. And it could always be both, of course, love and money tied up in the same situation. But the only time I saw Amanda shaken was when I mentioned her financial involvement with Frith's stables. Anyway, call it idle curiosity if you like—'

'Wouldn't dare,' Swilley murmured.

185

TEN

Sex at Noon Taxes

Porson was tired. His face was grey and his eyes pouchy, and his fidget level had fallen to a mere restless twitch as Slider made his report, the eyebrows surging now and then, the fingers drumming on the desk top.

'It doesn't sound as if you're much further forward,' he concluded when Slider paused. 'Isn't there *any* light at the end of the funnel? I've got to have something to tell Mr Wetherspoon.'

'We're working to identify the man who bought the plates, sir. We think Embry knew him. I'd like to put pressure on Embry, see if we can get him to cough, but it's not our ground, and the local police...'

Porson nodded. 'I'll see what I can do. Have a word with their super. We're all supposed to be on the same side.'

'Thanks,' said Slider. 'The trouble is we know those were the plates used in the crime, but we don't know that the man who bought the plates was the murderer. The killer could have bought the plates from him.'

'You want it to be this Frith character.'

'He's not dissimilar to the man on the CCTV footage. And he doesn't have an alibi for the time of the murder. Amanda Sturgess's car is a BMW seven, so he could have had access to that. It's actually gunmetal grey, not black—'

'But gunmetal can look black on a black-and-white tape,' Porson finished for him. 'But where's your motive?'

'The relationship between Frith, Sturgess and Rogers was complicated. Trouble is, we know so little about him – Rogers, I mean. I'm trying to find out what it was he was doing for a living, but I can't get anything more about this Windhover or the Geneva trust. The Swiss just won't co-operate. And I'm sure there's more money somewhere – what he was getting from Windhover doesn't feel like enough to me.'

'Wise instinct. *Cherchez* la cash.' He tapped his nose. 'This tells me there's more to it than wimmin. If this Sturgess woman had wanted to kill him over that, she'd had done it long since.'

'Of course, I've no real evidence she was in on it at all. But she has been extremely unhelpful from the beginning, refusing to answer questions and lying in reply to several of them.'

Porson shook his head. 'On the other hand, that sort don't like co-operating at the best of times. You haven't got enough even to question her hard. Especially as she's well connected, and she does this charity thing. The press'd have a picnic day if we went after a pillow of society like her. We know the murderer was a man, so it'd need a bit more than innuendo to link her with the crime.'

187

'Yes, sir,' Slider agreed glumly.

'On the other hand, there's no bricks without fire. She's hiding something or she wouldn't lie. What about this scandal Rogers was involved in? The press haven't cottoned on to that yet, but they will. Then the flood'll be let loose, and we'll be caught like Canute with our finger in the dyke.'

'It was all kept very quiet at the time, and it was a long time ago,' Slider said. 'They might not spot it. But I've got a feeling it could be important. I'm trying to find out what it was all about—'

'Yes, a little bird told me you were,' Porson said, his gaze sharpening. 'Not sure about your approach. Can't have civilians doing police work.'

How was it the old man always knew everything? Slider wondered. He was a little nervous himself about Emily, but he'd had time to think it over and realize that not only could it do no harm, but that he couldn't stop her anyway. 'She's an investigative journalist, sir. You said yourself the press are going to get on to it sooner or later. It's a matter of public record. And any journalist who's seen the newspaper archives could follow it up if they were interested. Probably some will. Nothing we can do about that.'

'Oh, is that how you're playing it? Well, watch your step. Make sure she doesn't use our computers.'

'She won't, sir. But it's useful extra manpower. And no overtime.'

Porson was not beguiled. 'I don't know anything about it,' he said. 'And you'd better not, either, if you know what's wise for you.' He got up and surged restlessly to the window and back. 'If you're wrong about Sturgess being in on it, you'll have wasted a lot of time while the killer was getting away.'

'We've got nothing else to go on, sir.'

Porson drummed his fingers on the desk in thought. 'You've got that hand-print off the bonnet of the parked car. You can rule Frith in or out once and for all if you get his fingerprints for comparison.'

'I did think of that, sir. But even if Frith isn't the murderer, he could still be involved in some way. And it doesn't rule out Sturgess as the instigator. She could have used someone else to do the job, and Frith might or might not have been a go-between. And if we fingerprint Frith, he's bound to tell her, innocent or guilty, which will warn her we're looking at her.'

'Innocent or guilty?' Porson said. 'There's another possibility – that Frith was acting on his own – had you thought of that? Apparently Rogers wasn't his flavour of the month.'

'But if Sturgess is innocent, why is she lying to us and refusing to answer questions?'

'Buggeration factor, plain and simple. That sort likes throwing her weight around.' He thought some more. 'In any case, I reckon she's got to know something's up by now. You told her you were looking at Frith when you asked her for his alibi. Get him in, get him printed, get it done.' He looked at Slider cannily. 'You'd have done it by now if you really thought he was the murderer.'

Slider was surprised for a moment by the insight. Yes, it was true. There was some part of him that had felt Frith wasn't the killer, and that hadn't wanted him ruled out because, frankly, they hadn't got anything else. And if Amanda had used an unknown professional, how would they ever find him, or prove the link?

'Yes, sir,' he said. 'I'll see to it.'

Emily had been in the game long enough to know that people were a lot more willing to talk to journalists than to the police. The idea of 'getting in the papers', which had horrified her grandmother's generation, was now seen as an undiluted good, and people would cheerfully tell her things that would have made her blush if she had not got used to it by now. It had not only been because she was interested and thought she might get a story out of it eventually that she had wanted to take on the job, but because she believed she could actually do it better. Connolly might be chatty and Swilley strangely intimidating, but as soon as they revealed who they were, fifty per cent of members of the public – maybe more – would become reticent, while to Emily they would be ready to reveal anything up to and including their operation scars.

So it did not surprise her to find herself with an appointment to meet Mrs Rosalind Taylor for lunch on Friday. They met at the Red Lion in Kingly Street, Soho, a short brisk walk from Harley Street but nicely anonymous: a dark-panelled pub with a pleasantly light and airy saloon bar upstairs that served food.

Emily got there first and secured a corner table and a couple of menus. Just past the appointed time she saw a tall, well-dressed woman come up the stairs and look hesitatingly around. It had to be her. Emily met her eyes and nodded, and she came over.

'Are you...?' she began nervously.

'It's all right,' Emily said. 'Sit down. Can I get you a drink?'

Mrs Taylor sat, divesting herself in a measured way of coat, scarf, gloves, handbag. 'Oh, just water for me, thanks. I can't go back to work smelling of drink.' She looked appraisingly at Emily. 'I'm sorry about all the cloak and dagger stuff, but my bosses wouldn't be happy about me talking to the press. Even about something so far in the past. They're fanatical about discretion – to a ridiculous degree, in my view. If they even knew I was talking to you it'd be instant dismissal. So you must promise to keep my name out of it.'

'Absolutely,' Emily said with warmth. 'I'd never be able to get anyone to talk to me if I couldn't promise that. Shall we do the food bit now, and get it out of the way? Then we can talk.'

The waiter came up and took their order: Emily went for the old-fashioned sausage sandwich; Mrs Taylor rather doubtfully chose the scampi and salad. She was very thin and looked as though remaining so was probably another demand of the job. She seemed in her forties, though under the professional, enamelled make-

191

up she might have been older. Her dark brown hair was innocent of any thread of grey, and was glossy and immaculately cut; she wore pearl earrings and a string of pearls around the neck of her blouse; her hands were well kept with short but painted nails, and a heavy diamond band next to her wedding-ring. And she exuded an air of calm and efficiency, so that to Emily she seemed perfect for a medical secretary.

'So, Mrs Taylor,' Emily began when the waiter had gone away.

'Oh, please call me Ros. Everyone does.'

'Fine, Ros, then. And I'm Emily.'

'You said – Emily Stonax – you weren't related to—?'

'Ed Stonax was my father,' Emily said, trying not to sound stilted about it. But she still found it hard to talk about him, except to those who had been closest to her during the investigation: Atherton, Slider and Joanna. It was perhaps part of why she felt so strongly for them.

'I'm so sorry,' Ros said, holding her eyes in a way that suggested she was used to dealing with extreme emotions. 'Was it tactless to mention it? But I thought him a fine journalist. You must be very proud to be following in his footsteps.'

'I miss him,' Emily said. 'But let's not talk about that. Tell me about when you were David Rogers's secretary.'

'Oh, I was never secretary to Mr Rogers. The papers at the time got that wrong, but it didn't seem important to correct it. Let me explain. You see, there were three doctors sharing the premises. There was dear old Dr Freeling – he's

192

retired now. Lovely man, lovely to work for. I was his secretary. We had the ground floor. Private general practice. Then there was Mr Rogers and Mr Webber upstairs. They were old friends. We called Mr Rogers the Beauty Doctor.' She smiled. 'It's a rather insulting nickname for plastics specialists who go in for that side of things rather than the reconstructive, but in his case we didn't mean it unkindly. It was mostly because he was so handsome – goodness, you'd get goosebumps just looking at him! But he was nice with it. Always polite and pleasant, not arrogant like some of these good-looking men can be.'

'I know what you mean,' Emily said, since she seemed to want encouraging at that point.

'He could wind anyone round his little finger. Well, I suppose in his line he really needed the bedside manner. His patients adored him. And then there was Mr Webber – Sir Bernard Webber he is now. The urologist.' She wrinkled her nose a little. 'He was supposed to be charming, too, but I never really took to him. Not that it mattered, because I had very little to do with him. And his secretary, Stephanie, spoke highly of him, but there was something a bit – I don't know...' She shrugged. 'I suppose he was more of a man's man. He was one of these clubbable types, do you know what I mean? On all sorts of committees, had the ear of important people, knew how to get things done. I always picture him leaning on a bar in some golf club buying drinks and telling after-dinner jokes.'

The waiter arrived with their food and she

stopped. When everything was arranged and he had departed, Emily said, 'Go on. About that day – the incident.'

'Oh, yes. Well, it was one of Mr Rogers's patients – a Mrs Lescroit. Young – in her twenties – and very pretty. I'd seen her go past my office when she came in – I always kept the door open and my desk faced the hall, because I had to sign for deliveries. And Dr Freeling liked me to know who was going in and out. Anyway, I saw Mrs Lescroit go up. She was slim, gorgeous legs. Made-up regardless and very well dressed – well, all the patients were well off. You don't run a Harley Street consultancy on low fees.'

'What had she come in for?' Emily asked. 'It said in the papers "a minor procedure", whatever that was.'

Ros wrinkled her brow. 'Do you know, I can't remember. Or perhaps I never knew. Something like the removal of a mole, was it? Anyway, it was after the procedure, and she was lying on the daybed in the ante-room, recovering.'

'She'd been anaesthetized?' Emily queried.

'Not a general, of course. She'd had a local anaesthetic, and an injection of Valium to keep her happy, so she was woozy but not unconscious during the procedure. Well, when the rumpus started my Dr Freeling told me to run upstairs and see what was happening. I dashed up and came into the middle of it. Mrs Lescroit said she'd been dozing lightly, and woke to find someone was touching her – you know, her down-theres.' She nodded, closed-lipped, to em-

194

phasize the awfulness of it. 'The vertical blinds were closed so it was dim in the room, and she was only half awake, and apparently she said, "What are you doing, doctor?" And he murmured to her, "Oh, call me David." Then she started struggling and he got up and hurried out, and she woke up properly and started making a hullabaloo. When I got there Eunice, Mr Rogers's nurse, was in there with her. Mr Rogers was standing in the corridor outside the room, and Mr Webber came out from his office, grabbed his arm and sort of bundled him into his room – Mr Rogers's room – and slammed the door. Seconds later he's out again and in the ante-room calming Mrs Lescroit down. It was amazing to watch him in action,' she added. 'He seemed to be everywhere at once, handling everything, talking to everyone, smoothing it all over. I got sent down to tell Dr Freeling it was all under control and to fetch some brandy.'

'For Mrs Lescroit?' Emily surmised.

Ros smiled. 'I wouldn't be surprised if it wasn't for Mr Webber. Anyway, Dr Freeling went up and there was all sorts of confabulation, but Mrs Lescroit insisted the police must be called and even the brandy wouldn't change her mind. So Mr Rogers got taken away. He looked terribly shocked. Claimed it was all a mistake. Well, he would, wouldn't he?'

'There must have been a terrible scandal,' Emily suggested.

'Well, there was and there wasn't. Of course, everyone in the business knew about it, and there was some stuff in the papers, but not nearly as bad as it might have been. In the end Mr Webber got it all hushed up, Mrs Lescroit agreed to a large lump sum and there were no charges. We were all sworn to secrecy – not that we'd have talked anyway. You don't keep your job in Harley Street if you're thought to be a blabber. There had to be a GMC enquiry, of course, but Mr Webber was very well in with them and he squared it so that in the end Mr Rogers wasn't struck off, provided he didn't work with patients any more.'

'What can a doctor do that doesn't involve patients?'

'Oh, lab work, research, lecturing, that sort of thing. Pharmacology. Pathology,' she added with a twinkle. 'I'm pretty sure Mr Webber fixed him up with something – they were great friends after all. I have an idea he became a rep for a pharmaceutical company, but I'm not sure,' she finished vaguely. 'He left our building and I didn't really keep up with him. And not long after that Mr Webber left as well. We got new people in, but I think the upset had been too much for my dear old Dr Freeling because he decided to retire – but not until he'd got me an interview for another job, round the corner in Devonshire Street. That was the sort of man he was, bless him. A real old-fashioned gentleman.'

'So everyone came out of it all right,' Emily mused. 'Quite an operator, your Mr Webber.'

'Not *my* Mr Webber,' Ros objected. 'But yes, he'd have made a great diplomat. He was the great fixer. Probably still is – don't know why I'm talking about him in the past tense. Not like

196

poor Mr Rogers. What a terrible thing – have you any idea why he was killed? One of those drug-crazed burglars, I suppose. You hear about it all the time these days, though somehow you never expect it to be someone you know.'

'So were you surprised at what Mr Rogers had done?' Emily asked, avoiding the question. 'He was a bit of a ladies' man, I gather?'

'Well, yes,' she said cautiously, 'but you couldn't help liking him. And it wasn't the sort of thing you'd expect of him. I mean, he was so attractive he could have had anyone he wanted – he didn't have to resort to groping patients. I know he was married, but there was plenty of talk about him having lady-friends. In fact–' she lowered her voice and her head and looked at Emily from under her eyebrows – 'there was a rumour going round that he was having an affair with Eunice, his nurse, at the time, though I don't know if that was true or not.' She straightened up. 'Given what a tartar his wife was, it was hard to blame him.'

'You knew her?'

'Oh, not really – only seen her once or twice, but she didn't look the sort to enjoy a cuddle and a giggle. Terribly high-nosed and haughty. Always looked down her nose at us mere minions. Though I suppose she had other qualities he married her for.' She sipped her water. 'But still, I was surprised that he messed about with Mrs Lescroit like that. He wasn't a bottom-pincher, in the usual way of things. At least, Eunice and Anthea, his secretary, had no complaints about him. Mr Webber was the one you didn't want to get in a lift with on your own. He was one of those people who always managed to accidentally brush against you as you passed, you know what I mean?'

'All that sort of thing's illegal now,' Emily pointed out.

'Oh, I know, but consultants are different. They are so powerful, and they all stick together like one big club. You'd have to be very brave to stand up to one of them, if you're just a lowly nurse or secretary.' She shrugged. 'Anyway, it was a bit ironic, really, for Mr Rogers to get caught like that on the very day his wife's in the building.'

'She was?' Emily said in surprise.

'Yes, she'd come to see Mr Webber about some charity thing she was involved with. Stephanie told me. Hoping to touch him for some money for it, apparently. I saw her go up just before it happened.'

'So she was with Mr Webber when it started?'

'She was waiting for him in his office – or in Stephanie's room, rather. Mr Webber had gone to the gents or something. He was on his way back when the fuss started.' She sighed. 'Poor Mr Rogers. His wife divorced him not long after that, and I suppose that was what triggered it. I know it was a terrible thing for him to do, and that he was lucky not to have been struck off, but I must say, I've always wondered whether Mrs Lescroit made a mistake – she was only half awake, and a bit dopey from the Valium. Maybe she saw him leaning over her and just imagined the touching. And because of her Mr Rogers lost

198

pretty much everything, his wife, his house, his career, everything.'

'And now his life,' Emily murmured.

'You don't think that could have had anything to do with the Mrs Lescroit thing, surely?' Ros looked startled. 'It was so long ago.'

'No, I don't suppose a vengeful husband would wait ten years to make the point,' Emily said.

'And as I remember, Mrs Lescroit was a divorcée, anyway,' said Ros.

'So, if you were all sworn to secrecy,' Emily asked, 'how did it get into the papers?'

'*I* didn't say anything,' Ros said stoutly. 'If Mrs Lescroit had accepted money, I didn't see it was anyone else's business to blow the whistle. I suppose she might have talked, even so – told her best friend or something.' She thought a moment. 'Or maybe it was Eunice. I know she wasn't happy about it being hushed up. Mr Webber had her in his office for ages, according to Stephanie, talking to her a like a Dutch uncle. And soon afterwards she left – got a more senior position at some private hospital, according to Anthea, with much better pay. Stephanie always reckoned Mr Webber got her the job to shut her up.'

'It was a lot of trouble to go to for Mr Rogers.'

'Well, they were friends from way back. And, like I said, he was a man's man.'

'Do you know what hospital it was?'

'That Eunice went to? No, not offhand. I didn't really see her after that day. Well, Mr Rogers wasn't seeing any more patients so he didn't need a nurse. And she had holiday entitlement to

199

use up, so she took that instead of notice.'

'I wonder if Stephanie would know.'

'I shouldn't think she knew any more than me. But in any case, you can't ask her,' Ros said, 'because she's not around any more. She was in an accident. She got knocked down and killed on her way home late one night.'

'Oh, I'm so sorry,' said Emily.

'It was an awful thing,' Ros said, staring at her hands. Here at last was something that could disturb her professional composure. 'It was a hit-and-run driver, so they never even found out who did it. Not that that would have brought her back, but at least it gives you a sense of—'

She paused so long that Emily felt obliged to suggest, 'Closure?'

She looked up. 'Yes, I suppose that's what it is. It doesn't make the thing right, but it allows you to move on.'

'What about Anthea? Would she know any-thing more?'

'I don't know. She emigrated to Australia soon afterwards, and I've never heard anything from her since. So what's your interest in this old story? It isn't much of one, really. Is it just be-cause poor Mr Rogers is dead?'

'That's right,' Emily said. 'I thought there might be something I could work up – not straight away, of course – that would be in bad taste – but eventually. Something about the playboy doctor brought low by a single fleeting impulse. But I'm not sure, now, that there's really an angle to work from.'

'No, it's all rather sad and sordid,' Ros agreed.

'I feel a bit guilty now for wasting your time.'

'On the contrary, I feel I've wasted yours,' Emily said, not to be outdone in gallantry.

Ros smiled. 'Oh, I've enjoyed it. It's nice to get out for lunch once in a while. I usually just have a yogurt and an apple at my desk. Very dull. It's nice to have someone to talk to for a change. I googled you, after you telephoned me, you know,' she confessed, 'and read a couple of your pieces. You're quite a writer! I always wanted to write. I think I could have been good at it if I'd ever had the chance.'

So for the sake of the cover story, Emily let her wander down that byway, talked about a journalist's life, and encouraged her to start jotting down 'some of the funny things I've seen' that would 'make a terrific novel'; and this beguiled the time until suddenly Ros looked at her watch and jumped up and said, 'Oh, my God, I shall have to dash! There are very old-fashioned looks given if one dares to be even a minute late. Thank you so much for lunch. It's been lovely meeting you. And if you do decide to write the story, I'd love to see a copy.'

'I'll send it to you first, to check the facts,' Emily promised her solemnly.

She told her story to a small audience over tea and buns back at the station.

'She was there at the time?' Swilley exclaimed. 'Amanda Whatserface? And she never said a word about it?'

'Maybe she's just too ashamed,' Emily said. 'Can't bear talking about it. It needn't be any-

201

thing sinister.'

'Maybe she's just too arrogant to talk about it,' Connolly suggested. 'People like her don't like talking about their private lives.'

'It all sounds a bit strange to me,' Slider said thoughtfully. 'Why would Rogers suddenly turn into a groper?'

'You don't know it was sudden,' Swilley said. 'Only that he hadn't got into trouble for it before. He was a ladies' man, everyone says so. Maybe he just couldn't resist it whenever he saw it.'

'Well, I don't know that it's got us any further forward,' Slider said, dissatisfied. 'Except for knowing that Amanda was right there on the spot – which must have made the shock and anger greater.'

'And this Mr Webber comes out as the good guy,' Swilley said. 'Helping his mate out of a jam.'

'Maybe he was just trying to save the reputation of the practice,' Connolly said. 'Doesn't mean he's a heart of gold.'

'But still, there's something odd about it,' Slider murmured, deep in thought. He roused himself to praise Emily. 'You did a good job.'

'Thanks.' Emily looked pleased. 'I'd better get off, now. I have to get on with my Irish story for the Sundays. But I'll get these notes written up this afternoon and email them to you straight away. And, if you don't mind, I think I'll look into these other two women who were on the spot – Eunice and Anthea. Maybe they'd have a different take on it, if I could track them down.'

ELEVEN

Penguin Gavotte

Frith was looking troubled and anxious, but as soon as Slider appeared he chose indignant as his motif du jour.

'Look, what the hell's going on? I've got a business to run. I can't keep running back and forth to Shepherd's Bush. What is it you want that's so urgent?'

Slider tried direct for his. 'Your fingerprints.'

Frith's hairline slid back. *'What*? You are joking! My *fingerprints*? For Christ's sake, you can't really think I had anything to do with David's death. Why on earth would I kill him?'

'You didn't like him,' Atherton answered over Slider's shoulder.

Frith only looked angrier. 'What was there to like? He was a smarmy womanizer who made Amanda's life miserable, but it's *murder* we're talking about. You don't just murder someone because you don't like them. Ordinary people don't kill other people anyway. What world are you people living in? I wouldn't murder my worst enemy, let alone—' He ran a distracted hand backwards through his hair. 'I mean, come *on*! This is not the Wild West.'

203

'We want your fingerprints in order to elimi-nate you from our enquiries,' Slider said, cutting through the whirlwind.

'Oh.' Frith jolted like a man who has gone up the step that isn't there. He took a beat to think, and then came back with a revival of resentment. 'I don't understand why you should ever have considered me anyway. What did I ever do to have the police on my back for this *preposterous* notion?'

Preposterous. Slider liked it. A bit of hedgi-cation never done no one no 'arm, he thought. 'There were some superficial reasons for taking you into consideration,' he said, the still, small voice of calm. 'At the beginning of an investi-gation like this we have to take the broadest view and gradually whittle it down. I'm sorry you have been inconvenienced, but your fingerprints should settle the matter and we won't need to bother you again.'

'I've a good mind to refuse,' Frith said sulkily. 'The idea that you should ever have considered me ... What were these "superficial reasons"?'

'I'm afraid I can't go into that at present.'

'And you've caused me no end of trouble. People in Sarratt are looking at me sideways, I have three cancellations, and – what the hell did you say to Amanda? She's been giving me the silent treatment, looking at me as if—' Some-thing occurred to him. 'You didn't tell her about Sue?'

'No,' said Slider. 'We haven't spoken to her since you last came in. But before that we had asked her to confirm what time you left in the morning on Monday, because you had told your employees you were working from home and then going to an appointment.'

'You told her that? Oh God!' He buried his face in his hands. 'No wonder she's so frosty with me,' he said, muffled. 'What a mess!'

Slider was interested. 'You mean she hasn't spoken to you about that? About your whereabouts on Monday?'

Frith shook his head. 'Biding her time,' he mourned. 'She'll hold back until she's ready, and then pounce.' He emerged from his hands and stared gloomily at Slider. 'Oh well, since you've already ruined my life, you might as well have my fingerprints and get it over with.'

'Thank you, sir,' Slider said. 'It won't take a minute. If you'd come this way, please.'

Frith got up and followed him. 'It *wasn't* me, you know,' he said. 'I'm the last person. I've shot plenty of birds in my time. I even had a go at shooting wild pig when I was over for the Atlanta Olympics. But I could never shoot a human being – not deliberately.'

'That's interesting. I didn't know you were familiar with firearms,' Slider said.

'Oh God! Now what? You're not going to—?'

'Don't worry. As a matter of fact I think that if you *had* killed David Rogers in cold blood, you would have supplied yourself with a better alibi.'

'In cold blood? You mean—?'

'It was planned, yes.'

Frith was silent as they walked down the corridor to the processing area. As they turned in at the door, he said, 'You know, I'm almost sorry

205

for him now. David. He was a selfish bastard, but he didn't deserve that.'

'The thing that intrigues me,' Slider said as they went back upstairs, 'is why Frith and Sturgess haven't discussed this business.'

'He wouldn't discuss his dodgy alibi with her,' Atherton said. 'It would mean revealing that he had a mistress.'

'True, but why hasn't *she* tackled *him* about it?'

'He said she's giving him the cold shoulder.'

'But don't you think that's uncharacteristically indirect?'

'Too many long words.'

'Wouldn't it be more like her to jump on him as soon as he comes in and shout, "Where the hell were you on Monday?"'

'Maybe she doesn't want to know,' Atherton said after a moment's thought.

'Or maybe,' Slider said slowly, 'she's happy enough to have us chasing after him, knowing it'll get us nowhere.'

'We'll never know,' said Atherton, thinking that was an uncharacteristically long line in supposing from his boss. 'I don't suppose he'll want to tell her we've fingerprinted him, for the same reason – it'd open up the whole "where were you" debate. So they'll tiptoe round each other on the thin ice, saying nothing and darting frosty looks, in a sort of hostile penguin gavotte.'

Slider turned his head, and blinked. 'That conjures up quite an image.'

'It was meant to,' said Atherton. 'It's called

206

metaphor.'

'Come to think of it, there *is* something penguin-like about Sturgess, with that long neck and long nose.'

'Penguins don't have long noses. What are you doing tonight?'

'Beaks, then. Nothing. Joanna's home. Why? Do you and Emily want to come over?'

'Is that an invitation?'

'Why do you need inviting? You never did before.'

'Ah, but you're a family man now. It's different,' Atherton said, and Slider realized, with just a hint of wistfulness, that it was.

'Hello, is that Miss Connolly. Detective Connolly? I don't know what I'm supposed to call you.'

'This is Rita Connolly. How can I help you?'

'It's Cat here – Cat Aude. Um, I've got something – I don't know if you want it. I don't know if it's important. But I thought – well, you know, the investigation and everything, I thought you might be wondering where it is. So I thought—'

'What are we talking about here?' Connolly cut through the babble. 'What've you got?'

'His mobile. David's mobile.'

'We've that already,' Connolly said. 'It was in his jacket pocket in the dressing-room.'

'No, I've got it,' Aude said confidently. 'See, like I told you, when I ran back in the bedroom, after I realized what's happened, I was gonna phone the police, and his mobile was there on the bedside table, and I grabbed it, but then the man

207

started coming upstairs and I had to get away, and I dropped it into my pocket, and that's where it's been all the time. That bathrobe, you know, the one David lends me when I'm at his place – that's what I was wearing, and I took it off in the hospital and they put it in a plastic bag, and I took it home with me – well, that policewoman brought me clothes from home. And I've never taken it out of the bag since. But now I've come home again and I had to do some washing—'

'Wait-wait-wait – you're back home? In Putney?'

'Yeah, well, it was getting on me nerves being at me mum's. I mean, I'd got nothing to do, and no money, and me mum's, like, going on and on at me about David and how I ought to date a man of my own age so I've got some chance of getting married and giving her grandchildren – she goes on and on about grandchildren. It's like an obsession with her. Honestly—'

'But you were there for your own safety,' Connolly pointed out. 'Could you not put up with it a bit longer? Wait'll we catch your man?'

'No, I can't stick it. You don't know what she's like. And I have to go to work. I've got rent to pay and everything. You said on the telly that I didn't see his face so he's got no reason to come after me.'

'Well, I can't make you stay away, but I strongly recommend—'

'Oh, I'll be all right. But the thing is, do you want this mobile? Cos I could drop it on my way to work tonight. I go more or less right past.'

'You're going back to Jiffies?'

208

'I have to. I need the money. And some of the customers have been asking for me. As an enter-tainer, I have a responsibility to my audience.'

Gak, thought Connolly. But she said, 'You be careful. And about this mobile – are you sure it's David's? Because I told you we found that in his pocket.'

'Well, he must have had two,' Aude said cer-tainly, 'because there it was on his bedside table and it's not mine.'

'Right, so, we'd better have it.'

'And I won't get into trouble for not bringing it before? Only, I'd forgotten all about it.'

'Very natural, in the circumstances. No, you won't get into trouble.'

'If she's not worried, it's not our business to worry for her,' Slider said.

'No, sir, but she's a bit of a gom, for all her thinking she's so sophisticated. I just feel ner-vous for her.'

'We can't force her to stay in Guildford,' he pointed out. 'And I don't really think there's any danger. We made it clear she couldn't identify the killer. What about this mobile?'

'Like she says, your man must've had two.' She handed it over. 'It wasn't switched off so the battery's run down. Have to charge it up before it'll work.'

'There's a selection of chargers in the CID room. Put it straight on, then we can have a look at last number redial.'

'Yes, sir. But it occurs to me that no one could've rung it this week gone, or she'd surely have heard it ringing.'

'His death was announced in the papers,' Slider pointed out.

'But his name wasn't given until Tuesday,' Connolly countered. 'If anyone'd rung it Monday, there it was on a chair in the hospital room. And even after Tuesday, not everyone'd've known right off he was dead. Some people don't read the papers, and it'd take time for word to get about.'

'What's your point?'

'I'm not sure I have one,' Connolly said with a disarming smile. 'It just struck me as weird.'

'I'll take it under advisement,' Slider said gravely.

Many had been the brainstorming session, generally at Atherton's place, with him popping in and out of the kitchen, doing magic with a few ingredients, the Van Gogh of the limited palette, while Slider, and later Joanna, and later still Emily as well, sat by the fire inhaling large G&Ts for the better stimulation of thought. It wasn't the same at Slider's new house – couldn't be. The kitchen was too far from the sitting-room, for one thing. And there were no cats. Slider made the G&Ts just as large in the hope of getting back some of the old atmosphere. But with Atherton corralled in the kitchen, with Dad as skivvy (Slider had held his breath – Atherton had split up with his previous girlfriend Sue partly over culinary differences – but Dad was the soul of tact and an intuitive helper) the conversation had to be social rather than work-related until the starter had been eaten (potted shrimps with ciabatta toast) and they were all settled round the ten-pound table with the main course. It was a tomato, mushroom and goat's cheese tart with baby new potatoes and broccoli.

Dad was very impressed with it. 'It didn't take him any time at all to make it,' he marvelled. 'I could do that myself for you and Joanna if you needed a quick supper. Put it together in five minutes—'

'I cheated,' Atherton said. 'Used bought pastry.'

'How do you live with yourself?' said Slider.

'—and fifteen minutes in the oven,' Dad went on. 'All done while the potatoes are cooking.'

'Peruvian,' Atherton disparaged them. 'No taste, but they're quick. Can't wait for the Jersey Royals to come in!'

'Ah, now you're talking,' Dad said with approval. 'Can't beat the taste of a Jersey Royal – and a lovely bit of English asparagus with it. Bit of melted butter for both, and you've got a supper fit for a king.'

'How long has this been going on?' Emily stage-whispered at Joanna, with an amazed look.

'What, Fanny and Johnny here? I don't know.'

'I feel completely de trop.'

'Whatever you do, don't say the pastry's good.'

'Seems all right to me.'

'What did I just tell you?' She bared her teeth in a rictus smile at Atherton. 'Terrible pastry, this ready-made stuff,' she said loudly. 'Wish you'd had time to make your own.'

'You two are mad,' Atherton said elegantly. 'I'll talk to Bill. What about this mobile phone business?'

'It's a bit rum,' Slider said. 'Number redial lists the last five numbers dialled, and they're all the same. And there's only one number in the memory.'

'The same one,' Joanna hazarded.

'And 1471 gives the same number again.'

'So the conclusion is that, as he had another mobile as well, this one was a special one for contact with one person only,' Emily said. Slider nodded. 'Which sounds a bit criminal.'

'Like on *The Wire*,' Joanna said. 'The drug dealers. But if he only rang one number on it, why did he put it in the memory?'

'Because he was a dipstick,' Atherton said.

'I imagine he put it in at the beginning before he memorized it and forgot to take it out,' Slider said. 'It doesn't matter, anyway, because the target phone has been switched off – probably thrown away or destroyed by now – so we can't use it to trace whoever he was phoning. But it does make it look as though his new job was something on the shady side.'

'Can't you trace them from the number?' Joanna asked.

'It's a pay-as-you-go. Bought from a shop in the St George's mall in Harrow. Purchaser paid cash and gave a false name and address. We could take our photo, such as it is, of the suspect round there and see if anyone by some miracle remembers him, but it wouldn't help because they wouldn't know who he was or where he lived. So the phone is a dead end. All it does is confirm Aude's story that Rogers made a call from his dressing-room that morning, which we thought before was impossible because there wasn't one logged on his other mobile. But beyond that...' He shook his head. 'It did occur to me to wonder, however, whether that was what the killer was searching for,' he added. 'He look-ed in drawers, but didn't turf out the contents; and he didn't search downstairs. Which suggests he was looking for something specific and had an idea where it might be. People don't bury their mobiles deep under things in drawers. And he'd spoken on it already that morning, before the killer came round.'

'It was probably the killer he spoke to,' Atherton said. 'Or the killer's boss, if he was a hired hand.'

'If you can't trace the phone back, why would he worry about it?' Emily asked. 'He could just switch his own off or throw it away and that would be that.'

'I suspect,' Slider said, 'because it wasn't just a two-way thing. I suspect there were other people using the same link, and if he couldn't get Rogers's back, he'd have to change the whole system, get a new number and make sure every-one knew it. It was a nuisance rather than a danger.'

'So you really think it was a network, like on *The Wire*?' Joanna said.

'It's just a supposition,' Slider said. 'Aude says he got a call early in the morning and then look-ed worried and said he had to go in to work. So it looks as though he got instructions from his paymasters.'

'And was told to expect a caller, so that he would let them in without fuss.'

'And then they shot him,' Emily said. 'Nasty but efficient.'

'But doesn't that rule out the ex-wife, whatser-name?' Joanna asked.

'Amanda Sturgess? Not necessarily. She could have been part of the ring – if there was a ring – or the murder could have been quite separate and coincidental. Nothing to do with whatever he was doing for a living.'

'But you said the killer was looking for the phone,' Joanna objected.

'I *said* that was just a supposition. We don't know what he was looking for.'

'Maybe he was looking for a will,' Mr Slider put in, in his mild, unemphatic voice. 'You still don't know who inherits his millions.'

Slider smiled. 'Or where they are, if there are any.'

'P'raps these people paid him in cash,' said Mr Slider. 'He could have a hoard of it under the floorboards. You've never taken the house apart, have you?'

'We had no reason to,' Slider said, but he looked at his father thoughtfully. 'Now you men-tion it, everyone does keep saying he paid for things in cash. Maybe we should go back and have a rummage. I've always said there was some more money somewhere, if only we could find it.'

'But what were they paying him *for*?' Joanna

asked. 'I'm sorry, Jim, but this pastry *is* nice.'

'I'll kill you later for that,' Atherton said. 'I suppose drugs is the obvious answer.'

'It's got to be something that's worth a lot of money, if it was worth killing him for,' Emily said.

'Well, you'd think that,' Atherton said, 'but when it comes down to it, it's surprising these days how little people *will* kill for. However, Rogers walked the walk, so let's suppose for the moment that it was something lucrative.'

'Ros Taylor said that after Rogers's scandal, his friend Bernard Webber sorted everything out for him, squared the General Medical Council, and she thought he got him a job too. She said she thought he became a rep for a pharmaceutical company.'

'I wasn't thinking of those sorts of drugs,' Joanna said.

'Nor was I,' said Atherton, 'but a knowledge of legal drugs wouldn't do you any harm with the other sort. And there's no knowing that what he started in, he stayed in.' He looked at his beloved. 'What? You've got that expression – the mills of Stonax are grinding exceeding small.'

'I did a bit more research this afternoon on the other people who were there that day Rogers assaulted Mrs Lescroit. Ros Taylor we know about, and she was downstairs when it happened, only came upstairs when the rumpus started. Then there was Stephanie, Mr Webber's secretary, Anthea, Rogers's secretary, and Eunice, his nurse.' She extended a finger for each of the three women. 'Anthea,' she said, touching the first, 'was Anthea Maclean, an Australian girl from Melbourne who'd been over here for four years, three of them with Mr Rogers. She went back to Australia a fortnight after the episode, and for all I know she's there still. She got a job as a receptionist at the Royal Melbourne Hospital but she didn't stay there long, only eight months, and I haven't been able to trace her any further. Then there's Stephanie.' She touched the second finger. 'Ros Taylor said she'd died in a traffic accident, and I managed to find the reports of that. She was living in Finchley and she was killed on her way home late at night, after an evening at the cinema. She told her flat-mates she was going to the pictures but didn't say who with. She was run down by a van travelling at high speed, which didn't stop. No one was ever caught for it. And this was less than a month after the incident.'

'Are you saying——' Atherton began, but she shook her head at him.

'Wait till I finish. Then there's Eunice, the nurse.' The third finger. 'Ros Taylor said Eunice wasn't happy about the Lescroit business being hushed up, and she left soon afterwards and got a nursing job at a private hospital. I managed to trace that. It was a BUPA hospital at Bushey, and Bernard Webber was consultant urologist there, so maybe he helped her get the job. But she didn't stay there long. A bit less than six months. Then she committed suicide. Took an overdose.' She looked round the watching faces. 'The nurse's way out.'

'Are you trying to say you think Rogers had

216

them all killed?' Atherton said, seeing she had finished.

'Don't know about Anthea. She's probably all right – but she did heave off to Australia pretty sharpish.'

'What, afraid of being bumped off? Come on!'

'I *said*, I don't know about Anthea,' Emily said with a trace of annoyance. 'But don't you think it's odd that all three were got swiftly out of the way, and that two of them are dead?'

'It's always tempting to see a pattern in what is probably just coincidence,' Slider said.

'I'm just throwing it into the pot,' Emily said with dignity. 'I'm not claiming anything for it.'

'All right,' Slider said placatingly, 'but *if* it's not a coincidence, you're reasoning that the three women were witnesses to a cover-up worth protecting; and that to stop them talking they were dealt with.'

'It's possible, that's all I'm saying. Anthea encouraged to go home to Oz, where no one would be interested even if she did talk. Stephanie bumped almost straight away. Eunice bribed with a better job at higher pay, then nudged out of play when it proved she couldn't be trusted.'

'It sounds plausible,' Joanna said, 'but what could it have been that Rogers was afraid of? The main witness against him, Mrs Lescroit, had been bought off, and the GMC had given him the soft option. He was doing as well as could be expected. What was worth risking murder for?'

'*I* don't know,' Emily said, with a reluctant grin. 'I'm the researcher, not the writer.'

'Interesting as it is for a speculation,' Slider

said, 'I don't see that it gets us anywhere with the present case.'

'I was going to say that,' said Mr Slider. 'You want to know what he was doing last week, not ten years ago. There's a last bit of pie going begging. Can I cut a bit for anyone?'

'Not me, thanks, I'm saving room for pud,' Emily said.

'What do you mean, pud?' Atherton demanded.

'There's no pud?' Emily looked offended.

'Slave my fingers to the bone, and that's all the thanks I get,' Atherton grumbled.

'There is, isn't there?' Emily said, beguiling. 'I know you.'

'For God's sake, woman—'

'There's a bit of cake left from last weekend,' Joanna said hastily. 'Fruit cake. You could have that with a bit of Wensleydale.'

'Good idea,' said Slider. 'And a drop of malt to go with it?'

Joanna stood up. 'I'll get the gubbins, you do the malts.' Mr Slider stood up as well, and together they cleared the table and went out to the kitchen. It was when she was laying the stuff out on the table that she said, 'It occurs to me that you talked about four women in the building at the time of Rogers's assault. But weren't there five? Didn't you say–' to Slider – 'that it turns out Amanda was there as well?'

'Yes, that's right,' Slider said thoughtfully.

'So what did she get out of it? The others got new jobs and tickets home.'

'And killed,' Emily reminded her.

218

'Carrots and then sticks. But Amanda – nothing.'

'She wasn't a part of it,' Atherton said. 'She just happened to be there.'

'Yes,' said Slider. 'But it's funny how it all keeps coming back to her, isn't it? I wish I knew what she was hiding. She's involved, I know she is,' he added in frustration. 'I just can't work out how.'

'You's de boss, Boss,' Joanna said, patting his arm. 'You'll work it out.'

It turned into a lateish session. Mr Slider went off to bed around ten, saying he couldn't manage these late nights like the young people, and the others sat round the fire with more drinks and by unspoken consent left the subject of the case and talked about any- and everything else. And when finally Slider began stifling yawns, Emily goosed Atherton with a look and said they had better be going. 'Don't forget it's a school night.'

'Is it?' Joanna asked of Slider. 'Are you working tomorrow? Don't forget Kate and Matthew are coming to stay.'

'I hadn't forgotten. I shall have to go in, but I hope not to stay too long. There's stuff being looked into, but until we get answers there's nothing for me to do but make encouraging noises.'

'Can I look at your baby before we go?' Emily asked, and Joanna took her upstairs.

'I think she thinks babies are catching,' Atherton said to Slider when they were alone.

'Oh? Are you at that point already?'

219

'No use asking me,' said Atherton. 'Isn't that sort of thing always the woman's decision?'

'Well, you are allowed an input,' Slider said.

'Don't let's get smutty.'

'Seriously, do you want a child?'

'If I wanted one, I'd want it with Emily,' Atherton said after some thought.

'Very circumspect,' said Slider.

The telephone hauled Slider gasping and flapping out of a deep dream on to the dry shore of awake. The bedside clock said ten past three and it was as cold as the dead of night can be. He reached for the bawling receiver and had a moment of blessed silence before the voice of O'Flaherty, the night relief sergeant, took over in his ear.

'Are y'awake, Billy, me darling? Let me hear y' sweet voice, y' native woodnotes wild, so I can tell if y'r compost mentis or not.'

'I'd speak if you gave me a chance,' Slider muttered, hoping not to wake Joanna. 'This better be good, at this time of morning.'

'Tis not a chat I'm after, tis your company. I've had Detective Superintendent Gordon Hunnicutt of Notting Hill on the blower. Your witness, the Aude female, has bought it.'

The words cut through any remaining fog. 'Dead?' he said, not loudly, but sharply enough to make Joanna stir and wake. 'How?'

'Bashed on the head, poor little eejit,' O'Flaherty mourned. 'Dead as Dick's hatband. So y'd better get up, get out and get over here.'

'I'm on my way,' Slider said, slinging his legs

out of bed in the same movement as putting the phone on the hook.

Joanna sat up, shivering. 'It's so cold,' she mumbled. 'What's happened?'

'I've got to go in. Our witness, the Aude girl, has been bumped off.'

'Oh God. I'm so sorry.' Slider was already across the room, dragging clothes on. When he came back, half clad, to briefly kiss her goodbye, she grabbed him by the collar to keep him long enough to say, 'You're not to feel guilty about this.'

He detached her hand but kissed it before giving it back to her. 'Too late,' he said.

TWELVE

Hello Dubai

'Poor little beast,' Slider said to Porson. 'The only good thing about it is that it isn't our case, so we won't have to find the men to investigate it.'

Detective Superintendent Hunnicutt ('Two ens, two tees, please,') had made it clear that he didn't want other firms treading on his hallowed. Big, young and pompous, with a large, gleaming face and a head shaved to stubble to disguise the encroaching baldness, he was a whale on procedure – one of the new generation of promotees

221

who didn't just have a grasp of all the paperwork required these days, they positively revelled in it. Returns, censuses, reports, analyses, tables, graphs, flow charts, activity logs, productivity ratings – he loved it all. It was meat and drink to him. His overmastering joy was a meeting with a graphic display and a pointer; bullet points gave him an erection. Nothing in the realm of human activity – he had written an article about it on the Notting Hill police website – was of value that could not be measured. Measurement and analysis was what separated man from the animals, he ruled – though the parallel NH Copper's Blog had suggested it was actually the inability to lick your own balls.

'You needn't worry,' Hunnicutt had told Slider graciously, 'we'll make sure you are kept informed of anything that may impact on your case. And of course–' the smile segued into a look of gravity – 'we expect you to do the same.'

'I'd love to impact on his case,' Slider said later to his NH oppo, DI Phil Warzynski, which was safe to do because they were alone at the time and Warzynski felt the same way about Hunniballs, if not a bit more so, since he had to put up with him every day.

'I'd impact on it with my trusty left boot,' Warzynski said. He had played stand-off half for the Met Police rugby team, and said boot was respected throughout the London League. 'But don't worry, Bill. I'll make sure you really do get anything as soon as we do. I take it you think this is part of your ongoing, and not just a coincidence?'

'It'd be a bit of a coincidence if it *was* a coincidence. I'll send you over my notes on Aude and a copy of her statement. The saddest thing is that she really *couldn't* have identified him, so there was no reason to off her.'

'He's being too clever by half,' Warzynski said. 'Overcaution is their downfall as often as carelessness. This could be a murder too far. All right, it was two in the morning and no one about, but there are surveillance cameras everywhere these days. We'll catch him on something.'

Slider hoped they would, though it was not certain that having another grainy photo of the man would help, since they didn't know who he was or what his connection was to Rogers.

To Porson he reported: 'Williamson, the manager of Jiffies, is really cut up, because he actually asked Aude to come back. Apparently he'd had a customer phoning up about Ceecee St Clair, saying she was his favourite artist and asking when she was coming back. When the call was repeated he rang Aude on her mobile and said her public was missing her and any time she felt well enough to return she'd get a hero's welcome. It played on her vanity, poor idiot, and back she came. Third call from the anxious customer, Williamson was able to tell him Ceecee would be dancing again that very night.'

'He didn't find the interest suspicious, then?' Porson grunted.

'No. He gets calls like that from time to time. Various acts have their followings. Of course, now he's kicking himself. Says he wishes he'd asked for the man's name.'

'Wouldn't've helped. He wouldn't've given the real one.'

'No. Warzynski pointed that out to salve his feelings. Anyway, it looks as though the "fan" rang Aude during the evening and made some kind of date with her. Williamson says he saw her talking on her mobile during a break – though I doubt whether that was unusual.'

'Wait a minute – how would the killer get her number?' Porson objected.

Slider almost sighed. 'She had a website. The number was there for theatrical agents to contact her.'

'Bloody Nora!'

'It's quite possible the killer posed as an agent when he rang her to get her to meet. I'm afraid she'd probably be quite uncritical about something like that. Anyway, she left the club just after two, and that was that. She was found in an access alley between two shops just off Portobello Road by a couple of blokes walking home after a party. She was lying just behind the wheelie bins. Warzynski says it looks as though she was killed at the entrance of the alley and dragged from there – it was only about ten feet. A single blow to the temple with a blunt instrument, hard enough to crush the bones. It must have been really quick, that's the only comfort. As they passed the end of the alley, one whack, quick drag, and away.'

'Easy enough if you've got the confidence,' Porson agreed gloomily.

'Yes. There was no real attempt to hide the

body, so he could have done it almost anywhere, just looking for a moment when there was no one else in sight.'

Porson thought, scratching delicately above his ear. 'Well, she wasn't much of a witness, so I doubt it'll make any difference to your case. Except that if he's killed again you've got two chances of catching him.'

'Twice as much human suffering,' Slider felt obliged to point out.

'But twice as much chance of chummy making a mistake. What's goose for the sauce is gander for the other. What lines are Notting Hill following up?'

'They're calling in all the local surveillance camera tapes, putting out Aude's picture and asking for witnesses,' Slider said, with the hopelessness that these things always generated in his voice. 'Not much else they can do.'

Porson nodded. 'Best leave it to them, put it out of your mind, carry on with your own case. As you say, the good thing is that this one isn't ours.'

So it was back to the grindstone. Slider, having lost most of the morning over at Notting Hill, rang Joanna, rather shamefaced, to say he would not be back soon. 'Can you cope? I'm sorry to have to ask you.'

'Nothing to it,' she said blithely. 'With your dad here. Any idea when you'll be through?'

'Not really. But unless something breaks, I should be able to take tomorrow off.'

'Tush! Don't say that. Don't you know the old

225

saying?'

'Any particular one in mind?' he asked.

She told him: '"What makes God laugh? People making plans."'

'Comforting thought,' he said. 'Someone wants me – gotta go.'

'*I* want you – but go anyway.'

It was Swilley at the door. 'Come in,' Slider said to her enquiring look. He liked the fact that she had a sheaf of papers in her hand: it looked hopeful.

'I've been looking into the various property sales and purchases, like you asked, guv, and it's quite interesting. Even more interesting when you add the dates in.'

She held up the papers and raised her eyebrows, and he made a space on his desk and invited her round. It was a perilous venture, for marriage hadn't done anything to impair Norma's looks, and having her leaning over him at close quarters only emphasized how nice she smelled. Since the baby (which was seven months old now, a girl they had called Ashley: Ashley Allnutt – how Atherton had rolled his eyes!) she had been wearing her blonde hair in a jaw-length smooth bell, and it swung forward as she bent and brushed against his ear. Made it hard to concentrate. Come on, he was only human!

'Now,' she said, indicating the table she had laid out in her large, clear handwriting, 'you see the incident in Harley Street happened in June ninety-eight.'

'Good title for a movie,' Slider said. *'Incident*

in Harley Street, starring Sidney Greenstreet.'

'Who?'

'Infant! Go on.'

'Oh. OK. And Rogers moves out of the marital home six weeks later, in July.'

'How did you find that out?'

'Connolly's contact at The Boot, Maureen. She remembers it because it was at the same time her brother was getting married. Anyway, the divorce is filed for in September, so Amanda didn't waste much time. Now, I've managed to track down the London flat. That was sold in the September, for around two-fifty according to the estate agent. The house takes a bit longer – that doesn't sell until January, and it goes for one point one million.'

'So that's around one and a quarter million for the two, give or take,' Slider said.

'And assuming Amanda gets half – she said they shared the money equally – it gives her six-two-five to play with. She buys the house in Ealing, also in January, for three-four-nine-nine-fifty.' She snorted in derision. 'These stupid estate agent prices. Who do they think they're fooling?'

'Well, us, apparently. Anyway, so far so good. Amanda buys a house and has some change left over.'

'You'd think that, wouldn't you?' Swilley said. 'But look here.' She tapped a finger against an entry. 'Frith buys the stables in October – that's *before* Amanda gets the big money from the house. Frith only got ninety thousand for his house. The stables went for two-ninety, but the

227

agent who sold them said they needed a lot of work – he'd have had to spend at least fifty thou on them. And then there's buying the horses. The agent reckoned it out for me, and Amanda must have put in at least three hundred thousand.'

'She must have—'

'Let me finish, boss. The Decree Nisi comes through in March the next year, and the Absolute in September, and in between the two Amanda sets up the agency. Now I haven't got access to her finances, but I've spoken to a contact of mine that says she'd have needed around two hundred kay in set-up costs.'

'Why so much?'

'Because she *buys* the building. And then she'd have had to have the modifications made for disabled access. Then there's equipment, stationery, wages, utilities. All in all, I reckon our Amanda comes up a quarter of a million short over the three transactions. So where did she get the money from?'

She straightened up – somewhat to Slider's relief – and he said, 'It's a good point. She may have money of her own, of course. Or she may have taken out a loan.'

'There's no mortgage on the Ealing house, and only a small one on the stables. I haven't found out about the agency building yet. It's a bit delicate. I don't want the estate agents asking her if it's all right to tell me.'

'No, I understand.'

'But even if there is a mortgage on that, it's not likely to be as much as two-fifty. There's a big black hole in there somewhere.'

'Hmm,' said Slider. From out of memory came a voice saying, *What did Amanda get out of it?* Oh, right, that was Joanna last night, talking about carrots and then sticks. He looked again at the dates. It all happened quite quickly after the scandal. And she didn't wait long after chucking out her husband before investing in Robin Frith. If Frith sold his house to buy the stables presumably he was living with her from that time – October. Three months after Rogers moved out, one month after filing for the divorce, and a generous year before the divorce was finalized. That could have got her into trouble with the courts, had Rogers wanted to contest the divorce. But he had gone pretty meekly, it seemed. Prompting the question, equally, *what did he get out of it*?

Was it possible that there was something in that incident, the Lescroit fumbling, that had turned a profit somehow for the Rogerses? No, not possible, of course. But it was the incident that triggered everything else, and he still could not help feeling there was something about it that he ought to know and didn't.

The agency, he thought. As soon as she was shot of Rogers, she had invested in the two things she cared about, Robin Frith and the agency. Well, one assumed she cared about them. Where the cash resides, there shall your heart be also. 'The agency,' he said aloud. 'What does it cost to run? Does it make money? Presumably it must do, if they pay the Fraser girl a wage. And Nora Beale, unless she has money of her own. But does it make enough for Amanda to live on as well? Because otherwise, where does she get her income? Unless she has private money or lives off the stables, the agency is her living. I'd really like to have a look at the books of that little venture. It's damnable that we can't touch her.'

Swilley thought for a moment, and said, 'What about the Fraser girl, boss? You said she was all cut up about Rogers and didn't care much for Amanda. Maybe she would find out what you want to know. She's in there, in the office. If she's alone at some point...'

'Norma, you're a genius. Get on to that, will you? I want to know if the agency makes a profit, and if not, who pays for it. And if Amanda Sturgess draws a wage. And anything else about the financial side you can squeeze out of her. She might come across woman to woman if you sympathize with her loss. Make her feel she's the real widow.'

'Yeah, boss. I know. Have we got an address for her? Weekend's the best time to make a start on her. That's the loneliest time for someone like her.'

'Good thinking,' said Slider. He considered the psychology of that. 'Take some Kleenex with you.'

'Inspector Slider?' said a cut-glass voice that felt like a very pointed fingernail being run down his spine. 'This is Amanda Sturgess.'

'Yes, I recognized your voice,' Slider said, concealing a tremor of interest. 'What can I do for you?'

230

'I – ah – wondered how your – investigation was coming along.'

'We are making some progress,' Slider said, and stopped to allow the silence to bloom. He wanted to know why she had phoned him. It wasn't to enquire after his progress. Leave her enough silence and perhaps she would cough up something interesting.

She did not speak at once, but Slider was an expert at the game and could outsilent anyone. 'Have you any – are you interested in anyone in particular?'

'I'm afraid I can't divulge any details,' he said.

'Oh, but surely – to me? He was my husband, after all. And I assure you I am discreet.'

'I'm sorry. It would be unprofessional of me to reveal operational matters to anyone outside my team. You of all people must see that.'

'Oh. Yes. Quite,' she said, without questioning what the last sentence meant. 'I just wondered...' A long pause. Slider believed he could feel her working herself up for a revelation – but perhaps that was only what he hoped was happening. In the end she said, in a different, brisker voice, 'I was wondering about the funeral. Whether you wanted me to make any arrangements.'

'The body is not being released at the moment,' he said. 'When the time comes I shall of course bear your kind offer in mind.' She didn't respond, and after a moment he said, quite gently, 'Is there anything you wanted to tell me? I can come and see you if you don't want to talk on the phone.'

It *almost* worked. He was sure it *almost*

231

worked. But then he heard her draw in a breath, and she said in the old, arrogant, sure tones, 'I have nothing to tell you. I don't know what you mean. I was merely enquiring about the funeral, and as it is, there is nothing more to say. Good day to you.'

And she was gone. Slider put down the phone. Had she been going to confess? Was she trying to find out if they were still following the sparkly lure of Frith? Was she protecting someone else? Or her own skin?

He shook his head at himself. You're good at identifying the questions. How about finding some answers?

McLaren was back from a long session at Stanmore police station, and the news was mixed.

'They bin watching Embry a long time, guv,' he reported. 'They're pretty sure he's up to something, but so far they've not got the evidence to move on him.'

'Up to what sort of something?' Slider asked.

'His old game of ringing,' McLaren admitted. 'All right, that's no use to us. But they've got word from their snouts that there's something else going on. They think he could be dealing in stolen goods, or else smuggling – cigarettes is big in that part of the world. Things going in and out his yard in the boots of cars. It's the perfect set-up for moving gear around – nobody goes to his yard on foot, do they? And nobody questions motors going in and out. Handy for the motorway, but out of the way enough—'

'But they don't have anything specific on him?' Slider interrupted. 'Presumably not, or they'd have moved by now.'

'They want *us* to give *them* anything we get,' McLaren said. 'They're assembling a dossier. They liked the number plate thing but want hard evidence on it. And,' he added with an attempt at brightness, 'they weren't surprised when I suggested he might be shifting guns as well. He's got some right tasty friends, and they said that would fit in with their profile of him.'

Slider sighed. 'Has Fathom come up with anything?'

'No. Firearms department don't know him. But then they wouldn't, if he was any good. But Stanmore's gonna open a new line of enquiry. If he's into firearms, they can get extra men on the case. It'll go multi.'

'Stop trying to soften my heart.'

'One thing,' McLaren offered, as if as a consolation prize, 'when I showed them the picture of our suspect, Mick Lonergan – he's the DS – said he was sure he'd seen him somewhere before, but he couldn't place him.'

'Hallelujah,' Slider said.

'He looked through his files, his most recent cases, but he couldn't work out why he knows him, but he's definitely ringing a bell,' McLaren went on doggedly. 'So he's taken copies and he's gonna put it round his snouts. We could still get a tickle, guv. He definitely sparked something – I could see in his face.'

'All right,' Slider said. 'We'll just have to hope. For now, though, it looks as though Embry is a dead end. Keep in touch with Stanmore over it.'

'Yeah, guv, will do. They're really going for him – say he's a blot on the landscape.'

'Well, they can put more into it than we could,' Slider said. But where do we look next, he wondered. Leads were all running out.

'Guv,' said Mackay from his desk as Slider passed through the CID room on his way back from the loo. 'I've been wondering – do you think Stanmore could be Stansted?'

'Too hilly,' Atherton answered for him across the room. 'You'd never find enough flat land for a runway.'

'Have manners,' Connolly rebuked him. 'Let the man speak, willya?'

Mackay ploughed on patiently. 'The Aude female said Rogers said he worked in a hospital in Stansted. I'm wondering if she misheard, or misremembered.'

'Not the sharpest tool in the box, I understand,' Atherton said. 'Could be the next Mrs McLaren?'

'Well, if she'd never heard of Stanmore – but everyone knows Stansted,' Mackay offered. 'Because of the airport.'

'It's a thought,' Slider said. 'Have you any other reason for supposing it?'

'Well, guv, I keep looking as hospitals, in between other stuff, because it got me that there was no hospital in Stansted. I kept widening the search, and when I got to Stanmore I thought about the names sounding similar. And there are two hospitals there. There's the Royal National Orthopaedic—'

'Except that Rogers wasn't an orthodpod,' Atherton said.

'We don't know what he was,' Hollis said, drifting up. 'If he was a drugs rep he could have been visiting any hospital.'

'But Rogers told Aude he was a consultant *at* a hospital.'

'Sure God, he was trying to get the ride offa your woman,' Connolly said with a bit of a gust. 'He'll tell her what'll go down best. Consultant's going to get him into her pants quicker than rep.'

'But then why pick on Stanmore?' Atherton said. 'If he was going to lie he could have made it any hospital. Why not one she might have heard of, Bart's or Thomas's or Hammersmith Hospital?'

'The point *is*,' Mackay said loudly, trying to get the attention back, 'like I said there are two hospitals in Stanmore, the Royal National Ortho-paedic, and the Cloisterwood Hospital. That's a private one. And it's having a fund-raising Gala Day next month, with a garden party in the after-noon and a dinner and dance in the evening.'

Slider was there. 'Aude said Rogers was going to take her to a big promotional party at his hospital.'

'Yeah, guv.'

'Well done. You could be on to something.'

Connolly was already clattering full speed at her own computer, calling up the hospital's site. 'Cloisterwood Private Hospital. It does cosmetic procedures—'

'Plastic surgery to you and me,' Hollis said.

'Rogers *was* a plastic surgeon,' Fathom said excitedly, trying to look over Connolly's shoulder.

'Until the GMC said he couldn't touch patients any more,' Atherton reminded him.

Connolly went on reading. 'And it does gender reassignment.'

'You what?' said Fathom.

'Saving Ryan's Privates,' Atherton clarified.

'Sex change. Wouldn't you like to go for that, Jez?' Connolly said with a sweet smile. 'They turn your lad inside out and stuff it up inside—'

Fathom went pale. 'Shut up! That's nothing to joke about!'

She went on reading from the screen. 'And they do transplants. Kidney, corneal.' She looked up. 'Is that a bit of a strange combination, would you think? Plastic, sex-swap and transplants? As in, "Hello, I'm Doctor Death, the eye, nose and bladder man."'

'It's a private hospital,' Slider said, 'and they're all things that people are willing to pay big money for.'

'Especially foreigners from countries where the culture is less laissez-faire,' said Atherton. 'Imagine being an Iranian wanting a sex-swap-op.'

'You'd hop on a plane and bop along to the sex-swap-op-shop,' Connolly said, still clattering.

'Or countries where the very rich have scads of money, but the medical facilities aren't so advanced,' Atherton concluded. 'Plenty of those.'

'Here's the staff,' Connolly went on. '"Our illustrious consultants." Smiling pictures – Janey Mackeroni, aren't they the sinister crew? I wouldn't let them take out a splinter. And ... no David Rogers,' she concluded, having scrolled to the end.

'But there is – go back,' Slider ordered. 'There is one name we know. There, look. Director of Surgery, Sir Bernard Webber.'

'Rogers's pal,' said Hollis.

'And benefactor,' said Atherton. 'Which perhaps explained why the Cloisterwood leapt to mind when he was spinning a line to Ceecee St Clair.'

'Maybe he did work there,' said Hollis, 'just not as a consultant. They don't list all the staff. Maybe he was working in a lab or the mortuary.'

'Or parking cars,' Fathom offered.

Connolly rolled her eyes. 'Yeah, they'd pay him highly for that, you gom!'

'He could have been their PR man,' Atherton said. 'Didn't someone say he took rich foreigners to that club? Showing them the hospitality. Maybe he was reeling in the customers. That would pay well.'

'That would fit in better with the Rogers we know about,' Slider said. 'Being charming, wearing nice suits, wining and dining and beguiling the punters.' He looked around at his crew, who had all picked up amazingly in the last five minutes. 'All roads lead to Stanmore. Our murderer went there after the shooting. The number plates came from there.'

'Not quite all roads,' Atherton said. 'What

about Suffolk?'

'What about it?' Mackay objected. 'We've only got that bint's word for it he went there. And it was probably just a leisure thing anyway.'

'One red herring at a time,' Slider said. 'We have to find out if Rogers did have a connection with Cloisterwood first.' He looked at his watch. 'Find out if Sir Bernard Webber is there today, and tell him I want to come over and see him. And–' to Connolly – 'see what else there is about him on the Internet. Let me have a few facts under my belt before I go.'

'Here, sir,' Connolly said, placing a printed sheet in front of him. 'All I've been able to get so far. Age fifty-six. On his second wife. Two kids from first marriage grown up and gone away. Lives in a gin palace in Letchmore Heath.'

'How do you know it's a gin palace?'

'I looked it up on Goggle-at-my-house – aka Google Earth. Called The Boydens. Gak! I hate people who call their houses *The* something. Massive modern place. Private cinema, indoor swimming pool, tennis courts. Ugly as a dog's arse. Sure it looks like a golf hotel in Antrim.'

'You've a cutting tongue on you, Detective Constable. Go on.'

'He's consulting rooms in Harley Street, present position Director of Surgery, Cloisterwood Hospital, as we know. Hobbies, golf – there's a surprise. Fishing – and another. And flying – has his own light aircraft at Elstree Aerodrome. Other positions, Deputy Director of Standards, General Medical Council; Member of the Health

Service Advisory Group; Member of the Pharmaceutical Oversight Board. Jayzus, you'd think they'd want to get rid of pharmaceutical oversights, not have a board for them! Quite the political player, too. He's been Special Adviser to the Department of Health – that musta been a bit of a jolly: did an eighteen-month fact-finding tour of China, the Middle East, the Sub-Continent – what's that when it's at home?'

'India and Pakistan.'

'Oh, right – and South America. Nice work if you can get it. He's also been Cabinet Special Adviser on Care Implementation, and Deputy Chair, Select Committee on GP remuneration. On the GMC website under his interests it's listed he's a member of the Labour Party, but we might have guessed that – he got his knighthood in 2003 for helping to shove through the new GP contract.' She looked up at Slider. 'You'd want to watch yourself, guv, tangling with that class of a player. He's friends in high places.'

'I eat people with friends in high places for breakfast,' Slider assured her. He held out his hand. 'Can I have that?'

'Work away,' she said, handing it over. 'If you get into trouble, you can write a cry for help on the back and turn it into a paper aeroplane.'

'Or fashion it into a pistol and frighten my way out?'

She considered. 'Forget that,' she concluded. 'Just do a legger.'

239

THIRTEEN

Bedside Manor

This part of Middlesex was simply lovely: gentle inclines, rich rolling pastures, fine mature trees, old hedgerows and wide verges. In the grounds of the Cloisterwood Hospital there was a prettily-shaped small lake, reed-fringed, from which skeins of ducks rose with joyful clamour. It looked like an eighteenth-century landed gentleman's idea of the Garden of Eden.

Part of the hospital building – the part you first came upon down the long drive – was a white-stuccoed early Victorian house of large windows, tall chimneys and gracious aspect, presumably the country residence of the original owner of this artful landscape. The modern, functional buildings that had been added to turn it into a hospital had been politely tucked away at the back, as was the car park, which was full of BMWs, Mercedes and Audis, not to mention a generous sprinkling of Rollers and Bentleys. In the corner a discreet notice pointed the way to the staff car park, and Slider, feeling his common old car would look less out of place there, modestly followed it. Ah, this was better. Minis and Micros and Meganes, Golfs, Fiestas and

Focuses, and even a couple of MPVs, together with a fair and reasonable degree of scruffiness and dilapidation, allowed him to park with more confidence.

Webber's office was in the old building, and he was shown into it by a slight, pretty girl in a lavender uniform dress and told that Sir Bernard would be with him very shortly. Slider anticipated a power-wait, but in fact it was only two or three minutes, barely time to take himself to the window and look out over the parkland to the lake, before the door opened behind him and a voice said, 'Nice view, isn't it? Even lovelier when the chestnuts come into bloom.'

Slider turned. Given Webber's eminence, status, and connections, Slider had been quite prepared to dislike him. He had expected cold briskness, arrogance, finger-drumming impatience with Slider's inferiority and the waste of valuable time he represented. But the Webber approaching him across the room was perfectly relaxed and smiling, holding out his hand with such an air of cordiality that Slider shook it without even a momentary shrinking.

'One of the perks of my position here,' Webber went on, joining Slider at the window. 'I got to choose my own office. I've worked in so many modern buildings – and of course no one wants to house the medical side of things in old buildings. But an office like this was always my dream. We had to adapt the house to a certain extent, but I think we did it tactfully – don't you? You see how we matched the mouldings and cornice – that's actually a false wall there. And

241

the door is a copy.'

While obediently looking at the things that were being pointed out, Slider was getting a look at Webber himself. He was a little taller than Slider, but not a tall man; fifty-six, as Slider knew, but well preserved, with only a little tell-tale thickening of the body to betray him. His hair was thick and wavy, brown sprinkled so attractively with silver it might have been deliberate. His face was firm-fleshed, authoritative and genial, and, if not exactly handsome, near enough to it to be deemed so with the aid of his fine clothes and immaculate *toilette*. The eyes, crinkled often in smiles, were a faded blue and very clear, as if their owner were a clean-living outdoorsman. With the natural-looking, light tan of the skin and the capable hands, it made Slider think of him at the helm of a racing yacht.

But the best thing of all was the voice, deep, warm and with a perfect accent – clean English but not over-posh – inspiring absolute confidence. It was the sort of voice you wanted to hear on a 747 saying, 'This is the captain speaking.'

Architecture was one of Slider's interests, and he was happy to allow Webber to tell him a little about the history of the house in the few minutes before the door opened and another slim, pretty girl in the same uniform came in with a tray.

'Ah, tea,' Webber said with an air of rubbing his hands. 'I took the chance that you would have a cup with me. Unless you would prefer coffee?'

'Tea is fine, thank you.'

Webber led the way to an armchairs-and-coffee-table configuration to one side of the room, where the girl was laying it out and pouring for them. Georgian silver teapot, fine china, and there was a plate of shortbread as well. Slider sipped his tea: it was good.

Webber, looking at him for his reaction, said, 'Kenya. I alternate with Darjeeling, but you've caught me on my Kenya day. I take my afternoon cup quite seriously, you see. It's the only way to treat the king of beverages.'

Slider put down his cup and smiled politely, suddenly wondering why all this charm was being expended on a lowly policeman. As if he had heard the thought, Webber let the smile go in favour of a serious look, and said, 'Well, I'm sure you're a busy man, and I know I am, so perhaps we should get on with it. Would you like to tell me why you've come to see me?'

Given that Slider was from Shepherd's Bush, Webber must have known the subject for debate, but he said, 'I'm looking into the death of David Rogers. I believe he was a friend of yours.'

Webber looked sad, but not heartbroken. 'Poor David! It's a shocking business. Yes, we were friends and colleagues some years ago. I was a mentor of sorts to him in the early days, and we worked together at one time, but we've rather drifted apart in recent years.'

'Why would that be?' Slider asked.

'Why did we drift apart? What an odd question! Why does it ever happen? The human condition is fluid, friendships form and break, lives

243

go off in opposite directions. One wakes up one day and finds oneself in a different place with different people.'

Slider cut through this happy horseshit. 'Was it because of the trouble he got into? The scandal over a patient?'

Webber looked put out by the bluntness. 'Not directly. I didn't drop him, you know. In fact, I did everything I could to help him.'

'You represented him with the GMC,' Slider suggested.

'Not precisely that, but I used my influence there. Otherwise the outcome could have been much worse for him.'

'Why would you do that?' Slider asked. 'Why protect a doctor who molests a patient? Surely there are ethical considerations which must override friendship?'

Webber blinked and put down his teacup. 'That's very blunt. If not a touch hostile.'

'I didn't mean to be hostile,' Slider said. 'I'm trying to understand the situation.'

'Well, I don't see what it has to do with David's death, but I'll tell you: David vehemently denied any wrongdoing, and at the time I wasn't convinced that the woman hadn't made a mistake. She was only half awake, and may have misunderstood what David was doing, or she may have exaggerated, or even made it up entirely, to get attention. I have to tell you there are a lot of women like that – or perhaps I don't have to.' He looked enquiring. 'I imagine policemen meet them as well.'

'I understand you got him a job afterwards.'

The washed-blue eyes sharpened. 'Who told you that?'

'Someone who was a friend of his at the time.'

'Who?'

Slider didn't answer that. 'Did you, in fact, get David Rogers a job?' he insisted.

Webber seemed reluctant to admit to this act of kindness. 'I – again, I used such influence as I had to promote his chances of obtaining a position. It couldn't be directly in medicine, but there was a pharmaceutical company looking for someone on the PR side – someone who understood how doctors think, who could advise on advertising and promotional campaigns. David had all the right qualifications: he was young, personable, intelligent. Sadly, however, he didn't stick at it. I think he was there about a year or eighteen months before he left. I don't know what he did after that. I lost contact with him entirely. I've no idea what he's been doing in recent years.'

'So when did you last see him or speak to him?'

'I can't remember. Not for years.'

'You disapproved of his leaving?'

'I was – disappointed. I'd gone to some trouble to help him and I felt he should have stuck at it. But perhaps he had a better prospect somewhere, I don't know.'

'So you didn't offer him a position here?'

'Here, at Cloisterwood? No, he has never been on the payroll here.'

'He seems to have told people he worked here.'

245

Webber looked grave. 'I'm sorry to hear that. We depend greatly on our good name and – look, I'll be frank with you. At the time of David's trouble I believed his protestations of innocence. But since that time, I've rather changed my opinion. His reputation with women – his shabby treatment of his wife – his unreliability. It's all of a piece. He didn't seem to be able to resist women, and I've come to believe that that poor Mrs – what was her name? Lindsey? Leicester?'

'Lescroit.'

'That's it. I'm afraid that she was probably right all along, and I feel bad about having persuaded her away from making charges. David wasn't to be trusted, either with women or a job. It's a great pity, because he was a talented surgeon. But I couldn't possibly have someone so unreliable associated with my establishment here.'

'I see,' Slider said. It seemed he had stumbled into another dead end. Rogers had merely been boasting, borrowing his old friend-and-mentor's success to make a rather dim bird. Shabby. Yet he had been doing *something* that pulled in the readies.

He tried a curve ball. 'Can you tell me something about the Windhover Trust?'

There was no flicker in Webber's face. He looked politely enquiring. 'Windhover Trust? I don't know it.'

'It's a branch of the Geneva Medical Support and Research Foundation.'

'Ah. Well, I *have* heard of them, vaguely, but I've no idea what they do. I don't have any dealings with them.'

'In what way have you heard of them, then?'

'I've seen the name somewhere – in a medical journal, perhaps. Usually these grand-sounding foundations are connected with the drugs companies. There is very large money to be made in pharmaceuticals, with government spending involved. Think of what was spent on Swine Flu vaccine during the last panic. Aids and malaria programmes run into billions. I expect that's where you'll find its activities concentrated.' He put down his cup, empty now, with an air of finality. 'Well, if there's nothing more I can help you with?'

'Not at the moment.'

The farewell handshake was being offered now. 'If you have any more questions, don't hesitate to ask,' Webber said, guiding Slider gently towards the door. 'I'll do anything I can to help catch the killer. For all his faults, David was a very loveable man, and a good doctor. I'm sad and dismayed at what has happened.'

A good doctor gone bad: that was the verdict. So Slider thought as he made his way out through the luxurious surroundings, which bore no resemblance to a hospital – well, they weren't supposed to, were they? The wide front hall, with its reception desk and seating areas and floral arrangements, looked like the foyer of a very exclusive country hotel. A man in fine Arab robes was standing impassively in the middle of the floor. A thin, anxious man who was obviously his assistant or courier was talking to a receptionist at the desk while three of his wives sat resignedly on the reproduction Empire chairs and a chauffeur carried in amusingly copious luggage from the enormous Rolls Royce just outside.

Slider stepped round the sheik, who did not deign to notice he was in the way, and made his way back to his car, which was looking more of a carbuncle every minute. There was money to be made in medicine all right, and it was evident the Cloisterwood Hospital had found one way of doing it. David Rogers had presumably found another, but what was it? Cloisterwood was a washout. But there had to be something, some connection, with Stanmore. If the answer wasn't here, he didn't know where next to look for it. He got in his car, reaching the exit at the same time as an MPV which, surprisingly, stood back for him to go first – not what you expected of MPVs, especially when they were black S line Audi Q7s with blacked-out windows. Surely there should be another word for this kind of four-by-four, some title to suggest their sleek, powerful and threatening street presence. MPV was too school-run-mum. Must be the staff motor for the Arab gentleman, he thought. Or maybe transport for inferior wives. A man of that wealth would want the best even for the last car in his cavalcade. What it must be not to have to count the cost of anything, thought Slider, who had never in his life even flown business class, let alone first.

He had to stop for petrol, and took the opportunity to ring the factory to see if anything had happened. 'Yes,' said Atherton. 'Something has. A bloke rang, says he's a solicitor and he's got something to tell about David Rogers. Seemed a bit cagey about it. Wants someone to go round.'

'Tell him to come in,' said Slider. 'Where is he?'

'Harrow.'

'Oh. Well, I'm practically there,' Slider said. 'I suppose I could drop in on my way past.'

'You sound glum. Webber no good?'

'He was perfectly charming, but he says Rogers didn't work for him and he hasn't seen him or spoken to him for years. Disapproves of his womanizing.'

'Brings the game into disrepute, eh?' said Atherton. 'So it's another dead end?'

'Took the words out of my mouth.'

'Then you need a bit of cheering up. I was going to see the solicitor myself, but you have him, with my blessing.'

'Oh, thank you,' said Slider, with irony.

'It may not be another dead red herring end,' Atherton reasoned.

'Likewise it is better to travel hopefully than to arrive. Give me the name and address.'

It was actually in Harrow Weald, and very easy to find: Slider turned off the A410 Uxbridge Road into the High Road, and there it was, on the left, opposite the bus depot, above a shop. It was very eye-catching, the London stock bricks having been cleaned of generations of soot so that it was the only upper storey in the terrace that was pale yellow instead of black. The name was painted on the window in large letters in black outlined in white, two words one above the other, curve and reverse curve so they made an open circle: MARICAS SOLICITOR. He wasn't taking any chances on losing trade because someone couldn't locate him.

Slider parked the car and walked back to the door, hospitably open, between a Chinese take-away and a betting shop. Upstairs there were two offices, the reception office being the one with the painted window. Here a middle-aged woman wearing a heavy cardigan over her shoulders was typing so vigorously the empty sleeves swung and jiggled to the movement. She looked up with polite and friendly enquiry as Slider entered.

'Mr Maricas? He's expecting me. My name's Slider.'

'Oh, right.' She came out from the desk and led Slider back down the passage to the closed door of the back room. She tapped and opened it. 'Mr Slider for you,' she announced.

The room couldn't have been a greater contrast to Webber's antique-furnished, thick-carpeted, gracious hidey hole. There was lino on the floor, a cheap, battered desk that looked as if it had been bought second-hand, some very incommodious office chairs, one with a large stain on the seat and the other with a cigarette hole, a table covered in box files and folders, and a plethora of filing cabinets, standing around awkwardly in every available space like people at a badly organized party given by someone they didn't know very well. The window was smaller than the one at the front and so dirty that Slider could get no idea of what it looked over.

The man behind the desk stood up and shoved his hand out eagerly. 'Henry Maricas,' he said. Slider shook it – it would have been churlish not to – thinking this had been a bad day for someone who didn't like touching members of the public. 'Can I get you some coffee or something?' Maricas offered with automatic hospitality.

'Nothing, thanks. I've just had some tea.'

'Oh. OK. Well, do sit down.'

Slider chose the seat with the hole in it – you never knew what that stain might be – and said, 'You wanted to see me?'

Henry Maricas was younger than Slider had expected – probably in his thirties, but he looked even younger, because of his thin, eager face and the silky mouse-coloured hair worn a little too long, so that the forelock flopped schoolboyishly forward over his brow and had to be shoved back every now and then. His skin was transparently pale, so that you could almost see the blood running about under it, and his eyes, surprisingly, were very dark, almost black, and fringed with thick dark lashes. His suit looked rather worn and crumpled, and his long-fingered, knuckly hands looked grubby, but given the amount of dust lying around this room it was hardly surprising. When he had stood up, he had towered over Slider – a good six foot three, he thought – but he was too thin for his height, which added to the air of gawky youth. He was, indeed, so thin that Slider wondered if his business was not doing well enough to support him. But his accent was pure Eton-and-Oxford, and there was something about his manner which gave Slider the impression of one of a long line of legal beagles, a son who had gone into the family profession as a matter of course.

'Well, not you specifically,' Maricas said with an apologetic smile, 'because I didn't know you existed, so to speak, but someone from the case. The David Rogers case, I mean.' And he glanced at the door as if to check that it was closed.

'I am the investigating officer,' Slider said, exuding calm. He felt absurdly fatherly already towards this nice young man. 'I'd be happy to hear anything you have to say about David Rogers.'

Maricas nodded. 'First I have to explain to you that I've been away – on holiday, in fact, skiing in Davos – my family always goes at this time of year. I only came back this morning, which was why I didn't know anything about it – about Dr Rogers being dead. There's only me and Maggie – my secretary–' he nodded towards the other office – 'and she didn't know anything about my dealings with him so she didn't alert me. It was only when I was looking through the papers today – she keeps them for me when I'm away, so I can check on anything that's come up – that I saw the report that he'd been killed. Otherwise I'd have come forward right away.' He frowned. 'Or, I suppose I would. It's hard to know what's the right thing to do when it's a case of murder. It was murder – I mean, there's no doubt?'

'There's no doubt, I'm afraid.'

He gnawed a finger. 'Then I suppose I ought to

tell you first, before I do anything about it.'

'Why don't you tell me what your relationship was with Dr Rogers?' Slider helped him along. He used that title since it seemed to be what Rogers had used with Maricas.

He pulled himself together. 'Yes, of course. I'll tell you the story from the beginning. You see, Dr Rogers came to see me about eight months ago. He was a walk-in – said he'd seen my sign from the road, and that he wanted someone to draw up his will.'

'His will? You have his will?' Slider couldn't help himself. The whole business about the next of kin had been dragging at them since the beginning.

'Yes, that's what I'm telling you. He'd brought in his previous will, which left everything to his first wife—'

'Amanda Sturgess.'

'That's right. But he'd divorced her and remarried and wanted to make sure his new wife would get his estate rather than Ms Sturgess. I explained to him that his old will would automatically be nullified by his remarriage, and that unless he had children or other relatives, his second wife would automatically inherit. But of course it's always better to have it written down, and he said that's what he wanted. He didn't want there to be any doubt about it. So I made up the document for him. He didn't have any other relatives, as it happened, so it was very simple, just leaving everything to his current wife.'

'I didn't know he had one,' Slider said. Maricas handed the will to him across the desk, and he read it. It revoked all previous testamentary dispositions, named Henry John Duval Maricas as his sole executor, and left all his property, whatsoever and wheresoever situate, to his wife, Helen Marie Aldous of 23 Station Approach, Southwold.

Southwold. Southwold as in Suffolk. Now they had the Suffolk connection. Slider looked up. 'The next of kin. You don't know the trouble we've been to, trying to find out who his next of kin was. His ex-wife offered to arrange the funeral because we didn't know of anyone else. Are you telling me this person doesn't know about Rogers's death yet?'

Maricas looked unhappy. 'Well, I haven't told her. I've explained why. If it had been a normal death or an accident I would have got on to her straight away today, as soon as I knew, but in the circumstances I thought I'd better speak to you first.'

'I wonder *she* hasn't contacted *you*.'

'She may not know he's dead yet. Not everyone reads the papers, you know. Or he might not have told her about me. People can be very funny about wills. They don't like to think they'll ever be needed.'

'But I suppose he had a copy of it,' Slider said. 'I wonder why we didn't find it. We had all the papers out of his house. His London house, I mean – presumably he owns the one in Southwold.'

'He bought it, but he'd already gifted it to his wife, so it's hers now.'

Hollis had been right, Slider thought. There

254

was a whole other establishment – the 'house in the country'. Probably all his missing gubbins were there. 'Perhaps he keeps his copy of the will there,' he said.

'He told me that he was putting a copy in his safe at home. I just assumed he meant Hofland Crescent, because that's the address he gave me as his. Southwold was always "my wife's house".'

'We didn't find a safe,' Slider said, more to himself than to Maricas.

'Presumably it was a concealed one,' said Maricas, smiling a little, but still looking anxious. 'He was a very cautious person.'

Slider nodded. They hadn't stripped the house, because there had seemed to be no reason for it. If there was a safe there, what else might they find in it?

'I haven't told you everything yet,' Maricas went on. 'He said the reason he had come to me for the will was that he didn't dare go to anyone who knew him. He insisted that I must keep the whole business secret. I had to type it out myself, and when he came to sign it, he came in a taxi and brought the taxi driver up to be the other witness. He didn't want Maggie to witness it because he said he didn't trust women. "They always talk," he said.'

'But why all the secrecy?' Slider asked. 'Did he explain that?'

'He said–' and here Maricas looked faintly apologetic – 'that he was involved in important but dangerous work, and that there were people who might attack him through his wife if they

255

knew of her existence.'

'That's a bit James Bond,' Slider said.

'I know, that was my thought too,' said Maricas, 'but he seemed quite sincere about it. I'm sure he believed it. I said if someone was threatening him he should go to the police, and he said that would be fatal. They mustn't know he was wary of them, he said. And he said he was trying to get himself out of it, but it would take time and be difficult and dangerous, because everyone knew what the fate of whistle-blowers was.'

'Whistle-blowers?'

'That's what he said. He wouldn't tell me anything about what he was involved in, and frankly, although I believed him at the time, because he was obviously nervous, afterwards I thought he must be making it up. Exaggerating for effect, you know – to make himself important. But now—' He looked seriously into Slider's eyes, his own brown ones troubled. 'But now, it looks as though he wasn't kidding. I mean, someone cared enough about what he was doing to kill him.'

'Yes,' said Slider. And he thought about that single bullet to the back of the head. Too professional. Amanda had said there was a woman at the bottom of it, but it was much more likely to be money, wasn't it? Putting aside the secret agent notion, had he been involved in some illegal but lucrative business, lucrative enough to kill him if he looked likely to pull the plug on it? But what the heck *was* it?

'I feel so bad that I didn't believe him,' Maricas said. 'So you see why I thought I should speak to you before I did anything?'

'Yes, I think you did quite right,' Slider said, and Maricas looked relieved.

'He was very worried for his wife – afraid for her. He thought they'd go after her to get at him. He said no one knew about her and it had to stay that way. She even kept her maiden name so no one would connect her with him. So I was worried that if I contacted her now it might somehow draw attention to her. But she'll have to be told – if she doesn't know already. And other people will have to know, if the will is to go through probate. I mean, she won't get his money until then, and he must have wanted her to have it, or why the will?'

'It's a tricky problem, I see that,' said Slider. And he thought of Cat Aude. If the witness who was no witness had been murdered, in how much more danger was a wife? He might not have told his wife all about his 'business', of course, but the murderer or murderers wouldn't care about that. They'd eliminate her anyway, just to be on the safe side. 'You have no idea what it was he was involved in?'

'No, he never said. Didn't so much as give a hint.'

'And do you think he told his wife about it?'

'I don't know. Really, I have no idea. I suppose if *anyone* knows, it would most likely be her. But he went to such pains to keep her secret, maybe he wouldn't have wanted to burden her with the knowledge.'

'And "women always talk",' Slider mused.

Maricas gave a quick, unhappy smile. 'So

what's to be done?'

'You'll have to leave it with me,' Slider said. 'Say nothing to anyone about this.'

'I've kept his secret this far. You can trust me.'

'I know I can,' Slider said.

'But what will *you* do?' Maricas asked anxiously.

'I don't know yet. Once we have the murderer behind bars, I think Rogers's wife will be safe.'

'But how will you catch him?'

I haven't the foggiest, Slider thought. But what he said was, 'We are following up lines of investigation.'

FOURTEEN

Beauty in the Eye of the Beer Holder

'You'd better go yourself,' Porson said. 'Normally I'd disignore this James Bond bollocks as so much fantasy, but given that the Aude female was offed as soon as she raised her head, we can't afford to assume there's no threat to the wife. Otherwise we ought to involve the local police, out of courtesy if nothing else. But the less people know about this the better. What about this Maricas?'

'I think Rogers got lucky. I'd say he was a hundred per cent. It seems to me that Rogers picked him because he was the first solicitor he saw – the office is very eye-catching when you turn into that road—'

'But what was he doing on that road in the first place when he lives in Shepherd's Bush?'

'It's the first major turning off the main road when you're coming from Stanmore,' Slider said. 'There's got to be some connection with Stanmore, but if it isn't the Cloisterwood, I don't know what it was.'

'Well, don't raggle your brain about that now. The wife might know. She might know everything, in fact. What else have you got to follow up?'

'Swilley's going after the agency – trying to find out how it's financed.'

'You think that's important? You still think Sturgess is involved?'

'We haven't got any other suspects. And the presence of a new wife makes her more interesting.'

'The presence of a new will leaving everything to the new wife makes Sturgess less of a suspect,' Porson pointed out.

'If she knew about it. Rogers seems to have been at pains to keep it secret. And the old will left Sturgess everything.'

'Point. Anything else?'

'I want to have a look round Rogers's house, see if I can find that safe.'

'You'd better do that before you go and see the wife. Might be all sorts of things in there.'

'Yes,' said Slider. 'I thought I'd go now, and go down to Southwold early tomorrow. Sunday's a good day to catch people in.'

'Good thought.' Porson's brows lowered themselves in thought over his eyes. It made Slider think of someone in a cave drawing the branches down to hide the entrance. His pronouncement eventually was, 'Be careful. Rogers could have been a fantastacist, or he could have been involved with some foreign secret service, or industrial espionage, or smuggling. But whatever it was, they've shown themselves to be ruthless. Don't dick about with your safety or the woman's.'

'I'll be careful,' Slider said.

But first, to the house in Hofland Crescent, where Slider and Atherton were met by their expert on safes and safe-cracking, Bill Adams, inevitably known as 'Burglar Bill'. He was a big man with a big presence, shrewd eyes, and the hands of a surgeon, an analogy improved by the presence of a stethoscope poking out of the top of his kit bag.

'But first we have to find it,' Slider said, to curb his eagerness to get cracking. 'It can't be anywhere too obvious or Bob Bailey's lot would have stumbled across it.'

'Essence of a hidden safe,' Adams said, 'is that you *don't* stumble across it. Though it's amazing how often people choose the obvious places. There's a sort of psychology that wants your friends to know you're important enough to have one. It's showing off.'

'Well, our Dirty Doc was a whale on showing off,' Atherton said. 'Where do you recommend we start looking?'

'Leave it to me,' Adams said, with an air of

rubbing his hands. 'I like a challenge. Though it probably won't be much of one.'

It was interesting to walk round behind him as he checked the usual places – peeping behind paintings, lifting rugs, examining cupboards. The dressing-room got him interested because there was a lock on the door – 'Why would anyone want to lock up their suits?' – but in the end he found it in the bathroom. The presence of a false wall was not in itself suspicious, he explained, because there were all sorts of pipes to be hidden, but this one was on the wrong side of the bathroom. The mirror over the basin was the sort that turned out to be a shallow cupboard containing medicines and spare razor blades; but the whole cupboard was further hinged and swung out from the wall, revealing the safe sunk into the space between the false wall and the brickwork.

'Nice,' Adams said. 'Not seen that one before. And cute – your average burglar wouldn't think of the bathroom.'

'And private,' Slider added. 'If there was anyone else in the house – as there often was, Rogers being fond of female company – he could go in there and lock the door to access it without anyone wondering.'

'Right enough,' Adams said. 'I hadn't thought of that aspect.'

'Now you've found it, can you open it?'

'Oh yes,' Adams said easily. 'It isn't a serious safe. Concealment was the real security. I'll have it open for you in a brace of shakes.' Shortly afterwards, a satisfying clunk having been heard from the door, Adams stepped back and said, 'Be my guest.'

Slider hardly knew what he had expected to find in the safe, apart from a copy of the will. That, however, was not there: what was there was was money, cash, in fifties and twenties, bundled and held together some by rubber bands and some by paper sleeves.

'Well,' said Atherton appreciatively.

'What's your boy done – robbed a bank?' Adams asked after a windless whistle.

'I wish it were that simple,' Slider said.

'We did keep hearing that he paid cash for things,' Atherton remembered. 'So this was where he kept it. Got to be ill-gotten gains – you don't keep your money in the house, unless you're a barmy old lady with fourteen cats.'

'Presumably he was paid in cash,' said Slider, 'for whatever it was he was doing. Or partly in cash.' He removed the bundles, doing a rough count as he went. There was close on a hundred thousand in there.

'Talk about your mad money,' Atherton said. 'So what now?'

'We take it into safe keeping,' Slider said. 'Until we find out where it came from. If it isn't dirty, the widow gets it. Look around for a bag, will you. There's probably something in the dressing-room that will do.' He turned to Adams. 'Will you just check round the rest of the house, in case he had two safes? I'm going to have a walk round, in case there's anything else of interest.'

* * *

262

Swilley was in his room when he got back, to report that she had made contact with Angela Fraser, who was 'more than willing' to help out.

'She loves it that someone's taking her seriously, poor cow,' she said with scant sympathy. 'She's pretty sure she can get a look at the books on Monday. Amanda's apparently not coming in, and she can do it when Nora goes to lunch and she's alone in the office. I've told her to be careful, but I think she would have been anyway – she's scared shitless of Amanda at the best of times.'

'Does she know what to look for?'

'Anything about how the place is financed, a list of donors, a rough idea of how much comes in and how much goes out, anything that Amanda draws personally.'

'That should do it.'

'And if she can get it into a conversation with Nora, she's going to ask how the agency was set up, where the money came from.'

'Good. And you're liaising with her how?'

'She's going to ring me on Monday when she goes out for her lunch – she goes when Nora comes back.'

He got home late and tired to find a family game of Monopoly going on before the fire, with Joanna, Matthew and Kate on the floor and his father in the armchair, leaning forward to shake the dice on to the board.

'What a wholesome picture,' he said. 'You look like an advert for Bournvita.'

'What's Bournvita?' Kate asked.

'It's a chocolate biscuit,' Matthew told her.

'No, that's a Bourbon,' Mr Slider corrected. 'Hello, son. Hard day?'

Slider nodded. Joanna had got up and came to kiss him, giving him a quick look of concern.

'Yuk!' Kate shouted. 'Get a room, you two.'

'Is that all the hello I get from you, brat?' Slider said. 'No kiss, no hug?'

'It's my turn next,' she excused herself. 'Come on, Grandad. Hurry up and move. You've landed on the Strand.' She snatched up the dice even before Mr Slider had finished moving his boot. She was very competitive, whatever she played – and lucky. Slider could see she had the biggest piles of money in front of her, and would have betted that she owned Park Lane and Mayfair, which both sported threatening hotels.

Slider looked across at his son, who smiled his small, reserved smile, and said, ''Lo, Dad.'

Slider longed to hug him, or at the very least to brush the hair back from his brow. But Matthew was at the age when any physical contact or exhibition of affection was excruciatingly embarrassing and likely to be responded to with a shamefaced, 'Gerroff!'

'How's it going?' Slider asked him.

'She's winning,' he said.

'I bet she's the top hat, as well,' Slider said.

'Yeah,' said Matthew. 'Miss Moneybags.' And they shared a warming look of complicity.

'Have you eaten?' Joanna asked him.

'Have you?' he countered.

'We waited a bit, but the children were hungry, so we ate about half an hour ago. I'll get you something.'

'Oh no!' Kate wailed, looking up from landing on Community Chest and taking a card. 'You can't stop the game.'

'I won't be long,' Joanna said. 'You can take my goes.'

'It's not the same. It'll spoil it!'

Slider remembered the passion of childhood for the moment in hand, the outrage that grown-ups didn't care in the same way. 'I can get myself something. You sit down and play.'

'No, I'll do the getting. You sit down and play, take over my hand,' Joanna said firmly. She was right, of course. The children wanted to be with him – and he wanted to be with them, too, only he was tired and his head was full of the Rogers case and it was hard to summon up enthusiasm for Monopoly against that background. But he saw so little of them, he must make the effort.

'As long as I don't have to be the thimble,' he said, sitting down.

Kate looked into the box. 'You can be the battleship, Daddy. No one's being that yet. And it's your go next.' Suddenly she gave him a dazzling smile, and reached over and pecked him on the cheek, and his heart melted. She so rarely handed out favours, and for a very different reason from Matthew – his was diffidence, hers was a liking to be in control. She was utterly self-absorbed and a manipulative little minx, which he supposed was par for the course these days, but it made such caresses as did come his way even more to be treasured.

'Thank you, sweetheart,' he said, smiling.

'What was that for?'

'It's my birthday,' she said. 'Collect ten pounds from each player. Cough up, Daddy.'

When the game finally finished, Mr Slider went back to his own quarters and the children elected to watch television for an hour before bed. Slider finally got together with his beloved in the kitchen, where she did the washing up while he leaned against the wall watching her and having a small whisky, at her insistence, because she said he looked as though he needed it.

'So what's the bad news?' she asked.

'How do you know there's bad news?'

'Hey, it's me,' she said. 'I can read you like a book.'

'Probably not a best-seller,' he said.

'Best-sellers are overrated. You're more like a much-loved classic you come back to again and again. You're the *Pride and Prejudice* of husbands.'

He had to smile. 'Thank you,' he said. 'Couldn't you at least have made it something manly and full of testosterone-fuelled battles?'

'What would a woman want with one of those?'

'You have a point.'

'So what's the bad news?' she reverted. 'You have to work tomorrow?'

'Got it in one. I have to go to Southwold.'

'How long will that take?'

'I don't know. It's about two and half hours to drive it. What happens then depends on what we find.'

'We?'

'Atherton's going with me.'

'Oh.' She thought a moment. 'Well, I half expected you wouldn't be around. I thought, as it's supposed to be nice tomorrow, we'd go and have a picnic in Kew Gardens, have a good run around, and look at the Steam Museum on the way back. I wonder if Emily would like to join us.'

He pushed himself off the wall, put his arms round her and kissed the back of her neck. She stopped washing up for a moment to turn her head to him. 'What was that for?'

'I can't tell you how comforting it is that you don't give me hell for having to work,' he said.

'What use would that be?'

'No use. But some people would still give a person hell,' he said. 'Some people did.'

'Silly. We don't have enough time together as it is. Why waste it on hell?'

'Wonder woman,' he said, and let her go.

'Is the case going to break soon?' she asked. 'Is that what the trip's about?'

'I don't know,' he said. 'I can only hope so.'

Kate appeared in the doorway, eyes everywhere. 'Were you two smooching *again*?'

'It's only the second smooch of the evening,' Joanna complained. 'You make it sound like non-stop romance.'

'Well it's yukky when old people do it.'

'I thought you were watching TV,' said Slider pointedly.

'Adverts,' Kate said. 'I'm hungry again. Is there any cake?'

267

Kate was always eating, and was as thin as a rake. Good genes – or a hyperactive metabolism. Or both. Irene was the same. Long may it last, Slider thought.

'I could make everyone Bournvita,' Joanna said. She and Slider exchanged an amused look.

'I didn't know you had any,' Slider said. 'Do they still make it?'

'I've got hot chocolate. It's much the same.'

'Oh, yeah, hot chocolate,' Kate said. 'Cool!'

'Not, it'll be hot,' Slider corrected.

Kate looked scornful. 'You're not a bit funny, you know,' she said with imperishable dignity.

'Southwold, the last posh seaside resort,' Atherton said. 'Houses here cost as much as in London.'

'Didn't I read somewhere that the government's letting the coastal defences go?'

'Yes, and they say the rivers on either side of Southwold will back up and refill the marshes and the town will become an island. At which point,' Atherton said, 'the townsfolk will probably rejoice. Well, we've got a nice day for it.' The bitter north wind had dropped at last, and although it was overcast, at least it was dry. 'It was nice of Joanna to think of inviting Emily to the picnic. She was a bit miffed that I was having to work.'

'It'll be nice for Jo as well,' Slider said. 'They're going to play rounders after they've eaten, to wear the children out. It's a bit like having dogs – now there's no PT at schools you have to run them about until they're exhausted at the weekend or they chew up the furniture.'

It continued overcast until they reached the turn-off for Southwold, which had its own microclimate: you could see a clear division in the sky all along the coast, grey to one side and blue to the other. The sea sparkled, deep blue, and the leaves were further along here, with the hedges greening and the oak already in olive-yellow curls. 'I can see why people would want to live here,' Slider said.

Atherton shuddered. 'I'm with Norma on this one. There's no life outside London.' They were just entering the little town. 'There's Station Approach. Well, that was easy.'

Southwold had had a railway once, and at that time extra roads of late-Victorian and Edwardian terraced cottages and semis had been added around the ancient core of what would otherwise have remained effectively a village. A drive-past established that Rogers's house was a semi in dark red brick, with a slate roof and bay windows on both floors, a typical 1890s house, solid and adaptable, of the type known as 'London dog-leg' which could be seen in suburbs all over the country.

Slider went past again and then found a place to park in the next street. 'Did you see anyone about?' he asked.

'Anyone watching the place, you mean? No.'

'All right. Let's go. But keep your eyes peeled.'

Slider went alone up to the door, while Atherton stayed on the other side of the road, but there was no answer to his knock, and the place felt empty. He rejoined Atherton, looking at his watch. 'It's still church time. That might be where she is. I think we should wait for a bit and see if she comes back.' There was a little scrap of green more or less opposite the house, with a bench, presumably for the convenience of people waiting at the bus stop there. They sat down. 'Try not to look like a policeman,' Slider said.

'Try yourself,' Atherton said. 'I've got this.' He pulled out a newspaper from his pocket and unfolded it.

'Is that today's?' Slider said, surprised – they had started off early.

'No, it's yesterday's. I haven't read it yet. I thought I might have a chance to read it in the car, but it comes in handy now as a stage prop.'

'As long as no one notices it's yesterday's.'

Atherton rolled his eyes. 'Oh, please! Most people wouldn't notice if their own leg dropped off.'

There were remarkably few people about, and very few cars, and it was pleasantly restful, Slider thought, sitting in the sunshine, which actually had quite a bit of warmth to it, and listening to the sparrows bickering in nearby hedges while Atherton read his paper. He leaned back and half-closed his eyes, hoping they looked like ordinary people. He saw no sign of anyone who might be a villain, no men sitting in parked cars or loitering purposelessly within sight of the house. He hoped there was not a more efficient and professional surveillance going on, but he doubted there would be. If they had been going to kill the wife as a risk, surely they would have done it at the same time as Rogers.

Fifteen minutes later a woman came along the pavement on the other side of the road, and Slider knew instinctively that it was their quarry, even before she slowed. She cast a nervous glance around, but it passed with hardly a hesitation over the man absorbed in his newspaper and the one dozing in the sun, and she stopped before Number 23 and reached into her handbag for her key.

'It's her,' Slider said to Atherton without moving his lips. 'Let me go first – don't want to frighten her. Come over when I signal.'

Atherton observed with amused approval how Slider could move like a cat when he had to, was across the road in a flash and yet managed not to appear to be hurrying. The woman had her key in and the door was opening when Slider got up beside her, and Atherton saw her jolt with shock. But the guv was a very soothing and reassuring sort of bod. He was discreetly showing his warrant card, talking all the while, and the woman was looking at him with saucer eyes like a rabbit before a snake. Now she flicked a glance across at Atherton, nodded slightly; Slider gestured to him to come; and they went inside, leaving the door ajar for him.

They were in the hall when Atherton went in, shutting the door behind him. Slider was helping her off with her coat, he saw with amusement. Probably she had been at church. She wasn't wearing a hat, but she had on a smart dress and coat, and plain, low-heeled shoes. She turned to

271

look at Atherton with wide, anxious eyes.

'This is my colleague, Jim Atherton,' Slider
said. Atherton proffered his warrant card, but she
only glanced at it briefly: she had accepted Slider
now, and therefore what came with him. She
nodded to him, and turned her attention back to
Slider.

She was quite a surprise to Atherton. He had
expected a busty babe, if not a bimbo, or failing
that, at least a sleek and high-powered beauty.
This, after all, was the one of all the many that
Rogers had actually married and wanted to leave
everything to. But Helen Marie Aldous was
nothing you would pick out in a beauty contest.
She was not even terribly young – probably in
her late thirties or early forties. She was around
five-foot five, with an unremarkable figure – not
fat, but solidly put together – and dark brown
hair in the sort of practical, short, curled style
that Atherton had heard Connolly describe as a
'Mammy-hairdo'. As to her face, it was perfectly
pleasant, but if the original Helen's had launched
a thousand ships, this one would have been
looking at a couple of tugs and the Isle of Wight
ferry, tops.

Mind you, he thought on further inspection,
she might have gone up the shipping register a
bit in better times. She had obviously been crying a lot recently, and not sleeping too well: her
eyes were swollen and brown-bagged, and she
wasn't wearing any make-up. Her expression
was doleful, and her pale mouth drooped at the
corners, which made her look older. But even at
her best she wasn't going to be someone who

272

turned heads. Had Rogers been drunk when he met her, or did she have other qualities which spoke to the man who so far, it had to be said, had shown the depth of a rapidly evaporating rain puddle when it came to women?

She was looking at Slider earnestly, as if ready to read the truth or otherwise in his face when she asked, 'So it's true then? He is – dead?'

'I'm afraid so,' Slider said with such gentleness even Atherton was touched. 'I saw him myself.'

'I wasn't sure. There was just one mention in the paper, and then nothing. I thought it might be a trick. I suppose I didn't *want* to believe it.'

'I don't know if it helps at all,' Slider said, 'but it would have been very quick. He wouldn't have suffered. He wouldn't even have known it was coming.'

She looked up at him consideringly. 'No, I don't think it does help. Not much. Not at the moment. But one day it might. All I can think of is that he's not coming back. I'm never going to see him again.' She stared at nothing for a blank moment, her face slack, her hands loose at her sides, and then came to life again, as though a faulty relay had reconnected. 'Would you like a cup of tea?'

'Thank you. That would be very welcome,' Slider said. Atherton knew his methods: people with something to do with their hands talked more easily.

She led the way through the house. The stairs were straight ahead and the narrow hall dog-legged round them – hence the name for the style.

There were two reception rooms on the left, one with the bay window to the front and the other with French windows to the back. At the end of the passage, straight ahead, was the original kitchen and scullery, which had been knocked together and had an extension added, to make one large kitchen-breakfast room. It was a very nice room, bright and sunny, with white walls and an oak floor, expensive modern fitments with granite work surfaces, and at the far end a large refectory table in the breakfast-room section, which had French doors on to the garden. A glance into the two rooms they had passed had shown them well furnished in an upper-middle-class taste. It was a comfortable house, the rooms were a good size, and it was no longer a surprise to Atherton that David Rogers had felt he could, at least partially, live here. It was certainly a lot more homelike than the Radisson Suites style of the Hofland Crescent house.

'Can I help?' Slider was saying.

'No, I'm fine,' Helen Aldous said. 'Please sit down.'

Slider and Atherton sat at the table, one on either side, turning their chairs so they could face towards her, and she moved about, filling the kettle, putting it on, getting out teapot and tea caddy. 'Do you mind mugs? And Earl Grey or builder's?'

'Mugs are fine,' Slider said. 'And builder's, if you don't mind.'

Atherton would have had Earl Grey for preference, but Slider always had his reasons so he just said, 'Same for me.'

Slider, without even thinking about it, felt builder's was the choice of the likeable and reliable man you could trust and tell things to. It seemed to work. She didn't smile – she looked as though she'd never smile again – but she nodded as if in approval. Her movements about the room were brisk and capable. She didn't slump in her misery, and Slider thought this was from old discipline. The way she walked and carried herself, the movements of her short-nailed hands, the awareness of her eyes – except in those pulled-plug moments of utter despair – all said 'nurse' to him.

'Tell me how you first met David,' he said. He wanted to get her talking while she was still busy with the tea-making, but he wanted it to be the easy stuff first. The more she told him before she got to the hard part, the more the hard part would flow.

'That's easy,' she said. 'He was a doctor and I was a nurse. We met at the Cloisterwood – that's a private hospital in Middlesex.'

'Yes, I know it,' Slider said. His voice conveyed that there was nothing sensational at all in this revelation. 'I didn't know he worked there.'

FIFTEEN

Artful Dodgers

'He didn't,' Helen said. 'He visited from time to time, but I think that was just to see Sir Bernard Webber – socially, I mean. They were old friends.'

'So where *did* he work?' Slider asked, careful not to make it sound important.

'When I first saw him, I thought he was a consultant at another hospital.'

'When was that?'

'That would be – about seven years ago. In the spring of '03. I'd just gone to Cloisterwood from the Royal Free. It had been open about two years then. I wanted to get into plastics, but there were never very many openings in the National Health, so I thought I'd make the switch to private.' She poured tea. 'Do you take sugar?'

'No, thanks. Neither of us.'

'Well, that makes it easy. No, don't get up. I can manage.' She brought the three mugs over and sat down at the end of the table, between them.

'So you were on the plastics side at Cloisterwood,' Slider said, to get her going again.

'Yes.'

'And how did you meet David Rogers?'

'I bumped into him. Literally. I was going in the staff entrance as he was coming out and he cannoned into me, nearly knocked me over. I banged my funny-bone on the door frame, so I was hopping about in agony, but you couldn't want to be bumped into by a nicer person. He was so charming and apologetic, you'd think he'd broken my leg at least.' She looked up sharply. 'It wasn't phony. I was never much to look at, not like some of the glamour-pusses on the wards, but I've had my share of pick-up lines. Men always think nurses are easy. And I know a bad hat when I see one. David wasn't like that. He was just genuinely a nice man. He was really sorry for barging into me – and believe me, most consultants would have knocked you to the ground without thinking twice about it. And while he was making sure I was all right, we looked at each other and something just clicked.' Her face softened as she remembered it, and for a moment she looked almost beautiful. 'He asked if he could buy me a coffee to settle my nerves. I said I was just going on duty, and he said could he see me later, then. So we made a date. And it started from there.'

'He told you he was a consultant?'

'No, he didn't actually say so. But when we met later and I said I was on plastics, he said that was his specialty, and we talked about it, and it was obvious that he really knew his stuff. He told me about his training, and it was sort of implied he was still a consultant.'

'So you didn't ask him where he was working?'

'Not then. We had plenty of other things to talk about. I just assumed he was still at the hospital where he trained.' Again the sharp look. 'I know what you're thinking, but he wasn't trying to con me. Later, when it got serious between us, he told me all about it.'

'All about—?'

'About that woman. Mrs Lescroit.' She took a fortifying sip of tea, and went on, staring past them out of the French windows into the sunny garden. 'We'd been seeing each other about a year, not very regularly, but whenever he could manage it. He didn't come often to Cloister-wood, and when he did, I didn't usually see him, except at a distance. When we met it was always away from there. Nurses aren't supposed to go out with doctors so we had to keep it secret. It suited me, anyway. The other girls would have made my life hell if they knew anything was going on between me and him. Anyway, this particular time, we'd been away for the weekend – the first time we'd done that. We came here, as it happens,' she said, with the closest she'd come yet to a smile.

'To Southwold?'

She nodded. 'Got a room at The Swan. I thought it was lovely – I'd have expected Brighton. But David always liked quality. We had a lovely time. It was June, and the weather was perfect. The sea was a bit cold but I didn't mind that. We had lovely meals, and long walks. We talked and talked – he told me all about his child-hood, and how happy he'd been, and how won-derful his parents were. He didn't come from a rich home, you know.'

'I know.'

'I think that was one of the things that made a bond between us, that our backgrounds were so similar. We both got where we were though our own efforts, not because we had money or knew people. Anyway, that weekend was just wonderful, and then on Sunday morning when we were lying in bed he said he had something he must tell me.' Her expression wavered, remembering the moment.

'You thought it was something alarming?'

'I thought he was going to tell me he was married, to be truthful,' she said. 'I'm ashamed now to remember I thought that, because he was always straight with me. The things he didn't tell me to start with didn't affect me, you see. But now he said he was falling in love with me, and he wanted to get everything out in the open. And he told me about that woman accusing him of messing with her.' She looked at them, first Atherton, then Slider, a direct and clear look. 'He didn't do it, you know. It was all a mistake. The woman was confused, sedated and muzzy. I've seen people in that state, coming out of anaesthetics. They have images in their brains and in the half-conscious state they think they're real. David said he didn't do it and I believed him. But if it had gone any further it would have ruined him, even if he *was* proved innocent. People always remember. They say "there's no smoke without fire", and things like that. So the way it went was the best he could hope for. She dropped the charges in exchange for a big payout, and

279

Sir Bernard pulled various strings so David wasn't struck off. But he couldn't practise any more.'

'Yes, we were told about that. He wasn't allowed to work with patients.'

'That's right. Well, Sir Bernard – or I think it was only Mr Webber then – got him a medical PR job.'

'And that's what he was doing when you met him?'

'That's what I thought,' she said, and looked unhappily at her hands. 'I wish it had been, because everything would have been all right, if only he'd stuck with that. But I didn't know anything about it then. And soon after that week-end things started to fall apart and I had my own problems to think about.'

'Tell me what happened,' Slider said.

She drank some more tea, and went on: 'After David told me about the trouble he'd been in – well, I loved him more than ever, if you want to know. It seemed to me he'd been the real victim, and that he'd behaved the best of everyone. He was so relieved that I'd taken it all right. When he told me, he said, "I suppose you won't want to see me any more." When I told him how I felt, he hugged me so hard I thought he'd break something. For a couple of weeks we were very close, and I had a feeling he was going to ask me to marry him. And then it all blew up at work. I was called before the disciplinary committee for stealing drugs.'

'Surely not!' Slider said, and it wasn't just lip-service. He couldn't imagine this plain, transparent woman doing anything like that.

'Of course not,' she said bitterly. 'They found some of the drugs in my locker on a random search. *I* didn't put them there, but I could never prove it. Those lockers were child's play to break into. Either someone was trying to save their own skin by framing me, or someone wanted rid of *me* specifically – though I've no idea who. I wasn't really friendly with anyone but I didn't think I had any enemies, either. Well, I protested my innocence, but it didn't do me any good. I was sacked. But Sir Bernard intervened and said he wasn't satisfied that I really was the culprit. He said I still had to go, but nothing would be put on my record, and he'd get me another job. As long as no other evidence against me came up, he wouldn't tell. And he recommended I sever links with everyone at Cloisterwood. Well, that wasn't hard to do. I never really liked any of them. And one of them at least obviously had it in for me.'

'Did you ever find out who the culprit was?'

'No. I can't even guess. It could have been anyone. But anyway, that's how I left the Cloisterwood – and I wasn't *all* that sorry, if truth be told, because it was really the reconstructive side of plastics I was interested in, and at Cloisterwood it was all rhinoplasty and breast enhancement and ear tucks, silly rich women fiddling about with their bodies because they'd got nothing better to think about. It made me sick. You should make the best of what God gave you, in my opinion.'

'So where did you go?' Atherton asked.

'I went home to my mum at first, while I waited to hear about the new job. It was a dreadful time. I was miserable and angry – there's nothing worse than being accused of something you haven't done. I didn't hear anything from Sir Bernard for ages, and as time went on I started to think he'd just been blowing smoke. But I suppose it wasn't all that easy to arrange, and he was a busy man. Anyway, bless him, he came through in the end, and I got an appointment for an interview at the Norwich and Norfolk. My mum was upset I was going so far away. She said I should turn it down and find my own way, because the job wasn't even in plastics. But it was a very good job – in intensive care, which was the next best thing – and I didn't want to start again at the bottom doing agency work. And anyway, if I'd gone solo, how was I going to explain why I'd left Cloisterwood? No, I was pretty much bound to Sir Bernard – and grateful to him as well, I promise you. So I went to the interview, and I got the job.'

'And what about David Rogers?' Atherton asked.

She gave him a rather bitter look. 'You would ask that. It wasn't a good time for me. I was in a terrible state, and it was only after about a week that I realized he hadn't rung me. I hadn't told him I was going home to my mum's, but he had my mobile number. That was how he always called me. Anyway, I got it into my head that he'd heard about what had happened, and he'd cut me off.'

'Didn't you try to call him?' Slider asked.

'I was angry and upset. I felt he ought to call me. I wasn't going to chase after him if he had doubts about me. I'd sided with him over his scandal, and he ought to do the same with me. So I didn't ring. And then when he kept not calling, it became a matter of pride. I thought "if that's how little he trusts me, to hell with him". So I went to Norwich and I thought that was that.'

'But obviously it wasn't,' Slider prompted.

'No,' she said quietly, looking at her hands. 'I should have trusted him. One day – it would have been about eight months later – I came off duty and there he was, waiting for me outside. He'd tracked me down. It was a bit of a stiff meeting at first, with hurt feelings on both sides. It turns out *he* thought I didn't want to speak to *him*. He'd rung me at home – I mean, my flat – a couple of times and got no answer, and he knew I'd left Cloisterwood, so he assumed I was cutting him off and let it go. But then he heard somehow or other that I was at the Norwich, and decided to see if I still felt anything for him. So we started seeing each other again. He could only manage about once a week, because of his job – and the occasional weekend – but we were so happy when we were together. Then the following year – that was in '06 – he asked me to marry him. And that's when he told me about his real job.'

Slider felt such a surge of relief that they'd come to it at last, he almost fell off the chair. But such was his self control he was even able to say, 'Yes please,' when she asked if he'd like another cup. Atherton refused, and though he sat quite

283

still, Slider knew him well enough to know that mentally he was chewing his fingernails.

When the second cups had been poured, she said, 'Where had I got to?'

'David asked you to marry him.'

'Oh, yes.' She looked away again, into the past. 'I got off at two one day, and he took me for tea in the Assembly House. Then we went for a walk along the river. It was March, a cold day, with a nasty wind, but I never noticed it. We walked arm in arm and huddled up together, and to me it was as good as being on the beach in Spain in June. We found a bench in a sheltered spot and sat down. And he said he wanted to marry me.' She sighed unconsciously. 'I'd have said yes there and then, but he said that before I answered, he had to tell me some things. He said his job was very demanding and took him away a lot, and that even when we were married I wouldn't see much of him, maybe no more than I saw of him now. So I said what *was* his job, because it didn't seem to me that being in PR for a drugs firm was *that* demanding. And he said he hadn't been in the PR job for a long time. Just about the time we first met he'd started something else. He said it was secret and very important work, and he couldn't tell me more than that, because it might be dangerous, and he didn't want me involved. I said couldn't he trust me, if he wanted to marry me? And he said *I* had to trust *him*, because he'd never do anything to put me in danger.'

'Secret, important and dangerous,' Slider said, with an inward groan. 'What did *you* think it was?'

'Well, I couldn't imagine, and we argued back and forth a bit, but he was adamant he wouldn't tell me about it, and in the end I had to trust him, because I knew he'd never do anything wrong, and if I was going to marry him – well, I had to, didn't I? I had the feeling that he was in the secret service, because he hinted there were foreign connections – and after all, what else is that secret? But he never would tell me, not from that day to this.' Tears filled her eyes suddenly as she stubbed her mental toe on the fact that he was dead, something that had subsided in her mind while she talked to them. But she blinked the tears back hard, and got out a handkerchief and blew her nose with a determined honk. Slider was impressed by her self-control. There was more to this ordinary woman than met the eye.

'So you got married?' Slider prompted.

'In May, at the register office. He'd bought this house already and had it done up, and in September when my notice at the Norwich and Norfolk was up, we moved into it. And that first day he gave me the deeds, and said he'd had it made over to me, as my wedding present, so that whatever happened I'd have somewhere to live.'

'Whatever happened?' Slider queried. 'He was worried, then?'

'No,' she said. 'Actually, I don't think he *was* worried then. He said the job could be dangerous, but I don't think he really thought about that side of it. He seemed to be enjoying it. He was happy whenever I saw him. High-spirited, even.

Sometimes he was tired, but he never seemed to be bothered by his job. He always said it was wonderful to be home, and he complained he wished he could see more of me, but that was the only thing he complained about. Until about a year ago.'

'And what changed then?' Slider asked.

'Well,' she said, considering. 'I suppose looking back it might have been coming on for a while before that, but it was about a year ago I really started to notice it. He was quieter, thoughtful, as if he had something on his mind that was worrying him. Sometimes he'd arrive and he'd hardly have a thing to say. He'd sit staring at nothing for ages, or he'd go for a long walk on his own. If I tackled him about it he'd say nothing was wrong and try to snap out of it, but I knew. And then he started talking about what would happen if he died. He said he was having his will made up, to make sure I got everything. He brought a copy of it down one day and told me to keep it safe. That would be about last July. But it was only for about the last month or six weeks that he's been really worried.'

'In what way?'

'Really jumpy. Anxious the whole time. Hardly speaking to me. Jumping out of his skin if the phone rang. He said that his job was coming to an end and there could be danger in it. That the people he'd been working with might decide it would be safer if he couldn't talk. He told me he was afraid for me, too, and that I mustn't talk to anyone about him. Well, I didn't anyway, I never

286

had, but he was extra insistent. He said if anything happened to him I'd be taken care of, but I'd have to lie low for a while and not let on to anyone about our relationship. He even gave me extra money to tide me over in case he suddenly disappeared. It had me worried, I can tell you. You'd need to have seen him to know how tense he was. But still I never thought anything would happen. You don't, do you? Not until it does. And when I read that paragraph in the paper, I thought that the people who were after him were playing a trick, maybe to flush out his contacts or his colleagues or whatever. But then when he didn't come down this week, and I didn't hear from him, I started to think maybe something had happened. And then – and then you arrived.'

It took her some determined swallowing and nose work this time to regain her composure. Slider said, 'I'm so sorry for your loss. But I have to ask you, have you any idea at all who these people were that he was afraid of? Or what sort of work he was involved in?'

She shook her head, emerging from the handkerchief with a red nose and a look of exhaustion. 'None at all. He always kept that side of things from me, and I never asked because I knew that was the way he wanted it. He was too gentle and kind to be a secret agent, that's what I always thought, but he must have been tough underneath it all to have done a job like that. And of course I was important to him, because it was only with me he could show the other side of himself, the gentle side. But in the end it got to him – the double life. That's what I think. I'm

287

afraid in the end he was so worn down with it that he made a mistake, and they got him. I can't account for it otherwise.'

Slider could not make head nor tail of this. David Rogers, a secret service agent? Was it possible? If he was, he was the Niven James Bond rather than the Connery or Craig. But he came up against the problem that if he *had* been, the investigation would have been taken away from them straight away. Six had its own way of dealing with these things. No, no, whatever was going on, it wasn't *that*. Secret and dangerous Rogers's job might have been, but the man who romanced Cat Aude and Angela Fraser wasn't doing important work for the country. He had been doing something that paid him handsomely in cash, and that was not the MI6 way. But on one thing he agreed with Helen Aldous – he *had* eventually made a mistake of some kind, and they *had* got him.

He asked, hoping for a new direction, 'Do you know anything about Windhover?'

'The *Windhover*?' she said. 'David's boat, do you mean? It's moored down at the Yacht Club.'

Slider blinked. 'His boat is called the *Windhover*?'

She nodded. 'Isn't that what you meant? He loved that boat. He really, really loved it. That's why he chose Southwold for us to live, because that's where he was keeping it. That was his one recreation – fishing. Lots of consultants play golf but he hated the game, and he never cared about skiing or shooting or any of those things. But the one thing he never missed when he came down was his night fishing on the *Windhover*.'

'He went night fishing?' Slider said, puzzled.

'He said it was the only real sport – sea fishing at night. Any other fishing was kids' stuff to him. He was passionate about it. I didn't begrudge him. I mean, we had little enough time together, but a man needs his hobby, and he worked so hard the rest of the time. He'd come down whenever he could get away, sometimes of a Tuesday, sometimes weekends, but whatever else happened he was always here on a Wednesday and he'd go out every Wednesday night in the *Windhover*. Then Thursday morning he was off straight from the harbour, so I never got to see his catch, but he said he was always lucky, always got something. He gave it away to whoever was in the harbour at the time. Well, he'd no use for raw fish in his sort of life – who'd have cooked it for him?'

Who indeed, Slider thought. Not one of his other women, that was for sure.

'Did you never want to go with him?' Atherton asked.

'I'm not keen on boats,' she said. 'I could get seasick crossing a bridge. I did go with him once, though. We'd not long been married, and he begged me to come with him because we had so little time together, he didn't want to waste it.'

Didn't occur to him not to go, thought Atherton. *Atta boy!*

'That was the time he got tangled up with that Dutch boat,' she went on.

'What was that?'

'Well, we'd been going for a while, and it was fun at first, rushing through the dark, standing at the wheel with David's arm round me, drinking champagne, with the wind whipping past. But eventually I started to get seasick – when it goes really fast it kind of skips and bumps on the waves, and my stomach was getting jolted. I told him I wasn't feeling too hot, and after a bit he says he'll stop. And he makes me a hot cup of tea and puts brandy in it and tucks me up in the bunk below with a hot water bottle. He was so gentle when he was taking care of me,' she said with a tremble of the lips. 'I think I dropped off for a bit, with the brandy, and being warm and relaxed. Anyway, I started to feel better, and I didn't want to spoil his night, so I thought about getting up and going on deck again. And then I heard another boat coming up fast. I sat up and looked out of the window, just as it sort of whirled round and came to a stop beside us. And a man started shouting something. I couldn't hear what it was. David shouted back, and it sounded as though they were having an argument. Anyway, after a bit the other boat starts up again and roars away. Then David comes down to see how I am.

'I asked him about the other boat, and he said it was some Dutchman making out this was *his* fishing spot and complaining David was in the wrong place. But David sorted him out. Then he said he was going to take me home, because I wasn't well. I said I was feeling a bit better and I didn't want to spoil his fishing, but he said he'd sooner see I was all right, so we went back. That was the only time I went out with him. It was really a man thing, his fishing, and he was better off doing it alone.'

Slider's mind was working so hard he wondered there wasn't smoke coming out of his ears. 'You don't happen to remember the name of the Dutch boat, do you?' he asked.

She raised her eyebrows. 'Why on earth do you want to know that? It was just some old—' She stopped as something obviously dawned on her. 'You don't mean,' she went on in a lowered voice, 'that he was meeting his contact? He wasn't fishing at all?'

'I don't know,' Slider said. 'The thought occurred to me.'

She thought. 'No,' she concluded. 'If I hadn't been seasick, what then?'

Atherton answered. 'There are lots of ways to make sure you were down in the cabin at the right moment.'

Still she shook her head. 'No, I don't believe it. He loved that boat, and he loved fishing.'

'*Do* you remember the Dutch boat's name, by any chance?' Slider urged gently.

'Well, as a matter of fact, I do. It was right under my nose, so to speak, when I looked out – it was about all I could see, with it being so close. It was called *Havik* – or however you pronounce it.' She spelled it for him. 'And there was another word underneath, a funny Dutch word beginning with I. Can't remember what that was. That would be the harbour, wouldn't it?'

'Probably,' Slider said.

'But you're quite wrong, you know,' she went on. 'Fishing was his passion. Fishing, and me – we were his real life. He kept his job separate, otherwise he wouldn't have had a life at all.'

'She probably wasn't wrong about one thing,' Slider said. 'She was his real life. Poor sap didn't have much else.'

'I'm trying to figure out what he saw in her,' Atherton said. 'I suppose she was a bit of a rest cure after Amanda Sturgess. And with slightly more brain than the jiggling jugheads.'

'She loved him,' Slider said. 'That was her attraction. She didn't see him as an investment or a means to social advancement or a meal ticket. She just loved him – enough to remain secret and be grateful for seeing him once or twice a week.'

'Hmph,' said Atherton. 'So did Aude and Fraser.'

'That wasn't love, that was delusion.'

'My point exactly.'

'No, I think there was more to this one. She said they came from the same background. Maybe he was reverting to the safety of his childhood.'

'You mean she reminded him of his mum? *That* I can believe.'

Slider wouldn't be baited. 'And she was a nurse and he was a doctor. They'd have had plenty to talk about.'

'Hmph again,' said Atherton. 'And what about this boat being called the *Windhover*? Was it a joke on Rogers's part, to name the boat after his paymasters? What is a windhover anyway? Sounds like a helicopter.'

'Country name for a kestrel.'

'Trust you to know that.'

'What are you so crabby about?'

292

'I hate this woman being taken for a mug. Secret agent indeed! What kind of a chat-up line is that?'

'You're just annoyed you didn't think of it first.'

Atherton's face split in a reluctant grin. 'At least with me it would be a credible story. So, harbour next?'

'Harbour next. And keep your eyes peeled.'

There was no sign of anyone watching the house, or them. Slider was fairly confident that whoever 'they' were, they had not yet caught up with the secret wife. Or, if they knew about her, they didn't think her dangerous, otherwise they'd have done her at the same time as Rogers. But he'd cautioned her to extra vigilance and warned her to speak to no one about David, and to ring him immediately if anyone tried to contact her.

'And what happens next?' she had asked him, looking utterly flattened, lost and doleful again, now that the stimulation of telling her story was over.

'We continue to investigate, until we find who did this and why. And take them into custody. At that point I will let you know, and then we'll be able to release the body to you for burial and you'll be able to file for probate of his will. Until then, you must just be patient and keep your head down.'

'I've been doing that for years,' she said. 'A few days longer won't make any difference.'

'A few days' was a nice piece of optimism, or trust in their prowess. Slider hadn't liked to mention at that point that if Rogers's money was ill-gotten, she wouldn't be getten it. At least she had the house – and how wise he had been to put that in her name straight away.

Southwold's harbour was a modest affair, lying to the south of the town on the River Blyth, stretching from the river's mouth nearly a mile upstream, but catering only for fishing boats, yachts and small pleasure craft. Those yearning for the delights and conveniences of a marina had to go further up the coast to Lowestoft, where there was every facility, including the Royal Norfolk and Suffolk Yacht Club in its grand white Edwardian clubhouse, looking like a cross between the Hotel Del Coronado and a vicarage conservatory.

The only facilities for yachtsmen in Southwold were the Harbour Inn, and upstream of it the clubhouse of the Southwold Yacht Club, which by contrast looked like a village cricket pavilion. The tie-ups were to rings in the harbour wall or rickety wooden jetties, and it was a brisk walk of a mile or so into the town for shops. The road along the harbour front wasn't even paved, but a spring-busting melange of ruts, potholes and jutting lumps of concrete.

'Now why would he choose this place, rather than a proper marina?' Atherton wondered as they picked their way past the puddles. It was too early in the season for the place to be seething with tourists, but there were a fair few Sunday visitors, idling along sucking ice-creams, and buying fish from the tar-paper huts that lined the road.

'Anonymity,' Slider said. 'He'd have thought he could slip in and out of here with much less scrutiny.'

'Could he?'

'Yes and no. Not much official scrutiny, that's for sure. But a lot of prying unofficial eyes. In a place like this everyone tends to know everyone else's business. On the other hand, they don't tend to interfere in it.'

They strolled along like tourists, keeping an eye out for the *Windhover*. Helen Aldous had told them she was white, with dark-blue dodgers with her name on them. 'They're new, he only got them a couple of weeks ago, only they misspelled the name. David was furious. Now they say it'll be six weeks before they can replace them. Not–' she suddenly remembered – 'that it matters now, I suppose.'

'It's surprising how often that happens,' Slider said now to Atherton. 'Our old super, Dickson, had a yachting friend whose boat was called *Oenone*, and when his dodgers arrived they said *Oneone*. He always called it the *One One* after that.'

'Not a bad name, actually,' Atherton said.

'There she is,' Slider said, spotting her at that moment.

The *Windhover* was tied up to one of the narrow wooden jetties that stuck out from the wall. This one had missing planks, a chain handrail on one side only, and, since the tide was down, a long drop to the grey, sucking water. Against the dilapidation, the boat rode the ebb-tide serenely, glowing with an almost feral beauty, though her dodgers, indeed, proclaimed to the world that she was called *Windhover*.

Atherton had stopped dead, as though struck by lightning. He was not a yachting man, but he knew a classy item when he saw one. It was big, sleek, sexy, white and powerful, bristling with antennae for every navigational aide and electronic entertainment known to man. 'That,' he said in a reverent whisper, 'is the dog's bollocks. That is the veritable reproductive organs of the absolute canine. What would you call that? You can't just call it a boat.'

'A power yacht, I suppose,' Slider said, admiring the rake of the superstructure, the fluid lines, the thrust and pointiness of the pointed end. 'Sixty foot, I'd say,' he remarked. 'Twin engines. She looks fast.'

'She looks like the rich man's ultimate wet dream,' Atherton said. 'We no longer have to wonder why David Rogers had a boat. It's an answer in itself.'

'Night fishing, though,' Slider said. 'I suppose it was an excuse of sorts. Shall we have a look inside?'

Helen Aldous had provided them with a key. Inside it was immaculate, still smelling new. It was fitted out with tasteful luxury – wood panelling, leather upholstery, brass lamps with acid-embossed glass shades, varnished wooden decks and thick carpet in the staterooms. It was not huge inside, but so well laid-out that it felt roomy. But the beds were not made up and there were no personal belongings stowed anywhere.

The cupboards were empty, and apart from soap and toilet paper in the heads, and a tin of biscuits and a bottle of brandy in the galley, it might just have come from the showroom.

'I suppose he brought everything with him, trip by trip,' Slider said. 'She said he went out on Wednesday night and came back Thursday morning, so he didn't sleep on-board. The galley looks as if it's never been cooked in.'

'What a waste,' Atherton said. 'It's hard to believe a man who frequents strip clubs and picks up pole dancers wasn't having tacky booze-fuelled parties and bonking cruises at every opportunity.'

The only thing of interest was found on the floor on the bridge: an enormous refrigerated cold box of white-painted aluminium, its plug lying next to the socket that would power it. 'You could get a lot of champagne in that,' Atherton said. But it was, in fact, empty as well as unplugged. 'He *must* have been having parties,' he complained. 'Why else all the chiller capacity?'

'To hold the fish he caught on his night fishing trips,' Slider said.

'Yeah, fish.' They exchanged a look. 'What contraband needs to be kept cold?' Atherton mused. 'Maybe he was smuggling caviar.'

There was nothing else to be gleaned from this ultimate empty vessel, which was sadly making no noise at all that might help them, just a gentle slapping of water against the hull and creaking of rope as she worked her moorings.

They teetered off the end of the rickety jetty on

to solid land again, and turned for one last, baffled look at Rogers's prize. And as if by magic a man materialized beside them: a short, squat man whose weather-pulverized face made it impossible to tell his age. He might have been sixty or eighty or anything in-between. He was hunched into a black donkey-jacket, his hands stuffed in the pockets; a battered and greasy black fisherman's cap was pulled down hard on his head, and a cigarette drooped from his lip, making him screw up his eyes against the rising smoke. With native politeness he did not meet their eyes, looking instead, with an air of indifference, at the *Windhover*.

'Thinking o' buying her?' he enquired.

SIXTEEN

Jewel Carriageway

'Is she for sale?' Slider asked neutrally.

'Wouldn't wonder,' the man commented, the cigarette wagging with his words. He unpeeled it from his lip and spat politely sideways away from them into the water.

Atherton was about to speak, and Slider froze him with a lightning glance and a hidden elbow nudge. Keeping silence invited confidences. In the absence of questions, a man eager to impart had to make his own timing. Eventually the man

had to speak. A casual glance behind him showed Slider that there were others of the local
fishing community, messing about by their huts
or laying out fish on their stalls, equally uninterested in Slider, Atherton, *Windhover* and
their new friend. You could tell they weren't
interested by the way they were pointedly not
looking at them, while their attention was out on
stalks. It was the country way, as Slider, a country boy, knew well.

'Ent bin down this week, th'ole doc. Never
misses.'

After a pause to show lack of interest, Slider
said, 'She's a nice-looking craft.'

The man grunted agreement, and then became
positively loquacious. 'Fairline Milennium Sea-
hawk, Mark II. Special job. Marine allymini-
mum hull. Twin three thousand 'orsepower
diesels plus a gas turban. She'll do sixty knots in
any sea. Carries more'n seven thousand gallons
o' fuel. Range like that, she'll take you to Nor-
way an' back on one tank. Lovely ole gal, th'ole
Wendover.'

He pronounced it like the Buckinghamshire
town. Slider reckoned he probably would have
pronounced the right name the same way, and
wondered whether the makers of the dodgers had
realized that and taken the line of least resis-
tance.

'She's a lady, all right,' he said.

'That is,' the man agreed.

'So you think she might be for sale?' Slider
said.

The man looked sidelong at him, and snorted

with faint amusement. 'Coppers, ent yer.' It was not really a question.

Slider shrugged non-committally. He wasn't giving the farm away. He looked to the left, towards the river mouth, and said, 'Tide's turning.'

'Slack water,' the man said, and the agreement seemed to create a bond between them. He took a last drag on his cigarette, threw it down and ground it out, shoved his hands back in his pockets and said, 'Knew he'd be in trouble sooner or later, that ole doc.'

'I'm afraid he's dead,' Slider said.

The man nodded as if he'd expected that. 'Never missed. Went out Wensdy night, come in early hours Thursdy mornin'. *Sport fishin'*,' he concluded derisively.

'Just an excuse?' Slider hazarded.

'Man like that, boat like that, don't go fishin' alone! Never had no parties in 'er. No drink, no girls.'

'So what *did* he do?'

He watched a burgee fill and crack straight in a brief, sudden air. 'Sometimes he'd go out same time as us. Set off 'ell for leather. Never see where he fished. Sometimes he'd come in same time as us. Come off with a big ole cool box o' fish every week. "Had a bit o' luck," he'd say. "Got some big ones," he'd say.' He snorted. 'Any fish he had, I reckon he bought at Macfisheries.' He seemed amused at his own wit.

'Did he ever show you his catch?'

'Never showed no one. Never saw what he 'ad in that box. "Got some beauties," he'd say. That went straight in 'is car, and off away, out o' town, quick as you like.'

Slider was having trouble with the cool box – that thing wasn't designed to be portable. 'That refrigerated box in the cockpit—'

'Not that one. Portable job. Kept th'electric one on-board.'

Slider had an image of Rogers coming in, tying up, emerging with his cool box on to an apparently indifferent harbourside, blissfully unaware of the dozens of eyes clocking his every movement. But if no one ever said anything, what harm?

'Dead, eh?' the old man mused at last, staring at the swirl of slack-tide on the brown-grey water.

'He was up to something,' Slider said indifferently to a passing seagull.

'Free trade, thass what we call it,' the old man said at the conclusion of some thought process. 'Suppose to be in th'ole Europeen Union, ent we? Suppose to be free movement o' goods. So how come a man can't bring in a foo bits an' bobs for hisself an' his mates without th'ole Customs and Excise persecootin' him?'

'Beats me,' Slider said. 'That's not my department.'

'Huh!' the man snorted, but it was aimed at the Customs and Excise, not Slider, who was still, as a man who could tell when the tide was turning, the acceptable face of the law.

'So the doctor was a free-trader,' Slider mused, not making it a question.

'He weren't sport fishin', thass for sure,' his new friend agreed, and then, as a final, huge con-

301

cession, actually looked at Slider and said, 'Coastguard bin watchin' him. You go and talk to coastguard.'

'Thanks,' Slider said. After a suitable pause, he nodded farewell and he and Atherton moved nonchalantly away. The old man remained where he was, staring up the river, to show he hadn't been talking to them at all.

The coastguard on duty, Steve Wilderspin, was a fatherly-looking middle-aged man whose firm face suggested a core of steel and whose level, noticing eyes wouldn't have been out of place on a policeman. He reminded Slider of Dave Bright. He examined Slider's and Atherton's warrant cards with professional swiftness, and showed no surprise when Slider asked him about the *Windhover*.

'We've been watching her for a while,' he said. 'We thought it was a bit odd the doc berthed her here, instead of the marina at Lowestoft. Nothing strange about a rich London consultant wanting a place in Southwold,' he was quick to add. 'We've got a few of that sort, I can tell you. Barristers, hedge fund managers, all sorts of top people. It's that kind of place. But *Windhover*'s a showy craft, the sort people like to show off when they've sunk that much money into it. And Doc Rogers wasn't showing her off to anyone. No parties, no pals down from London for weekend cruises. He didn't even join the Yacht Club. A man doesn't buy a super speed cruiser like that and then not talk to anyone about it.' His eyes crinkled with amusement at the thought. 'There was only half a dozen Mark IIs ever made, and four of them are in the States. Who ever heard of an owner not wanting to boast about that sort of thing?'

'You're right,' Slider said.

'And she's fast,' Wilderspin went on, 'and built for the open seas. What was he doing poodling about coastal waters with his once-a-week fishing trips? But on the other hand, a man can spend his money on anything he likes. It's a free country. If he wants to waste a power-craft like that, it's his business.' He looked at Slider. 'There's plenty of rich people with Maseratis and nowhere to let 'em out, am I right? And driving bloody great off-roaders around Kensington and Chelsea.'

'Exactly,' said Slider.

'So we just kept an eye on him. And we've never seen him bringing anything bulky off the *Windhover*. So unless he was smuggling diamonds—' He shrugged.

'You didn't ever try to inspect his luggage?'

Wilderspin's sea-faded eyes opened a fraction. 'Can't do that. Especially not to a respectable Southwold resident. No evidence against him.'

'What if you knew he was meeting another craft out at sea?'

'Ah,' Wilderspin said with satisfaction. 'That'd be different. Have you got something?'

Slider said, 'The one time he took someone with him he had a close encounter with a boat called *Havik*.' He spelled it. 'From a Dutch port beginning with "I".'

'IJmuiden,' Wilderspin said at once. 'Lay you

any money. IJmuiden port and marina – practically the first place you come to if you sail straight from Southwold to Holland.' He rubbed his hands together. 'That gives us something to work with. It could be diamonds, in that case. IJmuiden's only a stone's throw from Amsterdam, which is the biggest centre for diamond distribution on the continent.' He looked consideringly at Slider and Atherton. 'To find out anything more, I'm going to have to refer this upwards, to get co-operation with the Dutch coastguards. Is that going to mess up your case?'

'Can you hold off for a bit?' Slider said. 'I'm going to have to refer upwards as well. And if there is a big operation going on, we don't want to spook them before we've laid our hands on the murderer.'

'Fair enough,' Wilderspin said. 'Can't have people murdering our citizens with impunity.'

'Funny thing is,' Atherton said when they left, 'I'm pretty sure he meant Southwold citizens, not British citizens.'

'Wouldn't surprise me a bit,' said Slider from the depth of furious thinking.

Mackay was duty officer, and Hollis was there, doing a bit of office-managing on his own account, because he wasn't getting on with his second wife and liked to get out of the house when he could. Porson had arrived by the time Slider and Atherton got back, and they all gathered round him in the CID room, as he sat on the edge of Atherton's desk (always the tidiest) and fiddled with a biro, clicking the end in and out like Edmundo Ros on speed.

'Smuggling, eh?' he said thoughtfully, when they had told the whole story of the boat.

'Windhover being the name of the organization that was paying his salary, unless Rogers was just being clever about it, it's tempting to think they also bought him the boat, or owned it and lent it to him for the purpose,' Slider said.

'That would make it a criminal organization,' Hollis said. 'A diamond smuggling ring. They paid him a retainer through his bank and then a cash bonus on top whenever he did a job.'

'That works all right,' Mackay said. 'Explains why he had all the cash, and not too much on his credit card. But who were the jokers he was wining and dining?'

'Customers for the diamonds,' Hollis said. 'Rich Arabs and Indians and suchlike – the kind of people that *do* buy diamonds.'

'It explains Southwold and it explains the secrecy,' Atherton said. 'He's not going to tell his female conquests that he's a smuggler. Important secret work sounds much better for wifey, and consultant will do for anyone he's not going to know for long.'

'Talking of consultants, why did Sir Bernard Webber say he hadn't seen Rogers in years?' Slider said. 'Helen Aldous says Rogers dropped in from time to time at Cloisterwood to see Webber.'

Porson said, 'Aldous left Cloisterwood in – what was it, '04? You don't know that Rogers went there after that. That's years.'

'True,' Slider said. 'It's just that Webber seem-

305

ed keen to dissociate himself.'

'If he thought Rogers was a bad hat,' Hollis said, 'that's not surprising, is it, guv? He'd want to keep the reputation of his hospital spotless. And he *did* get him a job.'

'And he got one for Aldous,' Porson remarked. 'Bit of a night of shining ardour, if you ask me.'

'The consultant with the heart of gold. Can't be many of them around,' Atherton said.

'Don't be cynical,' Slider berated him.

'I wasn't really,' Atherton said. 'But what with Aldous saying Rogers was a fluffy white bunny rabbit, I'm just longing for a real baddy to turn up.'

'Sturgess,' Mackay said. 'Pin your hopes on her, Jimbo.'

'Ah yes, the Rosa Klebb of our story. But how do we tie her in with diamond smuggling? Can you see her as the Moriarty, squatting at the centre of a vast criminal web?'

'Not exactly living in the lap, is she?' Porson said.

'We do know she lied to us, that she had recent contact with Rogers,' Slider said. 'And that she had more money than we can account for – investing in the stables and the agency. And just because she isn't smothered in furs, it doesn't mean she's not spending. She could be using it for the benefit of others.'

'Giving it all to charity?' Porson barked, as though it was a ludicrous idea. Then he modified it. 'Well, maybe. Alterism can turn into an obsession. Doesn't do to misunderestimate these do-gooders.'

'The Bob Geldof syndrome,' Atherton said.

Porson nodded. 'They can be as capacious as anyone spending it on themselves.' He lapsed into thought, bending the biro now between his large, strong hands.

'Just have to wait and see what Norma comes up with,' Hollis said.

'Angela Fraser did say Sturgess is out networking all the time,' Atherton remembered. 'Supposed to be fund-raising, but who knows? Could be fund-spending. Or Moriartying.'

'Smuggling,' Porson pondered again, staring at nothing. The biro gave up and snapped in two with a sharp sound. He put the pieces down absently and said, looking at Slider, 'Diamonds are all very well, diamonds makes sense up to a point, but week in week out, year after year? That sounds more like something perishable. Something that gets used up so you need more of it. Get me?'

Slider nodded. 'I did wonder about that. There is something else Holland is famous for.'

'Drugs.' Mackay got there. 'And he worked for a drug company, didn't he?'

'Not the same kind of drugs,' Atherton said, as to an idiot.

Mackay looked indignant. 'I know that, but pharmaceutical drugs can get smuggled as well, can't they, new ones, or expensive ones not available on the NHS?'

'Recreational drugs make more sense,' Atherton said.

'Well,' Porson said, apparently coming to a decision and climbing off the desk, 'there's nothing more for you lot to do until I've spoken to Mr Wetherspoon and we've had a chat with the Excise boys. Their counterpoints in Holland might have something on this *Havik* boat. If they don't, we'll have to think again. Because–' with a sharp look at Slider – 'you only know Rogers met it once, and that was supposed to be an accident, which it could well have been. There's been a lot of leaping to conclusions going on, when for all you or I or the man on the Clapham omnibus knows, Rogers could have been out sport fishing after all.'

Slider's unhappy look said he knew that.

Atherton felt compelled to rescue his boss. 'Except that he was murdered, sir,' he pointed out.

'Yes, well,' Porson allowed graciously, 'except for that.'

Joanna came down to the kitchen early on Monday morning with George in her arms. A thin sunshine was mucking about with the stainless steel pots on the high shelf by the stove, and her missing husband was standing staring at nothing while the kettle emptied itself in steam over the ceiling.

'We need to get an electric one,' she said, reaching over and turning off the gas.

'Uh?' Slider said, jerking back to reality.

'Blue!' said George, holding out his arms with a beam of delight. It was a great thing in any life, Slider thought, accepting the surprisingly solid bulk into his own arms, to have someone who was always so unequivocally glad to see you. He looked at Joanna. 'I'm sorry I woke you up. I tried to get out of bed carefully.'

'I know you did. But I always know when you've gone. You having tea?'

'Please.'

'Peas,' George said. He took a good grip on Slider's ear so he could lean over his shoulder and watch his mother getting out mugs and tea bags. 'More!' he said urgently, pointing with his other hand, moist pink forefinger energetically poking from the dimpled fist. He had recently discovered the joys of pointing and did it assiduously.

Joanna held up his feeder cup. 'Do you want some milk, George?'

'Mum-mum-mum-mum-mum,' George said.

'I'll take that as a yes.' She set about the twin tasks of tea and milk and said gently to her spouse, 'Didn't sleep well?'

'Not much. Sorry. Was I restless? I tried to keep still.'

'I could feel you trying. The case, is it?'

'Yes. There are things I can't quite get to grips with.'

'You will, Oscar,' Joanna said with calm certainty. 'You look tired, though. Why don't you go back to bed for a bit? Maybe you'll sleep.'

Slider smiled. 'Not a chance. My brain's spinning like a teetotal, as Porson would say. I might as well use it to good purpose and go in early. If I read back over all the notes something might click.'

Joanna tested a spot of milk on her hand, licked it off and held out the cup to George, who

309

became urgent with morning hunger.

'Orbal! Blue! Ahmah!' he cried.

'This child has a remarkable vocabulary,' Slider remarked.

'Thank you,' Joanna said as she relinquished the cup – no harm in trying early for manners.

'Fank,' George said, beamed at his accomplishment, and rammed the spout into his mouth, sucking greedily.

'Did he just say thanks?' Slider asked, turning to look at Joanna.

'He does copy sounds,' she said. 'He said "door" the other day. And "ball".'

'Stone me, the child's a genius.' Slider gaped. 'He's barely more than a year old!'

'He's sixteen months,' Joanna said, amused. 'And that's what children of that age do. You just don't remember. Here's your tea. Give him to me while you drink it.'

He passed George over, started sipping his tea, and noted that Joanna, having hitched the baby on to her left side, was not only drinking her own tea, but was actually starting to make toast as well. So, she could do other things while holding a baby, but a poor imbecile man couldn't, was that it?

'Do you want a boiled egg?' she asked.

'I take it back. It's not the child that's a genius, it's you,' Slider said. 'The domestic octopus. If I could patent you I'd make a fortune.'

'One egg or two?' she asked, turning her head with a smile that melted his loins.

'Voluptuous siren,' Slider said. And to George, 'Let's hear you repeat that, boy.'

George unplugged himself from the cup, fixed his father with his blue gaze and said, 'Boy!'

'Close enough for jazz,' said Slider.

Connolly, first in, poked her head round Slider's door and said, 'Oh. I thought I heard someone. Morning, boss.'

'Must be telepathy,' he said.

'Is that right? What?'

'It was you I wanted,' Slider said. 'I have a job for you, but I don't know how you'll do it.' He explained. 'I thought of you because you're good at getting people to talk to you.'

She nodded, her eyes far away. 'I think I can see me way. Don't worry, boss. It'll be grand.'

'And of course – as quickly as possible,' he added.

Angela Fraser was what Swilley described to herself as 'wired' – tense, excited, but elated with it. She met her in Café Rouge, sufficiently far down the parade from the office to avoid being spotted if Amanda should happen to come back.

'She's been in a filthy mood since your blokes came in,' Angela confided, sitting beside Swilley on a banquette, at the back of the restaurant and facing the door. It was part of her new persona as a secret agent: she reckoned she could see anyone coming in before they saw her, and nip into the ladies, which was back here, if necessary. 'Snapping at everyone, complaining about the coffee. Can't get anything right for her. She sent back a letter because there was the tiniest little crease in the paper. She even bitched about one of the clients, and they're like gods to her, normally.'

'Has she given you any idea why she's in a bad mood?' Swilley asked.

'I'd have said it was grief over David dying if she was anyone else, but I don't think that woman's got a heart. I think she's worried, but I don't know what about. Unless—' The wide open eyes searched Norma's face. 'You think she had something to do with it, don't you? The murder.'

'I don't think anything,' Swilley said blandly. 'I just do as I'm told, and leave the thinking to my boss. He's good at it.'

'I liked him,' Angela said, settling down. 'He reminded me of this teacher I had at school, Mr Maltby. Maths. He was nice. I was rubbish at maths, but he always made you feel you could do stuff, you know?'

'Yeah, I know,' Swilley said. 'So what have you found out?'

'Well, there's a lot of stuff in Amanda's room, and she leaves it all locked up when she goes out.' She shook her head. 'I've never known an office where so much is locked away. I mean, salaries, yes, and staff files, but not anything else. What could she have to keep secret? We all know all the clients and their backgrounds. But I did get to look at the accounts. Some of it's in books that Nora keeps, and there's a lot more on her computer. It's security locked, but I know her access code.'

Norma was amused. 'How come?'

312

'She's a dipstick,' Angela said simply. 'She wrote it on a sticky label and stuck it on the side of her top right-hand drawer. Thinks no one'll ever find it there, but I've seen her checking it before she logs on. Anyway, I found out the main things you wanted to know. The first thing is that we don't get a government grant, which really surprised me. I'd have thought that'd be the first thing Amanda would go for, because the government's dead keen on getting disabled people back to work.'

'So where does the income come from?'

'Well, the companies pay a fee. The big ones have to employ so many disabled by law, so they pay us a retainer to find the right person whenever they need one, and the smaller companies pay on a case by case basis. And then there are donations. I guess that's what Amanda spends her time doing. It's mostly from private individuals, and one or two companies – manufacturers of mobility equipment and disability aids mostly – but the biggest donor is the Windhover Trust.'

Swilley looked enquiring. 'What's that?' she asked, to see if Fraser knew.

'Oh, they've been paying us a monthly donation since the beginning,' Angela said. 'It's a medical charity. I asked Nora about it once. Medical research and support, she said. I think they're something to do with one of the drugs companies,' she concluded vaguely.

'What would they get out of it – making such a big donation to you, I mean?'

'Well, I suppose it's good for their image,' Angela hazarded. 'And don't they get tax relief

313

or something? I think Nora said companies get their tax reduced for charity donations. And maybe Amanda collects data for them, or sends them customers. I don't know. That sort of thing would be what's in her private files, I suppose. Anyway, the Windhover's a big supporter – we could about survive on what they pay us alone. Oh, and I asked Nora about setting up the agency in the first place, like you asked me, and she said that was Windhover as well – gave Amanda a big lump sum to get the office building adapted and get the whole thing going.'

'They sound like the good guys,' Swilley said.

'Well, I guess they are. It's nice when you hear all the stories about these big multinational drugs companies, to know there's one that's doing something good, giving something back.'

'I expect lots of them do,' Swilley said. 'I expect a lot of these stories are exaggerated.'

Angela looked pleased at the idea of the world being a nicer place. 'Yeah, I bet you're right.'

'So that's the income,' Swilley prompted. 'What about the outgoings?'

'Oh, yeah, you wanted to know about salaries. Well, Nora gets £1650 a month – gross – which surprised me a bit because it's not that much more than me. I get £1350.'

Around twenty thousand and sixteen thousand respectively, Norma thought after a quick calculation. 'Is that about average?' she asked.

'I can't say about Nora – I mean, she's supposed to be an owner, isn't she? But mine is a bit above average. When you work for a charity you don't expect high wages.'

314

'And what about Amanda?'

'There wasn't anything about her getting a salary, either in the books or on the system – I suppose she'd be bound to keep that private. But in the bank account I did find a regular transfer to another account of ten thousand every month.' She screwed up her brow. 'But that couldn't be her salary, could it? I mean, that would be a hundred and twenty thousand a year. She wouldn't take that much, when it was a charity, would she? Only, I can't think what else it could be, because it's too big to be utilities or rates or anything, and if it was office supplies or something like that it'd be paid when the invoices came in, not monthly.'

'You're right,' Norma said. 'I wonder if it could be paying off a loan of some sort?'

'I don't know. I never heard of any loan – and a loan for what, anyway? Apart from the office and office supplies, we don't use anything else.' She shrugged the problem away, being essentially uninterested in it. 'Anyway, I made a note of the bank account number in case you wanted it. I suppose *you'd* be able to find out whose it was, wouldn't you?'

'Yes,' said Swilley. 'If it was important.' She smiled encouragingly. 'You've done very well.'

The last of the elation faded from Angela's face, and she slumped. 'Doesn't make any difference, though, does it? It doesn't bring David back.' Her lip trembled and she put her hand over it and pressed for a moment. When she removed it, a certain steeliness had come with further thoughts. 'If she did have anything to do with it,

315

I hope you get her! It makes me sick to think of her being all pious and smug and all the time she's done something like *that*.'

'Well, we don't know she's done anything,' Swilley said quickly. 'And you mustn't let her think you suspect her, whatever you do.'

'Oh, I won't,' Angela said easily. 'I can be as two-faced as the next person.'

SEVENTEEN

Butcher's Dog

Porson actually came to Slider's office rather than summoning him, proof of excitement. Because he was The Syrup, it wouldn't be revealed any other way. Except that – wasn't there something of a shine to the old boy's bumpy pate, and a sparkle lurking under the overhanging eyebrows?

'Well, someone took his finger out, wonders will never cease,' he said in his normal grumbling tone. 'Got some corporation for once in a blue moon, from the Excise opposite number, bloke called–' he inspected the paper in his hand – 'Wouter Zollars. Bloody Nora, what a name! Still, what wouldn't we give for more of his sort?'

'For a few Zollars more,' Slider said. He just couldn't help himself.

Fortunately Porson didn't notice. 'Right! None of that "them and us" bollocks from him,' he said. He was staring again at the paper. 'Blimey, I don't fancy standing up in a meeting and having to pronounce this lot. I'm not even going to try for you. You can have the phonetic version. I'm not the United Nations. Anyway, this Zollars knows the *Havik* boat all right. It's moored in the IJmuiden marina, like your man thought, and it's on their "to watch" list. It's registered to a Jaap Boeckman, but they reckon that's a pseudonym for a bloke called Jaheem Bodeker. You'd wonder why he'd bother changing,' he added in hurt tones.

'And Bodeker's someone they know?'

'You might say. He's a bit tasty. Up to all sorts of naughtiness as a lad, graduated into the diamond trade in his twenties, courier, got caught and ended up inside. Come out about ten years ago. Hasn't been in any trouble since, but he's one of those villains, you know in your gut they'll never change. You can't teach an old leopard new tricks. They've been watching him ever since, haven't caught him out, but friend Zollars'd bet his pension he's up to something. He goes down to the marina every Wednesday, supposed to be going out night fishing, but when we told Zollars about the meeting with the *Windhover* he come over all unnecessary and had to sit down in a darkened room for ten minutes.'

Slider reminded Porson of his own caveat. 'We only know about one meeting.'

'Both going out night fishing, the same night,

317

regular?' Porson said. 'One's a known courier, the other comes ashore with a box o' something no one ever gets a look at? Work it out, laddie. It's not rocket salad.'

'I wonder what they did this last Wednesday, with Rogers dead,' Slider mused.

'They must've thought about that before they offed him,' Porson said, 'because Bodeker – thank Christ I can say that one – went down as usual. Dutch police want him very bad. They're going to set up a big multi-agency operation and take him on the next run, let him get right to the boat with the goods on him and grab him.'

Slider looked aghast. 'But if they do that we'll lose our end of it. They'll close it down and we'll never be able to catch the rest of them.'

'Never mind,' Porson barked. 'That part of it is out of our hands now. The big boys have taken our ball and we can't play.'

'We've got two murders on our books.'

'You've got the hand print off the motor.'

'But no one to match it against. And even if we could get the murderer, there's little hope he'd give up his boss – the top man.' Slider fiddled unhappily with his pen. 'There are still lots of things I want to know. I've got ongoing investigations—'

'I know that,' Porson said, slightly more sympathetically, 'and there's no reason you can't go on trying to tie up loose ends, as long as you don't frighten the horses. Because if anything we do spooks the gang and the operation goes wrong, it'll be all our bollocks on a platter. I don't like this set-up any more than you, but we've got Europol and the Excise boys and God knows who else getting involved now, and that lot's too rich for our blood. We're not even second division. We're Noddy and Big Ears. Just remember that.' He headed for the door, but turned when he reached it to say from beneath seriously-levelled brows, 'If you do anything that throws a spaniel in the works, I'm not going to bat for you, not this time. I mean it. You listening to me?'

'Yes, sir,' said Slider.

When Porson had gone he lapsed into thought again.

Wonder who played Rogers's part on Wednesday/Thursday? Couldn't have used Windhover *or that old boy in the harbour would have said so: you can bet he and a few others were watching her once they heard about Rogers being murdered. A different boat, a different harbour. Must have been another small inlet – too much scrutiny at the bigger harbours.*

He twiddled his pen. *If I'm right, speed is of the essence.* He swivelled his chair and stared out of the dusty window at the blank sky. Speed is of the essence. And always the same day of the week.

Norma came in and made her report, and was disappointed that her boss seemed so distracted, he wasn't even moved by the revelation that Windhover was behind the agency. She eyed him curiously. 'You knew that already, didn't you?'

Slider roused himself. 'No. No, I didn't. But I'm not surprised. I *know* she's involved somehow, I just haven't figured out *how* yet. You've got that bank account number? Right, get on to the bank and get them to tell you whose name it's in.'

She nodded. 'Are we going after her?'

'Not now. Not yet. There are other things going on. We have to be careful. And I don't know yet—'

She waited but he didn't finish the sentence. 'You look tired, boss,' she said eventually.

'Didn't sleep much last night.'

'Have you had lunch?'

He looked at the clock in surprise. 'Is it that time?'

'Want me to get you a sandwich?

He roused himself. 'No, thanks, I'll go up to the canteen. I need a change of scene.' Maybe it would create a change of thinking.

Connolly found him there, toying with a portion of moussaka. He looked up at her resentfully.

'Aubergines,' he said. 'I mean, what's that all about? It's not a shepherd's pie and it's not a lasagne.'

'It's an abomination,' she said, to humour him.

'And look at this salad. It's all frisée.'

'I hate that yoke. You'd cut your mouth on it. And it tastes like shit.'

'It's the astroturf of lettuce,' Slider said. 'All right, gripes satisfied. Did you get anything? I see you did. Sit down.'

'Piece o' cake,' Connolly said modestly, sitting down opposite him. 'I shared a flat with two nurses for six months so I can talk a good talk.

And I've a friend who's an agency nurse. I borrowed one of her dresses and just walked in.'

'Into the Cloisterwood?' Slider asked in alarm, remembering Porson's final warning.

'No, no, not there,' Connolly said in a tone that implied the words 'you eejit' had been left out. 'The Royal Orthopod. I'd a stuck out like a sore mickey in the private hospital. I wouldn't know what agency they use, if they use one at all. But in an NHS hospital the trick is to find two nurses wearing the same thing. So anyway, seeing as I got there about lunchtime, I went up to the staff canteen and got talking to some o' the nurses.'

'No trouble getting them to open up?'

'Are you kidding? They wore the ear offa me. The Cloisterwood is all they talk about. Mostly it's the money – how much the patients pay and how much the staff are paid and why couldn't they get a piece of it and the wickedness altogether of the private sector. And when I got on to kidneys! It was all, the queue-jumping, and the rich foreigners getting in ahead of our people. It'd make your head bleed. Nurses are the great levellers.' She eyed the cold moussaka with which he was fiddling, despite the defensive crust it had grown. 'Would you not leave that? It'd break your teeth. It's like the horny plates on a Tasmanian devil.'

Slider smiled. 'A Tasmanian devil doesn't have plates. It's furry.'

'So what's that giant lizardy thing?'

'Never mind,' Slider said, and pushed the plate aside. 'Look, no hands. Go on with your report.'

'Well, after all the bitching it wasn't hard to

work them round to specifics, especially as I told them me anty was on a waiting list for a kidney. I had their hearts scalded with her sufferings! Anyway, kidney transplants at the Cloisterwood are done on a Thursday. They start at ten o'clock, and go on through the day, two operating theatres working at the same time, so they'll do eight or sometimes ten altogether. The op takes about two hours if there's no complications.'

'Eight or ten. That sounds like a lot.'

'I thought so. I wondered about it, eight kidneys a week for the one hospital? But all the nurses said was that rich private patients could always get what they wanted, it was the rest of us eejits that had to queue up and suffer. It was all part of the bitching. When I asked about me anty they said the NHS waiting list is two years minimum, and even then you've only a fifty-fifty chance of getting an organ. So you can see their point of view – especially when I asked what it'd cost to jump the queue, and they said these people'd be paying over a million for that one little bit of meat and a few tubes o' gristle.'

'And a chance of a normal life.'

'Well, there is that, I suppose.'

She stopped and looked at him intelligently, and he roused himself from mental arithmetic to say, 'You did very well. And you're sure no one suspected you?'

'God, no. That lot of Miserable Margarets don't mind who they complain to, as long as they can ride some ferocious crying-shame. By the way, I also found out that the Cloisterwood does corneas of a Friday, same system, non-stop, only it's a quicker op so they only use the one theatre. But they get through about the same number.'

'Corneas on a Friday,' Slider said.

'Makes you think,' said Connolly.

They walked downstairs together, and Slider found Atherton in his office.

'You're becoming very elusive,' he complained.

'I went to the canteen for lunch.'

'Good luck with that. Did you get any?'

'Not really.' He waved at the windowsill. 'Have a pew. I've things to tell you.'

At the end of it Atherton wrinkled his nose and said, 'I've heard of two lips from Amsterdam, but kidneys and corneas? Wouldn't they go off?'

'I checked. Properly refrigerated, kidneys can last forty to fifty hours, and corneas ten days.'

'But where do they come from?'

'You may well ask.'

'I did,' Atherton pointed out. He pondered. 'Not diamonds?'

'Porson himself said it sounded more like something perishable. There'd be no need for a regular day for diamonds – in fact, doing diamonds on a schedule would make it more dangerous – more likely to be spotted.'

'Well, you don't expect criminals to be intelligent.'

'IJmuiden is a short distance from Amsterdam airport, by a fast motorway link. Speed would be of the essence.'

Atherton thought a moment. 'But it's all supposition. We actually have nothing to connect

Rogers with Cloisterwood, apart from Webber being his old pal.'

'I want you to get on to the Hendon ANPR, see if you can trace Rogers's car from Southwold the Thursday morning before he was killed. He'd probably use the most direct route, A12 and M25, if he was coming back to London. If he wasn't—' He shrugged. That was whole-new-ball-game country.

'Right,' said Atherton. 'But it probably was London. Even if it was fish in that cool box, or an entire mixed grill, where would he go with it but London?'

'He could have another wife tucked away somewhere for all we know.'

'You don't believe that,' Atherton said. He headed for the door, then turned back. 'It could still be diamonds.'

'I know,' Slider said. 'In a way, I hope it is.'

Phil Warzynski rang from Notting Hill. 'I promised you I'd keep you up to date,' he said, 'but don't let Hunnicutt know, or he'll have my guts for garters. He doesn't want anyone else muscling in on his ground.'

'You're a mate,' Slider said. 'Everyone here seems to have forgotten that poor girl.' He had himself, for a bit, but didn't let on, of course.

'Grapevine says you've stumbled on to something big,' Warzynski said hopefully. 'There's a certain buzziness in the big brass dining-room – talk of Europol...'

'I can't say anything,' Slider said. 'Sorry, but it wouldn't just be guts they'd turn into garters.'

'Oh well. I won't be hard-nosed about it. You can have my bit of gen for nothing. Two bits, actually. Nothing too exciting, but you're welcome to them. First off we've got a motor seen hanging around before the murder, parked up just past Portobello Mews. It might be nothing, or it might be the villain. You know how these things go. Somebody noticed it because it drove up and parked and no one got out, and after waiting a bit it drove off. If it *was* chummy, he could've been sussing the place out before going to park.'

'Did they get a number?'

'No, that's why I warned you not to get excited. It was a black four-by four – MPV type, not Land-Rover type – with black windows. Sounds like a drug-dealer's wheels,' he added, free of charge. 'Any use to you?'

Slider remembered something. 'Could it be an Audi Q7?'

'That sort of thing,' Warzynski agreed. 'Witness was a woman so it's no use asking her for make or model. She was looking out the window on the way to bed. If she'd waited a bit she might've seen something useful. Oh well.'

'It's better than nothing,' Slider said encouragingly.

'Is it? My day hasn't been wasted then. The other bit of gen is about the victim's mobile – we checked 1471, and it went to another mobile. It was pay-as-you-go.'

'Of course,' Slider said. 'It's time they tightened up on that.'

'Gets my vote. The good news is, we were able

to triangulate the signal.'

'They haven't chucked it away?' Gloriosky, they'd made a mistake! Bliss it was in that dawn to be alive.

'Don't go mad,' Warzynski warned. 'The bad news is it's a hospital, so tracking down the actual individual will be a job and a half, especially when they're moving about inside.'

'I don't mind. In fact, I bet I can guess which hospital.'

'The Cloisterwood Hospital in Stanmore? You were expecting that?'

'Hoping for it. It doesn't give me the answer, but it's a help. Thanks a lot, Phil.'

'Welcome,' Warzynski said, with questions sticking out all over his voice.

'When I can tell you,' Slider promised, 'I'll give you the whole story, I promise. Over a drink. At least.'

'I'll hold you to that.'

Slider put the phone down and thought a moment, then looked up a name in the great file of notes that had been decorating his desk all day. Lonergan. That was it. Detective Sergeant Mick Lonergan. He rang Stanmore nick. With a name like that he was expecting an Irish voice, but it was your basic Middlesex when Lonergan came on.

Slider introduced himself. 'A couple of my lads were over your way looking at Embry's yard.'

'Oh yes. That squatty little toerag! Well, I've nothing new on him for you, sir. But it's building up nicely. We'll get him. He'll make a mistake 'sooner or late. They always do.'

'Yes,' said Slider, thinking of the mobile.

'It'd be nice to clear that blot off our ground. Our intelligence says he's supplying all the criminals in a wide area – wheels, shooters, information, even false documents – every bloody thing. What we need is a big multi-agency operation to catch him with the goods and close him down.'

Slider shuddered at the words. 'As you say, he'll make a mistake one day. But it wasn't him I wanted to ask you about.'

'Oh yes?'

'I wanted to pick your brains. You told one of my men you thought you recognized the photo he showed you, of the man we were interested in, the one who bought the false plates from Embry.'

'Yes, that's right. I remember. Dark hair, big build. I know I've seen him somewhere but I can't place him. It's on the tip of my mind, but—'

'I wondered whether he could be anything to do with the Cloisterwood Hospital – whether that's where you saw him.'

'No–o,' Lonergan said thoughtfully. 'I don't think it was that. I don't think I've ever been over there, tell the truth. We don't get a lot of trouble from it.' This was a joke. 'Drunks and fights and so on.'

'Oh well, it was just a th—'

'Wait a minute, wait a minute,' Lonergan said in a eureka tone. 'You're not wrong after all. I've got it! It wasn't *at* the hospital I saw him, but it

327

was to do with the hospital. He's a chauffeur. I caught him on a double yellow outside the Council Chambers one day, waiting for Sir Bernard Webber.'

'He's Webber's chauffeur?' That wasn't what he expected. 'What car was he in? A four-by-four?'

'No, it was a Jaguar. That's what caught me out at the time, because I'd have known Sir Bernard's Bentley anywhere. I told this joker to move on and he refused, then when I said I was going to ticket him he said he was waiting for Sir Bernard, so of course I had to let it go.'

'You did?'

'Well, he's a bit of a local hero, Sir Bernard. He's put Stanmore on the map with the Cloisterwood, plus he's into all sorts of charities, on every committee God made, and he supports all the local events and stuff – most of it wouldn't happen without him. He's very generous. People round here wouldn't hear a word against him, so we'd never hear the last of it if we moved his car on and made him walk.'

'But it wasn't his car?'

'Not his personal one, but it was a hospital car, one they use to collect patients from the airport or the station. They've got several, apparently. I suppose the Bentley was in dock for some reason.' The facts caught up with him and he paused, and then said in an uneasy voice, 'You're not telling me that he's your suspect, sir? Not Sir Bernard's chauffeur?'

A friendly warning to Webber from the supportive local police could jeopardize everything.

Slider said, 'No, it can't be. It must be a mistake. The picture my lad showed you – it wasn't very clear.'

Lonergan seized on this. 'That's right. It was blurred and grainy. You couldn't really tell who it was. I thought it looked like this chauffeur bloke, but now I think of it, it wasn't really anything like him.'

'No, of course not,' Slider said comfortingly. 'Oh well, never mind. It's another dead end.'

'There's not any trouble down at the Cloisterwood, is there, sir?'

'No, no trouble. Just trying to work out what the connection with Stanmore is.'

'Embry's yard,' Lonergan said promptly. 'That's what the connection'll be. This bloke you're looking for is a pal of Embry's, sir. You can bank on that.'

'I'm absolutely sure he is,' Slider said. 'Thanks a lot, you've been a great help.'

'I haven't told you anything,' Lonergan said in a puzzled tone.

'No, but you've set me straight about a few things.'

He got up and wandered out into the CID room. Hollis was standing at Atherton's shoulder, reading over it, and they both looked up as he came in.

'Got that ANPR trace, guv,' Hollis said. 'On Rogers's car.'

Slider read the quizzical expression on his face and tried to straighten up and be brisk. I must look like a road accident, he thought.

329

Atherton swivelled round and read off the printout. 'Picked him up just after four a.m. on the A12, at the junction with the Aldbrough turn-off. Then the Ipswich roundabout. Couple more pings before he comes off the A12 on to the M25. Comes off the M25 at the A1, Barnet Way. Pinged him at the Northway Circus turning on to the A41, and then it's our old friend the camera at the A410 roundabout for Stanmore, smile please, turn your head and cough, and out goes he.'

'He must a been tanking it, guv,' Hollis said, 'because he did the lot in less than two hours.'

'From these lips to your ears. From Southwold straight to Stanmore with a box of fish. Don't it make your heart sing?' Atherton enquired.

'Maybe the fish was poorly,' Hollis tried in his jollity. 'Took it in the A and E and said, "Here's the sick squid I owe yer."'

Slider didn't even notice. 'Speed would be of the essence,' he said.

Atherton nodded. 'A hospital would be great cover for diamond smuggling. But I'm beginning to see it your way. If it wasn't perishables, why risk it? Even in the middle of the night there can be traffic cops around, especially in the outback where they've nothing else to do.'

'What are you going to do, guv?' Hollis asked. They were all looking at him, hopefully, like dogs who've heard the rattle of the lead being taken down. His eye wandered, his brain having forgotten to tell it what he was looking for. It came to rest on Connolly, who half rose, ready to be of assistance.

'Just one more little job for you,' he said.

'Yes, guv,' she said smartly.

'You made some friends at that hospital. Can you use the connection to find out the name of Sir Bernard Webber's chauffeur? He's a good-looking bloke, so you could pretend you fancy him, if that helps. And when you get his name, run it and see if he has a criminal record.'

'I'm on it,' she said cheerily; like a good lieutenant, not asking any questions.

Swilley came across. 'That bank account, guv – it is Amanda Sturgess's all right. They didn't like telling me, but when I said I didn't want to look at it, only know whose it was, they eased up a bit.'

'Good. Thanks.'

'What was that about a chauffeur?' she enquired.

'Bank account?' said Atherton.

'Gather round, people,' Slider said. 'It's time I filled you in on recent developments – not the least of which is that we're forbidden to do any more sleuthing until after Thursday morning, so you can all have early nights until then. But – and this is important – you're not to speak about any of this to anyone. Not your mum, your aunty, your spouse, your lover and especially not the press. Because if one word gets out we could all end up in the Tower.'

Slider had not noticed how quiet the whole place had gone, but one by one the minions had departed. Connolly, almost the last, brought him the final piece of information: the man who chauffeured Sir Bernard Webber, when he didn't drive himself, was Jerry McGuinness, forty-five or thereabouts, unmarried but according to rumour living with a woman, though no one had ever seen her, in a former farmhouse on Harrow Weald.

'I've looked up the house on Google,' Connolly said, 'and it's a desperate sort of a kip, middle a nowhere, down the end of a long track. Humpy little cottage covered in ivy, with a bunch o' derelict sheds falling down all round it. Can't see a woman living there voluntarily, but there's no accounting for folly. Nobody's sure exactly what he does,' she went on. 'He drives the hospital motors – there's several, including a Beamer, guv – but apart from that there's a feeling he's Webber's odd-job fixer and trusty bagman. Known to be well in with the big cheese, goes way back with him apparently. General opinion is he's fit as a butcher's dog, but a bit scary with it. Likes to give the girls a thrill, flirting with them, but doesn't take it any further. For which they seem to be glad and sorry in about equal proportions.'

Butcher's dog, Slider thought. *Yes, that was apt. I am not the Butcher but the Butcher's dog.* 'Interesting,' he said.

She cocked a sympathetic eye towards him. 'He's got no record, guv. So we can't check the murderer's hand-print against his.'

'It's only what I expected,' Slider said, and lapsed into silence.

At last she said, hopefully, 'Is there anything else you want me to do, guv?'

'No, thanks. Not just now,' Slider said absently.

It wasn't the answer she had wanted, but there was nothing for it but to shrug, turn away, and say, 'Goodnight, then.'

Slider didn't even hear her. Deep in the notes, he was unaware of his surroundings until, looking up, he found Atherton leaning on his door frame with an empty CID room behind him.

'Not gone home? Did you want something?'

'I know you're about to do something,' Atherton said, 'and, at the risk of going all Rin Tin Tin about it, my place is at your side.'

Slider looked at him thoughtfully for a long moment. 'There is something you can do.'

'Hah!' said Atherton. 'I knew it. You're going solo again, and after Mr Porson's forbidden you!'

'No, in fact Mr Porson said I can tie up loose ends. As long as I don't frighten the horses.'

'Loose ends? Horses? No still waters or barn doors in this cliché-fest?'

'It cuts us out, you see,' Slider said. 'The big operation. Unless the Dutch courier sings about this end of the chain, and they're not likely to press him on it when they want to wind it up the other way. And we can't do anything this end, because we don't know who the new courier is, or where he's going out from. They won't use *Windhover* again.'

'No,' said Atherton. 'Too many eyes watching, now Rogers is a celebrity for being murdered.'

'New courier, new boat, new harbour.'

'Needle in haystack.'

'And I don't just want the courier. I want the brains behind it.'

'So – what, then?'

'We have to get the whole story, everything, from the beginning. From someone who knows. Someone with the moral courage to do the right thing.'

It didn't take Atherton more than a few seconds to work it out. 'You're going to see Amanda Sturgess? You think *she* has moral courage? Or do you think she's the brains behind it?'

'We'll see.'

'I hope we will. And what do you want me to do? Come with you?'

'No, I think she'll talk better one to one. I want you to get Frith out of the way.'

'I'm not going to befriend that ass's arse.'

'You can make it official. Find out how much he really knew about the whole business. That's something that's been exercising me. I think he was ignorant of it all, but I'd like to be sure.'

Atherton considered. 'But you'll give the secret signal if you get into trouble, so I can rush to the rescue?'

Slider raised an eyebrow. 'What am I, a weakling? She may be tall, but I could take her any time I wanted.'

Atherton shuddered. 'Choose another simile.'

'Not that sort of taking.'

'Even the thought of it...'

Amanda Sturgess looked terrible. She had aged ten years in a week. She was grey-faced and drawn and her eyes were haunted. Slider felt an inward quiver of satisfaction that he was on the right track. He had waited across the road in his car until he saw Frith stamp out, looking annoyed, to keep his enforced tryst with Atherton, then made his way through the windy darkness to the lit house. He rang, and she answered the door. The sight of him brought a sort of dread to her expression.

'I'd like to talk to you,' Slider said, quite gently.

She rallied. 'I have nothing to say to you,' she said, with an attempt at the old, cold arrogance. It almost worked.

'You *will* talk to me,' he said. 'Either here or down at the station.'

'You threatened me once before,' she said, nostrils quivering. 'You need to know that I am not a woman to be bullied.'

'Then, in God's name, how did you get mixed up with all this?' he cried. Her face flinched as though he had slapped her. 'They killed your husband!'

'My ex-husband!'

'And his girlfriend – an innocent woman. She had nothing to do with it, but they killed her anyway.'

'Why should I care about her? She was a slut. She got what she deserved.'

'You don't think that,' he said, looking at her seriously. She met his eyes, but her own grew nervous again, 'And two others at least – the secretary and the nurse from Harley Street. How many more have to die?'

'I don't care,' she cried weakly. 'Go away and

335

leave me alone!' She tried to close the door, but he had his hand on it.

'In your own self-interest, then,' he said. 'Don't you think they know you are now the one weak link? How long before they come after you?' She stared at him, holding on. Perhaps she even thought death would be a relief? No, she didn't really believe she was in danger. But he had another lever. 'What do you think will happen to your agency?'

That hit home. 'You can't touch that! You wouldn't! We do good work. It's *important* work.'

He inched closer and lowered his voice so that she had to stay near to listen. 'Financed by criminal money? We'll take it apart, close it down. The publicity will obliterate its reputation and your work.'

'Not my agency! You wouldn't!'

'I *will*. Unless—' Now she was listening. 'If you help us, I might be able to keep the agency out of it. You could find a new way of financing it, keep it going. I understand you're an expert fund-raiser. If, that is, you are free to fund-raise.'

'What are you talking about?'

'If I can arrange an amnesty for you in exchange for your information.'

'Amnesty?' Pale as she was, she whitened at the implication.

'You are right in the middle of this,' he said with soft implacability. 'You are implicated right up to the hilt. You will be arrested, charged with the rest of them. The illegal importation of human organs. Plus at least two murders.'

'I didn't kill anyone!'

'That's not the way the law sees it. You don't have to pull the trigger to be guilty. You knew all about it and you didn't try to stop it. That makes you guilty.'

Now she looked appalled. 'I can't,' she whispered. 'I can't go to court. I can't be on trial. It would kill my parents.'

'Then you must help me,' he said simply. 'Talk to me, tell me everything. But it has to be now. This is your only chance. After this, it will be out of my hands.' He watched her for a moment, and then started to turn away with a shrug.

'No, wait!' She seemed to crumple. 'Oh God, how did it come to this?' She swayed, and Slider thought he might have to grab her. But she was made of sterner stuff. She straightened herself, stepped back, and said, with a ghost of the old hostility, 'You'd better come in.'

EIGHTEEN

Organ Involuntary

He followed her over the threshold and closed the door behind him. There were lights on all through the ground floor, and it seemed they must have been having supper when Atherton rang, because the dining table was only partly cleared and there was a smell of food fading away in the kitchen. She walked straight to a cupboard in the corner of the sitting-room and took out a bottle and two glasses.

'I need a drink,' she said tersely. 'You?'

'Thanks,' he said.

She did not offer a choice, but poured whisky into both glasses and handed him one, innocent of ice or niceties. This was not a social occasion. It was the cowboy's slug of hooch before prairie surgery. She shot her slug straight down her throat and refilled, not offering more to Slider. Then she seemed to see the untidiness of the kitchen, took two swift steps and switched off the lights in there. He was glad she still had the spirit to be house-proud. It gave him more to work with.

They sat in armchairs facing each other. Slider sipped. She looked at him coldly. 'Well,' she said. 'What do you want to know?'

He didn't need to think. He had his starting-place long thought out. 'The Lescroit woman's accusation. You were there that day. What actually happened?'

A spot of colour came into her cheeks. 'What a thing to—! What makes you think I was there?'

'Please,' he said. 'This is going to take forever if you go the "what makes you think?" route. I know nearly everything. You are going to tell me the rest – for the sake of your clients, remember, if not your own skin. What happened that day?'

'The woman accused David of molesting her,' she said rigidly.

'But it wasn't David, was it?'

She looked at him as if she would have liked to

338

kill him, but she said, through gritted teeth, 'No.'

'It's not the sort of thing David would do,' Slider went on conversationally. 'He could get all the women he wanted without that. It was Bernard Webber who was the bottom-pincher, the one who brushed up against the secretaries in confined spaces.'

She glared. 'You don't have to go on.'

'Webber was out of his room – gone to the lavatory, apparently. But in fact he had slipped into the room where the woman was recovering.' Her cheeks were scarlet, her eyes bright with mortification, or rage, or something. 'She woke up, or half-woke. She said, "What are you doing, doctor?" 'And he said, "Call me David."'

'*I know*!' she cried.

'How do you know?'

'Because he told me.'

'You were in his room when he came back in.'

She nodded, and swallowed, as if it were difficult for her to tell this part. 'I'd just arrived. I was waiting for him. Then I heard the noise – the woman shrieking. He came in. He said, "There's the devil to pay." He said, "We can all still come out of it all right if you go along with whatever I say."'

'He asked *you* to cover up for him?' Slider said. 'Why did he think you would do that?'

She squeezed her eyes shut, and said, her lips rigid, 'We were lovers.'

'Ah,' said Slider. It was the last piece in his jigsaw. He'd pretty much worked out what it would look like from the space it left, but coming from her, coloured with the shame she still felt, it was bright and compelling.

She opened her eyes and, as if having got over this hurdle there was nothing more to fear, she sat up straighter and began to talk.

'We'd been lovers for some time. He was – still is – fantastically attractive; and things had been going badly between David and me. I told you before about his women. He couldn't leave them alone. It wore me down. Bernard was sympathetic – an old friend I could lean on. At first that's all it was. He was the only person I could really talk to, who knew David too, and liked him. But I was – lonely. And hurt. Sympathy drifted into comforting, the comforting became physical.' She looked at him. 'I'm not proud of it. I know I let myself down. I never intended to be unfaithful to David. But—'

'These things happen,' Slider said neutrally. He knew better than to offer her sympathy. 'You'd gone there that day to see Webber?'

'I told Stephanie – Bernard's secretary – it was about fund-raising. Bernard was always generous with charities. I knew David had a procedure, so I'd be able to see Bernard alone. Then all this blew up.'

'What made you go along with blaming David for the trouble?'

'Oh!' she said in frustration, 'I know how it looks. But it was the only way. Bernard explained it all logically. He said the Lescroit woman was convinced it was David and wouldn't change her mind. He said *he* had the influence and the money, he could get David off, but David couldn't get *him* off. He said if he took the blame

340

there would still be people who thought it had really been David all the time, because of his reputation. So they'd both be ruined, and his sacrifice would be for nothing.'

'Sacrifice?'

She had the grace to blush slightly. 'You must remember I was angry with David for what he had done. He was out of control around women. Even if he didn't touch the Lescroit woman, it was only a matter of time before he had some kind of affair with a patient and got struck off.'

Slider nodded, as if accepting the point. 'And what did David say to Webber's arguments?'

'David never knew,' she said. She looked away from him. 'He thought the woman had just been confused and imagined it all. He swore to me that he didn't touch her, but he knew he was in trouble all the same. When Bernard said he believed him and promised to make it all right, David was – grateful.'

Slider thought she was ashamed of that: perhaps uniquely in the whole mess, was she ashamed that David had been grateful for being stitched up?

'So he got David a lighter sentence from the GMC, and he got him a job,' he said. 'What did you get?'

She hardened her gaze. 'Money,' she said in a cold voice. Slider continued to look at her steadily, and she went on, 'I was divorcing David. The Lescroit business was the excuse but I was going to anyway. I had to get away from him. I hated him by then. Oh, you don't know, you can't imagine what it was like for me! David had betrayed me and broken my heart. Bernard was my rock. He helped me through everything. And his money – a friend's money – meant I didn't need to take anything from David. I told him I would pay it back. But he laughed and said he wouldn't hear of it.'

'You were still Webber's mistress?'

'For a time. But after all the fuss died down, after the divorce came through, Bernard sold the practice, got a government contract and went abroad.'

'How did Robin Frith fit in with all this? Weren't you involved with him long before the divorce was finalized?'

She looked annoyed. 'What business is it of yours?'

'Everything is now my business,' he said, unmoved. 'I thought we had established that.'

'I don't see what it has to do with anything,' she went on, with extra high dudgeon to compensate for co-operating, 'but it was Bernard's idea that I should cultivate Robin. Felicity – Bernard's wife – was having suspicions about me, and he wanted to divert them. She thought I was divorcing David for him. Bernard had already decided to divorce Felicity and he wanted it to be amicable, otherwise it would have cost him dear. So she mustn't think there was anything between Bernard and me. Robin was a smokescreen.' She shrugged. 'He'd always been in love with me, and I knew I could control him, so it worked very well.'

God, she was a cold one! Slider thought. 'So Bernard wasn't divorcing in order to marry

342

you?'

'God, no. He'd decided on it long before we were involved. And marriage was never on the cards between us. I wouldn't have wanted it any more than him. He and Felicity separated just before he went abroad and I didn't see him for almost two years.'

She stopped, her eyes inward. When he saw she was not going to resume unprompted, Slider said, 'It was on his tour abroad that he got everything set up, wasn't it?'

She came back from her reverie. 'Yes, of course. His government status opened all sorts of doors. He told me he saw the whole thing, complete, in one single flash, and after that it was just a matter of setting up the processes. It came to him one evening in Beijing. He was talking to some little Chinese government functionary, who told him about the state executions.' She gave him a defiant look. 'The Chinese government sells the organs quite openly, you know. They don't make any bones about it. These are all condemned criminals. Why shouldn't they repay their debt to society in a practical way?'

Slider didn't get sucked into that. 'He set up the Geneva Foundation. And the numbered Swiss bank account to handle the money. There'd be no questions asked or answered about either. But there had to be a British arm, so that end would look legitimate.'

'The Windhover Trust. It *was* legitimate. Then he worked out the quickest route for the organs – Hong Kong, then Amsterdam by plane, and then by speed boat to England, exchanging at sea where there was no one to see it happen.'

'And on his other travellings he was working up customers,' Slider suggested. 'The Middle East, India, South America...'

'Of course. He had to have agents to direct the patients his way.'

'And the last stage was to get the organs from the coast to Stanmore. He offered that job to David.'

'Yes.'

'Did you know he was going to do that?'

'I was there at the meeting. That would be in the March of 2001. Bernard asked me over to his place one evening – his new place. He and Felicity were divorced by then, and we were seeing each other from time to time. When I got there, David was there too. I thought for one horrible moment he was trying to reconcile us. But it was a business meeting, not a social one. He had the whole network set up by then, except for the last leg. David hated his current job, so he jumped at it. Bernard would pay him a basic salary through Windhover, just enough not to rouse anyone's suspicions, enough to pay tax on, and the rest he'd get in cash – lovely, untraceable cash. Plenty of it. David could live the kind of lifestyle he liked, and the work was negligible. Once a week, courier the goods to London, that was all. Later, Bernard asked him to entertain clients as well, but I always thought that was more to keep David occupied than because it was really necessary.'

Why did he offer the job to David? Was he uniquely qualified for it?'

344

'Good Lord, no,' she said scornfully. 'In fact, Bernard has this chap – a sort of factotum—'

'Jerry McGuinness?'

She raised her eyebrows. 'Oh, you know about him?'

'How did Bernard meet him?'

'Jerry? Oh, he picked him up on his travels when he was doing his tour abroad. Got him out of some kind of trouble with the police in South America. Brought him home. Jerry's forever grateful. Completely loyal.'

I am not the butcher, but the butcher's dog, Slider thought.

'Plus, of course, Bernard pays him well,' she concluded indifferently.

'So, why David, then?'

'To keep him quiet. Bernard thought that sooner or later he was bound to work out what had really happened that day in Harley Street, and he wanted to have him thoroughly bound by unbreakable ties. I think he was wrong – I don't think David would ever have suspected. He wasn't sharp enough – and he loved Bernard, as a friend. He trusted him. But also,' she said thoughtfully, 'I think Bernard really wanted to do David a favour. He loved him, too, you know.'

'And you were guaranteed money for your agency for ever.'

She looked sour. 'You're going to blame me for taking the money.'

'Not at all. It's perfectly understandable.'

'We do good work.'

'And Windhover gets a good cover story.' She

345

didn't answer, only gave him a cross look as though he was taking unfair advantage. 'But didn't the illegality of the whole thing bother you?'

'Illegality?'

'You must know that it is illegal to import organs in that way.'

'Oh! But that's just a technicality. Why on earth *shouldn't* we import organs? The government could change the law if it wanted to. When you think of the misery of people waiting for transplants ... What Bernard does is *good*. He saves lives, and gives people the chance of a decent life.'

'Only people who can pay large sums of money.'

She positively scowled. 'Don't you think rich people have the same right to life as anyone else? Do you measure a person's worth by how much money they have? It's not a moral virtue to be poor. It doesn't make you a saint.'

'Nor does being rich.'

'Whoever said it did? But the government could just as well buy these organs if it cared so much about saving the poor. In any case, Bernard's patients would all be on official waiting lists for organs if he didn't help them. Taking them off the list moves everyone else up. Everyone benefits. Oh, a man can spend his money destroying his body with drink and cigarettes and overeating, and that's his moral right! But if he spends it preserving his health he's some kind of monster!'

She had thought about it, he saw, many, many

346

times in the stilly watches of the night; had justified it to herself so that she could live with it for ten years, and never let out a word to a soul. In spite of her defiant words, she had a conscience, buried deep in there somewhere.

'Not everyone benefitted,' Slider said. 'What about the donors?'

'Condemned criminals? What would be the good of wasting the perfectly good organs? They would have died anyway.'

'Are you quite sure of that?' Slider asked in a deadly small voice.

The implications of the question could not have been new to her, but she must have shut them out in self defence. Now he saw the train of thought flitting through her face, taking the barriers with it. She sat rigidly upright in her chair, but her expression was a cry of desperation.

'And then there were the people who had to die to protect Bernard's secret,' Slider went on. 'Stephanie, Eunice, David, Catriona. They didn't benefit.'

He thought of Helen Aldous as well – moved away from Cloisterwood when Rogers showed an interest in her. Framed for stealing drugs – she had had a lucky escape.

'But it was—' she began to protest, and then saw the futility of it. She closed her eyes. 'Oh God,' she said. 'Oh God. What have I got myself into?'

'You know very well,' Slider said. 'You knew the day I first came here and told you David was dead. You knew who had killed him, and you knew what your part in it was. I could see it in your face.'

Her eyes flew open. 'He was going to blow the whistle on the whole scheme,' she cried. 'He rang me, he kept ringing me, and I kept trying to talk him out of it. He said he'd had a crisis of conscience. A crisis of cowardice, more like! He was afraid of getting caught, that was all. I told him there was no possible way he could be caught. But Bernard said he was a weak link, because of the women – he loved talking big to them and flashing his money. Sooner or later, Bernard said, he'd let something out.'

'You told Webber David was going to blow the whistle?

She whitened. 'I had to! I couldn't let it all be destroyed. I thought he would take David off the job – retire him. Give him enough money to be comfortable. David wanted to sail round the world on that boat of his. It would have taken him right out of the way. When Bernard said he'd sort it out, that he'd make sure David didn't spoil everything—'

'Webber said that? What were his exact words?'

'He said, "Don't worry, I won't let him spoil everything. Leave it to me, I'll sort it out."'

'And you'll swear to that?'

She looked at him whitely. 'Does it come to that?'

'It comes to that. It's him or you.'

Her mouth hardened. 'Then it's him.' And weakened again. 'But, oh God, you don't understand. We were *lovers*.' Slider waited. She said,

'I never imagined he'd kill him! I swear, I thought he was going to buy him off. It wouldn't have been difficult. He could always make David do what he wanted.'

'But he couldn't leave David like that,' Slider said. 'A man who likes women and tells them things? He couldn't take the risk. You don't make weak links comfortable – you eliminate them. And when I came to tell you David was dead, you knew that was what had happened. Bernard had him killed.'

'Yes,' she whispered.

'Then he had David's latest girlfriend killed as well, just in case. Now he must be wondering whether you can safely be left, knowing everything, as you do, and perhaps having doubts – because whatever you thought about the transplants, you never expected it to come to murder. David's death shocked you. Have you told Webber how you feel about that yet? Because if you have, I'm afraid time is running out fast for you.'

'No,' she said. 'I haven't said – anything. We've hardly spoken since – it happened. We're not lovers any more – haven't been for years. We're just friends. We've only talked once or twice but – not – mentioned—'

'You spoke with your friend and your husband's murder wasn't mentioned? Don't you think that was odd?' She bit her lip but didn't answer. 'If killing David was necessary, logic demands he has to kill you, too. Probably it's because of your relationship that he's even hesitated. Perhaps he's fond of you. But he was

349

fond of David, too.'

'He's a good man,' she said. It sounded puzzled. 'He's a good man, a surgeon. He saves lives. He only ever wanted to do good. I don't understand how he could get from there to killing David. His friend.'

Megalomania, Slider thought, though he didn't say it aloud. When power allows you to sidestep the rules and decide for yourself what's right and what isn't, the logical end is defending that right to decide. If you are right, anyone who stands in your way is obviously wrong, and must be removed from the path of the greater good.

She was flagging now; her hands shook as she took a tissue to blow her nose. He must get her moving while he could.

'Webber must be stopped, before there are any more victims,' he said. 'Whatever you think about the organ transplants, you know that murder is wrong. You must come with me now to the station and make a statement about this whole business – every detail.'

She looked up at him, startled out of some train of thought. 'I can't,' she said.

'You will,' he said. 'Only if you come in now, voluntarily, and tell us everything, help us to stop this man, can there be any hope for you to avoid implication in his crimes. We can protect you from him,' he said. 'And we may be able to save something from the wreck.'

'My agency,' she said. She sounded dazed.

'But you have to come now. A full statement.'

It took her two attempts to get out of the chair. She seemed dead weary. He helped her find her handbag and coat, turn off lights. As they went towards the door, he thought of one other thing he had wanted to ask, and might perhaps not have another opportunity to do, because it was not likely that he would be the one to conduct the formal interview at the station, not with the international implications of the case.

'Why did David call the boat the *Windhover*?' he asked. 'Was it because the company bought it for him? Did it come with the name? Or was it a joke?'

She didn't seem to find the question odd. Probably she was beyond discriminating now. 'No, he called it that. He loved that poem. We all did Hopkins at school in those days. "I caught this morning morning's minion." You know?'

'I know,' said Slider. '"Dappled dawn-drawn falcon in his riding."'

'He said it was a beautiful name. *Windhover*. He imagined the boat riding over the waves like a kestrel.' She shook her head. 'Idiotic! I could understand if it had been sailing yacht – a sloop or something. But it was only a motor-boat.' She closed her eyes a moment in pain. 'But he loved that boat, he really did. More than any woman.'

Commander Wetherspoon, their boss at Hammersmith, was a tall, thin man with grizzled, tufty hair that gave him a mysterious resemblance to an Airedale terrier. His squarish, chalky-pink face was fixed in lines of rigid disapproval and his eyes were frosty as he looked down his nose at Slider and said, 'Well done.'

He disliked Slider intensely, as Slider well

knew, and hated having to speak even two words of commendation. It was obviously at Porson's insistence that he had brought himself to this sorry pass. He couldn't find it in his heart to say more, so Porson had to take over the attaboy and do it properly.

'Could have saved us a diplomatic incident,' he concluded. 'The Home Secretary's relieved. Our European counterbands too – they'll be grateful. We've got a whole new ball curve now.'

Wetherspoon gave Porson a scornful look – he didn't like the old man either – and dismissed Slider with a curt nod. Slider removed his thorn from Wetherspoon's side, closing the door quietly behind him, secure in the knowledge that he'd hear it all later.

The fact of the Chinese government's involvement had, as Porson put it, opened up a whole new can of wax, as far as the European side went. Things got very hot very high up and very quickly. The Justice Commissioner had rushed into meetings with the High Representative and the two of them had bearded the head of Europol and the Excise Commissioner. The upshoot was, Porson explained, that Europe didn't want to upset the Chinese so near the date of the next trade round. The elegant, feline EU Trade Commissioner had mopped his brow and pleaded on the one side, while the tough, swarthy Dutch Excise Chief had torn his hair and howled on the other. Then the Assistant Commissioner, Specialist Crime Directorate, Metropolitan Police and the Deputy Commissioner, Specialist

Operations, Metropolitan Police, had had a word with the Commissioner, Metropolitan Police, who had a friendly chat with his Dutch opposite number and put the Home Secretary in to bat, with instructions to block everything until stumps.

The result was that the Euro lot were not going to scoop up Jaheem Bodeker until after he had done the exchange at sea, which meant that the Met and the SCD – the Specialist Crime Directorate – were going to have the chance to clean up their end after all.

It was, as Amanda Sturgess revealed during her night-long questioning, Jerry McGuinness who had taken over Rogers's courier role. As Slider had guessed, there was a new boat, not quite as lovely as the *Windhover*, but adequate – the *Marlin*, an Albemarle 360XF sport-fishing power-craft, small but fast – and a new harbour, Maldon, slightly further from IJmuiden, but closer to London, and equally posh and irreproachable. McGuinness would have no difficulty in handling the boat, even if the sea was rough. He was the sort of man who could work any kind of machinery. Amanda had spoken of him, with a sort of shudder, as capable of anything, an invaluable right-hand man.

'I'd like to keep her in custody,' Porson said of Sturgess. 'Best way to make sure she doesn't tip off Webber. But if she doesn't show up at her usual places, it'll be a dead giveaway that something's up. Do you think we can trust her not to blow the gaff?'

'No,' said Slider. 'Maybe. I don't know. She

353

knows she's in trouble but she half thinks we ought to leave Webber alone to get on with his good work.'

'And they were lovers.' Porson looked thoughtful. 'Funny she didn't mind about him fiddling with that Lescroit woman.'

'I think she thought he was so wonderful that he was allowed the odd weakness.'

'The great man must have his little procavities, eh? Well, I suppose we'll have to take the chance. Make sure she knows that if she doesn't keep it buttoned she's for the high jump.'

'Her agency seems to be the only thing she cares about protecting. I'll work on that angle.'

But she seemed resigned to it now, and accepted her instructions with docility.

As the plans progressed, the Deputy Commissioner, Specialist Operations – who as a woman knew all about not being loved by her superiors – insisted that Slider should be allowed to be in on the operation; in fact, should be in at the kill. 'It's only fair,' she said, as Porson reported to Slider. 'Without him we'd have no chance of a crack at Webber, and Europol would be blundering into the Chinese end of the thing in blindfolds.'

It was a big operation, involving levels of coordination that had to be set up in an unusually short time – normally these things were planned for months, but since Bodeker was being taken out, it had to be this Wednesday or never. Surveillance teams would watch McGuinness all the way to Maldon on Wednesday night, see him go out in the boat, and eventually back in to harbour. Officers would be watching other ports up and down the coast in case the plan had been changed. An officer would be stationed at Hendon on the ANPR computer, reporting on the return journey of the car: it was thought too risky to tail it too closely. At that time of night, a professional like McGuinness would be all too aware of anything keeping a constant distance behind him.

Once he hit the Stanmore turn-off, a relay of motors would check that he did in fact end up at the hospital. Slider would be part of a group hidden in the grounds, who would move in once they had been told the car had gone down the drive. They would all be wearing Kevlar jackets and be armed.

'I hope it won't come to it,' Porson said as he briefed Slider, 'but there's a lot at stake. This is a big money operation. They've offed two people already, and I wouldn't be surprised if this McGuinness type went tooled-up as a matter of course. But keep it under your hat. Don't want any whisper getting out we've got a big op going down.'

On the night, everything was in place. The hands-off surveillance worked: the *Marlin* went out and came back in to Maldon; McGuinness, driving the hospital Jaguar, drove back to the A12 and followed the same route Rogers had taken on his last run. He was clocked turning off towards Stanmore, and Slider, waiting in the chilly mist under the trees behind the staff car park, finally received the radio word that the target was on his way. The March dawn was still some way distant; it was black and cold and his stomach felt very peculiar, though that could have been hunger – he had been waiting for four hours, and it was an even longer time since supper. There were four of them strung out along that side, and the other three, who were all from specialist units, looked oddly at him from time to time, as if they were too polite to ask what a plod like him was doing mixed up in this big-boys' game. His team leader, Corby, who was from the SCD, went so far as to advise him to hang back 'when it went down' and let them take the action. He meant it kindly.

There were another four officers on the other side, ready to close the trap once the car had passed through the visitor's car park into the staff one. Because of the buildings, it was not possible for Slider to witness the car's arrival – that was reported in terse radio bursts from the other team. But when the word came – *Marlin's in the net. Big Shark's in the net* (how they loved their codes!) *Go, go, go!* – Slider's team were closer and were the first on the scene, emerging from between the buildings under the yellowish car park lights to where the Jaguar stood close to the annexe building. The fire door had been propped open, and behind the Jag were McGuinness, reaching into the open boot and lifting out what looked like a large, heavy cold-box, and Sir Bernard Webber.

The Big Shark, Slider thought, with a clutch of excitement. Supervising this last stage of the operation. But of course it would be. Doubtless always had been. The fewer people who were in on this end of the scheme, the safer they would all be. Webber would know that now if he never had before.

It was only a fleeting thought: Slider's adrenalin was pumping as fast as his legs. As he pounded across the tarmac, he saw McGuinness turn his head, thrust the box into Webber's arms, making him stagger, and reach under his leather jacket. The thought flicked through his mind: *so he does go armed.*

Corby, to Slider's left, shouted, 'Gun!' almost at the same moment as the other team arrived from the other direction, and its leader, Nicholson, shouted, 'Armed police! Stand still!' There was a dull gleam in the lamplight as McGuinness brought out the gun. Slider's stomach clenched. Webber had recovered his balance, turned towards the fire door with the box.

There were two explosions in quick succession. The first was McGuinness, firing at Corby's team. Slider felt something pass him in the dark and out of the corner of his eye he saw Corby drop. *Christ*, he thought, with a jolt of his stomach. The second shot was from Nicholson, a warning. It struck the tarmac near McGuinness with a little puff of grit and pinged off the car's wheel arch with a brutal sound that made Slider wince. *Oi, not the Jag!*

Nicholson's voice was an adrenalin scream. 'Armed *police*! Drop the *gun*! Stand *still*!'

Corby was up on his elbows, apparently unhurt: he had dropped in reaction. He was aiming

357

his pistol at McGuinness. 'Drop the *gun*!' he yelled. 'Don't be a fool. You're surrounded.'

It all seemed to be happening at once. McGuinness fired again at the same instant as Corby spoke. Slider had no idea where that shot went. Contrary to myth, it is extraordinarily difficult to hit a moving target, even one as big as a policeman. At the sound of it Webber stopped in his tracks, perhaps unsure if he was being shot at. Slider saw him swivel his head jerkily from one side to the other. Adams, on Slider's right, had his gun on McGuinness too. McGuinness looked over his shoulder at the other team, then back. His gun moved, covering Slider for a breathless moment, then Adams, and then slid on and up as he raised his hands in surrender.

A cold sweat of relief bathed Slider as he left McGuinness to the others and ran, feeling clumsy with his unfamiliar Kevlar armour and sidearm, to get himself between Webber and the fire door. He wanted to make sure he caught him with the goods, red-handed.

Webber's head flicked round at the movement, and his eyes widened slightly as he recognized Slider. 'You,' he said, with a sort of weary disgust; and then, 'You don't know what you're doing.'

'Put it down,' Slider said.

Webber was horribly calm. 'I'm not armed,' he said. 'I have to get this inside. Let me past, please.'

Slider shook his head. 'It's going nowhere. Put it down.'

'You don't understand,' Webber said with a

358

touch of cold impatience. 'This box contains human organs for transplant. I must get them into the proper storage facility.'

Behind him, McGuinness had been relieved of his gun and was being searched, while two others of the team were looking in the car for any more weapons, Slider saw, while never taking his eyes from Webber's.

'*You* don't understand,' he said. 'It's over.'

'Get out of my way!' Webber ground out.

'You're under arrest,' Slider said.

'Don't be ridiculous,' Webber said, his colour high. 'You can't arrest me.'

McGuinness, hands on head, was staring at Slider and Webber, watching the scene play out, as if ready for his cue to jump back in. Slider could smell his sweat, and Webber's aftershave, sharp on the flat, oil-tainted car park air.

'I have patients in there–' Webber jerked his head towards the hospital building – 'waiting for these organs. Waiting for a transplant that will transform their lives. Have you any idea of the suffering of these people? How long they've waited? How few organs there are available? And you want me to *waste* these? What are you, a man or a monster?'

'That's exactly what I was going to ask you,' said Slider.

Webber's calm was suddenly fractured. '*I'm not the villain here*!' he shouted. McGuinness stirred, and was still again. 'I'm a surgeon!'

'And I'm a police officer and I'm arresting you for the illegal importation of human organs,' Slider said.

'That's just a technical violation. An excise law! We're talking about people's lives.'

'I made a rough calculation,' Slider said. 'A million apiece for kidneys, half a million for corneas. Minimum. Six hundred million a year. Not a bad income, even if it is gross.'

'Do you think that's what this was about?' Webber cried. 'Money? Do you really think it was about *money*? I'm a humanitarian.'

'You've cleared your conscience very nicely on that score,' Slider said. 'But what about David Rogers – your friend. And his girlfriend Catriona Aude. How do you justify killing them? How do you justify murder?'

The word – murder – went home. Slider saw it jolt Webber. Had he believed they didn't know? That he had got away with it? But suddenly here it was, on the air and in Slider's face. And he quailed. His eyes flitted first one way, then the other, as though looking for escape. 'I didn't m–murder anyone,' he said, and his voice jittered horribly.

Slider pushed the knife home. 'You're finished, Webber,' he said quietly. He looked at the great consultant with open contempt.

Clumsily, still clutching the box, Webber swivelled on his shiny, expensive shoes. 'I didn't!' he cried. His eyes found McGuinness. His voice was high with panic. 'It was *him*. *He* killed them.'

McGuinness looked, just for a moment, as if someone had punched him in the solar plexus. He gaped for air. 'Shut your mouth, you fucking idiot!' he hissed.

But Webber seemed encouraged by the words. He grew eager, tried to point, hampered by the box. 'I swear it! He did it! *It was him!*'

McGuinness's jaw gritted, his eyes narrowed. He didn't say anything more, but he gave Webber a glittering look as kindly as black ice on a hairpin bend.

Vaughan, the fourth in Corby's team, was approaching with handcuffs. Webber saw them, and the last barrier of horrible realization was crossed. The humiliation made it all real. Under Slider's eyes he actually seemed to shrink, his sleekness became somehow rumpled. His fine clothes, his money, his status, could not protect him now. He was just another grubby criminal.

Slider's adrenalin was high, singing through his blood of triumph. End of the trail. He had his man. It felt good – *he* felt good. He could leap high buildings in a single bound. But there were procedures to follow, and the lads could probably do with finishing up so they could get some breakfast. He could savage a bacon roll himself.

'All right, let's just have a look in that box, shall we?' he said.

Webber looked as though he might weep.

What with debriefings, meetings, interviews, reports verbal and written, forms filled in, more meetings, even more meetings, and bringing various senior figures of increasingly head-spinning importance 'up to speed' on the case, the rest of the day disappeared into a confused kaleidoscope with all the hallmarks of a repetitive dream. Slider never did get a bacon roll. In fact, he couldn't remember getting anything to eat at all, though tea undoubtedly entered his system at some point, and Porson thrust an electric razor at him when they were in the car together being driven to Hammersmith through the twilight to hobnob with the gods.

One of said gods was Assistant Commissioner Congleton himself, head of the Specialist Crime Directorate, a man so senior you could get faint breathing the same air as him. Slider attributed to that the fact that he actually fell asleep in the ante-room when asked to wait outside for a few minutes. Porson, when he emerged, looked at him kindly as he struggled up to consciousness.

'Not much longer,' he said. 'They want you to hang around a bit in case of questions – the AC's briefing the Home Secretary on the phone at this moment in time – then you can get off and finish the paperwork. Everyone's very chipper. Mr Congleton's as pleased as a dog with two willies. He spoke to the head of the CPS while I was in there, and he says they're definitely going to run with the murder charge against Webber. Public interest, plus it showcases a nifty bit of police work and does 'em all a bit of *bon*. So well done.'

'I'm glad,' Slider said, struggling to sound it. 'They think we've got enough evidence?'

Porson used his fingers. 'The motive, hot and strong. Sturgess's testimony that Rogers was going to pull the plunger and Webber saying he'd sort him out. McGuinness bang to rights and testifying on oath that it was all on Webber's say-so – it was clever the way you got Webber to stuff him right in front of everybody,' he said in parenthesis. 'He's as mad as a wronged wife. "After all these years, after all I've done for him,"' he parodied in falsetto. 'He's singing like a canary on cannabis.'

Slider nodded. He had read the first deposition. A phrase from it came swimming up from memory: 'I'd have taken it for him if he'd kept his mouth shut. I owed him one. *I* would never have shopped *him*.'

'Didn't even have to offer him a deal,' Porson gloated. 'Says he just wants to make sure Webber goes down, the ungrateful bastard, eckcetera eckcetera.'

'I know, sir,' Slider said. 'But I'm still a bit worried that it's just his word against Webber's.'

'Of course, you don't know. It must have been while you were with the IAB. McGuinness volunteered his bank statement. He's on the Windhover payroll: basic salary – plus a bloody great bonus, one after Rogers got offed, and another after Aude. He's willing to swear what they were for, and since Windhover is a one-man band, Webber has to explain it or suck it up.'

'That's good,' Slider said reflectively. Webber was going down. But just for a moment he thought of those people waking up in Cloisterwood Hospital to be told that their transplant operation had been cancelled, that they were back on dialysis until they died. Everything had the defect of its virtues. But right was right and indivisible. And Helen Aldous was safe.

'It's enough,' said Porson. 'With everything else, they'll make it stick, laddie, don't you

363

worry.'

He turned away, and turned back. 'Oh, and by the way, while they're at it, Mr Wetherspoon says we should have a shot at the other two women, the secretary and the nurse, see if we can find enough evidence to bring them home to Webber as well.'

'McGuinness hasn't mentioned them, has he?'

'Not yet, but if we work on him the right way...'

Slider got his tired brain to grips. 'It sounds as though they've got it in for Webber.'

Porson positively grinned. 'Mr Wetherspoon met him once at a fund-raiser in Hammersmith Town Hall. Webber snubbed him.' He lowered his voice to a conspiratorial whisper and accompanied it with a wink. *'Not posh enough.'*

Crikey, Slider thought, impressed. Webber might be a cold-hearted murdering egomaniac, but it took some cojones to cut Mr Wetherspoon on his own turf.

'You didn't tell me there were going to be guns,' Joanna said when he finally, finally got home. She looked at his grey face and red-rimmed eyes but she couldn't help herself – she still had to say it. 'You didn't say there would be shooting.'

'Thought it better not to,' he said. 'What would be the point of worrying you?'

'I'm your wife. It's my privilege to worry.'

'Well, no one was hurt. And we got the baddies. Doesn't that warrant a "well done, darling"?'

She relented. 'Of course. Well done, darling.

Do you know what the time is? I thought you were never coming home. I don't know what to offer you – tea, breakfast, lunch, dinner, a drink?'

He didn't need to think. 'Tea,' he said prosaically. 'I seem to have been talking all day. My mouth's like the bottom of the budgie's cage.' She went to put the kettle on, and he followed her into the kitchen. 'I'm sorry I couldn't tell you anything about it beforehand, but it was all deadly secret, in case the villains got wind of anything.'

'I'm always tipping off villains,' she said. 'Well known for it.' But she knew that wasn't the point. She put out mug, tea bag, spoon, and then turned to put her arms round him. 'Tell me about it.'

So he told her.

'I suppose Webber did have a point,' she said when he got to the end. 'He was doing good things, even if he went about them the wrong way. Excise rules are just local customs – excuse the pun. How does that stack up against human lives?'

'He had two people murdered to protect his right to decide that the law didn't apply to him,' Slider said. 'Probably another two as well, years ago. If he hadn't been stopped, who knows how many more he would have had to eliminate?'

'Point,' said Joanna.

'And then there are the original donors,' Slider said. 'China still has people executed for political dissidence, you know. Does holding up a placard outside Westminster mean your kidneys are automatically up for grabs?'

'Point again. Pay no attention to me – I'm just flappin' m' gums.'

He drew her closer. 'Forget the gums, how about the lips?'

'I thought you were tired?'

'Never too tired for you.' But he rested his head on her shoulder, cheek to her hair, eyes shut – not the pose of a rampant lover. 'Do you know Hopkins' poem, "The Windhover"?'

'Only about the most beautiful poem ever written,' Joanna said. '"A billion times told lovelier, more dangerous, O my chevalier."' She waited for elucidation, then said, 'Never heard of it. Why?'

'We say it's always about love or money,' he said, growing warm and comfortable behind his closed eyes. 'This was both. Webber had the money, and Rogers had the love.'

'You're not making a whole lot of sense,' she told him kindly. The kettle poured steam and she reached out to turn it off – carefully, not to disturb him.

'He was a bit of an ass and a bit of a villain,' Slider said. 'But I'm glad he had some love. Not all the women, I don't mean. The boat. Even if it didn't have sails.'

'In fact,' Joanna said, 'I just thought I'd mention that you are actually asleep at this point in time.' He very nearly was. 'By the way,' she said, because he'd have to wake up to get himself to bed, 'Atherton phoned.'

'Hmm?'

'He said to tell you they're going to mount an

operation on Embry's yard next week. A multi-agency sting, he said. They're going to shut him down for good.'

'Good,' said Slider, rousing himself. He opened his eyes, blinking at the brightness. And yawned cavernously. 'God, poor old Stanmore! Another upheaval. Seek a better life in the suburbs, eh? I bet they'll wish they really were Stansted.'

'You're still not making sense,' Joanna complained.

Slider shook his head. 'You had to be there,' he said.